The
S...
CR...
Collection

D0403971

ALIEN VENGEANCE

ALIEN VENGEANCE

BY
SARA CRAVEN

MILLS & BOON LIMITED
Eton House, 18-24 Paradise Road
Richmond, Surrey TW9 1SR

First published in Great Britain in 1985
by Mills & Boon Limited

© Sara Craven 1985

Australian copyright 1985
Philippine copyright 1985
Reprinted 1985
This edition 1992

ISBN 0 263 77773 1

Set in Monophoto Times 11 on 11pt.
19-9204-51606

Made and printed in Great Britain

CHAPTER ONE

'YOU say there's still no message for me?' Gemma
Barton looked her incredulity at the desk clerk.
'Are you sure?'

'Quite sure, *thespinis*.' The man spread his hands
apologetically and smiled at her, his teeth very
white under the heavy Cretan moustache. 'It is
important this message? It worries you that it has
not come?'

Gemma gave a slight shrug. 'Actually, I'm more
disappointed than worried,' she returned. 'But I'll
get over it. The only problem is I don't quite know
what my plans are until I do hear from my
brother, and tonight is the last night of my
booking here.'

'No problem,' came the instant assurance. 'It is
early in the season still, and there is room if you
wish to stay. You have only to let us know.'

Well, that was reassuring at any rate, Gemma
thought as she walked across the foyer and
through the archway into the breakfast room. Not
that she was sure she wanted to stay on in
Heraklion even though the hotel was cheap and
friendly and spotlessly clean. As she had another
ten days to spend on Crete, she might as well make
the most of them and travel further afield—
especially if Mike continued to be conspicuous by
his absence.

He was and always had been the limit, she
reminded herself ruefully as she helped herself to
fresh bread rolls, and poured orange juice into her
glass. Mike was mad on botany, and generally

oblivious to anything else, and the world's worst correspondent, causing their mother, Gemma knew, hours of silent worry when he vanished into the wide blue yonder on his everlasting field trips.

This prolonged visit to Crete was part of a postgraduate study he was doing, and it had been his own idea that Gemma should join him for a holiday, instead of making one of a party to Ibiza with some of the women she worked with.

'This is the place,' one of his scrawled missives had told her. 'Away from the tourist bits, the living is dirt cheap, and I've fallen on my feet, residing in the lap of luxury half way up a mountain. You could do the touristy things for a couple of days, then come and see the real Crete with me.'

'The real Crete,' their mother had snorted. 'That mountain he mentions is probably all his dirty laundry.'

Gemma was inclined to agree, but at the same time the idea of going to Crete had taken a definite hold on her. While she was still at school she'd read Mary Renault's *The King Must Die* and the exploits of Theseus and his fellow bull dancers at the Minoan court had fired her imagination.

And she wasn't going to pass up the chance of going there, even if it did mean dealing with a backlog of Mike's dirty shirts and socks.

So, she'd fixed her flight, and written to tell him, not being amazed or aghast when she received no reply except a postcard of the harbour at Chania with a laconic 'Great' and his initial scribbled on it.

It was rather a blow, however, to arrive at Heraklion airport and find he wasn't there to meet her, but she supposed she could have expected it

with Mike's track record, and was glad she'd taken
the trouble to book herself a few nights' bed and
breakfast at a hotel not too far from the harbour.

That very first day, even before she had
unpacked, she'd written again to Mike—briefly
reminding him that she'd arrived, and giving the
name and address of the hotel and its telephone
number. Each day since she'd expected to hear
from him, but there'd been no word at all. Gemma
wasn't a child any more. She didn't need a big
brother to hold her hand, particularly on Crete
where the people, she was sure, must be among the
friendliest and most hospitable in the world. She
knew Mike was there to work, and if he was too
busy to get away, and regretting his rash
suggestion then all he had to do was say so.

There was plenty she could do. She'd made
friends with a young couple, fellow-guests at the
Hotel Ariadne already, and they were talking
about hiring a car and taking a leisurely trip right
round the island, staying at tavernas en route. If
Gemma cared to share the petrol costs, she was
welcome to go with them, and she was sorely
tempted.

But—she did want to see Mike, or at least talk
to him so that she could take reassuring news
home to her mother, who was still rather low after
a lingering virus infection she'd acquired in the
early spring.

As she turned away from the buffet with her
food, she saw James and Hilary waving madly at
her from a table in the corner of the room, and
went over to join them.

'Ignore James,' was Hilary's greeting as she sat
down. 'He was introduced to *raki* last night and
the friendship developed rather too quickly, so
he's feeling a little fragile today. Says he can't face

the bus ride to Knossos. But I'm still going,' she added swiftly, seeing faint disappointment on Gemma's face. 'I hope you are too.'

'I wouldn't miss it,' Gemma said, giving the wan James a sympathetic grin. 'Firewater was it?'

James groaned. 'I only noticed the fire. Hilly, of course, stuck virtuously to *ouzo* and is fine. There's no justice.'

His wife wrinkled her nose at him and turned to Gemma. 'Takis says the bus to Knossos leaves regularly from the harbour.'

'Then Takis is a liar,' James said, taking a cautious sip of coffee. 'He knows as well as we do that Cretan buses run as and when they feel like it. I don't know why they even bother to have a timetable.'

'Hangovers don't suit James. They make him so jaundiced,' Hilary said regretfully. 'The first couple of days we were here, he thought it was wonderful that nothing ever happened when it was supposed to. Said it was the first real holiday he'd ever had.'

'I still say that,' James maintained. 'And Takis doesn't believe in buses anyway. He told me so. He says you should be able to walk the five kilometres or so to Knossos like they used to do in the old days—two big strong girls like you.'

'Carrying bundles of firewood on our heads, no doubt,' Gemma said drily. 'There are times when Takis asks for a punch in the throat.'

'Well, don't expect Penelope to give him one,' Hilary advised cheerfully. 'She thinks the sun, moon and stars shine out of him, and she'd probably walk to Knossos and back carrying him on her head if he asked her to.'

'Cretan men have got it made,' James said moodily. 'They don't allow any women's liberation nonsense to interfere with their basic rights.'

Hilary giggled. 'And nor do you, darling, nor do you. In fact, you and Takis have a lot in common, and you can spend a lovely day together drinking coffee under the awning and discovering what it is while Gemma and I acquire some culture.' She looked at her watch. 'We'll meet in the foyer in twenty minutes shall we? Then, with any luck, we'll get to the Palace before it's too hot.'

'It's too hot already,' said James.

He had a point, Gemma thought as she and Hilary threaded their way along the busy streets leading to the harbour a little while later. Only idiot tourists rushed round risking sunstroke. Her skin was already beginning to tan, in spite of the filter creams she used to protect it, and on her first day in Heraklion she'd invested in a cheap straw hat.

The tables in the shade of the pavement cafes were already doing a roaring trade, she saw, and the aroma of coffee and cooking food mingled with the all pervasive fumes from the traffic. All around them worry beads clicked in an eternal rhythm, and voices hummed and rose on notes of laughter or expostulation. There never seemed to be any muttered conversations, Gemma thought with amusement. If a Greek wanted you to know something, he let you have it full blast.

They were equally uninhibited in other ways too, she reminded herself, aware of the frankly appreciative dark-eyed glances pursuing Hilary and herself as they walked along. At home she would have found such openly expressed admiration both embarrassing and a nuisance. Here, it was distinctly heartwarming to be regarded as if you were Aphrodite rising from the waves.

To their surprise, the Knossos bus was already there and filling up when they arrived. They found

seats without difficulty, and paid the few drachmas
for the fare.

They were both quiet as they set off, Hilary
checking the cartridge in her camera, and Gemma
wondering what it must have been like to have
been part of the Athenian tribute to King Minos,
and to have started the weary trudge in the sun to
Knossos knowing that danger and probable death
awaited them there.

She was very glad, she thought, that she lived in
the 1980s instead of a couple of thousand years
B.C. and that no danger waited for her at
Knossos, or anywhere else on Crete.

Even as the thought formulated in her mind, a
slight shiver went through her, as if a hand had
been laid on her shoulder and a warning voice
breathed in her ear, 'Be careful. No Greek would
ever tempt the fates and you shouldn't either.'

It was an odd, disturbing little moment, as if a
sudden shadow had passed across the sun, then
Hilary made some idle remark about the suburbs
they were passing through, and it was gone.

As journeys went it was relatively dull, the bus
passing through the usual urban sprawl. Hilary
mentioned the projected trip to the White
Mountains and asked if Gemma had given it any
further thought.

'I'd love to come,' Gemma admitted. 'And I
can't wait forever for Mike to get in touch. After
all, I don't even know if he got my last message.
Perhaps this mountain retreat of his has no
telephone, or the mail only gets delivered once a
month.' She sighed. 'Or more probably, Mike's
gone prancing off up some crag after a rare herb,
and hasn't given me another thought.'

Hilary sent her an amused look. 'Does he do
things like that?'

Gemma nodded. 'Constantly.'

Hilary chuckled. 'Then I suggest you set him a deadline, say midnight tonight. If he's not in touch by then, you come with us. How about that?'

'It sounds good to me,' Gemma agreed. She glanced round, aware of an unusual stir. 'What's everyone looking at? We're not there yet are we?'

'The most amazing car is following us,' Hilary said. 'They're all lost in admiration, I suppose.' She grimaced slightly. 'Thank God James isn't here, or he'd be off the bus by now and interrogating the driver about cylinders and camshafts and all the other things he finds so fascinating.' She eyed Gemma narrowly. 'Do they fascinate you too, or do you consider a car to be an unreliable lump of tin, designed to get one from A to B, like me?'

Gemma grinned. 'I think I occupy the middle ground. But I must admit it is a beautiful car— Italian, I think. It must have cost a fortune.

Hilary shrugged. 'Well, the gentleman behind the wheel looks as if he can well afford it,' she commented casually. 'You admire the car, and I'll admire him.'

The car, Gemma thought, was worth a second or even a third look. Not even the inevitable coating of Cretan dust could detract from its sleek, powerful lines. The top was down, so she was afforded a full view of the driver, but she was not particularly impressed, she told herself.

He was undoubtedly Greek, black haired and olive-skinned. His eyes were masked by sun glasses, but they did not disguise the fact that he was classically, almost startlingly good-looking.

In fact, Gemma allowed judiciously, he would almost have been beautiful, but for the tough uncompromising lines of his mouth and chin.

She thought that he must be aware of the fact that he was under close scrutiny from the bus, but preferred to appear arrogantly unaware of the fact.

'Pseud,' she thought dismissively, but watched with unwilling approval as he, at last, overtook the bus with maximum leeway, but minimum effort. He wasn't her type, but he knew his car and how to handle it.

'I expect he's one of those Greek tycoons one reads about,' Hilary said dreamily. 'Maybe we'll meet him, stumbling round the ruins at Knossos. If he's smitten, and invites you to cruise on his yacht, I hope you won't feel bound by our prior invitation.'

'He's more likely to be someone's chauffeur, joy-riding on his day off,' Gemma said crushingly. 'And if he does have a yacht, it will probably be already crammed to the gunwales with starlets.'

Hilary sighed extravagantly, 'Oh, Gemma, you're so prosaic sometimes. Don't you like to fantasise a little?'

Gemma smiled. 'Why, yes, but my fantasies don't centre round macho Greeks driving cars like virility symbols.'

Hilary gave her a curious look. 'Just for the record—is there anyone serious?'

Gemma shook her head rather wryly. 'No one,' she admitted. 'They used to say that it was women who wanted to get serious, who always had marriage in mind, but it seems to me that every man I meet wants to rush me into—into some kind of commitment or other, and I'm just not ready for that. Perhaps it's a fault in me but I like to take my relationships slowly—one step at a time, but they seem to want—instant *rapport*.'

Hilary smiled drily, 'You're right to be cautious.

I used to be that way myself, then I met James and within a month we were engaged. Don't freeze them all off, Gemma, or you could miss out on something wonderful.'

Gemma laughed. 'Not so far, I haven't, and that I can guarantee, I'm afraid.' She leaned forward. 'It looks as if we're nearly there.'

On leaving the bus, they walked down the narrow road towards the Palace, skirting the tavernas and souvenir shops, threading their way gingerly between the cars parked at the side of the road.

There was traffic edging down the road all the time, and in spite of herself, Gemma found she was watching out for an opulent dark blue sports car.

'I'm letting Hilary's nonsense get to me,' she told herself severely.

'It's too hot for much culture,' Hilary said as they queued up at the admission gate behind a party of French, who'd arrived with their own guide and were arguing noisily about numbers. 'I vote we belt round, then go and find something cold to drink.'

But inside the gate, it was like stepping into a different world. There were trees and shade, and Gemma saw that people were moving more slowly, talking more quietly, as if in respect of the fact they were present in one of the ancient places of the earth.

Even Hilary seemed subdued as they walked up the causeway towards the Palace ruins. It was all so much vaster than Gemma had imagined and not even the amount of restoration work which had been carried out, and the crowds of people wandering about could affect the power of its atmosphere.

By mutual consent, they decided not to attach themselves to any of the official tours which were being conducted round. Instead they walked quietly through the remnants of corridors and courtyards, past the remains of sacrificial altars, trying to come to terms with the size of the place.

They looked at restored frescoes, glowing in the brilliant sun, and wandered through dark state chambers where once King Minos and his Queen had sat in splendour.

Hilary was busy with her camera, making Gemma pose for her against painted columns, beside the big pottery jars, tall enough to conceal a man, and near the great Bull's horns carved in stone, a chilling reminder of the Minotaur myth.

It was while they were standing studying the fresco of the Lily-Prince that Gemma first felt they were being watched. She told herself she was being silly. There were dozens of other people around, all doing the same thing as themselves. It was the young Priest-King with his plumes and flowing locks which was the real centre of attention, as a casual glance around confirmed.

All the same she was glad to be back in the open air again.

Hilary looked around at the clustering hills and tall cypresses which bordered the enclosure fence like sentinels. 'It can't have been too easy to defend—in a valley like this,' she remarked dubiously.

'They wouldn't have had to,' Gemma said. 'It wasn't a fortress. It was a symbol of how powerful and mighty the Cretan empire was. People came here to pay their respects, not attack.'

Hilary grinned. 'They probably came to admire the drainage,' she said. 'It says in my book that the Queen's apartments had the first recorded flush loo. I like that—a homely touch among all this fallen splendour. And talking of splendour, just look at that.'

In a corner, rooted among fallen stones and rubble, a huge bush was just beginning to break into delicate blue blossom.

Hilary pushed Gemma gently. 'Go and stand by it, love. I want one last photograph.'

Gemma obeyed, waiting while Hilary adjusted the camera, muttering to herself, and motioned to her to alter her position fractionally.

'Remember, don't smile,' Hilary cautioned. 'Just look up when I say your name.'

Gemma stared down at the dusty ground. She heard Hilary call out, 'Gemma' and glanced up, trying to look into the sunlight without blinking, and saw a figure standing behind Hilary, tall and dark in the brilliance. She knew him at once. It was the driver of the car which had followed the bus Hilary's supposed tycoon. He was the last person she had ever expected to see again. But even as she registered all this, her shocked mind told her something else—that he was terrifyingly, blazingly angry. She felt her face go rigid, as if she was bracing herself against some blow, and heard Hilary groan.

'I may have said "don't smile", but there's no need to look as if you'd just seen Marley's ghost Wait one second while I take another.'

Gemma closed her eyes, passing the tip of her tongue over her dry lips. When Hilary spoke again, and she looked up, the man had gone

She thought feebly, 'It's the sun. I'm seeing things.'

But she knew she wasn't. On the face of it, he was an unlikely sightseer, but he'd been there.

And anyway, she adjured herself impatiently, it

was wrong to judge by appearances. Perhaps he wasn't a chauffeur or a wealthy playboy, but an expert on the Minoan period.

His unexpected appearance could be rationally explained, but she couldn't justify to herself that odd sense of his rage she'd experienced as he looked at her.

She hadn't simply been surprised to see him. She'd felt threatened- -frightened even. And yet there was no logical reason for it. They were strangers to each other—she knew they were.

She thought, 'If I'd ever met him, I'd remember. And now that I've seen him again, I have a feeling I won't forget him in a hurry.'

Hilary joined her, putting her camera back into its case. She said, 'Are you all right. You look a bit green round the gills. Is it the sun?'

Gemma forced a smile. 'Maybe. What about that cold drink you mentioned?'

All the way back to the gate, she had to resist an impulse to look over her shoulder and see if he was following. She told herself that she was being a complete idiot. She was imagining things, that was all. The sun, the power of the ruins, her worry over Mike had all conspired against her suddenly, and knocked her off balance. A cold beer, she thought, and something to eat would restore her normal equilibrium.

They bought some postcards and walked slowly back up the hill, turning thankfully into the vine-covered shade of one of the tavernas. The waiter was playing water from a hosepipe on to the floor, and the air smelled fresh and cool as they sat down.

They ordered beer and souvlaki—little chunks of lamb grilled on skewers and served with french fried potatoes, and a Greek salad of cucumbers, tomatoes, peppers and fetta cheese, dressed with herbs and olive oil. Gemma sat and looked through the guide book, while Hilary wrote a couple of postcards and changed the cartridge in her camera.

Other people started to come in. Some Germans took the next table, and one of them had a radio playing music softly. The beers, when they arrived, were ice cold and Gemma began to feel relaxed.

Then Hilary said under her breath, 'Hell's bells. You're never going to believe who's just walked in.'

Gemma put down her glass. She said too brightly, 'Not the mystery tycoon?'

'As ever was.' Hilary's tone sharpened. 'My God, he's looking right at us. Supposing he comes over . . .'

Gemma remembered the force of the curious anger. She said, 'He won't come over.'

'No, you're right,' Hilary conceded. 'He's taken one of the far tables, but he's facing this way, and it's you he's looking at.' She grinned. 'Maybe that cruise is on, after all.'

Gemma's mouth was dry, and she took another sip of beer. 'I really don't think so.'

The food was on its way, but she wasn't hungry any more. She was remembering how she'd felt she was being watched near the corridor of Processions—how he'd appeared out of the blue when Hilary was photographing her, and now here he was again—as if he was following them.

If she could look at it from Hilary's light-hearted viewpoint, it would almost be flattering, but somehow that wasn't possible.

She pushed her food around, going through the motions of eating, but her appetite had died on her completely.

This, she told herself stormily, is really ridiculous—allowing a total stranger to put me off a meal I'm going to have to pay for anyway.

With a feeling almost of defiance, she ate the last few morsels of lamb, and mopped up the salad juices with a piece of crusty bread, before asking the attentive waiter to bring her some ice cream.

As she did so, she looked towards the stranger for the first time, and realised with a tremor of apprehension that he was watching her. He'd removed his dark glasses, and without their concealment, she had to admit he was stunningly attractive, his swarthy face brooding and enigmatic.

Their glances met—locked, and Gemma felt her cheeks redden as his firm lips twisted in a contemptuous little smile, and the dark eyes looked her over in an insolent, overtly sexual appraisal.

Mortified, Gemma tore her gaze away. She thought savagely, 'If I went near any yacht of his, I'd sink it.'

Hilary said in an undertone, 'He can't take his eyes off you, Gemma.'

'Don't I know it.' Gemma pushed away the remains of her melting ice cream. 'Do you think we could have the bill, and get out of here?'

But this wasn't as easy as it sounded. The waiter was clearly upset by their intended departure. He offered them coffee, he offered them more beers, he offered cigarettes from his own pack, produced with a flourish from his shirt pocket. Gemma smiled tautly and refused, and asked for the bill, all the time tormented by the burning conviction that the stranger was deriving sardonic amusement from this little piece of by-play.

As they left, amid the waiter's lamentations,

Gemma found herself praying that they wouldn't be followed.

She could hardly believe the state she was in. She thought impatiently, 'Oh, get a grip on yourself. There's nothing sinister in all this. We're two girls on our own, and he's the predatory type. He probably thinks he's God's gift to the female sex, and that his technique is infallible.'

To do him justice, with his looks, she doubted whether he would have many failures.

But all the same, she felt on edge all the time they were waiting for the bus to come.

Hilary said teasingly, 'Your problem, Gem, is that you don't know when you're on to a good thing.'

Gemma shook her head. 'He is not a good thing,' she said. 'Believe me.'

The bus came at last, and as she climbed aboard, Gemma took a last jittery look over her shoulder. The stranger, however, was nowhere to be seen, either on foot or in his car.

She felt an overwhelming sense of relief. Soon, she'd be back in the safe anonymity of Heraklion, and tomorrow she'd be driving towards Chania with James and Hilary on the next stage of her holiday, and she'd be able to put this oddly annoying series of incidents out of her mind.

But as she went into the hotel, Takis the manager hailed her from behind the reception desk. 'Ah, Kyria Barton. There is a message for you.' He turned to the pigeon holes behind him and extracted an envelope. It bore the single typed word 'Gemma'.

She thought, 'Mike—at last.'

She smiled at Takis. 'When did this arrive?'

'Just after you and Kyria Trent had left for Knossos. Spiro says there was first a phone call, and he explained you had gone out. Then when he came back from coffee, this letter had been left for you.' Takis nodded paternally. 'This pleases you, *ne*?'

Gemma tore open the envelope and scanned the single typewritten sheet within.

'Dear Gemma,' it said. 'Something has come up which prevents my meeting with you in Heraklion as you suggest. Perhaps instead you could come here to the Villa Ione in Loussenas. There is only one bus a week, so I suggest you hire a car and a driver. Make no attempt to drive yourself, as the road is very bad in places. Michael.'

'Is it good news, or bad news?' Hilary asked.

Gemma shook her head. 'I'm honestly not sure. He wants me to join him, but he sounds very curt about it.' She sighed. 'Perhaps I'm being a nuisance. Maybe I'll drop him another line, telling him to forget it and make the trip to Chania after all.'

She handed the note to Hilary, who read it through in silence. Then she said, 'You don't think he's sick or in trouble of some kind?'

Gemma groaned. 'That's just what I was wondering. Knowing Mike, it could be both, but he wouldn't want to spoil my holiday by involving me.' She bit her lip. 'I'm going to have to hire this car as he says and go to him.'

'You'll do nothing of the kind,' Hilary contradicted. 'We'll drive you to this Loussenas, wherever it is. If it's in the mountains it should be spectacular, and we're in no great hurry to get to Chania in one day.'

'I can't ask you to do that,' Gemma protested.

'You haven't asked,' Hilary said firmly. 'I'm telling you what's going to happen. And James will say exactly the same, so no arguments.' She gave Gemma back her note, and added a comforting pat on the shoulder. 'And now I'm going up to have a shower. Takis, I hope the water is at least lukewarm.'

'At this hour of the day, *kyria*, it may even be hot,' Takis assured her graciously.

'In that case, I'll have one as well,' Gemma said.

But once in her room, she made no immediate attempt to use the miniscule shower cubicle attached to it.

Instead, she sat on the edge of the rather hard mattress and read Mike's note again. It was odd, she thought, and totally unlike his usual breezy scrawls, and it made her uneasy.

She uttered an impatient exclamation, and got to her feet. Instead of inventing problems, she should be thankful that Mike had taken the trouble to type, rather than expecting her to decipher his normal hieroglyphics.

It was the events of the day which had made her uneasy, and nothing to do with Mike at all. He was probably hale and hearty, and far too interested in his plants to spare her more than a passing thought. And if she was to mention when she saw him that his note hadn't been very welcoming, he would simply look injured and say, 'Well, I told you how to get here, didn't I?'

She sighed, and began to unbutton her dress. If she showered quickly, she would have time to do her packing before dinner, as James and Hilary would probably want to make an early start in the morning.

She was glad she was going to Loussenas with them, and not some unknown driver, she told herself.

And tried to suppress the thought that, fond as she was of Mike, she would far sooner be going to Chania tomorrow than the Villa Ione.

CHAPTER TWO

GEMMA had the same feeling, but doubled and re-doubled in spades, the following day as she stood beside the battered signpost stating Loussenas was one kilometre away, watching James reverse the car with infinite care.

They'd wanted to drive her to the door, but she wouldn't allow it. The road was getting steeper all the time, and deteriorating at every yard into a lacework of potholes. They'd been climbing, it seemed, since the moment they'd left the main road. At first, it had been easy to admire the scenery, but as the road narrowed, and hair-pinned, they all became very quiet, and started averting their gazes from the sheer drop only a foot or two from the car wheels.

Gemma found herself wondering all the time what they would do if they met another vehicle coming down, but by some miracle that problem did not arise.

The little hamlets they passed through, each with its gleaming church, were a relief. They'd stopped in one and drunk lemonade under the awning of a taverna, telling each other that Loussenas couldn't be much further now, although the truth was they had no idea how far it was. They'd asked Takis, but he'd only given the map a cursory glance, stabbed it with his finger and said, 'Loussenas is somewhere above here.' And that, it turned out, had been putting it mildly.

So when they reached the signpost, Gemma had insisted on getting out. The road was

22

slightly wider just here, sufficient to turn the car anyway.

'I really don't like leaving you.' Hilary had peered at her worriedly. 'If Mike is as absent-minded as you say, he might have forgotten you and gone off somewhere, and then where will you be?'

'Stuck,' Gemma returned robustly. 'But it won't happen. He's living at this villa, after all, so someone will be expecting me.'

Hilary looked unconsoled. 'If only we knew where we were staying tonight, or if the villa had a phone, we could keep in touch,' she wailed. 'It's so wild up here. God knows how many thousands of feet we are above sea level. Much higher, and we'd need oxygen.'

'Understating the case as always,' James said wryly. His fingers closed warmly round Gemma's wrist. 'When we get to Chania, we're hoping to stay at the Hotel Dionysius. If anything goes wrong, leave a message, and we'll get back somehow and take you off this bloody mountain.' He paused. 'And you have our address in England, so whatever happens, we want to know how this little adventure turns out.'

They drove off, Hilary waving frantically. Gemma waved back until the car rounded the first bend and vanished from sight. As she started up the road towards the village, she could still hear the sound of the engine growing fainter and fainter, until at last there was nothing but her own footsteps.

In fact, no sign of life but herself, plodding up the road, and a large bird that might have been a buzzard wheeling and circling against the faultless arc of the sky.

She sighed and transferred her case to her other

hand. It was hardly the hilarious reunion she'd
envisaged.

She didn't hurry, but she was tired and
breathless by the time she reached the first houses.
About half a mile earlier, the ground had levelled
out into a small plateau. The land had been
cultivated, and there was a little cluster of
windmills, their sails turning gently in the breeze.
Two women were working in one of the fields,
black-clad, with the familiar head scarves round
their hair and faces, but they didn't look up or
make any sign as Gemma passed, and she found
this odd. In every other village they'd passed
through in the car that day, there'd been waves
and smiles from almost everyone, from the
bearded priest to the smallest toddler.

A donkey was grazing a small patch of scrub at
the side of the road, and it turned its head, fixing
her with its mild, incurious gaze as she walked
past. Further on, goats were tethered, and bee
skeps droned sleepily on a wide ledge.

The village road was now a track, its stones
cutting uncomfortably through the thin soles of her
sandals. It was little wonder so many Cretans wore
boots, she thought ironically.

She put down her case and looked about her,
flexing her tired hand. All she could see were
village houses, many of them single-roomed by the
look of them, and hardly likely to qualify as villas.
The doorways were dark, and the window shutters
closed, like so many blank eyes staring at her, she
thought with a little shiver.

And there was no one about. The place was
deserted. There was a tiny kafeneion, but there
were no men sitting at its tables in the shade,
drinking coffee, and arguing about politics. Each
house had its own verandah, but there were no

women gathered in groups to chatter and weave the rugs and linens for which Cretans were famous.

Many of the villages they'd passed through had stalls beside the road, displaying their weaving and embroidery, but presumably Loussenas attracted too few tourists to bother.

The Villa Ione couldn't be far away in any direction, but Gemma wished there could be just one friendly face to ask, if only to dispel this growing sense of uneasy isolation which was pressing down on her.

The Cretans were among the most hospitable people on earth. Love for the stranger in their midst was bred into them. She remembered Takis warning them all that if they were offered food and drink anywhere, they should accept, even if they suspected it was all the host possessed. To refuse, he said, was hurtful, and damaging to Cretan pride.

The villagers of Loussenas, Gemma thought wryly, must be the exceptions to that rule. There were people in the houses, she was sure. She could sense movement in the shadowy interiors, but it was clear no one intended to welcome her, or offer as much as a drink of water, even though the well was there, at the end of the street, and a stone's throw from the bright blue door of the little church.

There was nothing for it, but to go on.

Again, she had the feeling that she was being watched. She groaned inwardly. Why had she had to come all the way to Crete simply to discover she was paranoid?

Beyond the church was the priest's house, and beyond that again the ground rose, and through a clump of straggling trees, she saw a high white wall.

Standing in its own grounds, she thought, this desirable residence must be the Villa Ione.

There was a narrow gate in the wall, and a copper bell hanging beside it. The sound was sweet and pure as she rang it, and it echoed endlessly into the stillness, but at last there was nothing left but silence.

Gemma sighed. '"'Is there anybody there?' said the Traveller",' she muttered, and tried the gate. It opened with a faint squeak to the first pressure of her hand, and she stepped inside.

The garden was quite small, but it was well-tended and bright with flowers. The house itself was a good size, the living quarters built over what Gemma assumed had once been a byre and would now be a garage, with a flight of steep steps leading up the side of the building to the terraced entrance. The steps were worn, but in good order, and the whole house looked as if it had just been freshly painted white. Gemma, looking up, saw solar heating panels in the roof. Loussenas might be a backwater, but one of its residents knew about modern technology, it seemed.

There were some Greek letters carved into the stonework at the bottom of the steps, and she peered at them, wishing she'd taken the trouble to learn the alphabet before she came. They looked as if they might spell 'Ione' she decided, and started up the steps.

The little terrace was tiled in a warm terracotta shade, and tubs and urns of geraniums and cyclamen had been arranged round its edge. Splashes on the tiles indicated that someone had been busy with a watering can not long before, and her spirits rose.

She went to the open door, and called a tentative, 'Hello.'

Nothing. No voice, no step, just silence.

Out of the corner of her eye, Gemma caught a faint movement. She swung round, and saw a cat peering at her round one of the urns. It was a typically scrawny specimen, grey and white, and striped like a zebra, with eyes that looked almost twice the size of its pointed face.

Gemma crouched down, and snapped her fingers gently. 'Are you the welcoming committee?'

The cat arched its back as if offended by the suggestion, and vanished in one sinuous movement.

Gemma shrugged and rose to her feet. 'That figures,' she muttered aloud.

She stepped over the threshold, and looked around. She seemed to be in the main room of the house. It was large and airy, and windows, which she suspected were a recent addition, filled the far wall, giving a spectacular view of the valley beneath. The furniture was wooden, and simply designed, and the cushions, rugs and hangings were all hand-woven. One rug, a sunburst in shades of crimson and gold, had been used dramatically as a wall hanging. An archway led through into a small dining room, and beyond this was the kitchen.

It was clean, but very simple with few concessions to modernity apart from the small sink unit, and a tiny refrigerator and cooker, both run off bottled gas she noticed.

There were lamps in all the rooms, suggesting that the Villa Ione had no electricity, and there was no sign of a telephone.

There was a scrubbed wooden table in the middle of the kitchen, and in its centre, a folded sheet of paper anchored by a pottery candleholder

She picked it up and opened it out. Five typed
words. 'Make yourself at home, Gemma.'

'Oh, thank you, I will,' she said ironically. 'I will
also have to stop talking to myself, or it could
become a nasty habit.'

She opened the fridge. It might be small, but the
interior was crammed with food, while the bottom
shelf, she was relieved to see, was devoted to cans
of beer and soft drinks. She opened a Coke and
drank it gratefully, straight from the can.

She kicked off her sandals and wandered back
to the living room, enjoying the cool feel of the
tiles under her burning feet.

In a way, she could understand why Mike
preferred to remain holed up here, rather than
submit to the noise and bustle of Heraklion. She
perched on the wooden arm of the sofa and stared
through the window, wondering which of the
stark-looking crags her brother was scrambling
about on, looking for specimens, and wishing that
just for once he'd given up the hunt to be there to
meet her.

Still clutching her can of Coke, she climbed the
flight of wooden stairs leading out of the living
room to the next floor. Straight ahead of her, a
narrow passage led to glazed doors opening on to
another terrace, equipped with sun loungers. Two
large bedrooms, each with its own small bathroom,
flanked the passage, again very simply furnished.
Each room contained little more than a double
bed, built on to a stone platform in a corner of the
room, a large chest of drawers, and an alcove with
a hanging rail behind a woven curtain, which
presumably acted as the wardrobe. In addition,
each room had its own small balcony.

One room was clearly in use already, and in the
other the bed had been freshly made up with an

attractive blue-and-white bedcover in a Cretan design.

Gemma fetched up her case, and extracted her toilet bag. There were towels, thick and soft and smelling of herbs, folded on a chair, inviting her to make use of them. Well, she thought, with a mental shrug, she'd been told to make herself at home, and she could think of nothing more homely than a shower. She felt hot, tired and sticky, and a little depressed, and showering would refresh her as well as helping to pass the time.

If there was no electricity, perhaps there was no piped water either, and the expensive bathroom fittings were just for show, she thought with a little grimace as she fiddled with the controls of the shower.

But water there was in abundance, and at just the right temperature, she realised with satisfaction, revelling in the sensation as it cascaded through her hair and down her body. It was wonderful to feel the tension seeping out of her, she thought, turning off the water and languidly wringing the excess moisture out of her thick rope of blonde hair. She took one of the towels and wrapped it round herself, sarong-style, anchoring the free end securely. She couldn't use her hand-drier, but she could dry her hair just as well in the sun, and the little terrace at the end of the passage was sufficiently secluded to preclude her needing to get dressed again just yet. If there was nothing else to do, she could always work on her suntan.

She collected one of the paperback novels from her case that she hadn't even started on so far, and padded along to the terrace.

The view from here was fantastic too, the rocky peaks around and above her gleaming white and silver in the sun, but shimmering into a blue and violet haze in the distance. Away down to the right in the valley, she could see the muted sheen of olive groves, interspersed with terraced areas of cultivation, and the harsher green of cypress and scrub. It was a bleak landscape in many ways, but dazzling too.

Everywhere on Crete you were aware of the mountains. The God Zeus had been born in them, although there was some dispute about the actual location. Each peak, each cave had its own myth, its own mystery, and closer to her own times, Gemma recalled, the mountains had provided shelter not only for newborn gods from murderous fathers, but for ordinary mortals—Cretan partisans and their British comrades-in-arms in the last war.

Gemma had hoped to climb up to the cave on Dicte where Zeus was said to have been suckled by the goat Capricorn. She'd thought Mike might take her there. He wouldn't be interested in the myths, but he could look for dittany and other herbs while she looked at the cave, or so she'd reasoned, but she hadn't bargained for the fact that he was living in such a remote place.

She would come back, she knew suddenly, probably next year, and explore all the places she hadn't yet seen. Crete was in her blood already, as she'd somehow always expected it could be. Given a few days, she supposed she might even get to love this uncharacteristic, unfriendly little village. Perhaps its very remoteness had made the inhabitants suspicious of outsiders—and yet, and yet all the stories she'd heard other tourists tell suggested just the opposite. One couple at the hotel in Heraklion had got lost on a moped trip, ending up in a village that seemed at the back of beyond and further. The villagers had feasted them royally, and driven them ceremoniously, moped and all in someone's truck, back to the nearest main road, refusing all offers of payment with smiling dignity.

She sighed. It made the attitude of the inhabitants at Loussenas all the more difficult to understand. But perhaps her imagination was playing tricks again. Maybe those houses had been empty after all, and all the villagers had gone off to market or somewhere, on the one bus a week Mike had mentioned. He would explain when he arrived, she told herself drowsily.

Even in the shade, the terrace was blissfully hot, and the lounger she was occupying the most comfortable place in the world. Every time she looked at the printed page of her book, the words seemed to dance oddly, and it was much easier to let it drop to the floor beside her, and think of nothing except how warm she felt, how relaxed . . .

Too warm, and too relaxed to be struggling up this rocky path which got steeper and more difficult with every step she took, but at the top was the cave she was searching for, the pinnacle of all her dreams in some mysterious way, so she had to keep going.

The cave entrance reared up in front of her, as high and wide as a palace gate, and for a moment she hesitated, peering through the darkness. She wanted to turn and run, but instead, she found her feet carrying her forward. And the cave wasn't as dark as she'd thought at first. There were wall torches flaring every few yards, just as there would have been at Knossos, and she thought 'I must tell Hilary.'

She was excited and frightened at one and the same moment, and the light was almost glaring now, it was so bright, and the only darkness was the man's tall figure, waiting for her, commanding her, drawing her to him. She was close to him now, close enough to feel his hands closing on her, his breath warm on her face, and she looked up and felt the scream rising in her throat as she saw for the first time the great golden bull's mask which hid his face . . .

Gemma sat up with a strangled gasp, staring round her, trying to orientate herself. She must have been asleep for some time, because the sun had moved round, and her struggles had been real because the towel had become unfastened and slid down to her hips. She made a face and stood up, securing it again. It was just as well there was no one around to see her, she thought, and time she got dressed again anyway.

It was then that she heard it—the unmistakable slam of a car door near at hand, and footsteps somewhere below. She almost sagged with relief. Mike, she thought. At last.

The terrace door was closed and she thought, 'That's odd because I left it open . . .' but it wasn't really important. She flew along the passage and down the stairs, almost jumping the last few in her eagerness.

She began teasingly, 'And about time too . . .' then stopped dead, words and movement halting in the same astonished second.

She knew him at once. It was the stranger from Knossos, but looking very different from the sophisticated Western guise of the previous day. No expensive knitted casual shirt, or elegantly tailored cream pants today, but what looked like full Cretan dress from the soft leather knee boots to the dark red embroidered jacket, and the sash enfolding his waist. Only the black headscarf was missing. He'd left the thick dark hair which clustered, curling, close to his head, uncovered.

For a dazed moment, Gemma thought she was still in the middle of that strange dream, then she felt the solid curve of the newel post under her hand, and knew that it was all only too real.

She said, 'What are you doing here?' And what would she do, she asked herself, if he didn't speak English?

Only it seemed that he did.

'Waiting for you,' he said, adding with soft deliberation. 'To awaken.'

Helpless, humiliated colour flooded her face as she assimilated what he had said. He'd seen her on the terrace, asleep and half-naked, and he was letting her know it.

'Why do you blush?' came the cynical question, cutting across her embarrassed silence. 'Your compatriots show as much of their bodies on our beaches every day.'

'Perhaps, but I don't,' Gemma said tightly. 'And what gives you the right to walk in here and spy on me?'

'The right of ownership,' he drawled. 'This house belongs to me.'

Gemma's lips parted but no sound emerged. She stared at him, utterly appalled. 'My God—then—there's been the most terrible mistake. You see, I thought this was the Villa Ione . . .' She stopped abruptly, her forehead creasing. 'But it must be—or how would there have been that note?'

'It is the Villa Ione.'

She stared at him, still frowning. 'Then you must know Mike. Do you know where he is—when he'll be back. He can explain everything . . .'

'That I would doubt.' His voice was even, but there was an underlying coldness which worried her. 'I do not know where this—Michalis is, but my information is that he left the island—several weeks ago.'

'Left?' Gemma repeated stupidly. 'But that can't be true. He's here. He wrote me that note– two notes. I can show you.'

He shook his head. 'Do not put yourself to such trouble, Kyria Barton. I wrote those notes.'

There was something terribly wrong. Her whole body felt as taut as a bowstring. She said thinly, 'You did? But why?'

He shrugged. 'To make sure that you would come here, *thespinis*, why else?'

'You knew I was coming?' Gemma felt her way carefully. 'Then Mike must have told you . . .'

'He has told me nothing. How could he when I have never met him? But he left the letter you wrote him from England in the room he was using.'

'And you read it? A personal letter addressed to someone else?' Her breathing was fierce. 'This may be your home, *kyrie*, but that's utterly despicable.'

He was unmoved. 'You have a saying I believe—that the end justifies the means.'

'Well, I don't happen to believe that,' Gemma said tautly. 'I don't know what the mistake is, but there's obviously been one. I'll get my things and leave at once.'

She turned and went swiftly back up the stairs to the room she'd thought was hers. Her case had gone from the floor. For a moment she stared at the space it should have occupied, then she ran across to the bathroom and looked inside. The clothes she had discarded before her shower were missing too, although her toilet bag was still there.

She flew back into the bedroom. He had followed her upstairs, and was standing in the doorway, leaning almost negligently against the jamb.

She said, 'My case—all my things—they've gone. Someone's stolen them.'

'They have not been stolen,' he said. 'They are quite safe and will eventually be returned to you.'

'Eventually,' she repeated almost hysterically. 'But that's nonsense. I want to leave right now.'

He shrugged again. 'I regret that will not be possible.'

There was another silence. Her mind worked feverishly, discovering and rejecting possibilities. She said, 'If you intend to hold me to ransom, then you're wasting your time. I work for my living, but I have no spare cash, and neither does my family.'

For the first time, he looked faintly amused. 'I do not need your money.'

It was hardly likely that he would, she thought bleakly, remembering that car, the designer clothes, the thin gold wristwatch he'd been wearing the previous day. Now, he might look like a peasant, but his voice was educated, and his English superb.

She said slowly, 'Then what do you want?'

'The payment of a debt.' His voice was laconic.

She was utterly bewildered. He'd just said it wasn't money . . .

'Did Mike go off owing you rent? Is that what you mean by debt? Well, I can understand your annoyance, but I'm sure it's just an oversight. You said yourself that Mike had left some things behind, so it's obvious he intends to come back, and settle things for himself.'

'I hope that he does,' he said softly. 'In fact, *thespinis*, I am counting on it.'

She felt cold. She resisted the impulse to hug her

arms round her body in case she betrayed to this man how frightened she was.

She said, 'You may be prepared to wait around for him, *kyrie*, but I'm not. You had no right to ask me here under false pretences. I only have a limited time on Crete and I'm anxious to make the most of it. I'd like my things back now, and directions to the nearest telephone please.'

'And who would you telephone?' The amusement was deepening, she could feel it.

'The friends who brought me here,' she said clearly. 'They offered to come and fetch me if anything went wrong.'

'Then it is unfortunate that you will not be able to make contact with them.'

'But I know where they're going to stay,' she protested. 'All I need is a telephone, and there must be one in the village, if there isn't one here.'

'Yes, there's a telephone in the village,' he admitted almost casually. 'But it is of no consequence, Kyria Barton, as you would not be permitted to make use of it.'

She glared at him. 'And just who would stop me?'

'I would,' he said. 'And so would the people in the village. You see, *thespinis*, they also wish you to stay. To repay in some small measure the heavy debt your Michalis has incurred among them.' He paused. 'How much do you love him?'

She was tempted to reply, 'When he involves me in situations like this—not at all,' but she knew instinctively this wasn't a moment for flippancy.

And how could she describe to this intimidating stranger the kind of exasperated fondness that she normally experienced for Mike? How could she explain that her main reason for seeking him out was to put her mother's mind at rest? She could only be thankful that her mother was hundreds of miles away, and would never know that Mike seemed to be in real trouble at last.

She said with a calmness she didn't feel. 'Enough.'

His eyebrows rose. 'So lukewarm? And yet you came all this way just to be with him.'

'I came all this way to have a holiday. Visiting Mike was intended to be a fringe benefit—a minor one,' she said, adding, 'Not that it's any damned business of yours.'

He looked grimly at her. 'It is my business, *thespinis*, at this moment to discover the depth of your feeling for this man, and his for you.'

Gemma gasped. 'We're brother and sister for God's sake. How do you expect us to feel about each other?' she demanded indignantly.

His dark brows snapped together thunderously. 'What is this story?' he asked contemptuously. 'His name is Leslie, and yours is Barton.'

Gemma sighed. 'He's my half-brother. My mother was married before, but her first husband was killed in an accident at work.' It killed her to have to explain a syllable to this swine, but she would recount her entire family history if it would only get her out of here. 'A year or so later, she met my father and married him, but Mike kept his own father's surname. Now, do you see and now will you let me go?'

He said silkily, 'After what you have just told me, *thespinis*? It makes my reasons for keeping you here doubly potent, believe me.'

She felt incredibly weary suddenly. She said, 'I might, *kyrie*, if I knew what those reasons were. As it is, I'm tired and fed up with the whole affair. I don't know what Mike's supposed to have done, but whatever it is, I'm not responsible for it.'

'I will tell you what he has done,' he said gently. 'He has seduced a girl from this village, abused the trust that was placed in him, and the hospitality he was shown.'

Gemma's lips parted in disbelief. She said angrily, 'There isn't a word of truth in it. Mike wouldn't do such a thing. He's not that sort of person.'

'He is not completely a man—is that what you're saying?'

'No,' she denied furiously. 'But he's no womaniser and never has been. He has a girl in England, but it isn't a serious relationship. I—I'm sure they don't sleep together,' she added, annoyed at having to discuss such a subject with a stranger.

'Then he should have treated Maria with equal honour.' His voice was chilling. 'Your defence of your brother is natural, *thespinis*, but it does not impress me. Maria is to have his child.'

Gemma heard him with dismay. In the books she'd been reading before she came away, she'd learned that on many of the islands the old ways still prevailed, and that a woman's honour was sacrosanct, especially before she was married. She could imagine the kind of slur illegitimacy would confer in this kind of tightly knit community.

She bit her lip. 'Has she said so—accused him?'

'Not at first,' he said grimly. 'But ultimately she confessed everything. How they had met in Chania when she was there working in her uncle's hotel, how she suggested he should use the villa as a base for his work, and brought him here. No one thought wrong of it. The villa was unoccupied, after all, and he made himself popular in the village. Maria's mother came each day to cook and clean for him, until she fell and hurt her leg and the doctor said she must rest.' He paused. 'So

Maria took over her duties. Her family did not wish it. A marriage had been arranged for her with the son of the headman of the next village, and Maria should have been occupied in learning from her mother how to be a good wife. Already her groom's family had been displeased because she had worked for a while in Chania, and had demanded more dowry.' His eyes were like obsidian, dark and menacing. 'They were right to question. Maria had taken your brother as her lover in Chania, and he had persuaded her to bring him here so they could continue the affair in secret.' He shrugged. 'Who knows—perhaps she thought this Michalis would marry her. She knows better now. He has gone, and her bridegroom and his family have repudiated her. She is ruined, and the honour of her family and her village is tainted.'

'But you don't believe that, surely?' Gemma appealed. 'You're a man of the world—you know how things are.'

He said quietly, 'Perhaps, but the people of this village do not. My father was born in this house. He and Stavros were friends, and he was godfather to all his children—Maria too. My father is dead now, and I am head of my family, so in his trouble, Stavros and his kin look to me.'

'But I don't understand what you can do,' Gemma protested. 'I'm sure it's a terrible thing for them all, but you haven't heard Michael's side yet.'

'No,' he said. 'Because as soon as Maria told him there was to be a child, he ran away. He knew, your brother, what Stavros and his sons would do to him if they caught him. But they still seek vengeance.' He paused again. 'And that is why, sister of Michalis, you are here.'

'But I can't do anything.' She spread her hands in appeal. 'If the baby is Michael's, then I'm sure

my family will help in some way—with money. of
course, or helping Maria make a fresh start where
things aren't quite so—rigid.'

'No.' He shook his head. 'Whatever her fault,
Maria is our own, and will be protected by us.
Yes, you will pay, my girl, for what your brother
has done, but not in cash. You will pay in kind—
in shame, and your family's shame. You will stay
here and work in this house as my servant, as
Maria worked for your brother, and I shall take
you as and when I please, as he took her.'

His voice deepened, driving the bitter words like
sharp nails into her bewildered mind. 'This is my
revenge, *thespinis*, for your brother—for your
family—to know what it is like to have a beloved
child despoiled, taken for pleasure by a man who
has no intention of marriage. Perhaps in turn they
will also suffer the knowledge that she too carries
a child of an alien race in her body.'

CHAPTER THREE

SHE stood very still. There was silence in the room, and he seemed suddenly to have receded to a great distance. She wondered detachedly whether she might be going to faint. She hoped she might die. She hoped anything might happen to her except the kind of horror he was threatening.

Stay calm, she adjured herself frantically. Keep talking—reason with him—don't let him see you're on your knees, because there has to be a way out of this.

She said in a voice she barely recognised as her own, 'I think I've heard enough. I don't know whether this whole thing is meant to be some kind of ghastly joke, *kyrie*, but if so it's in the poorest taste.' She paused. 'And if you wanted to scare me and upset me, then you've succeeded. But that's as far as it goes. If Mike has really caused all this havoc, then he must sort it out for himself. I sympathise, but I'm not getting involved, and I'm certainly not staying in this house on any terms whatsoever.'

'Bravely spoken,' he approved sardonically. 'But the choice is not yours. I thought I had made that clear.'

'But you can't keep me here against my will.' By a superhuman effort she kept her tone level. 'I should run away.'

He looked at her mockingly. 'In this climate, *thespinis*? And naked and barefoot. I don't think so.'

She began, 'But I'm not naked...' then

41

stopped, as she read the message in his dark gaze. She stepped backwards, clutching defensively at the towel. 'You wouldn't.'

'I advise you not to put it to the test,' he said. 'Besides, where would you run to—the village? They would send you back.'

'But they can't be the only people around. There's a bus and . . .' her voice tailed off as she saw his mouth twist derisively.

'The bus called yesterday, *thespinis*. It will not be here again for a week.' He shrugged. 'Who knows—perhaps by that time I will have had enough of you anyway.'

'And I've had enough of you now,' Gemma flared at him. 'You must be out of your mind to threaten me like this. You can't really imagine I'm going to hang around here so that you can—rape me.'

'I have no intention of raping you, *thespinis*,' he said gently. 'I shall use no more force towards you than your brother did to Maria,' he added huskily.

She swallowed. For one terrible moment, she'd had an image of those firm lips crushing hers, parting them—the lean, brown hands caressing and intimate.

She said on a whisper, 'Touch me and I'll kill you.'

He laughed. 'You have spirit. I approve of that. Our time together should prove more pleasurable than I anticipated.'

'There'll be no time together.' Gemma closed her eyes wearily. 'If you do any of the things you've threatened, then I shall go to the authorities. You can't hope to get away with it. We're not living in the Dark Ages.'

'And what will you tell these authorities? That

you went to Knossos and picked up a rich Greek for a little adventure, and found you were out of your depth? Because that is what I will tell them. And the waiter in the taverna will confirm my story. He saw us watching each other, and he believes your hurried departure was only to lure me on. He told me I was a fortunate man, and wished me well,' he added.

'How nice for you,' she flashed. 'Perhaps if he'd known what you really intended, he'd have told you that you were off your head.'

'Perhaps,' he smiled a little grimly. 'But we shall never know.'

'Why were you at Knossos anyway?' Curiosity got the better of her.

'I needed to see you before I put my plan into operation. When I rang the hotel and was told you were catching a bus to Knossos, I decided to follow. The hotel said—two English girls travelling together. You were not hard to pick out.' He paused. 'And then, your companion called you Gemma, and I was sure.'

Shakily, she remembered the photograph, and the waves of burning anger reaching her.

'Wasn't the trip a little unnecessary,' she asked coldly. 'As you'd apparently already made up your mind what you were going to do.'

'Ah,' he said softly. 'But you might have been ugly or undesirable.'

She swallowed, 'And if I had been, you'd have—changed your plan?' Her voice shook. 'My God, I wish I had a harelip, a hunchback and a squint.'

'Such a combination might have given me pause,' he admitted mockingly. 'As it is——' His eyes went over her again, stripping, assessing, while the angry colour flared in her face. 'As it is, I have little to complain about. You are a little skinny for my taste, but in a situation like ours, one cannot have everything.'

She was mute with rage and humiliation, her hands curling instinctively into claws at her side, a movement which was not lost on him.

He smiled faintly. 'Scratch me in passion, little cat, but not in anger, or you will be sorry.' He pulled back the cuff of his full-sleeved white shirt and examined his watch. 'It is time you began your duties.' He saw her flinch slightly and laughed out loud. 'No, not that. My needs at this moment are a little more prosaic. You may cook me a meal.'

She said steadily, 'I'll see you in hell first.'

He lifted one shoulder negligently. 'As you wish. But you should consider—if you do not cook, then you also do not eat.' He glanced around him. 'It is a pleasant room, *ne*, but I think you would soon grow tired of its four walls.'

And he meant it, she recognised bitterly. She glared at him. 'How do you know I can cook?'

'I don't require gourmet food. There is a leg of lamb to roast, and a salad to make. You should be capable of that at least.'

She was capable of that, and more. She'd been well taught at home, but that was no reason why this—this bastard should benefit from her skill.

She lifted an indifferent shoulder. 'I'll try, but I hope you won't blame me if it's ruined.'

'I hope I shall not have to,' he said quite gently, but there was a warning implicit in his words. He turned and walked away, and she heard him go down the stairs, leaving her alone.

Gemma drew a deep breath and sank down on the edge of the bed. She was trembling violently inside, and her heart was pounding as if it threatened to break through her breastbone.

She bent her head, staring at the tiled floor, and began to breathe deeply and rhythmically, deliberately calming herself. At the moment, she was vulnerable, totally on the run, but that could change, and she could change it.

She began to think. The first sign she'd had that she was not alone had been the slamming of some vehicle's door. Had he really brought that fantastic car all the way up those appalling mountain roads, she wondered incredulously. But if he had, then it was parked near at hand, and that meant that the keys weren't far away either. He was probably carrying them on him, she decided judiciously, and once he was asleep, she could go through his pockets and find them. She tried not to contemplate what it would be like driving an unfamiliar vehicle in bare feet down that snake of a road. She also tried not to think about the events which might precede his falling asleep, because if she did so, then her courage might evaporate entirely.

She sank her teeth into her soft lower lip until she tasted blood. Oh God! Why hadn't she obeyed her first instinct and gone with James and Hilary? She would have been safe then—or would he still have pursued her?

She got up and went into the bathroom. She washed her face and hands in cool water, then rewrapped her towel sarong, fastening it firmly with some safety pins from her toilet bag.

If this was all the covering she was to be allowed, then she would make damned sure it was secure, she told herself, flicking her hair back from her face.

The Cretan was lounging on the narrow sofa when she went downstairs, looking through a newspaper, a glass of ouzo at his elbow He didn't even glance up at her as she walked through the living room, and out into the kitchen.

Presumably, Gemma thought bitterly, he was used to a woman's presence about the place, both in the kitchen and the bedroom.

She managed to light the oven, then found the joint of lamb from the fridge and put it in a roasting pan. After a brief struggle with herself, she added seasoning, and then inserted some slivers of garlic, alternating with sprigs of rosemary she had found growing in a pot on the windowsill, into slits she had cut in the skin. She dribbled olive oil from a jar over the meat and set it to roast.

It was while she was slicing tomatoes for the salad, that she first noticed the knife she was using. An ordinary kitchen knife, but the blade was pointed and sharp, and it was a line of defence she hadn't considered. If only she'd been wearing normal clothing, she could have hidden it somewhere, but a towel had very few hiding places, she thought ruefully. She needed something with long sleeves so that she could slide the handle under the strap of her watch and let the blade rest against her arm.

And she knew with sudden excitement, exactly what she could use. She gave a slow, triumphant smile. Her captor might think he held all the winning cards, but the last trick could be hers, after all.

She'd hoped she could slip upstairs again unnoticed, but when she came back into the living room, he was clearly waiting for her.

He gestured imperatively, indicating the seat beside him. 'Come here, Gemma.' He saw her hesitation, and the dark brows lifted arrogantly. 'Do you intend to make me fetch you?'

No, she didn't, and that was for sure. Fighting down the signs of inner rebellion, she walked over to the sofa and sat down beside him. If ever she'd needed that knife, it was now, and the damned thing was in the kitchen.

'Would you like me to fill the time until supper with some housework, *kyrie*?' she asked coolly. 'Or have you other plans for me?'

He said softly, 'Little wasp. Has no man ever taught you to sweeten your tongue? My plan is that we should talk a little, get to know each other- -even . . .' he paused, as if uncertain how to continue.

'You mean you intend to woo me a little?' She put a world of exaggerated surprise into her voice and expression as she faced him. 'But surely that's unnecessary- for what you are planning?'

He looked at her with a glint of anger in his eyes. 'Quite unnecessary. I'd thought only that it might ease the situation for you, perhaps.'

'Nothing,' Gemma said bitingly, 'could ever do that.'

She wished the sofa was bigger. He was resting his arm along the back of it, and his hand was too near her bare shoulder.

'Then that is a pity,' he said. 'I thought, you see, that we might indulge ourselves, you and I, with a little pretence. I thought we might pretend that yesterday at Knossos, I had joined you at your table for lunch, and afterwards driven you and your companion back to Heraklion, and that later you and I had dinner together.' His voice deepened and softened. 'And that when I suggested you might allow me to drive you into the mountains today, you agreed. So that we have spent the whole day alone together, walking and talking, and now we are here—and our meal is

cooking, and we both know it is too late for me to
take you back to your hotel—and we are content
that it is so.' His voice sank almost to a whisper.
Gemma felt his fingers on the nape of her neck,
under the fall of her hair, stroking her skin softly
and sensuously. 'And you are waiting, Gemma
mou, for me to kiss you.'

He had moved while he was speaking, she
realised with a jolt. He was so close to her now
that their bodies were almost brushing. If she
turned her head even a fraction, then their lips
would meet . . .

She had no intention of doing any such thing, of
course, only his warm hand smoothing her skin
was dangerously, treacherously compelling. She
could feel an answering warmth, deep inside her
body, an excitement constricting her throat.

She fought it away fiercely. 'Enjoy your
egotistical fantasies, *kyrie*,' she said huskily. 'But
they don't alter a thing. As it happens, I wouldn't
walk to the end of the street with you—in
Knossos, or anywhere else. And now, if you'll
excuse me, I have potatoes to peel. Your primary
requirement is still for food, I understand.'

'At the moment,' he said between his teeth, 'my
most crying need is to give you a beating you will
always remember. You had better get out of my
sight.'

Her impulse was to run like a hare, but she
made herself saunter, head held high as if
indifferent to the very real threat in his voice.

Once in the kitchen, she sagged against the table
with a barely stifled whimper of relief. Just for a
moment or two there, it could have been so easy,
so fatally easy to let him get to her.

No matter how much she hated him, there was
no way she could deny his attraction. Physically,

he was one of the most devastating men she had ever seen. He would have turned heads on any street in the world, and under normal circumstances, he wouldn't have given Gemma Barton, with her fair hair, grey-green eyes and chain store clothes a second look.

And no matter how much he might charm her now, no matter how skilfully he might exercise that potent sexuality, that seductive expertise, she couldn't forget that he was taking her only for some twisted motive of revenge.

And that was her safeguard, Gemma realised painfully. Because she was beginning to realise that if this stranger who had forced his way into her life had wanted her—really wanted her—for herself, then she would not have known how to resist him.

Gemma put the final touches to her appearance, and contemplated her reflection with satisfaction.

The towel lay discarded on the bed, and in its place she was wearing one of the Cretan's own shirts which she'd filched from his room. She'd had a quick look for the car keys too while she was there, but hadn't dared spend too long in case he came upstairs and caught her.

It was dark by now, and he'd lit the lamps downstairs, creating little intimate pools of brilliance against the encroaching shadows.

Soft lights, Gemma thought caustically, but at least there'd be no sweet music to accompany them. And no sweet talk either. He'd barely addressed a word to her, except to ask when the meal would be ready.

His shirt was too large for her, of course, but she'd belted it in with a piece of rope she'd found in one of the kitchen drawers, and rolled up the

sleeves a little, making sure they still hung down
over her wrists, hiding her watchstrap, and the
knife now tucked into it. She would have to be
careful not to scratch herself on it, but its mere
possession gave her new confidence in herself.

If he laid a hand on her now, he could lose it,
she told herself defiantly.

She'd managed to take a quick look outside
too, and seen that he hadn't brought the sports
car, but a small jeep, which might prove more
manageable.

She tugged at an errant strand of hair, nervously
flicking her tongue over her dry lips, an image of
the man lying stabbed and bleeding on the floor
while she searched his pockets for the keys taking
nervous hold on her mind. Well—if it happened,
he'd asked for it, she assured herself.

With one last jittery glance in the mirror, she
went slowly downstairs. The living room was
empty, but as she paused at the foot of the stairs,
he came through from the kitchen, bending a little
to negotiate the doorway. He saw her and stopped,
his brows snapping together incredulously as he
noticed how she was dressed.

Gemma took the initiative. 'I hope you don't
object, *kyrie*.' She allowed what was almost a
coaxing note to enter her voice, as she circled
briefly and gracefully in front of him. 'But I have
to wear something—and beggars cannot be
choosers.'

'Beggars usually content themselves with
something less than my best shirt,' he said coolly.
'But wear it for this evening.' He gave her a thin
smile. 'I can always reclaim it later. Now serve me
this meal.'

She murmured a meek word of acquiescence
and slid past him into the kitchen. It smelled

wonderful, she had to admit, and she had cooked Lyonnais potatoes and green beans in addition.

She had set a place for him in the dining room, but had laid her own knife and fork on the kitchen table. After all, he'd told her she was to work as his servant, and the hired help wouldn't normally expect to eat with the master of the house. Besides, while she was getting dressed, another little surprise had occurred to her.

She carved the lamb into thick slices and arranged it on two platters, adding a helping of beans to each. Then she took her own serving of the browned and savoury potatoes, before lifting the top layer of the remainder and adding a hasty handful of salt. It looked innocently appetising, but what it would taste like made her eyes water just to think of it as she added it to his platter.

At the very least, he would complain. At best, he might actually be ill, she thought vindictively, and she would be able to protest in wide-eyed innocence that in England people liked their food well-seasoned.

When she took his food into the dining room, he was pouring wine into two glasses.

'You are not hungry?' He looked questioningly, as she set down the single plate.

'I was going to eat in the kitchen.'

The firm lips tightened. He said coolly, 'No. You will eat in here at all times. Is that understood?'

'Perfectly.' Gemma kept her voice expressionless. She fetched her plate and took the seat opposite, watching under her lashes as he picked up his fork.

He said, 'You haven't taken much food.'

'I've plenty,' she returned hastily. 'And anyway, I'm on a diet.'

'Then you should not be. You are already too

thin as I have told you.' Calmly he reached across and swapped her plate for his. 'It looks delicious,' he added, and began to eat.

She could have ground her teeth in disappointment, but she picked up her own fork and began her meal. The lamb was succulent and fragrant with the herbs she had used, and the beans too were perfect, but she was careful to steer clear of the potatoes.

He must know, she thought, but how could he? He'd not been in the kitchen during the dishing-up process.

'You should eat some potato. It is excellent.'

'Potatoes are my least favourite vegetable,' she returned, forking up a gingerly fragment and trying not to wince at the taste.

'And yet you took the trouble to cook them in this special way for me. You are a paragon among women, Gemma *mou*.'

She didn't have to look at him. The note of unholy amusement in his voice was enough. She picked up her wine glass and raised it to her lips, then jerked away, looking at it with acute suspicion. 'What is this?'

He laughed. '*Retsina*. Resinated wine—but a mild one. It is quite safe to drink. I have not doctored it in any way.'

She put down her glass. 'I think I'd prefer water.'

'As you wish.' He wasn't ruffled in the slightest. 'There is bottled water in the refrigerator, although it is safe to drink from the taps.'

When she came back, he had finished and pushed his plate aside and was peeling himself a peach from a bowl of fruit on the table.

She began to clear both plates, and he halted her. 'Do you intend to starve yourself before my eyes? Or are you sulking because your ploy with the food did not work?'

'I don't know what you're talking about,' Gemma lied coldly. 'And if I have no appetite, is it really any wonder? I'm worse than a prisoner here.'

'At least have some fruit.' He pushed the bowl towards her, but she refused with a curt shake of her head. He sighed. 'Gemma, I am not a barbarian. If I promise you that tonight you will sleep alone, will you eat something?'

She gave him a startled look. 'Why should you promise any such thing? And how do I know you'll keep your word anyway—after all the deceptions of the past couple of days?'

'I'll keep my word,' he said. 'And I have my reasons, but I do not mean to share them or my bed—with you tonight.'

A wild hope was beginning to stir in her. She stared at him. 'How long will this reprieve go on for—a day—a week—longer?'

He shrugged, the dark face enigmatic. 'Until I decide otherwise, Gemma *mou*.'

She swallowed. 'I don't believe that. I think you're having second thoughts. You—you have to be. You've just said yourself that you're not a barbarian—but to keep me here like a slave is—inhuman.' She paused, her wide eyes fixed on his face in passionate appeal. 'Prove you're not a barbarian. Let me go—please.'

He didn't answer, and she went on, her courage rising, 'If you take me back to Heraklion tomorrow, that will be the end of it. I won't tell anyone or go to the police. After all, I don't even know your name.' She moistened dry lips with the tip of her tongue. 'You talked about pretending earlier—well, we can pretend this never happened.

You—you can tell your friends some story—say that I ran away—anything. They'd have to believe you.' She paused again, eagerly scanning his face, his eyes, for some softening, some answering warmth. 'You can't convince me that you really want to be involved in this sordid little vendetta. You don't even belong here. It's not your concern.'

His clenched fist struck the table, making the crockery dance, and Gemma gasped, shrinking back.

'You talk like a fool, *thespinis*. You—from your safe, conventional English town—what do you know of me—of any of us? If you find this affair sordid, then it is a member of your own family who has made it so. If he needed a woman, he should have gone to a brothel, or sought out one of his own countrywomen who understand how such games are played.' His eyes were grim as he surveyed her. 'You think that to be here with me is the worst that could happen? You are wrong. You are lucky that your brother still lives, and you are buying his life, make no mistake about that. Now, do you still want to run away?'

'Yes,' she threw at him recklessly. 'Because I'm not convinced by this—any of it. Mike's been tried and condemned in his absence, without being given the slightest chance to defend himself. And what about this innocent Maria? It doesn't sound to me that she was exactly unwilling. You've said yourself he didn't rape her.'

'It is precisely because of that, he is not a dead man at this moment,' he said. 'And take care how you speak of Maria to me. To us, the innocence of our girls is their protection, and so it should have been to your brother who was accepted as a friend by the village. He was trusted and he betrayed that trust, and ran away rather than face retribution. The firm mouth curled cruelly. 'But you, Gemma *mou*, will not run away. You have my guarantee on that.'

She got to her feet slowly, trembling in every limb. 'And you have my guarantee that I'll do anything—anything to get away from you. I loathe and despise you for doing this to me. And I know why you're letting me off the hook tonight—because you're such a bloody egotist you think if you wait long enough I'll fall into your arms. Well, forget it. Anything you take from me will be by force. And rape can't be any worse than the contamination of having to live under the same roof with you.'

He stood up too, his chair crashing violently away. Two long swift strides, and he was round the table, towering over her. Before she could move, his hand had hooked into the open neckline of her shirt, dragging her towards him.

He said between his teeth. 'Your frankness does you credit. So you can have no objection if we dispense with one source of contamination at least.'

His hand moved downwards, freeing the buttons as it went. His fingers grazed scorchingly against the soft mound of her breast, and she bit back a cry, as if his touch had actually branded her flesh. And knew in that moment, that if she allowed this to continue, allowed him to strip her as he was intent on doing, that she would be branded for life anyway.

Her fingers fumbled wildly under her sleeve, then the knife was safely in her hand.

She said hoarsely, 'Let me go—don't touch me, or I'll use this. I swear I will.'

He stepped back, looking down ex-

pressionlessly at the dangerous glitter of the
blade between them.

He said, 'Use it then. Do you know how?'

Her fingers clenched round the hilt in an effort
to stop their trembling, her breathing constricted,
she watched in disbelief as without haste he
unfastened his own shirt down to the waist, pulling
the material free of his waist sash so that his chest
was completely bare.

His skin was smooth and brown, his chest
shadowed with body hair growing down to a vee
across his flat stomach. Gemma stood as if
paralysed, the knife pointing stiffly towards him.
Her mouth was dry, her pulses slow and heavy.

He said again, his voice quiet. 'Do you know
how?'

His hands reached and took both her wrists,
drawing her towards him. He placed her free hand
over the strong rib cage, her other hand just
beneath, the tip of the blade resting against his
skin.

'Strike upwards,' he advised coolly. 'Like this.'
The pressure on her wrist increased fractionally,
and as if mesmerised, she saw a bright bead of
blood appear under the tip of the knife.

She gave a choking, frightened cry and jerked
backwards, throwing the knife away, hearing it
clatter across the tiled floor.

Her legs buckled and she sank down to her
knees, covering her face with her hands, her
tortured breathing tearing at her lungs.

His hands were on her, lifting her inexorably to
her feet, and she struggled feebly, moaning 'No.'

His hand twisted in her hair, stilling her,
imposing a reluctant submission. His dark face
seemed to swim in front of hers. She could read
the purpose in his eyes, and a cry of protest

formed in her taut throat, never to be uttered as his mouth came down, fiercely, ruthlessly on hers.

She couldn't think, or breathe. She wanted to stay totally passive, impervious to any demands he might make of her, but his lips parted hers with a sensual dominance which enforced a response in spite of herself.

As she capitulated, shaking, yielding her mouth to the sweet erotic abandonment of taste and touch, the violence in him gentled. The agonising tug on her hair faded, and his hand slid down to cup the nape of her neck, his fingers working warm and sensuous magic against her skin. His other arm closed round her, drawing her forward until her bared breasts brushed against the warm muscular wall of his chest, her sensitive nipples excited unbearably by the subtle friction of his body against hers.

She'd never been kissed like this before, she realised dazedly. Never been held in such an intimate embrace, and her body's reaction startled and bewildered her.

She could stay in his arms forever, she realised with a shattering sense of shock, if only he would go on kissing her like this, go on exploring every secret her soft mouth had to offer with such heart-stopping completeness.

And when at last he lifted his lips from hers, she felt almost bereft. Her eyelids flickered open, and she stared up at him in utter confusion, the bruised grey-green depths of her eyes betraying her inner turmoil.

His face was taut, cast in lines as harsh as the mountains which surrounded them. For a long moment he looked down into her face, his gaze burning into hers, then his hand slid, unhurrying, the slim curved length of her body, curving with sensuous mastery round the swell of her hip, urging her forward slightly so that their thighs touched, and she was made compellingly aware of the fact that he was deeply and passionately aroused.

Shudderingly, incredulously, she felt her whole inner being clench in response and desire.

And then she was free—no contact between them at all, and she was ashamed to realise that it was he who had stepped away.

He said harshly, 'You had better go to your room, while I am still capable of keeping my word to you.'

She swallowed convulsively, then turned and went away from him towards the stairs. At the archway, she turned and looked back.

He hadn't moved at all. She could see the rapid rise and fall of his bare chest as he fought to control his breathing, and below his ribcage, that tiny smear of blood. Her hand stole up to her throat in shock as she absorbed the full force of everything which had happened between them.

His voice came to her soft and remorseless. He said, 'It will not be rape.'

Gemma gave a small inarticulate cry, and ran from him—up the stairs on legs which threatened to betray her at every step, and into the illusion of safety offered by her room.

CHAPTER FOUR

GEMMA sat for a long time on the edge of her bed, staring blankly into space, trying to come to terms with what had just happened, and failing by a mile.

She could offer neither explanation nor excuse for herself. This was a man she had cause only to hate. A man whose name she did not even know. A man who was using her as the instrument of a vengeance she did not even comprehend.

Why then, in spite of everything, had she fallen into his arms?

For a moment, she'd even had the upper hand, but her own cowardice had let her down. Gemma shivered. She couldn't have killed him, she thought, but she could have hurt him, incapacitated him sufficiently to allow her to make her getaway unmolested. Now she was back to square one, or worse.

She thought her defiance had surprised him, but there would be no element of surprise in future. He would now be prepared—on the watch for anything she might do.

But he had no idea that she could drive, she told herself, trying to rally her spirits. And her next plan had to be to find the keys of the jeep, even though the prospect of having to negotiate that mountain road in an unfamiliar vehicle frankly appalled her.

But what other choice did she have, without shoes to walk in, or indeed, proper clothes?

Once inside the jeep, she reasoned, she would be

safe until she got to Chania. She'd find James and Hilary somehow, and Hilary would lend her anything she needed. She would have to enlist James' good offices over her missing passport and travellers cheques, she realised ruefully, and sighed out loud. God, what a mess it all was.

And when she did get away, there was still the problem of Michael to contend with. Somehow she would have to find him, wherever he'd gone, and warn him to stay out of Crete for good, even if he claimed he was innocent of the accusation. If her unknown captor was right, it would be all too easy for any determined and vengeful persons to stage an accident in these mountains.

She looked at the flickering flame of the little lamp beside her bed, and her lips twisted. She'd found it alight when she came in, and realised that he must have done it while she was occupied in the kitchen. Before, she thought, he'd come to the decision to let her sleep alone that night.

She shivered again. She couldn't count on being allowed another respite, which made her need to escape during the next twenty-four hours not just imperative, but overwhelming.

Those few agonisingly passionate moments in his arms had taught her things about herself that she had never known, could never have guessed. In the past, although she'd had a number of boyfriends, she'd always regarded herself as something of a cool customer. It had always been simple enough to call a halt when more than kisses were sought, and this was why she'd always fought shy of any closer commitment. In a way, she'd almost been afraid that there might be something lacking in her, which would make her a bad bet for any man seeking a normal loving relationship with a wife. So, while the kissing had been enjoyable enough, she'd never been tempted to go further.

Except tonight, she thought, putting tentative fingers against the swollen fullness of her mouth.

Decent men, with perfectly honourable intentions, had wanted her, and she had sent them away without one pang of regret. Why in hell, she asked herself despairingly, had she had to learn her first lesson in desire from a stranger who cared nothing for her, who was only taking her to satisfy some primitive notion of justice?

Yet he himself was far from primitive, she thought wonderingly. He might wear peasant clothing, but everything he had, including the shirt she herself was wearing, was of the finest quality. He was educated and sophisticated—so how could he lend himself to this barbarity?

And all the time, as she sat there, watching the little flame and thinking, she was listening for the moment when he would come upstairs.

He'd promised—but would he keep that promise, she thought, her heart thudding oddly. After all, he'd brought her to the brink of surrender as his own instincts and experience must have told him. Wasn't it more than likely that he might decide to follow up the advantage he'd gained?

And if he came upstairs and saw a light under her door, mightn't that provide the final prompting he needed?

With a burst of nervous energy, Gemma blew out the lamp. Moving quietly in the darkness, she washed her face and cleaned her teeth in the bathroom. The shirt she removed and hung over a chair. It might once again be all she had to wear tomorrow, she thought wryly. She turned back the coverlet to the bottom of the bed, and slipped under the thin sheet, welcoming its fresh coolness against her heated skin.

But she couldn't relax. Tensely she lay looking up at the ceiling, and waiting for what might be.

It wasn't a very big house, and in the quiet night air every little sound seemed magnified. She could hear him moving around downstairs—even, she thought, hear the chink of a bottle on a glass. It sounded as if he was drinking, and she wasn't sure whether this was a good thing or a bad.

And it was while she was trying to decide, that exhaustion finally claimed her, and she fell asleep.

When Gemma awoke, it was early daylight. For a moment, she was totally disorientated, staring round her wondering where she was, then memory came flooding back, and she sank back against the pillow with a little groan.

The events of the past twenty-four hours might just have been some awful dream. Now, she knew, it was all only too real.

She wondered what had woken her. It was at least an hour before she normally stirred. She slid out of bed, and, naked, padded over to the window, opening the shutters a cautious fraction. She could see the road leading down to the village quite plainly, and walking down it, away from the villa, was a girl, dark-haired and wearing a red dress.

As Gemma watched, the girl swung round in her tracks and stared back at the villa. Even from that distance, Gemma could see that she was a vibrantly pretty girl, although her looks were currently marred by a sullen expression, and her shoulders had a dejected droop as she continued to trudge down the track.

Gemma pursed her lips in a silent whistle, then grabbed the shirt from the chair, and thrust her

arms into the sleeves, her fingers clumsy with haste
as she tried to fasten the buttons. She needed to
talk to that girl, and fast.

She let herself quietly out of her room, and
slipped stealthily down the stairs.

The sun pouring in through the light curtains
illuminated the living room with merciless emphasis. Gemma's nose wrinkled as she surveyed the
bottle and used glass which stood by the sofa, the
ash tray, overflowing with butts, and the general
disarray of cushions and rugs. But she didn't have
time to worry about that now, she told herself
impatiently, and if she could just talk to that girl
for a few moments, she might never have to bother
about it at all.

She'd expected to have to wrestle with bolts on
the door, but to her surprise it wasn't even locked.
She opened it with care, gritting her teeth as the
hinges squeaked slightly. Not that it mattered, she
thought optimistically. If that bottle was anything
to go by, her captor should still be sleeping it off
at noon.

'You're going somewhere?'

Gemma almost screamed. Certainly she jumped,
whirling round, her heart thudding painfully. And,
of course, he wasn't sleeping anything off. He was
standing in the archway watching her, hands
resting lightly on his hips. He looked the worse for
wear, however, his eyes narrowed against the light
as if it hurt him, and she hoped that it did. His
hair was dishevelled too, and he hadn't shaved.

'I was just letting in some fresh air,' she returned
defensively. 'Or perhaps you don't think it's
necessary?'

He shrugged as if fresh air or poison gas were
all the same to him. 'Do as you wish,' he said
flatly. 'And then you may prepare breakfast.

You will find fresh bread in the kitchen,' he added shortly.

'Oh?' Gemma was intrigued in spite of herself. 'How did that get here?'

'One of the villagers brought it.' His tone was impatient. 'Now, if you have no more questions, I will go and finish dressing.'

She said, 'I saw a girl from my window. I thought that perhaps it might be Maria.'

'Then I advise you not to think,' he said unpleasantly. 'Just do as you're bidden. And call me when breakfast is ready,' he flung at her over his shoulder, as he turned towards the stairs.

'Certainly,' Gemma returned coolly. 'And where would you like breakfast—in the dining room —on the terrace?' Or thrown at you, she added silently.

He shrugged again. 'On the terrace will do perfectly well.'

'And when I do call you,' she went on cordially, 'what do I say?'

He frowned. 'What do you mean.'

'Well, I don't know your name,' she said. 'So how do you wish to be addressed. Sir, perhaps? My lord? Your majesty?'

The frown deepened to a scowl. 'I recommend you to guard your tongue, *thespinis*. I am not in the mood for your insolence this morning.'

'So I've noticed,' she returned drily. 'Sexual frustration and a hangover seems to be a lethal mixture.'

His eyes narrowed dangerously. 'What do you dare say to me?'

'Nothing,' Gemma said hastily. 'A little joke, that's all, but out of place. I'm sorry.'

He looked at her for a long, disturbing moment. 'I think you will be,' he said at last, and went upstairs.

Gemma drew a deep breath, and expelled it shakily. She was a fool to provoke him, even mildly, under the circumstances. She would have to keep her natural sense of mischief firmly under control, she decided wryly.

She tidied the living room hastily, clearing away the debris from the previous night, and shaking up the cushions and hanging the rugs to air over the terrace balustrade.

Then she went into the kitchen. The bread was on the table. It was still warm, and it smelled wonderful, Gemma thought ecstatically, as she emptied a carton of orange juice into a jug, and filled a dish from the tin of jam in a cupboard. There was fresh coffee, but she wasn't sure how to make it in the Greek manner, so she compromised with instant.

She carried the tray out to the terrace and set it on the table, covering the food with a cloth as a safeguard against the inquisitive wasps which were already gathering.

Then she went upstairs. Her hand was raised to tap on his door, when it opened suddenly, startling her. Downstairs, he'd been wearing a pair of faded denims and nothing else as far as she was aware, but now he had changed once again into the Cretan dress, minus the jacket he'd been wearing the previous day. He'd shaved, and his hair was wet from the shower, and she could smell the cool, damp fragrance of his skin.

He was one of the most physically arresting men she had ever seen in her life, Gemma thought dazedly, looking at the way in which his damp hair clung curling to the shape of his head, the length of the lashes which shadowed eyes as black as onyx, the sculpturing of that wickedly experienced mouth . . .

She said huskily, 'Your breakfast is ready,' and turned swiftly to escape downstairs, only to be brought to an abrupt halt by his hand on her arm.

He said silkily, 'Perhaps the day should begin here. *Kalimera*, Gemma *mou*.' And bending his head, he brushed his mouth lightly across hers.

As a kiss, it was over almost as soon as it had begun, but it left Gemma with the bruising, shameful knowledge that she had wanted it to go on. Her pulses were pounding, and breathing was suddenly difficult. She did not dare look at him again, merely turning and almost stumbling in her haste to get downstairs.

By the time he joined her on the terrace, she had almost regained what rags of composure were left to her.

His eyes flicked over her, travelling frowningly from her aloof expression to the empty plate in front of her.

He said, 'The bread is good, Gemma. Take some.'

'I'm not hungry,' she informed him defiantly.

'Nevertheless, you must eat, or you will make yourself ill.' There was a steely note in his voice.

Gemma raised her eyebrows. 'Yet only twenty-four hours ago you were threatening to let me starve.'

'It still seems to have much to recommend it,' he said grimly. 'However, I have allowed humanitarian counsels to prevail. Besides,' he added with a shrug, 'a girl weak from hunger is unlikely to prove very stimulating as a companion in bed.'

Gemma's lips tightened. She was incredibly hungry—the sun, the air, the appealing fragrance of the bread all putting an extra edge on to her normally healthy appetite. Now, she was damned if she would eat as much as a crumb in front of him.

She said glacially, 'But then providing you with that kind of entertainment is the last thing I have in mind.'

'So—what is the first?' He sounded politely interested, no more.

'Getting out of here,' she said between her teeth. 'And putting you in jail where you belong.'

'An ambitious scheme.' He didn't sound particularly perturbed. He spread jam on to a slice of bread and ate it with every appearance of enjoyment.

'But not an impossible one.' She hesitated. 'After all, you can't hope to get away with this. I'm not completely alone in the world. I have a return flight to take—a job at home in England— my family. If I don't return when I'm supposed to, then enquiries will be made. You must see that.'

He shrugged, 'And when these enquiries are made, Gemma *mou*, what will be discovered? That you were here with me. That we were lovers. It is a story as old as time, and will surprise no one— except, perhaps, your family, and it is my intention that they should suffer through your dishonour anyway.'

Her voice thickened. 'They don't deserve that.'

'Nor did Stavros and his wife,' he said coldly. 'It is something this brother of yours should have considered before he seduced Maria.'

She lifted her chin. 'So—what would satisfy them? If Mike married her?'

'Do you think that is likely?'

Gemma bit her lip. 'No,' she said honestly after a moment's thought. 'He's still a student. He can't afford to get married to anyone for several years yet. Although I suppose he'll have to contribute something to the baby's support,' she added frowning. She was silent for a few moments, staring down at the empty plate in front of her, tracing its pattern with her forefinger. Then she said, her voice unsteady, 'If you're determined to punish Mike through me, can't you leave it at that?'

'I'm not sure I understand you.' He drank some coffee.

The colour deepened painfully in her face. 'If I—agree to—to let you do what you want to me, will you let me go afterwards—when it's over?'

His mouth twisted wryly. 'I have had more beguiling invitations, *matia mou*. Why should I agree to any such thing?'

'I've told you—I have a life in England to return to—a career. I want to get back to them,' she said fiercely.

'And a man too, perhaps?'

The words of denial were already quivering on her lips, when Gemma scented danger in the apparently idle question.

She said, 'That's none of your concern.'

'You think not? Yet I am naturally interested to know whether you will come to me a virgin, or some other's willing pupil.'

She tried for nonchalance. 'Of course there have been men.' She shrugged. 'As you've implied yourself, things are different in England. We—we don't lead the same sheltered lives as your girls.'

'Is that a fact?' He leaned back in his chair, surveying her through lazily narrowed eyes. 'But if you are so free with your favours, Gemma *mou*, why the virtuous protests?'

Gemma could have ground her teeth in frustration and temper. She had been certain that he'd wanted her to admit she was a virgin—that for some reason, probably to make his revenge totally complete, she supposed bitterly, it was important to him. It had been a long shot, but she'd hoped that if she claimed experience, hinted that he would be one of a long line, he might find it sufficiently distasteful to bring about a change of mind where she was concerned.

She said sharply, 'Because I prefer to have a choice. Having forced me into this situation . . .'

He laughed. 'What force have I used?' he challenged. 'Within the confines of this house you move freely. I have not tied you to my wrist—dragged you screaming into my bed. There are no marks of violence on your skin—no bruises.'

She met his glance defiantly. 'Not yet.'

'Not ever.' He lifted a dismissive hand. 'Why should I use brute strength when I know a little patience will succeed in bringing me everything I desire from you?' His eyes met hers, steadily, unsmilingly. 'As we both know, Gemma *mou*,' he added softly.

The silence between them seemed to crackle. Gemma swallowed quickly. 'You—you revolting egotist,' she said.

His mouth twisted. 'So—if we are calling names—you, my lovely Gemma, are a little hypocrite. At Knossos you were as aware of me as I was of you. I need not have been honest with you. I could have sought your acquaintance, as if you were any pretty tourist to whom I was attracted—could have brought you here, seduced you, taken you body and soul—and then, but only then, told you the truth. It was a temptation, believe me, *matia mou*. Is that what you would have preferred?'

She sat very still, her mind considering and rejecting the all-too potent images his words had conjured up. She could imagine only too well how she'd have felt, falling asleep in his arms, sated with passion, believing herself desired, then waking to the ultimate cruelty of the truth.

It could, she realised stunnedly, have destroyed her—and the shock of that realisation drained the colour from her face. It contained implications she had no wish to explore—implications with the power to terrify her.

From a great distance, she heard him repeat quietly and remorselessly, 'Is that what you would have preferred?'

She said thickly, 'No.'

'That is what I thought.' He sounded as if the question had only been of minor interest to him. He drank the rest of his coffee, and pushed the cup away, glancing at his watch as he did so.

Gemma took herself in hand. 'An appointment?' she asked with heavy sarcasm. 'Please don't let me keep you.'

He smiled thinly at her. 'You could not, Gemma *mou*, if I did not wish to stay. And, as it happens, I do have an appointment—business to attend to elsewhere today. I hope you will not be too lonely.'

She stared at him. 'Oh, I imagine I'll survive.' She spoke calmly, but her heart was beating faster with the first stirrings of excitement. He was actually going to leave her here—alone. Of course, he'd be taking the jeep, she hadn't the slightest doubt about that, but there were other ways—there had to be . . .

'I expect you will.' His smile widened slightly. 'But to ensure it, I have arranged a companion for you.'

The balloon of hope inside her deflated as quickly as if it had been stabbed with a pin. She forced her face and voice to remain impassive.

'You're very thoughtful, *kyrie*. But I really don't need a surrogate jailer.'

'You think not?' He pushed back his chair and got up. 'But you need something, *pedhi mou*, to protect you from the consequences of your own recklessness. And I feel sure that if I left you here, completely alone, you would be tempted to be— very reckless.' He paused. 'As it is,' he added sardonically, 'I can relax and go about my business, knowing that you are here, safely occupied with your domestic concerns. Who knows?' He shrugged slightly. 'You might even miss me a little.'

Her pulses felt erratic. 'I wouldn't count on it.'

'You might also,' he went on silkily, as if he hadn't heard her last remark, 'give some further thought to the fascinating offer of your body you made me earlier.' He paused again. 'I am inclined to accept, so if you were not serious, now is the time to say so.'

'I wasn't serious,' she said.

'Very wise.' He sounded almost approving. 'You see, *agape mou*, I would have guaranteed nothing in return. You assumed, did you not, that I would be satisfied with one brief coupling which you would somehow endure?' He shook his head, smiling faintly. 'You are wrong, my lovely one, on all counts. Once I have you, Gemma, I intend to keep you—for a while at least. And it is also possible that once you belong to me, you will not want to leave either,' he added softly.

She wanted to say something shattering, something which would blast his ego, his self-esteem to smithereens, but no words came. Did he really believe, she found herself wondering shakily, that his physical enthralment of her would be so simple, so effortless as he implied? And knew, in that moment, that he did.

At last she heard herself say in a voice which did not seem to belong to her, 'You're mad—you have to be. It's the only explanation.'

'It's a crazy world, Gemma *mou*.' He paused. 'I will bring food for this evening with me when I come back. Is there anything else you require? Anything you would like me to bring you from the town?'

She raised her eyebrows in exaggerated surprise. 'Trying to buy me now, *kyrie*? Surely you're not losing faith in your own technique at this late stage.'

He looked at her for a long moment, bleakly, and in silence, his mouth firmed to a harsh line. Then he said, 'It was a gesture of goodwill, intended perhaps to ease the situation a little. But forget it.' He shrugged dismissively, and turned away.

Gemma bit her lip. 'I'm sorry,' she said stiffly. 'Actually, there is something—but I'm sure you don't have to go all the way to town for it.' She took a breath. 'I'd like something to wear, please, if only as an alternative to this.' She indicated the shirt, with a gesture of self-derision. 'It surely isn't too much to ask?'

'No.' He went on watching her. 'At least not when it is asked in the right way.'

'I said "please".' Her chin went up.

'I heard you, but I would have preferred the request to be made with a little more warmth.'

'Do you want me to go on my knees?' She fiddled with the dishes, piling them together fussily on the table, avoiding looking at him.

'No.' He paused again. 'I think I would prefer you to kiss me.'

'Go to hell.' Gemma spoke with bitter distinctness.

'As you wish. Then your request is refused.'

She stared down at the table. 'You mean—if I kiss you—and only then—you'll bring me something else to wear.'

'Why, yes, *matia mou*. That is exactly what I mean,' he said mockingly. 'Is it so much to ask?'

She swallowed. 'I'm not actually putting you to any trouble. You've got my luggage hidden somewhere, after all. You only have to open the case . . .'

'And you only have to walk a few paces across this terrace to me,' the tormenting voice returned. 'The decision is yours.'

Head bent, cheeks burning, hating him, she took the requisite number of steps. He didn't move, and she had to stand more or less on tiptoe to reach his olive-skinned cheek with her lips, briefly and awkwardly.

He said something terse and very violent half under his breath, and in his own language. His hands clamped down on her shoulders, forcing her to stay where she was. His eyes glinted down at her contemptuously.

'Is that what you call a kiss, Gemma?' he demanded harshly. His dark face seemed to swim before hers, and she closed her eyes on a little shaken gasp as his mouth fastened on hers, taking expert, insolent toll of its sweetness, his tongue exploring its every contour, every moist crevice. She couldn't speak, or think, or taste anything other than him. He seemed to fill the universe. She felt the deep inner trembling start within her, and knew that without that fierce bruising grip on her shoulders she would have collapsed on to the floor, her legs no longer strong enough to support her.

She was faint, she was going to die. Perhaps she
was already dead, and this was Paradise already
within her reach. The incoherencies rioted crazily
in her head, as the world tilted on its axis dragging
her down against the force of gravity into some
undreamed-of maelstrom of sensation.

She couldn't breathe, her head was being forced
back at an impossible angle, and when he let her
go the pain of separation was almost more than
she could bear.

She lifted her hand and touched her swollen lips
softly with her fingers, staring down at the tiled
floor at her feet, watching wild golden particles
whirl and dance before her wide and frightened
gaze, trying to control the ragged hurry of her
breathing, so that he wouldn't know—dear God—
what his exquisite brutality had done to her.

'So.' His own breathing didn't sound any too
sure. 'Now we begin to understand each other a
little.' His hand took her chin, forcing it upwards,
making her meet his eyes, darker than night,
harder than obsidian. 'Let our Cretan sun warm
you, Gemma, before I return tonight.' He added
grimly. 'My patience is not endless.'

He let her go, and she twisted past him into the
house, through the living quarters and into the
kitchen, as if it represented some sanctuary.

But there was no sanctuary, she thought, as she
turned on the tap letting the cold stream of water
play gratefully over her wrists and hands.

Not even where she most needed one—inside
her own heart.

CHAPTER FIVE

IT seemed a very long time before she heard the sound of the jeep starting up and driving away. But then she had spent most of it leaning against the sink unit, praying that he wouldn't follow her. She was on the ropes, confused and vulnerable, with nowhere to run, and nowhere to hide.

She moved at last, slowly and stiffly, as if she wasn't quite sure that her recalcitrant body would obey her, would observe the commands of her brain.

But her brain didn't seem to be functioning any too efficiently or it would have warned her, reminded her just how dangerous it was to provoke him.

She sighed tremulously, letting the tip of her tongue flick along her dry lips, exploring tentatively the slight soreness which still lingered. But that might be the least of her troubles before this long day was over, she thought, wincing.

She sighed again, but more sharply, bracing herself to fight the feeling of inevitability which threatened to overwhelm her.

He had said it would happen, that he would take and she would give, and she knew now how fatally easy it would be to let herself go with the tide, drown with him in sensual oblivion. She had never wanted a man before, and it was a terrible irony that it should be this particular man who was the focus of her first passionate desires.

She wished with all her heart that she really had the experience she'd foolishly boasted of. At least she might know how to cope with what was happening to her. Might be able to judge, to gauge the astonishing intensity of response he seemed able to arouse in her and which nothing in her life so far had prepared her for. She was ashamed of it, but she could no longer deny it existed.

She listened intently for a moment. She'd not heard any other voices, any sounds of movement but his while she'd waited in the kitchen like a cornered animal. Perhaps he'd forgotten to provide her with the alternative jailer he'd threatened her with, she thought hopefully, and if so—if so . . .

She went quickly to the stairs and up them, straight to his room. It would have been nice to have had her own things back to escape in, but under the circumstances she couldn't wait around for them to be returned to her. She would have to make do with whatever she could find.

She pulled back the curtain and scanned the hanging rail. It would have to be another shirt, preferably one even more opaque than the sample she was currently wearing. And not a rope belt either. One of his own sashes from the second drawer in the chest. She'd managed without underwear so far, and supposed she could go on doing so. But shoes of some kind were essential, and not those damned knee boots he favoured. The alternatives seemed to be sandals, or a pair of flat heelless mules. She tried them on. They were far too big, of course, but she thought if she stuffed the toes with paper, she might be able to shuffle along somehow. Anyway, she would try. This was her last chance, and she had to take it.

She changed into the clean shirt, belting it carefully round her slim waist tightly, and

frowning a little as she twisted and turned in front
of the mirror assessing the effect. It was perfectly
decent, just as the other one had been, she
thought, and it was only her own self-consciousness
about her lack of other attire that made her doubt
it. It covered her as adequately as any dress.

The mules were far more of a problem. It took
three-quarters of the Greek newspaper she found
down in the living room to make them stay on at
all, and they felt thoroughly uncomfortable as well
as restricting quite considerably her freedom of
movement. But then, she wasn't planning on
taking part in a hundred metre sprint, she
reminded herself. She wasn't going to hurry at all,
in case anyone was watching her. She was simply
going for a gentle stroll—up the mountain.

She wished she'd paid infinitely more attention
to Takis' map, then she might know if there were
other villages round about. Slightly more civilised
villages, she thought hopefully, where they didn't
conduct weird sexual vendettas . . .

Surely, there had to be something else, and,
eventually, someone else. Someone who would
help her. Loussenas, and its watching, hostile eyes,
couldn't be the end of the line.

She took a deep breath. There was only one way
to find out, she told herself resolutely, and
shuffled, cursing the unwieldy mules silently, to the
door.

For the moment, she thought the low rumbling
sound she heard was distant thunder, and paused,
scanning the cloudless sky with frank dismay. The
last thing she wanted was to be caught in a storm,
next door to naked. She wanted to escape, not die
of pneumonia.

The rumble came again, and she realised with
heart-stopping suddenness that it was emanating,

not from the Lord Zeus' displeasure with mankind, but from the throat of a very large dog.

She stopped dead, staring in dismay, and the dog looked back at her, lifting its upper lip in a snarl which was no more pleasant for being silent.

Gemma said in a voice of false cheerfulness. 'Hello then, boy, Good dog.' She extended a clenched fist for the animal to sniff, a gesture of confidence which it treated with contempt, snarling again, and this time adding sound to the performance. It was stationed slap in the middle of the terrace, and clearly had no intention of budging.

Gemma toyed with the idea of bribing the thing with the remains of last night's leg of lamb, but dismissed it. This particular Cerberus looked as if he meant business, and would require a far more substantial sop to be thrown to him than a few leftovers.

Aloud, she said, 'Cerberus is a good name for you, hell-hound,' and went back into the house. She stood for a few moments, watching the dog choose a patch of shade and lie down in it. But not, it seemed, to sleep. Massive chin on large paws, it lay and gazed towards the house, ears pricking attentively at every move she made.

A companion, she thought corrosively. The half was not told me.

Moving cautiously, the offending mules kicked into a corner, she began to tidy the house, to sweep and dust, to fill the long minutes with the mundane details of domesticity. And the dog Cerberus seemed to track every move she made with his unswerving gaze.

Once, and only once, she made an attempt to get past him to the steps, but he growled at her with such positive venom that she abandoned it almost immediately.

When she went upstairs, he rose, shook himself and padded after her. Gemma found it almost a relief. She'd been trying to gauge the drop from the terrace where she'd sunbathed that first afternoon—could it really be only yesterday? she asked herself in frank astonishment—and the dog's presence meant that she wouldn't even be tempted to try and risk breaking a leg, or worse.

The people who advocated death before dishonour had obviously never actually been faced with the choice, she thought with irony.

The dog lay in the passage and watched her as she moved from one room to the other, tidying bathrooms and straightening beds. As Gemma worked, she chatted to him as if he had been a pet instead of a jailer, and eventually was rewarded by a faint and perfunctory swish of the tail. But that, she thought wryly, was probably as amiable as he was likely to get.

In the Cretan's room she worked slowly, taking the time to look around her, now that the coast was relatively clear.

He was still very much a mystery, and this room—his domain—provided no clues at all. There were his clothes, expensive and of excellent quality as she'd already noted, but few other personal possessions—no photos, letters or papers to give any indication of his identity. She wondered if that was deliberate—part of the plan—or perfectly usual for the way he lived his life. A man, she thought, who travelled lightly because he travelled alone.

But that, of course, was pure speculation. He probably had a wife and six children somewhere. Perhaps he was with them at this moment, playing the part of the devoted family man, she thought with a little hostile snort.

And if this wife existed—did she know what he was doing in these days away from her? And, if so, would she care? Would her own desire for vengeance align with his, cancelling out all other considerations?

It seemed impossible. What wife could know that her husband was sleeping with another woman, whatever his motive, and endure that knowledge?

I couldn't, Gemma thought fiercely, and found that her hands had involuntarily clenched into fists at the idea.

She gave a small weak laugh. It seemed she was allowing her imagination to run away with her.

Besides, any woman who married a man like that was asking for trouble, and would deserve all she got.

But being in his room like this, she was forced to admit, was a strange sensation. Straightening his bed, shaking up the pillow, folding the linen sheet which was the only covering, was an only too forcible reminder of what the night could bring.

Gemma swallowed thickly. Simply touching the bed which held him seemed to conjure up an image so powerful that she had the odd feeling she had only to turn round, and she would find him there—waiting to take her in his arms, to draw her down beside him on to the bed . . .

The dog barked, gruffly, throatily and Gemma jumped, almost expecting that the Cretan had materialised beside her somehow, and that the dog was giving warning.

But Cerberus' attention had been engaged by something or someone downstairs, and as Gemma paused to listen, she could hear the sound of footsteps moving about, but not, she thought, those of a man.

The dog was already halfway down the stairs and she followed more gingerly. She heard the dog growl, then bark again, and a girl's voice speaking sharply in Greek. The dog's ears went down and his tail wagged. Whatever the girl had said, they were clearly magic words, Gemma thought.

She recognised her at once—it was the girl in the red dress she'd seen earlier, and she still looked sulky, her heavy-lidded dark eyes almost fierce as they met Gemma's.

Gemma said coolly and clearly, 'My name is Gemma Barton, and I think you must be Maria.'

The girl shrugged. She muttered, *'Then katava-leno.'*

Gemma's Greek was minimal, but that was one of the few phrases she'd managed to master. She said sharply, 'I think you understand perfectly well. And don't tell me that you and Mike only spoke Greek to each other because it's just not possible.'

There was a silence. Then the girl said, 'You are the woman of Michalis?'

'His sister,' Gemma corrected. *'Adelphi tou,'* she added for good measure.

'Sister.' The black brows snapped together frowningly. 'I do not understand.'

And Gemma did not feel capable of explaining all over again to someone whose knowledge of her language seemed limited. She sighed.

'Did Mike Michalis never mention that he had a sister? Didn't he talk about his family at all?'

Silence. Another shrug. 'A little maybe. But not a sister.'

'Nevertheless, that's who I am.' Gemma made herself smile, speak pleasantly, and was relieved to see the heavy frown lift a little, the sullen expression lighten.

'You know where Michalis has gone? You can help me?'

'I think I'm the one who needs help,' Gemma told her drily. 'Do you know why I have been brought here?'

The girl nodded. 'It is a punishment, although this was not my wish, you understand,' she added hastily. She put a protective hand on her abdomen in a curiously poignant gesture. 'My father—my brothers were so angry. They threatened many things—bad things.'

Gemma said gently, 'This is also a bad thing, Maria.'

Maria's eyes widened sceptically. 'To be here—with Kyrios Andreas?' She almost giggled. 'There are many —many women who would not think so, *thespinis*. Many who would be glad to take your place.'

'Including yourself?' Gemma asked sharply, irritated by the knowing gleam in Maria's eyes.

The girl drew herself up. When she wasn't scowling, she was incredibly pretty, Gemma thought, her figure full-breasted and voluptuous.

'Not I, *thespinis*.' She shook her head. 'The father of Kyrios Andreas was our *nonos* –our godfather.' She crossed herself. 'In his life, a good man, and important man. Always he was most kind to us. But I was not for his son. Never would my father have dreamed of such a thing. When Kyrios Andreas takes a wife, she will be a woman of wealth and property, as is fitting.'

So—his name is Andreas, and he isn't married, Gemma thought.

She said, 'Maria—whatever wrongs my brother has done you, I can't stay here. You must see that. I'm sure that if he'd known you were pregnant, he'd never have gone off like this and . . .'

'But it was because he knew that he went, *thespinis*.' Maria sounded almost matter-of-fact about it. 'If he had stayed, my father and brothers might have killed him. It was better he went. But he promised he would help, and he will.'

Gemma bit her lip. 'Are you thinking that he'll marry you, perhaps?'

There was a pause, then a negative shake of the head. Maria said flatly, 'It would not be fitting.' She did not meet Gemma's gaze.

She said, 'I don't believe that, Maria, and I know my parents wouldn't either, if you love each other. But there would be problems. Michalis is still studying. He can't afford to get married, for one thing. And how do you suppose he will feel if I'm forced to stay here with —with this— Andreas?'

Maria shrugged. 'As I said, *thespinis*, it was not my will that you should be brought here. I tried to tell them—to speak against it, but my father would not listen. All his words were of revenge for the harm done to the honour of our family. And for this revenge he goes to Kyrios Andreas, who is a brother to us in all but blood.'

Gemma flushed angrily. 'Why should he do that? I'm surprised your father didn't simply arrange to—pass me round the family.'

Maria looked shocked. 'He could not do such a thing, *thespinis*. It would cause shame to my mother, and to the wives of my brothers. Besides,' she added on a more practical note, 'our house is next to that of the priest. The *papa* would be angry to hear such talk of vengeance. But if he hears that there is a woman here with Kyrios Andreas, he will not think it strange, although he may shake his head,' she added quaintly.

Gemma was thinking rapidly, 'And if he knew the truth, he'd probably blow his top.' She looked appealingly at the other girl. 'Maria I'm not really dressed for visiting, as you can see, but you could ask the priest, secretly, to come here and speak to me. He'd have to help me if he knew what was going on.' She paused. 'Please Maria—if you care anything for Mike—do this for me.'

Maria spread her hands helplessly. 'I cannot, *thespinis*. Only today, the *papa* has gone from the village to visit his own father who is ill. He has driven to Heraklion in Kyrios Andreas' own jeep with him.'

Gemma said hollowly, 'Oh God,' and sat down on the bottom step. She looked up at Maria. 'When is he expected back?'

Maria shrugged. 'In a few days, perhaps, a week. I do not know. But do not agitate yourself, *thespinis*,' she added hearteningly. 'I have heard my mother say that Kyrios Andreas wearies quickly of his women. Perhaps by that time, you will no longer be here.'

Gemma's lips parted to say something blistering, then closed again. There was no point, she thought wearily, in venting her anger and worry on Maria, who probably thought she was making a lot of unnecessary fuss, judging by the aggravating note of reverence which entered her voice each time she mentioned Andreas.

So, he came from a wealthy and important family. Gemma supposed she might have guessed as much, and was forced to admit to herself that it only added to her problems. Presumably, he could be expected to have some kind of influence with the authorities, and she might have trouble getting her story believed.

She remembered bitterly his own cynical remark 'a little adventure with a rich Greek' and realised with something approaching despair that it was a

view it would be only too easy for other people to
share. Certainly, the truth sounded preposterous,
and who would vouch for the fact that she'd been
held at the Villa Ione against her will? Maria?
Never in this world, she told herself realistically.
Maria might not agree with her family's methods
of avenging their honour, but she would never say
so publicly.

She said slowly, 'You asked me where Mike had
gone, Maria. Have you really no idea yourself?
You must have seen him just before he left. Did he
give no hint? Leave no clue?'

Maria looked as if she was going to cry. 'None,
thespinis. All that I know is that he was going to
join a friend of his, nothing more.'

'You never heard him mention this friend's
name?' Gemma demanded. 'Was he another
Englishman.'

Maria shrugged evasively, her full lips pouting a
little. 'I do not think so.'

'A Greek?' Gemma prompted. 'A Cretan,
perhaps?'

Maria walked towards the kitchen with a
flounce of her red skirt. 'I will not answer all these
questions,' she flung back over her shoulder.
'Your brother promised to help me, and now he
has gone, and I do not think he will come back,
because he is frightened. He has broken his
promise to me, so why should I help you—*vromo
anglitha*,' she added venomously.

Gemma felt bewildered by this sudden change in
attitude. She said, 'I'm sorry, Maria, but I'm upset
too. I've been kidnapped, and that's a very serious
offence in my country. This Kyrios Andreas of
yours could be in big trouble . . .'

Maria sneered. 'Trouble? For you, perhaps,
thespinis, but not for Andreas. You say you were

kidnapped—but all the world saw you come here, walking on your own legs up to the villa, *po po po*. Who heard you scream? Who has heard you cry for help? No one, and if questions are asked that is what we shall say. We shall say that you were the *eromeni* of Andreas, and that you followed him here, and that you say terrible things about him because he has tired of you, because he no longer desires a pale skinny English girl in his bed.'

Gemma said acidly, 'Your command of the English language has improved amazingly, Maria. May I ask if you have a reason for being here, or did you just come to look me over?'

'I came for the laundry which my aunt will wash,' Maria said sulkily.

Gemma raised her eyebrows. 'Well at least that's one domestic chore I'm being spared.' She tried not to sound too defeated, but it wasn't easy. Maria had been a doubtful ally from the start, but Gemma had thought she might be prepared to help her in some way, if only for Mike's sake. But the girl was obviously bitter at his desertion, and Gemma supposed she couldn't blame her.

She said, more gently, 'Maria, I'm sure my brother will come back.'

Maria shrugged. 'I no longer care whether he does or not,' she said rudely. 'Now, I take the laundry.'

She took it, wrapped in one of the bed sheets from upstairs. She did not look at Gemma again, or speak, as she walked through the living area, and disappeared with a swing of her hips towards the terrace steps.

Impulsively, Gemma started after her. She couldn't let her go like this—when for a few moments they'd seemed so close to an understanding. Surely she could make Maria see that she wouldn't endear herself to Mike by allowing his only sister to become some stranger's unwilling mistress.

She was at the door, when she heard the dog's warning growl just behind her. She took another step, and felt herself held, the hem of the shirt she was wearing clamped in the animal's jaws. Its eyes gleamed at her malevolently. It was growling in its throat, and she could feel its breath hot on the skin of her thigh.

With a groan, she turned back into the room, and immediately felt herself released.

She said with great distinctness, 'You bloody animal,' and burst into tears.

No day had ever seemed so long.

The hands on her watch seemed to crawl round, each five-minute interval like an hour in duration. She was on edge all the time listening for the sound of the jeep, awaiting dreading his return.

At lunchtime, she made a sandwich, using some of the bread from breakfast with the lamb. She ate ravenously, surprised at her own appetite. She had started to believe she would never eat again. In fact, her own hunger made her ashamed, and she was thankful she was alone, and could indulge it unobserved.

She offered the dog some meat, but it refused point blank to take it from her hand. She put the lamb bone down on the floor and presently it carried it into a corner and began to gnaw, but Gemma wasn't fooled into thinking this might represent some kind of truce between them. She'd tried two more casual strolls towards the terrace steps, each time with the same result.

The dog had been polite but firm, she thought with irony. However, she was under no illusion that the politeness would necessarily continue if she persisted.

During the long afternoon, she remembered the paperback novel she'd taken to the sun terrace the previous day, and retrieved it, but it was no real help. The trials of the heroine seemed to pale into insignificance when compared to her own.

She debated about sunbathing; wondered what Andreas would do if she allowed herself to be burned raw; decided the attendant risks were too great, and sneered at herself for being a coward.

There was sun filter cream in her toilet bag. She used it, and for the first time in her life sunbathed nude, turning herself delicately and languorously in the hot rays, enjoying the sensation of freedom it gave her. This time, however, she was careful not to fall asleep.

The sun was already sinking down behind the mountain peaks when she went for her shower. Andreas—her mind used his name tentatively, more accustomed to thinking of him as the Cretan, or, more simply even, the stranger—had still not returned. Not that she wanted him to, she thought stormily. In fact, it would give her infinite satisfaction to know that he and his damned jeep were at the bottom of some precipice, with the buzzards already circling overhead. But his return would mean she'd have some decent clothes to wear again. Being only half-dressed like this made her vulnerable, undermined her morale, she thought, and it was no earthly use reminding herself that during the ordinary course of her holiday only a short while before she'd worn scarcely any more. That was different, and she knew it. And, presumably, he knew it too.

He'd worked out his plan of campaign very carefully, Gemma thought savagely. He knew exactly how to play upon her hopes, her fears, and, she had to admit, her desires.

She shivered as she stepped under the jets of the shower, but not simply because of the impact of the cool droplets on her heated skin. Oh God, but he was dangerous, and she'd known it from the first moment she saw him. Dark as the devil, arrogant as one of the gods of old in this land, powerful as the Lord of Life and Death who'd ruled in his bull mask at Knossos, taking tribute from the alien captives brought in chains across the sea.

Closing her eyes, she lifted her face to the cascading water, letting it pour through her hair and over her shoulders. Then with a little sigh of satisfaction, she turned off the flow.

There was no warning—none at all. The dog hadn't uttered, and the noise of the shower had effectually blocked out all other sounds.

She turned, reaching for a towel, and saw him standing in the doorway, watching her. He was smiling faintly as the dark eyes coolly assessed every inch of her naked body.

Her first instinct was to shrink, to cover herself somehow with her hands, her hair, yet something told her that such a belated and useless attempt at modesty would only amuse him further. It would be just another petty victory for him if she seemed to care too much about herself so completely. Far better to brazen it out, to let him think his presence here was immaterial because she despised him. Her eyes flared contempt at him, and her chin lifted defiantly as she scooped the heavy strands of damp blonde back from her face, and tossed them over her shoulders. The gesture arched her small high breasts, a fact he acknowledged with a mocking downward slant of his mouth.

Then he moved, stepping towards her, his purpose clear in the sudden intensity of his dark gaze, and Gemma moved too, at speed, all her bravado disintegrating as she grabbed frantically for the errant towel. Her foot slipped on the damp tiles, and she fell down on one knee, cracking the bone painfully as she did so. She cried out involuntarily and at once he was beside her, his hands under her shoulders lifting her effortlessly.

'You are hurt? Tell me . . .'

He carried her into the adjoining bedroom and put her down on the bed. The discarded shirt was lying there and she seized it and held it in front of her.

'Don't touch me.' Bright spots of colour burned in her face. 'Get out of my room.'

He'd been bending over her, but at her words, he straightened and stood back, the concern in his face giving way to overt amusement.

He pointed to the shirt. 'Isn't that a little late?' he asked, laughing.

That this was her own view as well made it no easier to bear. She glared at him savagely. 'Kidnapper, rapist and now Peeping Tom,' she hurled at him recklessly. 'What a full life you lead, *kyrie*, or should I say—Andreas.'

There was a brief electric pause. His mouth twisted. 'So—you have had a visitor. Once more, it seems, Maria's curiosity has outrun her discretion.'

'Oh, you mustn't blame her for telling me. She must have thought that, as your mistress, I would at least know your Christian name if nothing else about you.'

'It is not her place to think about such matters at all,' he said icily. 'What else did you discuss?'

She shrugged. 'Very little. Religion—briefly—

and the fact that she's no longer in love with Mike.'

'Did you think she ever was? You are a romantic, Gemma *mou*. Love does not describe the kind of brief, sordid association she and your brother shared. If they had—loved, he would have courted her with honour—asked her to be his wife.'

It was odd how those contemptuous words hurt her, more even than the pain in her bruised knee.

She said stonily, 'Then it's fortunate for them both that you've avenged the family honour and saved them the necessity of being miserable together. And now perhaps you'd let me have some privacy, because I'd like to get dressed.' She took a breath. 'I assume you've brought me some clothes.'

'I have warned you before about making assumptions, Gemma.' His tone was sardonic. 'By day, you are already adequately covered by what you can filch from my wardrobe. If you feel you need an alternative for the rest of the time—I have brought you one.'

He reached into his pocket, and produced a square packet which he tossed to her. She caught it awkwardly, one-handed, still clinging to the shirt with the other. A bikini, she wondered, or underwear. But, no. The parcel was too small, surely, and too heavy as well. She eased the outer wrapping with her thumbnail, and took off the paper. The decorated box inside was familiar. She looked down at the lettering almost stupidly. '*Shalimar?* But that's . . .'

'The perfume you brought from England,' he completed the thought for her.' It is a favourite of mine too. How nice, *matia mou*, that our tastes are the same.'

'Nice?' Gemma repeated dazedly. 'Nice? My God.' She jumped to her feet, regardless of her throbbing knee. 'How dare you do this? Haven't you degraded me enough already?'

'You find French perfume degrading?' His brows lifted. 'You must be unique.'

'It isn't the bloody scent.' Her voice throbbed with temper. 'It's the—the implication, and you know it. As an alternative to your loathsome shirts, I'm to wear this—and nothing else, I suppose. Your own private strip show. Well, I'll see you in hell first. If you like it so much, wear it yourself.' She threw the bottle at him, but he caught it adroitly before it smashed, to her chagrin. 'Or better still, keep it for your next lady. She may share your—your perverted appetites. I don't.'

'As you wish.' He put the box back in his pocket. His face and voice were expressionless, but she knew that he was angry just the same. He said, too gently, 'My appetites are quite normal, I believe. As for your own, my lovely one, I suspect that in spite of your protestations, they are still unawakened.' He paused. 'A situation,' he added with cool deliberation, 'that I intend to remedy later.'

He went out, closing the door behind him.

CHAPTER SIX

THE light faded out of the sky, and she watched it go with a kind of quiet desperation. The arrival of darkness seemed an omen of all her worst nightmares, and she was scared.

As soon as she was alone, she'd dressed hurriedly, fastening all the buttons on the shirt from throat to hem with finicking and ridiculous care, and winding the sash tightly round her slim waist. As if it would really make the slightest difference in the end, she thought despairingly.

Then she'd sat on the edge of the bed, one palm cupped round her sore knee and waited.

She could hear the sound of the shower from his room, and the silence when it ceased. Later, she'd heard the door of his room open, and his footsteps and in spite of herself, she'd shrunk back on the bed, staring at the door, anticipating its opening. But he'd walked past, without even the slightest hesitation, and gone downstairs.

That had been nearly twenty minutes ago, and now the delicious aroma of grilling meat was floating up to her, reminding her with potent cruelty just how long ago it was since she'd eaten that sandwich.

Gemma licked her lips. There was little point in remaining where she was, cowering in a corner until he chose to come for her, especially when she had no means of keeping him away. She'd even tried to shift the chest of drawers to block the door, but it had been too heavy for her, and she hadn't been able to budge it by as much as an inch

All she could do was go downstairs and hope somehow to find a way to persuade him to give her some further respite. She bit her lip nervously. Probably it hadn't been very wise to make him angry, to have thrown an expensive gift literally back in his face, but she couldn't honestly say she regretted it, she thought fiercely, her hands curling into claws. And anyway, it was safer to be on hostile terms with him. She could fight his anger with her own. It was when his voice gentled – when he came close to her—touched her—that he was most dangerous.

She shuddered, remembering the moment when he'd picked her up from the bathroom floor, his hands momentarily grazing her breasts as he did so. He hadn't even intended a caress, yet the shock of it had shaken her as if the earth had moved under her feet.

If she kept him angry, perhaps she could also keep him at arm's length, she thought.

The door to his room was ajar, and he'd left the lamp burning on the chest of drawers. Gemma paused, wondering whether she should extinguish it, and then she saw the bunch of keys lying next to it. Car keys, she thought incredulously. The keys to the jeep, there for the taking. She was already stretching out her hand, when she remembered she had no pockets to hide them in. Besides, if she took them now, and hid them in her own room, he might miss them. Whereas, if she left them where they were for the time being, and took them while he was asleep as she'd planned originally, then the first he'd know about it was when he awoke the next day, and found her gone and the jeep too.

But she was sorely tempted to grab the whole bunch and make a dash for it here and now. The main problem was still Cerberus. She hadn't heard a yelp out of him since Andreas had returned. but that didn't mean he wasn't lurking about downstairs, just waiting for her to make one false move.

And when she got downstairs, and realised that Andreas himself was on the terrace, cooking steaks on a charcoal grill, she was more than ever thankful that she'd decided to wait.

He had his back turned to her, seemingly intent on his task, but as she got to the doorway, he said coolly, *'Kalispera.'*

Gemma swallowed. 'Good evening,' she returned with an assumption of calmness.

'The food is nearly ready.' He gestured towards the table where a salad and a bottle of red wine were already waiting.

'So I see.' She paused. 'I gather I've been demoted from chef.'

He gave her an enigmatic look. 'Some of your recipes are a little too ingenious, *matia mou*. Who knows? You might have gone wandering in the hills today and found some hemlock.'

'With the Hound of the Baskervilles to keep me company?' she asked sweetly. 'Even I'm not that ingenious, *kyrie*. And where is Cerberus, by the way?'

'He has gone back to his master,' he said, 'who lives in the village, not the Underworld. You miss the dog perhaps? You would like to have him as a pet while you are here?'

'I can think of only a few things I would like less,' Gemma said, still sweetly.

'And I'm sure I don't even have to ask what they are.' He transferred the steaks deftly to plates and handed her one. 'I hope you don't intend to refuse this too.'

She would have loved to have had the moral strength to fling the steak off the terrace into the bushes, but she was so hungry she could have eaten the plate as well, so she merely smiled noncommittally as she watched him pour wine into her glass.

'You don't have a dog of your own?'

He shook his head. 'I am here so little, it would not be fair.'

'But then what is?' Gemma said blandly. 'I've seen a cat.'

'Did you feed it?'

She hesitated. 'Not really. I put down a few scraps this morning.'

'Then I am only surprised you have not seen a hundred cats,' he said. 'They are not the sleek pampered pets you have in England. Here, they breed, and they beg.' He gave her a sardonic smile. 'And now we have finished with the animal kingdom, Gemma *mou*, what safe topic do you suggest for discussion next?'

She shrugged. 'As far as I'm concerned, we don't have to talk at all.' She cut into her steak as if it were someone's throat.

'You have a gift for silence?' His brows lifted. 'An amazing quality in a woman.'

'My speciality.' She sipped her wine. 'As chauvinist remarks seem to be yours.'

'I specialise in other things as well,' he said gently.

She glared at him mutely over the rim of her wine glass. There was a long pause, then Gemma said abruptly, 'Did Michael have a special friend in the village? A man friend, I mean.'

'Not that I am aware of. He knew Stavros, of course, and Maria's brothers.' He took more salad. 'You have some reason for asking?'

'Not really.' She speared a piece of tomato. 'It was just something Maria said to me. She told me Mike had gone to meet a friend, and I got the impression this friend could be Greek.'

'It would be no one from this village.' He frowned a little. 'He no longer has friends here. But I believe he stayed in other places before he came to Loussenas.'

She sighed. 'I suppose he must have done.' And she had little chance of tracing any of these places, she thought despondently. Crete was a big island, and although she thought Mike in one of his infrequent letters had mentioned some place in the White Mountains, she couldn't be sure.

She said, 'I wouldn't be too sure that it's no one from this village. Perhaps not everyone thinks Maria's the wronged maiden her family like to make out. I think she knows this friend of Michael's because she got very angry when I pressed the point.'

'Perhaps Maria does not think it necessary to keep her temper with the sister of her seducer,' he said grimly. 'Anyway, she had no right to be here. I shall speak to Stavros tomorrow.'

Go and speak to him now, Gemma prompted silently, and the last you'll see of me will be the jeep's tail lights disappearing down the mountainside.

But, of course, he did nothing of the sort. When she had finished her steak, he asked if she would like some fruit. She was on the point of refusing when she remembered that even if she was no longer hungry, fruit would be a way of prolonging the meal. But when he made to refill her glass, she hastily put her hand over it. It was heady stuff, she'd discovered already, and she needed to keep her wits about her.

He cleared the plates and came back with a bowl of fruit, and two small cups of coffee, thick and rather bitter.

She said, 'Is this what we call Turkish coffee?'

'You may, Gemma *mou*, but we do not. Relations between our countries have been strained and worse for generations.'

'It's sad,' she said, half to herself. 'Turkey's such a near neighbour to Greece to be an enemy.'

'Everywhere in the world there are such problems.' He shrugged slightly. 'In the case of your own country, there is Ireland, I think.'

She took some grapes from the bowl, and began to eat them. They were the size of small plums, purple and thick with juice. There was silence between them, but the night was full of sounds— the chirping of cicadas in the undergrowth, the cry of a bird, far off, mournful and piercing, and closer at hand, music.

Gemma pushed back her chair, and went over to the balustrade. 'What's that?'

There was a moon, she noticed, a great golden ball swinging in the heavens on a chain of stars.

She heard him get up too. Was suddenly aware he was standing behind her, very close to her.

He said, 'The music? They are having a celebration in the village.'

'Don't tell me.' She kept her tone light, but she was acutely conscious of him, of his breath stirring her hair, the warmth of his body subtly penetrating her thin layer of clothing. 'They're having a public stoning.'

'They are good people,' he said quietly. 'Under other circumstances, Gemma *mou*, you would think so too.'

His hand closed on her hip, swaying her backwards so that she was actually leaning against him. She felt his lips touch her ear, his teeth gently grazing the lobe, and she tensed. His mouth moved downwards, teasing a sensitive path down to the curve of her shoulder. The music in the distance was playing an insistent, insidious rhythm, and her pulses echoed it, while the moonlight swam behind her closed lids.

His other hand cupped her breast, caressing its rounded softness, before his fingers sought the hardening thrust of her nipple through the fabric of the shirt. The barrier of the material between his seeking and her urgency was a delicately erotic torment. She was suddenly scorched by the memory of his hands brushing against her bare breasts, and the knowledge of how desperately she needed to feel his hands on her body again shook her to the soul.

If she moved, even slightly, turned fully into his arms, offered him her mouth, then there would be no going back—and no escape either.

She whispered, 'No' frantically, and pulled away from him. She'd made her plans and no shock of desire, no fever of the blood, was going to stop her now. But was the choice even hers anymore, she wondered as his hands came down on her shoulders, turning her to face him.

His voice was deep, urgent. It made her shiver. 'Forget, *matia mou*. Forget everything except that we are here together and we want each other.'

'I can't,' she said hoarsely. 'I can't forget. You- -you must give me more time —please. If you'll wait, I'll do anything you want, be anything you want— I swear it. Only not now, not yet, I beg you.'

She swallowed, waiting in a kind of agony for his reply.

She heard him murmur something which could

have been an obscenity or a prayer, then his hand took her chin, turning her face up to his.

'What are you trying to do to me, Gemma?' he asked huskily. 'Is this how you've treated your other men -putting them into hell while you offer them heaven?'

She shook her head, avoiding the intensity of his dark eyes. 'That—that was a lie. There's never been ... I've never ...' She stumbled to a halt. 'Oh, I don't expect you to believe me.'

'No, I think that is the truth—at last,' he said grimly. 'Does it also explain your reluctance, I wonder?' He shook his head slowly. 'That- I cannot believe. You are not a child, but a beautiful woman.'

She flicked the tip of her tongue along her dry lips. 'You said you'd be patient,' she reminded him.

He smiled wryly. 'And you catch me in my own trap, Gemma *mou*. If you remember too, I said my patience was not endless.'

She stared, as if mesmerised, at the open neck of his shirt and the black hair which shadowed the golden skin it revealed. 'I remember.' Her voice shook a little. 'But it won't be for much longer.'

'Is that a promise?' He was frowning slightly.

'A promise.'

'Then we have a bargain.' He paused. 'You are a creature of moods, Gemma. One moment a virago, screaming abuse at me—the next, a cooing dove. Which, I wonder, is nearest the truth— nearest the woman who lives behind your eyes?' He brushed a gentle finger across her lids. 'The woman who wishes to spend yet another night alone.'

He released her, and she stepped back, trying to

stem the flood of relief rising inside her in case it showed, and made him suspicious. But he turned away, pouring himself more wine, and she seized the opportunity to slip away. She washed the dishes and put them away, then went up to her room. She glanced into his room, and saw the keys still there on the chest. She gave them a longing glance, and hoped Andreas wasn't planning on spending half the night on the terrace drinking wine and listening to the music.

She didn't undress, but slipped as she was under the covering sheet. She was nervous and excited, but made herself relax, because she might have to wait quite a while. In the end, she dozed a little, and eventually woke with a start, convinced it was morning and her chance to escape missed completely.

But the room was still bright with moonlight, and the house was filled with a deep quietness.

She slid out of bed and padded to the door, opening it cautiously and listening. Still no sound.

She crept back into the bathroom and collected her toilet bag. It was all she possessed in the world, and she had no intention of leaving it behind, although it seemed she was forced to abandon the rest of her belongings for the time being. Including her passport and her travellers cheques, she thought, biting her lip. But she'd be back for them, bringing the authorities with her.

She tiptoed across the passage. His door was closed, but the handle turned easily and quietly under her fingers, and she slid into the room like a little ghost.

All she had to do was pick up the keys and go, but something impelled her to take one last look at him. He was asleep, half-turned on to his side, his skin very dark against the stark whiteness of the bedlinen. The rumpled sheet draped across his hips in no way disguised the fact that he was naked.

He looked younger, she thought with an odd little catch of the breath, with some of that proud arrogance muted by slumber.

For a long moment, she stood, staring down at him, her mind playing tricks, her imagination taking her down paths she had never before wanted to tread. Then, her lower lip caught in her teeth to bite back what might have been a sigh, she tiptoed to the chest and picked up the keys with infinite care.

She seemed to be saying goodbye with every step of the stairs as she descended. Her captivity had lasted hours rather than days, but already in some strange way the house seemed as familiar to her as—as her own home in England. She gave herself an angry mental shake. She should be thanking her stars she was escaping, relatively unscathed, not indulging in stupid and unnecessary nostalgia.

The jeep was parked off the track just under the wall. She approached it with a certain amount of trepidation. But—she could drive, therefore it followed that she could drive this, and the fact that her licence was in England, and she was not insured were details she hoped she would never have to discuss with anyone.

She slid in behind the wheel, and felt for the ignition. She tried each key in turn, and because it was dark and she was nervous, she missed the right one, and had to start again. This time, she counted them off in her head as she used them. And again, by some mischance, she missed.

Get a grip, she adjured herself silently, taking a deep breath. Third time has to be lucky.

He said, 'Those are the keys to my sports car, Gemma. Do you think I am quite a fool?'

She almost screamed, and the keys fell clattering to the floor of the jeep. She bent to retrieve them, but he was there before her, picking them up with one hand, clasping her wrist with the other.

His voice went on mockingly, 'You were almost convincing, my cooing dove, with your virginal fears. But at the same time, I was sure you could not resist the bait, if it was offered.' Insolently he dangled the keys in front of her. 'And I was right.'

Her voice shook. 'Damn you to hell.'

He grinned. 'The return of the virago. I am not sure I do not welcome it. I wonder how many other facets of your personality I shall discover before the night is over?' His grip tightened on her wrist. 'Now come with me.'

She had no choice. She realised now there had never really been one. She had been playing a game, but he'd been dictating the rules, every step of the way. And, when he wished, changing them.

In the living room, he had lit a lamp. He had dragged on a pair of jeans, but he was barefoot, bare-chested, and she looked at the lithe body which would soon possess her own, and knew that he had the power to possess her soul too. And she knew she could not let that happen. She remembered Maria's words, '*Andreas wearies quickly of his women*' with a pang. That was what she had to guard against—the moment when he sent her away, because he had no further use for her as an instrument of vengeance, or more damagingly, as a woman.

He said, 'You are shivering, *matia mou*.' He held out a hand to her. The gesture and the smile which went with it teased and beckoned. 'Let me warm you.'

She took a quick breath. 'No.' She turned away, turning her back quite deliberately on the outstretched hand, and the lure it offered of warmth, of laughter, of passion—and, ultimately, of a heartbreak which could destroy her.

He sighed sharply. 'Gemma, don't be a fool. You knew from the first . . .'

'Yes,' she said. 'You made the position perfectly clear. I know why I'm here, and I know what you intend to do.'

The smile was back in his voice. 'My sweet one, I intend to make love to you.'

She shook her head, staring blindly at the wall. 'No—not love. Earlier today, you spelled out exactly what it would be—"a brief sordid association". Those were your words.'

'Yes.' His tone roughened. 'But I spoke of Maria and your brother, not of ourselves. You misunderstood . . .'

'I've never misunderstood.' Her throat felt tight. 'I know why I'm here, in this situation. And I know that you'll never let me go until I've paid this—this unspeakable debt for Michael. So I will—pay. I accept that's the way it has to be.' She took another long breath. 'And I won't fight. I—I won't try and stop you. You can have me. But that's all you'll have.' She bent her head and stared down at the floor. 'So—so don't try and dress it up with talk of making love, or—or wanting because that's not part of it.'

'You think I don't want you?' There was an odd note in his voice.

'I don't think about it at all, because I don't care.' Her throat felt constricted. 'If going to bed with you is my passport out of here, then I'll go. But—please—no more cat-and-mouse games, and no more talk about making love. Just—do what you want and get it over with.'

There was a long and terrible silence, then he said very quietly, 'You do not know what you are saying.'

She nodded. 'But I do. There's no way you can make this easy for me, so I'd be grateful if you could at least be quick. If you wouldn't mind,' she added, like a polite child.

'But I do mind.' His voice was like molten steel. 'And you will mind too, Gemma. You are not made of wood, so why pretend that you have no feelings?'

'Because it's better to have none,' she said. 'If I allowed myself to feel something, it would be hate—hate for you for bringing me here, hate for myself, for being a woman.' She shook her head. 'I don't want to feel those things—they're damaging, destructive.'

'And indifference is not?' he challenged.

She said wearily, 'I don't know. But it's all I have.'

There was another silence, then he said with cold courtesy, 'Then let it be as you wish.'

They went to his room. She watched him straighten the bed, shake up the pillows, then turned away hastily as he began to unzip his jeans. If she'd secretly hoped that her defiant speech would kill any desire he had for her stone-dead, then she'd miscalculated, she thought wearily.

He said, 'I am waiting.'

She risked a quick glance. He was in bed, propped on one elbow, watching her, his eyes as black as onyx, and as hard.

Gemma cleared her throat. 'Would you put out the lamp please?'

'No.'

As she unwound the sash, she tried to comfort herself with the reminder that he'd seen her in the shower only that afternoon. That, outwardly at least, her body no longer held any secrets for him. But it did not prevent her from fumbling every button.

The walk across the room to the bed seemed the longest she had ever taken. She slid under the sheet and lay next to him, not touching. Her pulses sounded like thunder in her ears. She wondered if he could hear them too.

He put out a hand, and gently stroked a tress of hair back from her forehead.

He said, 'My Gemma, it does not have to be like this between us, and you know it. Turn to me, sweet one. I promise I will make you happy.'

And afterwards unhappy, she thought. When it's over.

She didn't look at him. 'No—this is how it must be.'

He said harshly, 'So be it then. Am I permitted to kiss you—caress you—or would that simply prolong your agony?' He paused, and when she didn't reply gave a short laugh. 'I see. Then, if nothing else, my dove, relax for me, otherwise you will feel pain.'

She felt pain already. It filled her heart and mind. It swamped the universe, but she welcomed it because it helped her to remain detached as his hand swept a slow, remorseless path down her body.

She had said she wouldn't resist, and when the long fingers stroked her thighs, she allowed him to part them, without demur. And he was keeping his side of their cold bargain too, she realised, dazedly accepting his almost clinical exploration of her most intimate self. Whatever she'd been expecting, it had not been this, she thought, trying not to flinch and failing.

He saw, of course. 'I am hurting you?'

Gemma bit her lip. 'You're very thorough.'

He said coolly, 'And you are very inexperienced In that, at least, you told the truth.'

She turned her head away and stared at the small flame flickering in the lamp. There was another small flame, somewhere deep inside her, barely alight, struggling for life, which she had to ignore. Because even this bleak, impersonal discovering of her was having its effect on her body's reflexes.

It would be so easy, she thought wretchedly, to reach up and draw him down to her, to put her lips against his face, his skin. So easy, and so fatal.

She stole a glance at him through her lashes. He looked stern- -remote, and when he moved over her, she was frightened again, because he was a stranger whom she had absolved of all necessity to be kind. And if he was brutal, she would only have herself to blame, she thought, her nails scoring tense crescents in the palms of her hands.

But when he'd said he could be patient, he had not lied, she discovered wonderingly. She might not have deserved consideration but it was there for her just the same. And skill. And an infinite control which reduced the initial pain of his possession that her taut, unyielding muscles had made inevitable.

And, as he entered her completely, she cried out, not just because of the hurting, but in amazement too that this joining of their bodies which should have been so traumatic was, in the end, so incredibly, miraculously simple.

He took a corner of the sheet, and gently wiped the tiny beads of sweat from her forehead and cheekbones, and in that moment she let herself acknowledge freely for the first time that she loved him. That the ultimate disaster which she had tried to avoid had already overtaken her.

And she acknowledged too, as he began to move inside her slowly at first, that this brief treasuring of his warmth and strength as part of her would be all of him she would ever have to remember.

Echoing his own words, she thought, 'So be it, then.'

As he reached his climax he groaned something—her name—some words in his own language, then rolled away from her burying his face in the pillow, while his harsh, ragged breathing slowly steadied.

Gemma lay beside him, not speaking, aching, wondering what she should do next. Go back to her own room, perhaps?

After a while, he flung back the sheet and got out of bed, crossing the room to the bathroom.

She heard the sound of running water. Perhaps this was a signal for her to take her leave she thought, lifting herself up, and wincing a little. But the next minute he was back, carrying a bowl of water and a small towel. He sat on the edge of the bed, and began to bathe her with the dampened towel, first her face, and then, drawing back the sheet, her body.

She saw without surprise that she had bled a little. It was strange, she thought, but oddly sweet to lie there, allowing him to perform this intimate, but at the same time impersonal service for her.

When he had finished, he put the bowl down beside the bed, and let the towel drop to the floor beside it.

She said quietly, 'May I go now?'

'No,' he said. 'You may not.' There was a note

in his voice which seemed to warn her not to press the point.

He lay down beside her again, pulling the sheet to cover them both, and blew out the lamp. His arm went round her shoulders, pulling her down to him, pillowing her head on his chest. His other hand closed round the curve of her hip, drawing her closer to the warmth of his naked body. Cradled against him, she felt the tensions and the misery slowly begin to ebb away. His skin felt like silk under her cheek, the beat of his heart like the pulse of the universe under her hand.

After what had happened, it was madness, she thought, to feel so safe, so comforted.

Yet, after a while, against the odds, against all reason, she fell asleep in his arms.

CHAPTER SEVEN

SHE awoke to the beauty of a dawn sky and the realisation that she was being watched. She turned her head a fraction and looked into his eyes.

He brushed his mouth lightly across hers, and she knew what had woken her.

'You have rested well?' he asked.

Her, 'Yes' sounded strangled, because the hand that had been resting on her hip travelled upwards, and was now cupping her pointed breast, his thumb lazily stroking her nipple, sending fierce shafts of pleasure through her.

'And I did not hurt you too much?' He bent his head, and trailed a pattern of tiny kisses around the breast he was caressing, taking the aroused rosy peak between his lips, and tugging it sensuously.

She gasped. 'What are you doing?'

He lifted his head and smiled at her. 'Making love to you, *agape mou*, as I should have done last night.' He kissed her other breast, his tongue moving against her skin, filling her with piercing excitement.

She said hoarsely, 'No.'

'Yes,' he contradicted her, a sudden fierceness in his eyes and voice. 'Last night, Gemma, you made me feel like an animal. You will not do so twice. From this moment, I want to feel human again, to feel as a man should do with his woman.'

'I'm not your woman.' It was the only defence she could think of, and a poor one as it turned out, because he only grinned at her sardonically, and flung the sheet which was her only protection off the bed.

'Tell me that later,' he invited. 'Much later,' he added huskily, and kissed her indignantly parted lips very slowly and very completely. When at last he raised his head, she couldn't think of a single thing to say. She lay back against his encircling arm and looked up at him, her eyes widening endlessly. Every nerve in her body seemed tinglingly awake, the blood moving slowly through her veins, as thick and sweet as honey. She was aware of that deep inner trembling, and knew now that it was desire, that her body was crying out for the fulfilment it had been denied.

He kissed her mouth again, her eyes, the swift unsteady pulse in her throat. She wondered helplessly how she could ever have thought his mouth hard, when it was like velvet against her skin, his tongue a sweet flame, setting her alight in turn . . .

His fingers caressed her, moulding every curve and plane of her slender body, and where his hand touched, his lips followed in an erotic pilgrimage which made her moan aloud, half in protest, half in yearning.

She moved against him restlessly, driven by instincts she still barely understood, kissing his shoulder, her small teeth grazing the smooth skin. She wanted to please him in turn, to create the same kind of delight for him, but she didn't know how, and then he took her hands and guided them to his body, and showed her.

She'd always considered herself a girl of her times, informed and intelligent about sex, know-ledgeable about the physiology of her own body. But now she knew how wide a gulf there was between theory and practice. No book, no lesson, had ever taught her that one man's hands caressing her breasts, one man's mouth unhurriedly exploring the hollow inside her hip bone could turn her responses to frenzy. Nothing had warned her of the pleasure, even pride, to be gained from feeling his own body quicken in answer to her first shy, unpractised advances.

She heard him groan her name, his face taut, almost fierce, then he was above her and within her, and they were one, driven and consumed by the same passionate, primitive hunger.

There was sunlight in the room, touching him like an aureole, turning his lean body to gold, and it was part of her too, she discovered —a great sunburst of sensation, exploding in the deepest core of her being, and rippling through every fibre of her in spasm after spasm of uncontrollable pleasure.

She cried his name, the sound torn out of her in a kind of agony, and heard him answer, then his mouth took hers in an endless kiss as the storm of feeling slowly subsided, and they slid, still locked together, into calmer waters.

A long time later, he said, 'Talk to me.'

'About what?' She still felt almost dazed, her body weightless with contentment. If his arm had not been across her, anchoring her, she would have floated, she thought idly.

'About yourself. This career you once spoke of, for example.'

'You won't find it very interesting,' she said. 'I demonstrate and sell electronic typewriters, and word processing equipment.'

'For yourself?'

'Heavens, no, for a company—Protechnics Limited. Graham employs a team of girls.'

'This Graham is your boss? Tell me about him.'

She tried to think what there was to say about Graham. Not that it was easy to think of anything except that Andreas' hand was stroking her arm very gently, tracing with one forefinger the delicate tracery of veins inside her elbow.

She said, 'Well—he's kind and practical, and a very shrewd businessman, although he's always moaning that the company's on the edge of disaster. We all like him.'

'Is he young?' He picked up her hand and carried it to his lips, kissing each finger in turn. 'Middle-aged? Married?'

She laughed a little breathlessly. 'He's nearly forty, and very much married, with three children. His wife works for the company too.'

'This is usual in your country for a wife to identify herself so closely with her husband's business?' His mouth caressed the softness of her palm.

'I'd say that would depend very much on the business.' It was getting increasingly harder to string coherent words together.

'Perhaps. And the children—you said three— what happens to them?'

'They're all at school. And Jennifer has an *au pair*.' She stole a look at him under her lashes, noting a slight tightening of his mouth. 'You obviously don't approve.'

He shrugged. 'How other men live their lives is hardly my concern. But remembering the needs of my own childhood, I am glad that my mother was always there. No nursemaid, however kind, could ever have taken her place.'

'Is—is your mother still alive?'

'Very much alive.'

'And were you an only child?'

'By no means.' He kissed the inside of her wrist very softly, making her pulses leap frantically. 'I have a brother and two sisters, all younger than myself.'

'So you're the head of the family.' Her voice almost cracked in her effort to keep it under control.

'Yes.' It was as if a door had suddenly closed. He kissed her hand again, and rolled away on to his back, staring up at the ceiling.

It was absurd to feel so bereft, she thought faintly. Absurd, and shaming too.

Downstairs, she was suddenly aware of faint sounds of movement. He slanted a look at her. 'Our breakfast has arrived,' he said lightly. 'Are you hungry?'

Her mouth felt dry. 'A little.'

'Then I'll fetch us some food.' He yawned slightly, and stretched, his body lithe and bronzed in the sunshine, making her stingingly aware of the superb play of muscle and sinew. He turned his head and looked at her. Looking at him. She glanced away but not quickly enough, it seemed. Because he said softly, 'Unless you have other plans?'

'No,' she denied hastily. 'None at all.'

He smiled at her lazily. 'Then let me teach you some Greek.' He paused. 'Say after me, *"Mine etho mazi mou"*.' He said the words again slowly, making her repeat them after him. 'Very good, *agape mou*. Now say, *"Se thelo poli"*.'

She complied, looking at him suspiciously. 'I already have a phrasebook. What am I saying?'

His smile widened wickedly. 'What you were too shy to say in your own tongue, my Gemma. You told me "Stay here with me. I want you very much".'

She gasped, 'Oh,' her cheeks burning. 'Oh—you're a bastard. And it isn't true.'

'Is it not?' The long arms captured her effortlessly, pulling her to him. He whispered against her lips. 'Then prove it . . .'

Gemma stepped out from the shower, and wound a towel round her body before going back into the bedroom. Andreas had opened the windows fully before going downstairs, and the sun was streaming in. She stepped out on to the little balcony, and stood drying her hair with her fingers.

She ached, but not unpleasantly, and at the same time she felt vividly, shiningly alive. The air had never seemed so clear, the colours of the rock, the sky, the foliage so sharp and new.

Glancing at herself in the mirror, she had almost been surprised to see she looked the same as usual. Well almost the same, she thought smiling a little. Her mouth looked slightly swollen, and there were faint marks on her shoulders and breasts and thighs which had never been there before.

Their last coming together might have started out in laughter, but it had ended in an almost savage urgency, her body matching his in the fierceness of its demands. When it was over, she had cried, and he had held her closely, comforting her as if she was a child.

She flexed her shoulders in the sun's warmth, narrowing her eyes against the glare. Only she wasn't a child any more. She was a woman, with all a woman's certainties, a woman's power. His woman.

Out of the corner of her eye, she saw a movement, a splash of colour which had not been there before, and she turned her head sharply, her attention focused.

It was Maria, her red dress sharply contrasting with the white dazzle of the rock she was silhouetted against as she climbed the track up the mountain.

Gemma frowned. It was obvious the Greek girl didn't want to be seen, by the way she kept glancing back over her shoulder towards the village path. At first, Gemma wondered whether she could be running away, but she seemed to have nothing with her in the way of luggage. And if she was simply on her way to visit another village, why was she behaving so furtively?

But Gemma thought, with a mental shrug, it was no concern of hers what Maria might be up to. And then stopped dead, her mind almost blanking out with shock. Because she'd almost— almost forgotten in the dazed aftermath of her first experience of passion, why exactly she was at the villa.

If it had not been for Maria she would have come to Crete, met Michael somewhere and possibly spent a few days sightseeing in his company. Because of Maria, Andreas had come into her life, not as her lover, but as an avenger, and now she had to face the bitter acknowledgment that their hours together in that bed had been primarily the exactment of that vengeance.

She shivered, as if a cloud had passed over the sun. He'd done exactly as he'd threatened he would do—taken her for his pleasure, without love or the promise of commitment, and now she was left with the shame of that knowledge.

It seemed ironic that only a few days before, she'd been complaining to Hilary how all the men she met seemed to want to rush into serious relationships.

I like to take things slowly, she reminded herself painfully, one step at a time. And yet here I am— over my head, and out of my depth.

And she couldn't even pretend she hadn't seen the danger, because she'd recognised it from the first moment she saw him.

She bent her head, and a sigh shook her whole body. Last night, she'd known exactly what she was doing. She'd fought her senses with her mind, and won a small, bitter victory. She should have gone on fighting, but she'd been betrayed by her love for him, and by the needs she hadn't even known existed in her.

But he'd known, she thought wretchedly. He was diabolically experienced. Every time he'd touched her, kissed her, he'd been gauging the sleeping sensuality within her, and planning how to awaken it.

At dawn, that was how, she thought stormily, when she was half-asleep and vulnerable, and bewildered by the gentleness he'd shown her. And she'd forgotten everything- everything except how much she wanted him.

She only hoped she would be able to forget everything that had happened between them as easily.

She started violently as his hands descended on her shoulders.

'What are you dreaming of?' His mouth brushed the side of her throat.

She said woodenly, 'I was just looking at the view.' She pointed. 'What's up that track?'

He shrugged. 'Very little. A few goats, many stones, and an old hut which the shepherds use. Why do you ask?'

'I thought there might be another village.' She turned back into the bedroom.

'Still trying to run away, Gemma *mou*?' He spoke lightly, but his eyes were narrowed.

'No.' She shook her head. 'As you mentioned, dressed like this I wouldn't get very far.'

'But with your clothes, and in the jeep, you could get as far as Aghios Nikolaos.'

Her heart seemed to miss a beat. 'You—you're letting me go?'

'No, little fool.' He dropped a kiss on her bare shoulder. 'I have to go there on business later, and I thought you might like to go with me.' He paused. 'Well? What do you say?'

She shrugged pettishly, moving away from him. 'What's the alternative. Another day alone with Cerberus?'

'Perhaps.'

'Then I'll go to Aghios Nikolaos,' she said ungraciously, and he laughed.

'You are indeed a woman of contrasts, *agape mou*. In bed, a passionate angel. At breakfast, a grudging shrew. I suppose I must thank God it is not the other way about.' He indicated the tray he had placed on the bed. 'Have some honey on your bread. Perhaps it will sweeten your temper.'

She bit her lip. 'You mentioned my clothes. Do you mean you're letting me have them back?'

'Your case is downstairs at this moment.'

'And my money? My passport?'

'Not those.' The dark eyes glinted. 'Nor your plane ticket to England.' He looked at her, half-smiling, half-watchful. 'Are you really so eager to leave me?'

She shrugged again. 'There isn't a great deal to keep me here—now that you've got what you wanted.'

'And you did not?'

'Oh, naturally.' She sat down on the edge of the bed, and poured herself some coffee. 'It's always been an ambition of mine to be deflowered by an expert. I shall remember it as the highlight of the trip.'

There was an electric silence, then he said silkily, 'But you have forgotten. It is my intention to supply you with a more tangible reminder of your stay here.'

Her cup clattered back on to the tray. She felt all the colour drain out of her face. Involuntarily her hand flew to the flatness of her stomach. 'No.'

'You have some reason for thinking you are immune?'

She had no reason at all, and she wished desperately she'd listened more closely to the information which would have told whether it was likely. She supposed it could be.

She had been so busy fighting her attraction to him, that she had indeed forgotten that last stark threat to make her pregnant.

He said, his tone dry, 'The idea does not seem to appeal to you. You would not like to carry my child under your heart?'

It was agonising to realise there was little she would like more, if only ... She snapped such thoughts off at the roots. They were futile, and could be heartbreaking.

She made herself meet his gaze, lifting her chin defiantly. 'I wouldn't carry it,' she said. 'In England, we have resources to deal with such problems.'

'But only within a certain length of time, I understand. How do you know I would let you go in time?'

She said in a low voice, 'Because I don't believe

that even you could be that cruel. You said you wanted my family to suffer? Just knowing that I was pregnant by a man they'd never met would be enough for that.'

The dark face was hard. 'Well, let us wait and see.'

She said almost inaudibly, 'Yes.' Then, more strongly. 'Could I have my case, please. I'd—I'd like to get dressed.'

'Then you shall.' From the doorway he looked back at her. 'Eat something, *pedhi mou.*' He sounded faintly mocking. 'To starve yourself now will solve nothing.'

She said coolly, 'I suppose not.' She reached for the bread, took a piece, added butter and honey, and bit into it, marvelling at her own outward calm.

But he was right about one thing, she thought as she listened to him go down the stairs. There was only one solution, as there always had been, and that was escape.

Back in her own clothes she looked and felt more like the Gemma of old, she decided, taking a critical look at herself in the mirror. He had left her alone to change, which she hadn't altogether expected, and when she heard him come back into the room, she tensed slightly, waiting for some sardonic remark. But although the dark eyes took in every detail of the plainly cut cream shift, and the low-heeled sandals which matched it, he said nothing.

He glanced at his watch. 'It is time we were going. It's a long drive.'

Gemma examined a fleck on one of her nails. She said, 'I've changed my mind. I'd prefer to stay here.'

'With Cerberus?' he asked mockingly.

'With anyone, or anything,' she said. 'I hope I make myself clear.'

'As the finest crystal,' he returned civilly, but she could detect an undertone of anger. He walked over to her and took her chin in his hand. He said, 'Do nothing foolish, my dove.'

She shrugged. 'What could I do? I imagine I'm still *persona non grata* in the village, you're taking the jeep, and I shall have my jailer. Getting my clothes back doesn't really make all that difference.'

He smiled rather grimly. 'You are wrong, believe me, *matia mou*. They make all the difference in the world.' He bent and kissed her on the mouth, then left the room and went downstairs.

Gemma unpacked her case, and put her things away, but in her own room, not the one they had shared. Defiantly, she shook out a simple broderie anglaise nightdress and arranged it on the bed.

She was just putting the last dress on the hanging rail, when she heard Cerberus bark below.

Andreas was in the living room waiting for her, his hand on the dog's collar. He said, 'Here is your companion.' He paused. 'Can I bring you anything from Aghios Nikolaos?'

'No thank you.' She would have loved some more books, but would have died rather than tell him so.

'A different brand of perfume perhaps?'

'No.' She glared at him.

For a moment it seemed as if he was going to say something else, but he merely shrugged, and went down the terrace steps, and presently she heard the jeep drive off.

She sank down on to the sofa, and began to cry

very softly, the tears running unchecked down her face and dripping on to her skirt.

She heard an anxious snuffling whine, and then Cerberus was beside her, pushing his formidable nose on to her lap, and presenting all the signs of a sheep in wolf's clothing.

She said brokenly, 'Oh Cerberus—I should hate him, but I can't. It's only been a couple of days, but it seems like a lifetime, and it will be too, because I'll love him until I die.'

She didn't seem to be making a lot of sense, but Cerberus seemed to understand, because he whined again and allowed her to put her wet cheek on top of his massive head. He smelled strongly of dog, and he was probably infested with fleas, but Gemma put her arm round his shaggy neck and hugged him and knew an odd comfort.

Presently she sat up, scrubbing the tears fiercely from her face with her hand. Andreas didn't give a damn about her. He was and always had been using her, as he'd made brutally clear, and it was no use sitting moping all day.

She got up, hooking two fingers into Cerberus' collar with what she hoped he would recognise as confidence. 'You and I,' she told him, 'are going for a walk.'

He couldn't have known the word, but perhaps he recognised the tone of voice, because to her amazement he trotted along obediently beside her. Once outside the house, she didn't even hold on to his collar any more. There was a slight contretemps outside the gate when Gemma turned towards the track up the mountain, when Cerberus clearly thought they should be going to the village, but that was soon resolved.

'You're a fraud,' Gemma told him pulling one of his ears. 'I let you terrify the life out of me yesterday, yet I bet at home you fetch people's slippers, and roll over and die for your master.'

He grinned, showing the kind of teeth night-mares are made of, and she said, 'And there again, perhaps not.'

The track proved to be very much as Andreas had said, only rather steeper and stonier. Gemma found it hard going. The stones kept slipping and rolling under her feet. Once she nearly fell, and another time twisted her ankle badly enough to have to sit on a boulder and swear at it.

Certainly it was the last sort of place that any pregnant woman should be scrambling about on, she thought, grimacing. She'd been thinking of Maria, but of course the same thing could apply to herself.

Could it possibly be true? She did some swift calculations, and realised it wouldn't be too long before she would have proof, one way or the other. It was a shattering realisation, underlining with humiliating force her own naïveté about the workings of her body and emotions. But then, how could she have expected her life to change so fast and so violently, she asked herself despairingly. Up to only a short time ago, her body had been her own private domain, and she'd been content for it to be so until she met the man she could love, until the tender leisurely courtship she'd envisaged took place, culminating eventually in a marriage when her white dress and veil would mean more than mere tradition.

She'd expected love to come to her like a gentle breeze blowing across the summer of her life—not a hurricane sweeping her crazily away, she thought helplessly.

She struggled up the last few yards of the track and emerged panting on to a small plateau. The view to the valley was dizzyingly spectacular, but was it this Maria came to see?

Beside her Cerberus barked excitedly, and took off towards what she'd first thought was a pile of stones under the cliff wall, but which Gemma now realised must be the remains of the shepherd's hut Andreas had mentioned.

It had been constructed out of the materials closest to hand, she thought as she approached. There was a low door, but no windows, and an apology for a roof made from brushwood.

Cerberus had vanished inside and was giving little muffled yelps, and she followed, bending to avoid cracking her head on what passed for a lintel. It was very dark inside, and it smelt of animals. Presumably on occasion the sheep and goats slept there along with their herders, she thought, wrinkling her nose, and this must be what was exciting Cerberus.

As her eyes became accustomed to the gloom, however, she began to realise the hut had been occupied and recently. There was a tin plate, still with traces of food, which Cerberus was investigating noisily, a water bottle, and reposing on a pile of scrub which had been pulled together in a corner to form a bed, a sleeping bag.

Gemma's mouth went dry suddenly. The pattern of the bag, dark blue with a red lining, was familiar. She half-knelt beside it, her fingers searching the lining just inside the zip until she found what she was looking for. She knew it was there, because she'd sewn it in herself, a long time ago, and not very neatly either. She looked down at the narrow strip of fabric, and the words 'Michael Leslie' danced before her eyes. Mike's sleeping bag. So he was here, living rough in this hut, hiding from Maria's family. She pressed her knuckles against her mouth like a frightened child. So this was why Maria was braving that awful scramble --because Mike was relying on her for food and other essentials.

She shivered. Had either of them considered what the consequences might be if Maria's relatives became suspicious of her daily jaunts and followed?

She remembered that stomach-churning drop to the valley floor, and felt sick. One of her main consolations had been that Mike was well away from Loussenas, out of immediate danger from Maria's justifiably resentful family.

She licked her dry lips. Yet here he was, within half a mile of the village, liable to discovery by anyone with the same measure of idle curiosity as herself.

And it hurt, too, to think that Maria must have told him she was at the Villa Ione and why, yet he'd made no attempt to help her, or even send her a message.

He must be terrified, Gemma thought, biting her lip. And he must have little faith that her sacrifice- -that the vengeance already exacted— would be enough to satisfy the blow to the pride of Stavros and his family. He must know that he was in peril, too.

Cerberus lifted his head, whined sharply and was gone, his body darkly silhouetted against the sunlit doorway. At the same moment, Gemma heard the sound of a footstep, and rose sharply, her heart thudding unevenly. She said shakily, 'Mike?' and moved into the sunlight. For a moment it dazzled her, but not enough to make her think, even for a minute, that it was really Mike standing in front of her.

The hands which gripped her shoulders, hurting her, were only too familiar.

His voice shaken by rage, Andreas said, 'What in the name of God are you doing here?'

'I came for a walk,' she said defensively. 'I thought you were going to Aghios Nikolaos. Why did you come back?'

'Because I didn't trust you,' he said bitingly. 'And it seems I was right. When I found the house empty, I remembered the questions you'd asked about the mountain, and followed.' He shook her. 'You little fool, this is not the place for a casual stroll. You could have fallen—injured yourself—and for what—a glimpse of a wilderness?'

She dragged herself free. 'Thank you for your concern,' she flashed. 'Is it for me, or for the seed you're so egotistically sure you've planted in me?'

His eyes blazed at her, making her shrink away from him. 'How dare you speak to me in such a way . . .' He stopped abruptly, clearly fighting the loss of his temper. There was a silence, then he said, 'I ask again, Gemma, what are you doing here?' He looked past her to the hut, his eyes narrowing. 'Or must I guess?'

She said in a thread of a voice, 'No . . .' but before she could intervene, he was past her, bending his tall body beneath the low door. She waited, trembling with apprehension, as long minutes seemed to drag past.

He rejoined her, his face set and grim. He said softly, half to himself, 'So this is where he has been—all this time. If Stavros had known—if we had all only known.'

She said urgently, 'Andreas—don't tell anyone—please.'

His mouth curled. 'You can plead for him—this worthless brother of yours? When he has been hiding here like a coward, letting you pay the price of his folly?

'Perhaps he doesn't know,' she said desperately. 'Perhaps he's only just returned.'

His glance was contemptuous. 'He has been there for days. Didn't you count the number of cigarette ends?'

She looked at him dazedly. 'Cigarette ends? But Mike doesn't smoke.'

He shrugged. 'Then he has started since you saw him last.'

'No,' Gemma said with conviction. 'He never would. He's a botanist—mad on ecology. He looks on cigarettes as a source of pollution—a health hazard. He wouldn't use them under any circumstances.'

His gaze was still sceptical. 'Fear can do strange things to a man.'

'Nor,' she said clearly, 'is he a coward.'

There was a brief tense silence as they looked at each other. Then Andreas turned abruptly, whistling to Cerberus who had retired to a safe distance and was sitting, watching them. 'Come.' His hand closed round hers. 'We will go down.'

Although she would have died rather than admit it, she was thankful he was there as she slid and slithered behind him down to firmer ground.

He didn't relinquish her hand, and she almost had to trot to keep up with his long stride. She was breathless and indignant by the time they reached the top of the terrace steps. He pushed her ahead of him into the house.

He said arctically, 'You have ruined your ridiculous shoes.'

Looking down, she saw that he was right. One of the straps on her sandal was hanging broken, and the leather was scuffed and spoiled. Her dress too was streaked with dust, and there were other marks on the skirt from where she'd knelt in the hut.

She said in a voice which quivered, 'I'll have to change.'

'Then do so quickly.'

She glared at him. 'Don't give me orders. Besides—I've hurt my ankle. I can't hurry.'

'Allow me to help,' he said. He picked her up in his arms as if she was a child, and carried her up the stairs to her room, setting her on her feet not too gently. His eyes scanned the rail of her clothes. He pulled out a dress, sleeveless and full skirted in glazed cotton and tossed it to her. 'Wear this,' he directed. 'I shall return in a few minutes. Be ready to leave with me then.'

She swallowed, fumbling for the zip of her dress. 'Where are you going?'

'To the village.'

'To—to tell them about Michael?'

He exhaled impatiently. 'That is not your concern.'

'Whatever he's done, he's my brother.' She slid the dress off her shoulders, letting it fall to the floor. She stepped out of the little heap of crumpled fabric, and walked across to him, putting a hand on his arm, raising her face pleadingly to his. He looked back at her expressionlessly, but she knew what he was seeing—her body, barely covered in the wisp of bra which lifted her breasts, the lacy triangle veiling her womanhood. She whispered achingly, 'Andreas—please don't give him away—for my sake. I'd do anything...' She paused, half-expecting him to draw her close, but he didn't move. She lifted her hand, sliding it inside the opening of his shirt, caressing the warm, hair-roughened skin with the tips of her fingers. She said again, 'Please . . .'

He touched her then, putting her away from him with a suddenness which robbed her of breath and sent the colour draining from her cheeks.

His eyes were cynical as they flicked over her. His voice sneered. 'Bribing me, Gemma *mou*? Then try offering me something I do not already possess.'

He walked past her to the door, and went out, leaving her humiliated and alone.

CHAPTER EIGHT

THEY travelled in silence. Gemma kept stealing sideways glances at him, but the dark enigmatic face revealed nothing.

She'd hurried into her clothes, expecting at any moment to see a group of grim-faced men with rifles pass the villa on their way to the hut, to hunt Mike down, but in the end Andreas had returned alone, walking slowly, clearly lost in thought, his face frowning as he stared down at the dusty ground. Perhaps they hadn't believed him, she thought, or maybe they were just waiting for him to get her out of the way before they started their search.

She wanted to ask what was going to happen, but couldn't find the words. And she couldn't plead with him again, she thought, the bitterness of shame sharp in her throat as she relived those few humiliating moments in the bedroom.

She had not, she realised, underestimated his skill as a driver, but her heart was in her mouth a few times as he manipulated the jeep round those dizzying hairpin bends. She found herself remembering James' cautious ascent, and had to resist an impulse to grab the side of the jeep to steady herself. In a way, she was almost grateful for that fast, relentless drive, because while she had the prospect of imminent death at the foot of some gorge to think about, she couldn't worry about Mike and what was going to happen to him when Stavros and his family caught up with him. Or, what was going to happen to her too, she reminded herself a little shakily.

She'd expected Andreas to take the broad national highway which carved its way across the island from Heraklion to Aghios Nikolaos, but instead, to her surprise, he turned the jeep on to a secondary road and began to climb again.

She ventured, 'I thought we were going to Aghios Nikolaos?'

'Later,' he said. 'There is something else I must do first.'

She recognised that he did not intend to tell her what this was, and she subsided into silence once more, turning her attention to the cultivated terraces and olive groves they were rapidly passing. Ahead of them she could see a cluster of roofs, and a church tower very white against the blue arch of the sky, and she felt the jeep began to slow as they entered the village street.

It was a pleasant street, lined with trees, the terraces of the single-storey houses which bordered it alive with flowers. Andreas pulled into the shade and stopped the engine.

Gemma asked, 'Shall I wait here for you?'

He shook his head. 'I don't know how long I shall be,' he said. 'There's a taverna in the square. Go and get yourself a drink.' He took some money from his back pocket and handed it to her, before striding away purposefully up the street.

She watched him arrive at his destination – a small pink-washed house, shaded by an enormous fig tree. Two women were sitting under the tree, clad in the traditional black, their heads bent over their embroidery. As he went in at the gate, they looked up, then rose to their feet, exclaiming in what seemed to be pleasure.

Andreas shook hands with them both with a certain amount of ceremony, then all three of them vanished into the house.

Gemma turned away in the direction he'd indicated as leading to the square, with a little mental shrug. They couldn't be part of his harem, she told herself ironically. Even from a distance, she could see they were both old enough to be his mother, if not his grandmother. So—perhaps they were something to do with his business. Maybe he was an entrepreneur in handwoven cloth and embroideries, and they were part of his workforce. And maybe too it was none of her business, she decided as she arrived in the square.

There was another surprise waiting for her here. It wasn't a large square, but it was a positive hive of activity. Outside the taverna long tables had been set up covered in snowy cloths, and people were milling around them adding cutlery, crockery and flowers, bringing chairs and laughing and talking at the tops of their voices.

The taverna owner seemed slightly harassed, but he brought the fresh lemonade she haltingly asked for. His English wasn't very fluent, but she managed to make enough of her questions understood to learn that there was a wedding. That the couple were in church that very moment, and that when they emerged there would be a big celebration.

Gemma said 'Oh?', and smiled and wished she'd stayed with the jeep after all. She felt very much as if she was intruding on a private occasion, and her fairness made her feel conspicuous, and deeply aware of the curious though friendly glances which were coming her way.

She lingered over her lemonade, wishing that Andreas would come and whisk her away, but by the time her glass was empty he still hadn't come to join her, and almost in desperation, she ordered another.

As the taverna owner set it down on the table, she heard him give a roar of pleasure and looking up she saw Andreas walking towards them, his face set and grim. At once he was surrounded by a grinning group of men, all vigorously shaking his hand and slapping him on the back.

Definitely an entrepreneur, and a successful one, Gemma thought judiciously. He probably kept the village supplied with work, but today he was annoyed because the two women had told him they couldn't manage some rush order.

It was some minutes before he disengaged himself and came to join her, dropping into a chair, and stretching his long legs in front of him.

He gave her a bleak look. 'Our trip to Aghios Nikolaos will be delayed,' he said expressionlessly. 'Hara and Petros are being married, and we are expected to stay and join the celebrations for a while.'

'But that's impossible,' Gemma protested.

His brows drew together icily. 'May I know why?'

'I should have thought it was obvious,' she said tightly. 'These are your friends, and it's a family occasion. I hardly think they'd welcome me if they knew the truth.'

'What truth is this?'

She bit her lip. 'That I'm—your mistress.'

He shrugged. 'You think not? Yet perhaps they are not as naïve, or as narrow-minded as you seem to suggest.'

In other words, they were probably quite used to seeing him with some enslaved female in tow, she thought raggedly.

He said on a mocking note, 'Don't look so stricken, Gemma *mou*. You are being asked to pass an hour or two in eating, drinking and dancing. Is that really so bad?'

Almost as bad as it could be, she thought. She didn't want to be with him like this, as if they were a couple and belonged together.

Besides, a wedding was altogether too intimate an occasion for them to share even on its fringe—too evocative of all the secret absurd dreams she hardly dared acknowledge even to herself.

'But perhaps the entertainment offered is a little too unsophisticated for your taste?' his voice continued remorselessly, flicking her on the raw. 'You were, after all, looking forward to the cosmopolitan delights of Aghios Nikolaos.'

She said unsteadily, 'Damn you, you know that isn't true. I'm looking forward to nothing.' As soon as the words were uttered, she regretted them, wondering if she had given away too much, but he seemed unaware of her slip.

'Not even to being reunited with your beloved brother? I thought you would be waiting eagerly to meet him again—almost as eagerly as I am myself,' he added grimly.

'Why?' she asked bitterly.

The firm lips were tautly compressed. 'So that I can be sure that justice has been done,' he said, half to himself.

'And how will you do that?' Her hands clenched together in her lap. 'By comparing scores –to ensure you've had me as many times as Mike had Maria?'

She could feel his anger as his mouth curled in a mirthless smile. 'An intriguing notion, Gemma *mou*. Are you now admitting that your brother is not the paragon you have always claimed? That you believe he did indeed seduce her and has been hiding like a coward on the mountain ever since, leaving you to pay the penalty?'

Gemma bent her head. 'I don't know what to believe any more,' she said wearily. 'All I know is that I'm not really in the mood for a celebration.'

'No more than myself,' he said coldly. 'Nevertheless, we must stay for a while at least. To leave when we have been invited would give offence, and these are good people.'

'Crete is full of them according to you,' she muttered, not looking at him. She sighed. 'All right then—we stay.'

She still felt agonisingly conspicuous as she sat and watched him move among the various groups who were gathering, seeing the pleasure and respect with which he was greeted, and wondering about it. He was still almost a total enigma to her, she realised unhappily. She'd begun to know his body intimately, but his mind was still closed to her.

This was the first time she'd seen him in association with other people—the first time she'd been obliged to think of him as a person in his own right with a life completely divorced from the Villa Ione and all its connotations. He had a family, friends, business associates while she— she belonged in a separate compartment of his life, and one that could be easily jettisoned when the time came, she reminded herself painfully.

She could hear music in the distance at first, then growing louder, and a few minutes later the musicians came into sight round the corner from the church, walking ahead of the bridal procession.

In spite of herself, Gemma felt her spirits lift at the intrinsic joyousness of it all. Everyone was happy, wreathed in smiles. The bride Hara was plump and not dazzlingly pretty by any means, but her dark eyes sparkled like the sun as she looked adoringly at the thickset young man by her side, and his protective air as he led her to the seat of honour at the table enclosed them both in a kind of beauty which went deeper than any surface charm.

Everyone was moving to the tables now, taking their places, but Gemma hung back feeling more of a stranger with every second that passed.

Andreas said harshly, 'Do you mean to sit there all day?' and pulled her to her feet in one easy movement, his hand firm on her waist as he guided her to a seat. People were grinning in welcome, making room for them, and Gemma's hand was shaken a dozen times or more. She was being swept along on a tide of goodwill which was almost overwhelming, absorbed into what seemed a vast group of women clustering around her. Their chattering voices rose and fell like birdsong, and the fact that she didn't understand a word of what they were seeing seemed irrelevant. With little admiring noises, they stroked her blonde hair, pointed to the fairness of her skin, and fingered the fabric of her dress, making it clear to her that she was welcome, and that they found her beautiful.

She had no idea what, if anything, they made of the fact she was there with Andreas. Probably it was just her own over-sensitivity which made her feel so wretched about the whole situation.

She found her glass being filled with wine, then filled again. Great platters of lamb baked in the oven with herbs and meltingly tender, were being brought from the taverna, with bowls of salad, and dishes of steaming fried potatoes fragrant with lemon. In spite of her half-hearted protests, her

plate was heaped with food. Eat, she was urged
mischievously in sign language, because a strong
man like the *kyrie* needs a strong woman, they
added with laughter, and Gemma found she was
laughing too. That in spite of the agonies of
heartache and worry, her mouth was watering for
the food. And that never in her life had she tasted
anything so delicious.

He was sitting further along the table from her,
on the opposite side, among the men, and she
found her glance straying to him over and over
again. He didn't seem to be enjoying himself
particularly. He was smiling and joining in the
conversation around him with what was clearly an
effort, and in between his face still held that
brooding bleakness. Was it just business worries,
she wondered, or was the quarrel they'd had
earlier getting to him?

She bit her lip, remembering his anger with her,
his contempt. The memories hurt, and she wished
that the pain could be deep enough to stop her
loving him. She wished something could burn out
of her for ever and ever the agony of this one-sided
relationship destroy it and make her whole
again.

The music which had been playing quietly all
during the meal suddenly swelled in volume,
taking on a more pronounced rhythm, and she
realised, as she was urged to her feet, that it was
time for the dancing. Amid laughter and hand-
clapping, the bridal couple led the way into the
middle of the square, and the others swarmed
around them forming an enormous circle, hands
joined. Gemma felt lost at first, her feet unable to
copy the intricate steps she was being shown, but
after a couple of circuits of the square, her body
began to adapt itself instinctively to the dipping,

swaying rhythm, and she was laughing, absurdly
pleased with herself when the dance came to an
end, and the rhythm changed.

Now, it was time to watch, because the men—or
some half-dozen of them were dancing alone, and
with a wrench of the heart, Gemma saw that
Andreas was one of them.

Everyone around her was clapping, accentuating
the beat of the music, and she joined in too, unable
to help herself. It was very different, she
discovered, from the exhibition dancing staged for
tourists in the Heraklion tavernas. This was no
folklore demonstration, but a joyous, strangely
powerful assertion of their masculinity by men
occupying what was still, primarily, a man's world.
The dance expressed their pride in their strength
and their virility with every sure, confident
movement, the muscular bodies an extension of
the music's rhythm. It was alien to anything
Gemma had ever experienced, alien even to her
own tentative beliefs about the equality of the
sexes, yet it moved her to her soul.

This pride, this certainty about the world and
his place in it was part of his birthright, she
thought, her mind faltering a little at the
realisation. That was why there was no self-
consciousness about the way the Greeks danced. It
was an expression of their belief in life itself.

She could feel tears springing in her eyes, and
turned away hurriedly, afraid that someone would
see. When she had control again, the dance had
ended and another circle was forming, but this
time she returned to her place at the table and sat
sipping her wine.

She knew she was being watched suddenly, and
turned her head. Her glance met his; locked. They
could have been alone. It was as if every sight and

sound around them had removed to some vague distance, enclosing them in a golden bubble of timelessness which, she knew dazedly, she never wanted to leave.

No one else existed. And she knew that no one ever would for her, and it made no difference at all that in terms of sanity they had known each other for such a brief time.

The passage of actual hours and days was only another irrelevancy, she realised with a kind of shock. And if at this moment, she was seeing him for the first time, she knew she would still want him as fiercely—a wanting that transcended mere physical desire.

She shared his bed, but what she wanted was to share his life, however alien to her, with utter completeness, and the depth and passion of that wanting frightened her, especially when she knew it applied to her alone.

There was no future in their relationship. None. And she was all kinds of a fool to even consider the possibility. She'd begun by fighting him. She'd even won some kind of hollow victory, then ruined everything by her rapturous, mindless surrender to his unexpected tenderness. He'd seduced her after all, she thought baldly, and she'd let it happen. In fact, she'd gloried in it, allowing herself to forget briefly exactly why he was taking her.

Only, she hadn't been permitted to forget for too long, she thought painfully.

Perhaps the harshness of his reminder to her of the stark reasons for his possession had been quite deliberate. Maybe, he was being cruel to be kind, stripping away any foolish illusions she might be harbouring about their relationship, and making her face reality.

He was an experienced man. She'd probably

betrayed her true feelings to him a dozen times as she lay in his arms—but never more so than at this moment, she realised with anguish.

With a supreme effort of willpower, she tore her gaze from his, concentrating her attention fiercely on the frankly unintelligible conversations going on around her, refusing with a kind of defiance to look his way again.

She'd succeeded so well that she almost jumped out of her skin when his voice beside her said almost laconically, 'It is time we were going.'

The dark eyes were aloof again, his face forbidding.

She said, 'Oh,' and paused. 'Then may I say goodbye. Everyone's been so kind to me . . .?' Her voice trailed away in appeal, and he nodded briefly before turning away, and striding off in the direction of the jeep.

They all seemed sorry to see her go. Even though verbal communication had been minimal between them, Gemma managed to establish that she was sorry too. One of the women darted away and returned breathlessly with a small flat package which she presented ceremoniously to Gemma. She could see she was expected to open it there and then, and did so. It was a tablecloth, she discovered, made of handwoven lace, produced with the skill and care of generations somewhere in this village. On the open market, it would cost a great deal, but this was a gift to her—a gift which it would cause offence to refuse.

And not just any gift either. The smiles and signs and gestures all around her were signifying that the present was intended for when she herself became a bride.

She was blushing painfully, her throat constricted as she managed, *'Efharisto—efharisto poli.'*

Her cheeks were still burning when she arrived back at the jeep. She'd bundled the cloth back into its wrapping, but all the same she was aware of Andreas eyeing it as she climbed into the passenger seat, his face coldly cynical as he did so.

'They have taken you to their hearts,' he said, as he started the engine.

'Yes,' she forced a smile. 'They shouldn't have done this.' She gestured almost helplessly towards her parcel. 'Obviously they'd made it to sell and . . .' She swallowed. 'I hope you didn't mind my accepting it.'

'Why should I mind?' His brows rose. 'I am glad you had the sensitivity not to offer to pay for it.'

'Did you think I would?' she demanded, stung.

He shrugged. 'It has been known. Your countrymen seem sometimes embarrassed by the generosity they are shown here, and try to respond by producing their cheque books.'

Gemma shook her head, 'Not me, I'm afraid,' she said too brightly. 'I priced some of the textiles during the first few days I was here, and a cloth like this would be totally beyond my means.'

'This job you have is poorly paid?'

Gemma shook her head. 'Not at all, but I can't afford to splash every penny I have on a holiday. I have to support myself when it's over, after all.'

'You live alone?'

'No, I live with my parents, but I pay my share of the bills. And I was thinking of finding a place of my own—in the autumn perhaps,' she added, remembering with a kind of amazement all the plans she'd been making in what seemed a lifetime before.

Hurriedly, she changed the subject. 'Where are we going now?'

'To Aghios Nikolaos.' His mouth curled a little.

'You will find it in complete contrast to the village we have just left.'

'And is that where you work? Where you sell your textiles?'

His sideways glance at her was sharp. 'What gives you the notion that I deal in textiles?'

She shrugged. 'It was just a guess. Those ladies you were visiting—I thought perhaps they might work for you.' She paused. 'I don't think I saw them at the wedding. Were they there?'

'No,' he said. 'They were not. Neither do they work for me in any way. I visited them because Soula used to live in Loussenas and I wanted news of her family.' There was sudden harshness in his voice. 'Does that satisfy your curiosity?'

She said stiffly, 'I'm sorry. I didn't mean to pry.'

'Does that mean no more questions?' he asked derisively, and she flushed.

'You ask enough,' she muttered defensively.

It was his turn to shrug. 'You are not obliged to answer,' he pointed out casually, as if it was of little interest to him whether she did or not, and Gemma subsided, biting her lip in chagrin.

At last, she said, 'If you're still angry about what I said this morning . . .'

'I am not,' he said briefly, and she was silenced again.

It was a long journey, and the broad national highway which cut its way across the island to Aghios Nikolaos although fast was not particularly interesting, Gemma decided. Nor was she overly impressed with the string of resorts which bordered the coast down to the Gulf of Mirabello. The Gulf itself was an intense shimmering blue as they descended towards Aghios Nikolaos. It looked almost unreal, Gemma thought. An artist's dream come to life with the bleached rock, and the dazzle of the buildings crowding almost to the edge of the dancing, glittering water.

Aghios Nikolaos was larger than she'd expected, and very much busier—the Crete of the tourist, with its streets lined with souvenir shops, offering leather and ceramics, and the crowded tavernas edging the harbour where pleasure boats and caiques jostled each other at their moorings.

After the seclusion of Loussenas, the noise of the traffic, the hubbub of voices and laughter from the people thronging the narrow streets seemed to batter at her ears.

She gazed around, trying to assimilate the cheerful, noisy charm of the place and caught sight of another glimmer of water.

She pointed. 'Is there an inner harbour?'

He shook his head. 'That is our so-called bottomless pool, where legend says Pallas Athene used to bathe,' he told her drily. 'I would not choose to do so myself.'

'Is it really bottomless?' Gemma craned her neck for a better view.

'It is deep enough,' he returned.

She was hoping he would stop and let her have a closer view, but to her disappointment he edged the jeep through the busy traffic round the harbour, emerging on to a broad promenade with hotels and tavernas on one side and the shining blue of the sea on the other, dotted with the sails of small boats and windsurfers.

He glanced at her. 'Don't you want to ask where we are going?' he challenged, faint amusement in his voice.

Gemma lifted her chin. 'It's really none of my business. I'm just enjoying the drive.' She paused. 'It's so wonderful to be allowed out of prison for a while.'

'Yet not every prisoner can boast a cell as comfortable as the Villa Ione.' The amusement was overt now. 'Or a jailer so aware of your needs,' he added cynically.

'So what is this?' she asked jerkily. 'My parole. Do you expect me to give my word I won't try and run away?'

'Is there really any need?' The words were softly spoken, but they burned her, because they told her quite unequivocally that he was aware of how she felt. That he knew that separation from him would be an agony for her. She could only pray that he would assume it was merely a physical infatuation.

She knew she should answer him somehow— snap back at him, try and build some defences, however precarious, but she couldn't think of a single thing to say. She wasn't even sure she could trust her voice. Instead, she concentrated her attention on the glamorous settings of the luxury hotels which fringed the outskirts of the little town.

The signposts indicated they were on their way to Elounda. It was one of the places she'd read about before she came—a little fishing village which had been rocketed to resort status by the popularity of the British television serial, *Who Pays the Ferryman*, which had been filmed there.

The road was climbing steeply, and when they reached the crest she almost cried out because the broad bay below them was so beautiful, the water shimmering from jade to turquoise, then melting to azure where it merged with the sky. There was a sprinkling of islands too, dominated by one eye-catching rocky mass.

Andreas said, 'That is Spinalonga. It was once a leper colony.'

Gemma shivered. Such a grisly reality seemed to

have no place in the fairytale vista ahead of her. 'How awful.'

'It is quite safe now,' he said. 'In fact it is an attraction for tourists. Boats visit the island regularly.' He paused. 'You don't approve?'

'I think it's a little morbid,' she said. 'After all you come on holiday to enjoy yourself—to escape even. It seems odd to deliberately seek out misery, even if it is in the past.'

'Yet you yourself visited Knossos. Do you believe that life there did not also have its dark side once?'

'No,' she said, with a little sigh. 'I suppose every age in history has its own brand of violence. But it wasn't all like that, I'm sure. It couldn't have been. The Lily-Prince for example . . .'

'Ah,' he said softly. 'Where I first saw you, Gemma *mou*.'

She bit her lip. 'I'd forgotten,' she lied.

He laughed. 'You did not know,' he told her, but in turn she could have told him that he was wrong. Even then her senses had warned her she was being watched, although in her wildest imaginings she could never have guessed why, or where it would lead.

He was signalling he was about to turn off the road. Leaning forward, Gemma saw a tall arched gateway surmounted by a display of international flags. There was a rope barrier across the gateway which a smartly dressed security man unlooped for them, saluting as they drove past.

'What is this place?' she asked.

'This is the Hotel Apollonissos,' he said laconically.

'Are you meeting someone here?'

'Several people,' he agreed. 'I hope that you will be able to entertain yourself in my absence. There are the usual water sports on the beach, or you could sun yourself by the pool, if you would prefer.'

'I think perhaps I'd better wait for you in the jeep,' she said.

'What nonsense is this?' He turned to her, frowning.

'No nonsense at all,' she returned levelly. 'I'm not dressed for the kind of activities you're talking about for one thing, and for another, I'd imagine, judging by the guard on the gate, that the management prefer to keep their facilities private for the use of guests only.'

'They are not quite as exclusive as that,' he said drily. 'You may bathe in the pool, or order a drink at the bar without fear of being thrown out, foolish one. As for your clothes ——' he shrugged. 'That can also be arranged. The hotel has an adequate boutique.'

'Adequate for millionaires, I expect,' Gemma said stiffly, glimpsing through the trees and shrubs which bordered the drive they were traversing, smooth lawns stretching down to a ribbon of pale sand along the edge of the sea. 'Perhaps you've forgotten that I happen to be a working girl. The Hotel Ariadne in Heraklion is more my environment.'

'Why denigrate yourself, Gemma *mou*?' he asked coolly. 'If I had thought you would be out of place here, then I would not have brought you.'

The jeep rounded a corner, and Gemma saw the hotel itself in front of them, an imposing two-storey building, dazzlingly white in the sunlight.

Andreas drove under another archway, and brought the jeep to a halt in a small paved courtyard, fragrant with green plants growing in huge stone urns. The air felt refreshingly cool after the heat and dust of the long drive, and Gemma inhaled thankfully as she looked around her.

He sprang out and came round to the passenger side, his hands closing inexorably on her waist as he lifted her down. 'Come.'

She hung back reluctantly. 'I really don't think I should. It all looks incredibly upmarket and glamorous.' She looked down at her simple chainstore dress with a faint grimace. 'I shall be totally out of place.'

He frowned swiftly, and she tensed, prepared for some blistering retort. At last he said, 'What do you want from me, Gemma? Reassurances about how beautiful you are? Do you not know that you fill my eyes?' He pulled her towards him almost fiercely, and his mouth took hers in a hard, bruising kiss in which the simmering anger she sensed in him was more evident than passion. When he let her go, she had to resist an impulse to cling to him, and was glad she'd done so when he said coolly, 'Now come with me quickly, because I am already late for my appointments.'

He opened a door, and she found herself in a broad corridor, floored with marble, the exterior wall made of glass to give panoramic vistas of the gardens. She would have liked to have lingered, but his long stride gave her no chance, and she was breathless by the time they arrived in the foyer. While Andreas went over to the long reception desk, Gemma stood staring about her.

There were stairs, she saw, directing guests to an open-air restaurant on the first floor, as well as lifts, desks for car hire and tourist information and an imposing shopping mall opening off the foyer itself. There were few people about. Most of the guests would be outside, she thought, soaking up the afternoon sun and other delights. Inside, there were no raised voices or loud noises, or even canned music. The whole atmosphere was one of hushed, unhurried luxury, and it made Gemma sigh a little. How the other half lives, she thought ruefully.

Andreas came striding back. 'I'll take you down to the pool area,' he told her. 'Dimitris, one of the under managers, is there, and he will look after you, and see you have everything you need.'

Gemma shook his hand off her arm. 'I can look after myself. I don't need another jailer.'

His mouth thinned. 'You need a beating,' he said softly and furiously. 'It is fortunate for you that I do not have time to administer it. Now, while you are here, you will keep a guard on that wasp's tongue of yours,' he added grimly.

His hand closed round hers, and this time she knew she wouldn't shake him off without a struggle, so she let him take her, seething, out of the foyer on to an enormous sunny terrace, and down a narrow flight of steps in the corner on to the lawns beneath.

She was aware immediately that they were attracting attention. Every step they took was being monitored in some strange way from beneath the sun umbrellas they were passing between, and Gemma couldn't imagine why.

Unless everyone knew they weren't guests at the hotel, and their presence was being remarked and resented, she thought forlornly.

She began to hope they would find this Dimitris soon.

He turned out to be a short, stocky man, talking to the waiters at the poolside bar, and when he saw them coming towards him, Gemma saw his jaw drop visibly, although he recovered immediately and came towards them smiling, and holding out his hand in greeting.

Gemma felt absurdly self-conscious as she stood waiting while they talked to each other. She didn't understand a word of what was being said, but it sounded as if Andreas was giving instructions rather than asking any favours, she thought, surprised.

And then a new voice intervened, female, husky and speaking good but accented English. 'Andreas—where have you been hiding yourself all this time? We have all missed you.'

She was beautiful, Gemma thought detachedly, a real Valkyrie of a girl with flaxen hair, and a figure bordering on the voluptuous and shown off to the best possible advantage in a tiny leopardskin print bikini. She was smiling at Andreas radiantly, and at the same time managing to give Gemma a look from her vivid blue eyes which was both hostile and dismissive. A clever trick, Gemma found herself thinking, and one which the newcomer had got down to a fine art.

Andreas turned to meet her, his smile easy in response. He said, 'You flatter me, Helga. I am sure your life is too full, too interesting, for you to have even given me a thought.'

She gave a little gurgle of laughter. 'Then you are wrong. We were only saying at lunch how cruelly you have been neglecting us.' She came even closer, putting a hand on his arm caressingly. 'But it is good to see you because I have an invitation for you. Tomorrow is my father's birthday and we are having a special dinner to celebrate. Both he and my mother would be so glad if you would join us.'

Her smile was winning, her fingers curling possessively on his dark skin. Gemma, watching, was shocked by a predatory impulse to do her violence.

He said, 'If only it were possible, but to my infinite regret, I have engagements for several days.'

She pouted appealingly. 'They will be so disappointed. We have hardly seen you at all this year.' Her glance flicked to Gemma. 'It is not kind to desert your—old friends.'

'Have I done so?' He lifted her hand to his lips. 'Then I apologise. Convey my respects to your parents, and assure them I shall have the pleasure of dining with them one night next week.'

Helga's eyes were heavy with seductive meaning. 'That will be good. We shall all look forward so much . . .' She paused. 'Now, won't you introduce me to your little friend?'

As a put-down, it couldn't be bettered, Gemma thought as she shook hands politely and murmured something. Helga's eyes were all over her taking in every detail of the cheap dress, and the simple sandals, and letting Gemma know what she thought of them with one derisive flicker of an eyebrow.

Andreas was looking frowningly at his watch. He pulled Gemma to one side. He said in an undertone, 'I have to go.' He paused, the frown deepening. 'You will be all right?'

She said brightly, 'Never better,' and watched him walk away round the edge of the pool. It needed all the strength she possessed not to run after him, begging him to take her with him wherever he was going, and she was proud of the control that kept her standing where she was.

She didn't know what his relationship had been with the gorgeous Helga, although she could guess. And the fact that her parents seemed to be around would make very little difference either. She was beautiful, sexy and very determined—a potent combination, Gemma had to acknowledge.

And next week—when her plane had left for England—next week he had promised to dine with them—with Helga for dessert, no doubt, she thought, her nails digging convulsively into the palms of her hands.

And she was all kinds of a fool to feel so bitterly, grindingly jealous because she'd known all along that she only existed on the fringe of his life, their relationship, such as it was, purely temporary, born out of bitterness and vengeance.

And when it was over, Helga and others like her would be waiting . . .

And I'll be waiting too, Gemma thought achingly. Waiting for the rest of my life.

CHAPTER NINE

GEMMA lay under the sun umbrella, pretending to read. Dimitris had been endlessly kind, producing a lounger and umbrella for her as if by magic, providing a selection of the latest paperback bestsellers for her to choose from, insisting that she had a long cool drink. But he could not persuade her to accompany him to the hotel boutique and choose a bikini to sunbathe in. Kyrios Andreas, he kept repeating almost plaintively, had left instructions. Kyrios Andreas would not be pleased if they were disregarded.

Gemma, however, remained adamant. She did not want to swim, she told Dimitris mendaciously because the glittering turquoise water looked infinitely cool and alluring, and she preferred to stay in the shade.

At last he shook his head sadly, said that if she required anything, she had only to tell one of the waiters, and took himself off.

She knew she was being an idiot, but she couldn't help it. She was conscious all the time of Helga's sharp blue gaze following her every move from across the pool, and there was no way she was going to strip and reveal all her body's pallid deficiencies in front of that sneering, suntanned goddess. Compared with Helga, she wasn't just slim, but thin, she knew despondently, and under the circumstances she preferred to remain covered, no matter how hot it was.

She found she was stealing covert glances at Helga from time to time, despising herself as she

152

did so. The German girl was spectacular and knew it, she thought drily, especially after she had casually discarded the top of her bikini. She wondered what Helga's parents, who looked portly, middle-aged and conventional, made of their glamorous daughter's antics, and decided after a few moments' observation that they regarded them with doting, uncritical fondness. And presumably if she wanted to spend part of her vacation in bed with a rich, sexy Greek that was all right too.

She bit her lip sharply. That kind of speculation was bad news. The last thing she wanted was to start building images of Andreas and Helga together, his darkness against all that golden splendour.

She tried to interest herself in her book. It was by one of her favourite writers, but the problems of the main characters seemed to pale into insignificance beside her own, and for once the plot failed to grip.

'Still all alone?' Helga asked with sweet malice. Without waiting for an invitation, she gestured to a passing waiter to put a vacant lounger next to Gemma's. She had her sunglasses with her, and a bottle of expensive oil. She looked as if she'd come to stay, as she stretched languorously on the lounger, and began to apply the oil to her full, firm breasts. 'It is wicked of Andreas to leave you for so long. But that is the way he is.'

She paused, and Gemma wondered drily whether she was supposed to say, 'Thanks for the warning.'

'Have you known him long?' Helga asked. 'And how did you meet?' She was eyeing Gemma almost incredulously.

Gemma said lightly. 'Not long. And I suppose you could say my brother brought us together.'

She could see Helga trying to work that one out, and failing, then the other woman said, 'You are here on holiday, one supposes.'

The supposition was correct, but what Helga really wanted to know was when she would be going home, and Gemma was damned if she was going to tell her.

She said, 'Yes, I've always wanted to come to Crete.' And launched into a spritely and specious account of the museums she'd visited and the antiquities she'd seen, sensing and enjoying her companion's rising irritation.

At last Helga interrupted shrilly, 'But you did not meet Nikolaides in such places. It is not possible. And you are not a guest in this hotel. Did you come on some package tour?' She made the idea sound like an insult, which was probably exactly what she intended.

And Gemma thought, 'I'm not the only one who's eaten up with jealousy. She'll be here when I'm gone, but she isn't sure of him.'

She said equably, 'No, I'm not staying here unfortunately. It's a beautiful place, isn't it. Do you stay here often?'

'We have stayed here each year since it opened,' Helga returned ungraciously. 'We spend usually a month, but sometimes it is longer.'

And you'd like it to be permanent, Gemma added silently. Well, you have nothing to worry about from me. I'm just passing through.

But all she said quietly was, 'It must be wonderful to have such freedom,' and saw with relief Dimitris almost hurtling towards them.

'Excuse me ladies,' he was smiling smoothly, the polite managerial mask well in place. 'But Kyrios Andreas would like you to join him in the penthouse, *thespinis*.'

She got up thankfully. She looked down at Helga, smiling faintly into the lovely, sulky face. 'Goodbye, *fraulein*,' she said politely. 'It was good to meet you.' It was certainly salutory. she added wryly.

Helga's smile in return was small and hostile. '*Auf wiedersehen*. And you may tell Andreas that if he wishes to change his mind about dinner tomorrow night, he need only arrive.' She paused. 'He will be more than welcome.'

'I'll tell him,' Gemma agreed calmly, and walked away.

As they went into the hotel, Dimitris said, 'I hope Fraulein Gretz has said nothing to upset you, *thespinis*. Her father is a very wealthy man, an industrialist from Stuttgart, and she is an only child who gets very much her own way.'

'And is consequently spoiled rotten,' Gemma concluded for him. 'I'd rather worked that out for myself.'

'She can be difficult,' Dimitris conceded discreetly. 'And Kyrios Andreas was not pleased when he saw she was talking to you,' he added.

She failed to see why, although she didn't say so to Dimitris. There was nothing Helga could have told her that she hadn't been able to work out for herself.

They didn't use the public lifts, to her surprise. Dimitris unlocked a door in the reception area, revealing a short passage leading to another. smaller lift.

'This goes straight to the penthouse,' Dimitris said, pressing a button.

Gemma was totally at a loss as the lift ascended. 'So, what's up there?' she asked 'Offices?'

'Just the boardroom, *thespinis*, and the apartment that Kyrios Andreas uses when he is at the hotel.'

'And does he stay here often?' she asked bemused, wondering what a permanent penthouse suite would cost in a hotel as luxurious as this.

'As often as he can, *thespinis*. Kyrios Nikolaides takes a close interest in the running of all his hotels, as his father did before him.'

She felt dizzy, as if the walls of the lift were closing round her. She said breathlessly, 'I don't quite understand, Dimitris. Are you saying this hotel actually—belongs to—to Kyrios Andreas—that he's the owner?'

As the lift doors opened, Dimitris gave her a slightly reproachful look. 'But of course, *thespinis*. How could you not know?'

'How indeed?' Gemma said ironically.

They passed the boardroom. She glimpsed a long polished table, and two secretaries gathering up papers. Then Dimitris was knocking at a door, and it opened and Andreas was standing in the doorway so close that she could have touched him, and yet in another way, they had never been further apart.

Her smile as she looked at him was forced, and she saw that he knew it, his eyes narrowing as she went past him.

It was a beautiful room, full of sunshine and colour, and light years away from the simplicity of the Villa Ione. There were huge windows on two sides giving panoramic views of the bay and the hotel gardens, including the environs of the pool. So that was how he knew Helga was with me, she thought.

She said in a wooden voice, 'Your hotel is fantastic. What a fool you must have thought me, chattering on about textiles.'

'I have never thought you a fool, Gemma.' His voice was quiet. 'Would you like some coffee? Or there could be tea if you preferred.'

'Or even champagne cocktails.' She went on staring out of the window as if the view fascinated her.

'Those too,' he agreed, sounding faintly amused. 'Is that what you would like?'

She shook her head. 'Coffee would be fine,' she said huskily. She paused. 'I can see why you were so sure the authorities would believe you, and not me. Kidnapping isn't the kind of thing you associate with respectable hotel owners.' She bit her lip. 'From what Dimitris says I gather you have a few of them.'

'There is another at Rethymnon,' he said. 'As well as those on Rhodes and Corfu.'

'The Nikolaides chain,' she said faintly. 'I should have realised when Fraulein Gretz mentioned your name. But even then I didn't make the connection.'

'You have heard of the hotels?' He sounded surprised.

'Heard, yes,' she said. 'But I never expected to set foot in one.' She smiled brightly. 'Another experience to treasure when I go home next week.'

There was an enormous sofa, like a divan, piled with cushions. He sat down and began to pour the coffee which was waiting on a low table.

He said, 'I think your return home is something we need to discuss.'

Her mouth was dry. 'You—you mean to keep me here?'

He shook his head. 'On the contrary, Gemma *mou*. I think it would be best if you went home almost at once. Tomorrow, if a suitable flight can be arranged.'

She took the cup he handed her. Her fingers didn't shake, which was amazing when she considered that her life had just fallen in ruins about her.

She said, 'Tomorrow would be perfectly convenient, I'm sure—for everyone.' She drank some coffee, and nearly scalded herself, but she kept smiling. 'You'll be able to attend Herr Gretz's birthday party. Your—Helga asked me to tell you the invitation was still open.'

'That is hospitable of her,' he said.

'I thought so too,' she said. In spite of the air conditioning, it was hot in the room, and yet she was so cold that any moment her teeth could start chattering. 'Do you think there's any chance of a reservation tomorrow?'

'I'll call down to our travel desk,' he said. 'Ask them to make some preliminary enquiries. It may be possible to transfer the unused portion of your return ticket.'

It all sounded very efficient, and she supposed she should thank him, but it was difficult to find the words when she was dying inside. She knew a terrible destructive impulse to throw herself at him—into his arms—down at his feet and plead with him not to send her away. And perhaps he sensed the loneliness in her, and the despair, because he said, quite gently, 'Gemma, believe me, it is necessary that I do this. I wish it was possible to explain fully.'

To explain what? That between her and the glamorous daughter of a wealthy German industrialist there was no contest?

And then, unbidden, from somewhere at the back of her mind, she saw the shepherd's hut, and an icy fear gripped her.

She said sharply, 'It's Mike isn't it—something

to do with him—and you don't want me to be here when it happens?' She ran her tongue round her dry lips. 'Or has it happened already? Your friend Stavros—has he found Mike? Harmed him?'

'No.' Andreas got to his feet and came to her. His arms went round her, but she stayed rigid in his embrace. 'It is not that, I swear. They would have to harm me first. But I have done you a great wrong, Gemma, and somehow I need to make amends. You must understand that.'

She shook her head wearily. 'I don't understand anything, and I haven't—not from day one.' She moved away from him, because even though there was only comfort in his embrace, her body was crying out for him just the same. 'Perhaps you'd phone about my ticket now.'

'Yes.' There was a phone on the table next to the tray, and she watched him lift it and dial a number. She didn't understand a word of the brief conversation which followed, but she felt that the sound of it would be imprinted on her brain forever.

He said, 'Kostas will phone us back as soon as he has news.'

'That's good.' She took a breath. 'It's a pity you didn't put my case in the jeep this morning. Then there would have been no need to go back to the villa.'

He shrugged. 'No problem.' He sounded casual to the point of indifference, she thought dazedly. The passionate lover who had caressed every inch of her body with his mouth and hands might never have existed.

But perhaps he never had, at that. Perhaps there had only been the cold-blooded avenger of Maria's honour, a role which he had not enjoyed, and now wished to forget with as little trouble as possible.

He talked of amends, but wasn't it more likely that, having exacted his vengeance, he was bored with her, and wanted to get his life back to its normal tenor?

She had known it would happen, expected it, but dear God, not so soon, she thought wildly.

She hurried into speech, trying to find a safe subject. 'This is a fascinating apartment. I'm surprised you can ever bear to leave it.'

'It's useful, but it does not afford a great deal of privacy,' he said drily. 'Would you like some more coffee?'

'No, thank you,' she said politely. She had hardly touched what she'd had, the taste of it as bitter as gall in her mouth.

She hurried into speech again. 'Could I see the other rooms?'

His brows lifted. He said coolly, 'It will be my pleasure.' He paused. 'Shall we start with the bathroom?'

She wouldn't have cared if he'd offered to show her the garden shed. She didn't want to see any of the apartment, but she had to say something, do something to fill this terrible aching void while she waited to hear whether she was being flown out the next day.

The bathroom was fantastic, tiled in black and gold with a huge sunken bath, and she couldn't think of a thing to say about it, so she made approving noises. The bedroom was vast too, the bed which dominated it covered by a spread of Cretan design in shades of blue and crimson.

Gemma stood in the doorway of the room and stared at it. Andreas was standing behind her, so close to her that she could feel the warmth of his body penetrating the fabric of her dress. She remembered the night she had stood on the terrace at Loussenas listening to the music from the village and the way his lips had caressed her neck and his hands touched her breasts. She was on fire for him, longing for him to draw him to her again with a depth of yearning which was physically painful. She wanted to turn into his arms, to feel his mouth on hers, parting her lips with passion. She wanted him to carry her to that bed.

But no amount of wanting could make it so, she discovered.

Instead, she heard him say, 'That completes the tour,' and her senses told her he had moved away back into the living room. After a moment, she did the same, avoiding his gaze, aware that her cheeks were unnaturally flushed.

It was almost a relief when the phone rang. Andreas lifted the receiver and listened, his face expressionless.

Then he nodded, uttered a swift word of thanks and put the phone down. He said, 'It is settled then. There is a plane just after four in the afternoon. You are booked on to it.'

Her mouth felt so dry suddenly, she was afraid her lips might crack. She said, 'Thank you. How—how will I get to the airport?'

There was an edge of impatience in his voice. 'I will take you there.'

'That's very kind of you,' she said politely. 'But I don't want to put you to any trouble, or inconvenience.'

His mouth tightened and he did not reply.

Gemma walked over to the other window, and stood rigidly staring out, fighting back tears with all her strength. He couldn't wait to be rid of her, it was evident, and all she had to ensure now was that she took her departure with some dignity. And bursting into tears, or revealing any other emotional weakness would be about as undignified as it was possible to get, she told herself.

At last he asked, 'Would you like to have dinner here, or return to the villa?'

Not looking at him, she said, 'Do you mean—actually here, or . . .?'

He said curtly, 'I meant in the restaurant. However, if you have no particular preference, it might be better if we returned to Loussenas.'

She said colourlessly, 'I would prefer that, too.'

'Then we had better be leaving.' He picked up the paperback she had brought up from the pool. 'Is this yours?'

She said, 'Dimitris gave it to me. I'd like to keep it to read on the plane, but naturally I'll pay you for it, when I get my money back.'

He said icily, 'You are all consideration. But perhaps you will accept it from me as a gift, as I understand you would take nothing else.'

She looked away. 'Just as you wish,' she said dully.

'We will not, I think, discuss my wishes.' His tone was grim. 'Now let us go.'

The sun had set by the time they reached Loussenas, and the Villa Ione was full of shadows. Andreas moved about lighting the lamps, but the shadows were still there, inside her, and she stood watching him, her arms wrapped across her body, hugging herself as if she was cold.

He said, 'Are you hungry?'

She thought, 'Only for you' but naturally she did not give the thought utterance. She shook her head. 'Not—really.'

'Then I suggest you get some rest,' he said. 'You have done a lot of travelling today, and you have another long journey to face tomorrow.'

She swallowed, lifting her chin. 'And—you?'

He turned away, making some adjustment to the shutters. 'I have to go down to the village,' he said at last. 'I will try not to disturb you when I return.'

If he had struck her across the face, the rejection could not have been more painful, or more final.

She licked her dry lips. 'To use your own words—you're all consideration,' she said tonelessly, then turned away and went upstairs.

From her window, she watched him walk slowly towards the village, his head bent, never glancing back even once. She shivered almost convulsively. Bitterness, anger, passion—she could have met all those, but not this chilly remoteness, telling her more plainly than any words that she had nothing to hope for from him.

As if I ever had, she thought wretchedly. That incredible sensual sweetness he had brought her the previous night had meant nothing to him. He'd made her respond, because his pride demanded it, that was all, but she was not and never had been 'his woman'. And now, she was an inconvenience, and an embarrassment on the edge of his life.

She took the clothes she had unpacked only a few hours before and thrust them into her case anyhow, humiliated tears burning behind her lids.

Then she showered and put on her nightdress, and got into bed, and lay staring into the gathering darkness. She felt weary to her bones, but her mind and senses were awake and crying out.

In a few short days her life had totally changed. She had totally changed. The self-contained girl, in charge of her emotions, in charge of her future, no longer existed, and she couldn't even be sorry.

Her hand slid wonderingly to the flatness of her abdomen. Perhaps the changes in her life would be more far-reaching than she could ever guess. She hoped there would be a child, in spite of the grief this would inevitably cause her family. And although the baby would have beèn conceived in an act of vengeance, it would be brought up in love no matter what the difficulties. She would manage somehow, and she would manage alone. She wouldn't use the baby as an excuse to contact Andreas again, as a fragile chain to keep him bound to her at any level of obligation. About that, she was adamant. When her plane left tomorrow, that would be the end—a break as clean as an amputation.

She sighed, her body twisting restlessly on the bed. But that was for the following day, and she had a long lonely night to get through somehow.

She had no idea how many hours had passed, but she was still wide awake, her mind treading the same painful tracks, when she heard him come back.

She listened to him moving about, then, her whole being tensing hopefully, expectantly, heard his footsteps on the stairs. She waited, staring at the door, willing him to come to her, her body one wild cry of yearning.

But without pause, without even hesitation, he went past her door and into his own room.

With a smothered groan, Gemma rolled over on to her stomach and lay still.

She lay for a long, dragging time, her pride, her self-respect fighting a bitter losing battle against the unending clamour of her senses.

At last, she slipped from the bed, and went out of the room, crossing the narrow passage to his door. It was closed, and she opened it quietly and went in.

He was awake too, and he turned his head slowly and looked at her, standing in the brilliance of the moonlight.

He said quietly, 'Go back to your room, Gemma. Go back now.'

She shook her head. 'No, Andreas *mou*. You're sending me away tomorrow, and I accept that, but let me have tonight.'

There was a taut silence, then he said harshly, 'You do not know what you are asking.'

'Oh, but I do.' She smiled, her mouth tremulous. 'You—you taught me too well, perhaps. Don't make me spend the rest of the night alone.' She paused. 'I'll never ask you for anything else—I swear it. No—demands on any grounds. But let me stay with you now.'

'Oh, God.' His voice was hoarse. 'Gemma— *agape mou*—I have done you the greatest wrong it is possible for a man to do to a woman. How much else do you want me to bear on my conscience?'

'Why should there be guilt?' she asked. 'Unless—you don't want me?'

He flung back the sheet and came across to her, his arms sliding round her body, fiercely, bruisingly.

'Not want you?' His voice almost broke. 'My sweet fool, how could I not want you?'

His fingers slipped under the narrow straps of her nightdress, pushing them from her shoulders, tugging them downwards until the garment lay in a white cloud on the floor. Then he lifted her into his arms, and carried her to the bed.

She was wild for him, the brush of his naked body against her own filling her with sensuous urgency. Her hands slid over his burning skin, paying tribute to the strength of him, the sheer animal grace, echoing without inhibition the passionate exploration his own fingers were making of her.

His head bowed to her breasts, his mouth taking one rosy nipple, then the other into sensual captivity, teasing the hardened sensitive peaks with his tongue until she moaned in pleasure and pleading.

He laughed in his throat. 'Patience, my dove, my tigress,' he told her huskily.

His mouth moved downwards over her trembling flesh, trailing fire, bringing every last sense to shattering, responsive life, making her shudder with delight.

His hands slid under her hips, lifting her towards him, silently demanding her acquiescence in the most intimate kiss of all, and she had neither the strength nor the will to deny him, her body convulsing in a shock of pleasure, a soundless scream tearing at her throat as his mouth possessed her.

She was mindless, dazed and rapturous with sensation, consumed by a sweet flame she had never dreamed existed, her body arching towards him, her head thrashing from side to side on the pillow. He moved, his body covering hers, glorying in the completeness of her acceptance of him, and she whispered her need in little broken words as she welcomed him into her, and went with him down the brief, explosive path to their mutual consummation.

And when it was over, she turned pliantly into his arms, pillowing her cheek against his sweat-dampened chest, and they slept.

And woke and made love again with slow, passionate intensity as the night began to take on the shimmer of the day. She clung to him, her hands raking at the smooth skin of his shoulders, the harsh hurry of her breathing matching his, her body poised on the edge of ecstasy, and realised with a kind of anguish that this was the last time she would ever fall through the stars to earth with him, and this agony of pleasure was their farewell to each other.

CHAPTER TEN

GEMMA woke first. For a long moment, she lay watching him, as if every line of that darkly arrogant face and strong, lithe body wasn't already committed to her memory, then moving very carefully so as not to disturb him, she slid out of his encircling arm, and out of bed.

This last time, she would make breakfast for them.

She picked up her discarded nightdress and slid it over her head. Although there was no one but himself to see, she still felt oddly shy about appearing naked in front of him.

She went silent and barefoot downstairs, and out into the kitchen, but the bread had not arrived. She filled the kettle and set it on the stove to boil. Later, she knew there would be pain as she faced the fact they would never meet again, but now, still wrapped in the aftermath of their lovemaking, she felt oddly at peace with herself.

And the sound of footsteps on the terrace, entering the villa was a disruption, although an expected one.

She turned her head, and called, 'Maria—I'm out here.'

Silence. She frowned a little moving towards the door. 'Maria?' Then stopped dead, her hand flying to her mouth with shock.

Michael stood just inside the dining room, his face a picture of stunned incredulity. He said on a whisper, 'Gemma? What the hell . . .?'

A wave of burning colour seemed to sweep up

from her toes, as she looked back at him. She could hear sounds of movement upstairs, and realised Andreas must have woken. At any moment, he could come down and find them . . .

She said hoarsely, 'Mike—you've got to get out of here, now. Which way did you come? Did they see you in the village?'

He looked at her as if she was mad. 'I don't know whether they did or not. What's the matter with you? And what are you doing here? Didn't you get my last letter?'

'Probably not,' she said shakily. 'But we haven't time to talk about that now.'

'Well, we need to talk about a few things,' he said austerely. 'For one, did you ask anyone's permission before moving in here? It's not for hire, you know. It's privately owned by some hotel tycoon called Nikolaides . . .'

'I know,' she interrupted hastily. 'And he mustn't find you here.'

'I've got permission,' he told her impatiently. 'Stavros, who's the head man in the village is a great friend of this Nikolaides and . . .'

'But not a great friend of yours—not any more.' She swallowed. 'Mike, I know about you—and Maria. They all know, and it's not safe for you to be here, believe me.'

He disengaged himself from his rucksack, dropping it to the floor with a thud. 'Oh, Maria,' he said casually. 'What's the little idiot been doing now?'

'Don't play games,' Gemma said bitterly. 'She's pregnant, and don't pretend you didn't know.'

He shrugged. 'Oh, I knew all right.' He sounded exasperated. 'But hell, I thought she'd be safely married by now. What's been the snag?'

Gemma looked at him, appalled. 'The snag,' she

said cuttingly, 'as you so winsomely put it, was her fiancé, who was understandably reluctant to take on someone else's child.'

'Not him,' he dismissed. 'I meant Kemal. I went to Chania to find him, and he was coming straight here to get her to marry her, even if it meant running away together. Don't tell me it's all gone wrong?'

From behind him, Andreas said grimly, 'Yes, my friend, it has indeed all gone wrong—very wrong.'

Mike swung round to face him, initial surprise giving way to wariness as he registered the fact that Andreas had clearly just emerged from the shower, and was wearing nothing but a towel draped round his hips. At once, his glance travelled swiftly and sharply towards Gemma as if assimilating her own lack of attire, and his expression changed to an amalgam of embarrassment and condemnation.

He said, 'Just who the hell are you? And what is my sister doing here with you?' He sounded defensive and rather young.

'Do I have to spell it out for you?' Andreas asked drily, but his tone held none of the triumph Gemma had expected from him now that he and Mike were actually facing each other.

Mike flushed. 'I suppose not,' he said with constraint. He didn't look at Gemma again, but the back of his head spoke volumes of disapproval and more.

'I have been hoping you would return,' Andreas went on almost conversationally. 'And so, I understand, has your friend Kemal, who has spent an uncomfortable time camping out in a shepherd's hut on the mountain.'

Mike frowned. 'What on earth for?'

Andreas' mouth curled. 'The car he was using broke down on the way here, and he had to abandon it, and with it, his romantic plans for an elopement in the teeth of Stavros and his family. Instead, he had to hide on the mountain, eating as and when Maria could smuggle him food, and waiting for you to come to his rescue yet again.'

Mike groaned. 'If that isn't typical,' he began furiously. 'I was sure it would be all cut and dried by now. God knows, I never wanted to get involved in the first place.'

'Then why did you?' the cool voice asked inexorably.

Mike grimaced. 'I met Kemal in Chania ages ago. He seemed a bit of a loner at first, but we used to eat in the same places, and got talking, and eventually he told me about this girl he was in love with from one of the villages. Only, he said, her family wouldn't hear of it because his father was Turkish, and his mother was considered to have disgraced herself by such a marriage. It didn't seem to make a lot of sense to me, but I felt sorry for him, and for her too, when I found out her family were planning to marry her off to some guy she hardly knew. But in the meantime, she was in Chania, working in some relative's hotel as a waitress, and Kemal was meeting her on the quiet.'

Gemma stood as if frozen, listening to the story unfold, hearing it at last make a kind of terrible sense in her mind. Maria's lover was part-Turkish, she thought, which would arouse all kinds of ancient enmities.

'It seemed an ideal arrangement,' Mike continued, 'until the family got suspicious and she was whisked back here to Loussenas. Kemal couldn't follow at once—her father had banned him from his house a long time before, and naturally he was nervous about showing himself in the village, but he knew I was planning to come to this area anyway to do some research, so he asked me to keep an eye on Maria—make sure she was all right, and that they weren't pushing this marriage at her.'

He paused. 'I could see why he wanted to steer clear of her father. Stavros is a formidable guy, although he was kindness itself to me, arranging for me to use this villa. I really didn't like deceiving him, especially when I found Maria was expecting me to act as a go-between for Kemal and herself. It was just after this that she found out about the baby. She knew all hell would break loose and she begged me to go to Chania and tell Kemal. Well,' he shrugged, 'I felt I couldn't refuse under the circumstances, and as it happened I'd just had a letter from a university mate of mine, Chris Hennessey, saying he and a couple of others were planning to take a caique across to Karpathos, and did I want to join them?' He shrugged again. 'You don't turn down a chance like that, so I wrote to Gem, telling her to postpone her trip for a month or so. It never occurred to me she'd come anyway,' he added in a tone of faint injury.

'The letter must have been delayed,' Gemma said. 'I never received it.'

Michael turned and looked at her, flushing a little. 'Okay, these things happen. But coming here is one thing. Getting yourself—involved with some guy you can only just have met is quite another.' He stopped swallowing. 'Gem, this isn't like you. It would just about kill the parents if they knew.'

She bit her lip. 'Do you plan to tell them?'

'No, of course not,' he denied heatedly. 'But all the same . . .'

'You must not blame your sister in any way,' Andreas said calmly. 'Your quarrel is with me, and me alone. Because of the lies Maria told her family after you had left the village, they believed you were the father of her baby.'

'I was?' Mike sounded outraged. 'But that's insane. I mean—she's a nice enough girl, I suppose . . .'

'Nevertheless, that is what she told them, and they believed her. She was terrified that if she told the truth, Kemal might come to some harm. As you said, Stavros is indeed a formidable man, and he did not take this damage to his daughter's honour lightly. He wanted—vengeance.'

'So?' Mike's eyes narrowed sharply.

'So—the letter Gemma wrote to you giving details of her travel plans was found in your room. And to avenge Maria's honour, and bring shame on you, as you, it was thought, had disgraced Stavros and his kin—to punish you, I—took your sister.'

There was a long silence, then Mike said unevenly, 'Christ.' He swung round on Gemma. 'Gem—does this bastard mean he—raped you?'

Her face burned. 'No.'

Her brother's usually gentle face was ugly suddenly, and she moved to him swiftly, gripping his arm, interposing herself between the two men. She said softly and urgently, 'Mike—I can't explain—I have no excuse at all, but it—wasn't rape. It—happened, and now it's over—all over, and I'm leaving this afternoon for home. And there's no need for anyone to know anything unless you tell them.'

His voice shook. 'Oh, my God.'

Andreas broke in swiftly, 'There is no name you can call me that I do not deserve. Nothing you can say, that I have not already told myself a hundred times. But by the time I came to suspect the truth, it was already too late.' The dark face looked suddenly haggard. 'At first, I couldn't believe we had all been so wrong. I thought Kemal had gone to the Turkish side long ago to join his father's people. So yesterday I spoke to his mother and his aunt, who live now in a village a little way from here, and they told me he had never left Crete. They told me, too, he was planning to marry, and would be bringing his bride to them soon.'

Gemma said half to herself, 'The house with the fig tree.'

He said quietly, 'Yes.' There was a long pause, then he said, 'There is only one way in which I can now make amends for Maria's lies and the terrible harm they have caused. In the absence of her father, I ask you Kyrios Michalis, for your sister in marriage.'

In a voice she barely recognised as her own, Gemma said, 'No,' violently.

One long stride brought Andreas to her. He took her by the shoulders, turning her to face him. 'What do you mean?' he demanded harshly.

'Exactly what she says,' Mike cut in. 'And who can blame her? Anyway, I'm here now, and she doesn't have to do anything you say again, you scum, no matter how many times you may have had her in your bed. She can do better than you, God knows, any day of the week.'

Gemma said softly, 'Mike—this is Andreas Nikolaides.'

And watched his jaw drop in shock. But he made a stout recovery. 'To hell with that. I stand by every word I've said. The best thing Gemma can do about a swine like you is forget you ever existed.'

'And is that what you wish, Gemma?' His hands were still holding her inexorably, his eyes grim as he stared down at her.

Somehow, she found the strength to tear herself free. 'Yes,' she said in a thread of a voice. 'I'm tired of obligations and—and honour, and making amends. I just want to get out of here—away from you. I want to go home.'

'So you keep away from her from now on,' Mike added fiercely. 'Leave her alone, or you'll have me to reckon with.'

Andreas' face was sardonic suddenly. He was taller than Mike, heavier, stronger, more muscular in every way. Mike's threat was on the face of it absurd, and Gemma cringed from the crushing words she was sure would come in reply, but all Andreas said was, 'Very well,' before turning and walking away, leaving brother and sister together.

The inside of her lower lip felt raw. Her teeth had almost met in the soft, moist flesh.

She said in a high, strained little voice, 'I think I'd better get dressed.'

'Don't you think we should talk first?' His face was unhappy as he studied her. 'I can see now why you wanted to get rid of me so damned quickly. You didn't want me to catch you with your millionaire—stud.'

Gemma winced, 'Don't.'

He flushed. 'I'm sorry, love.' There was real compunction in his voice. 'That was a lousy thing to say. But I can't relate you to—all this. You've admitted yourself he didn't have to use force, for God's sake. And yet you're no raver, and never have been. I—I just don't understand any of it.'

She said wearily, 'Nor do I, believe me. But I was not trying to chase you away because I was ashamed of anything I'd done. I was frightened for you, that's all. You see, I didn't know this Kemal even existed.'

For a moment he looked bewildered, then a quick frown spread. 'You don't mean you actually believed Maria's ridiculous lies about me?'

'No, I don't think I ever did,' she acknowledged quietly. 'I said from the first, that you'd never have seduced anyone and left them in the lurch. But—Andreas did believe it, and so did Maria's family. And I couldn't take it for granted that what Andreas had done to me would be enough for them.' She shuddered. 'I thought in spite of everything they might—kill you.'

He muttered something awkwardly, and patted her arm, then looked past her into the kitchen. 'There's a kettle there, boiling its head off,' he said with an attempt at lightness. 'Go and get some clothes on, and I'll make the coffee.'

She gave him a grateful smile and escaped upstairs.

Andreas was waiting in her room. He was dressed, she registered numbly, in smoothly tailored slacks, and a casual navy shirt which he was still buttoning. He looked at her grimly.

'Have you nothing to say to me?'

'What is there to say?' She dragged a tan-and-white striped dress out of her case, and tossed it on to the bed. 'Except that I realise now why you were having such pangs of conscience about me.' She paused. 'When did you realise this—Kemal was the one involved?'

'When you told me your brother did not smoke, I wondered,' he said. 'But even so, I was only guessing at first. I knew, of course, there had been some talk of love when they were both younger, which Stavros had forbidden even then. And when his mother moved from the village, I supposed that would be the end of it.'

'So, what will happen now?' she asked tightly. 'Does Kemal have a sister, or will Stavros and his men merely hunt him down in the mountains?'

'Neither.' A tiny muscle jumped beside his taut mouth at her bitter words. 'Last night, when I finally persuaded Maria to confess the truth to her family, there was much anger and sorrow, as you can suppose. But Stavros has agreed to the marriage, and Maria and one of her brothers went to the hut and brought him down to face his obligations.' His mouth twisted. 'He was a sight to be pitied.'

'Please don't ask me to try,' she said. 'And now will you please get out of my room? I'm waiting to get dressed.'

The dark eyes watched her. 'Last night you were naked in my arms,' he said. 'So, why this sudden desire for modesty?'

'Because that was last night.' Gemma stared at the floor. 'And this is today, and everything has changed.'

'Why, yes *agape mou*,' he drawled. 'For one thing, I have asked you to marry me.'

'And I have refused.' Gemma lifted her chin defiantly.

'May I know why?'

'I should have thought that was fairly obvious. If Mike hadn't turned up like this, you wouldn't have asked me. Yesterday, all you could think of was getting me off the island. Well, I prefer to stick to the original plan.'

'You don't understand at all,' he said with exasperation. '*Matia mou*, I felt I had to send you away, for your own sake, so that no word of this would ever leak out to involve us in scandal.'

'You mean, you didn't want your own involvement known,' she accused angrily. 'Everyone at the hotel yesterday was staring at me, wondering where you'd picked me up. I suppose I must be a disappointment after your usual ladies.'

'That is nonsense.' He was angry now.

'Is it?' Gemma pushed her hair back wearily. 'Not that it matters. So, please don't feel guilty on my account. As we've established already, it wasn't rape, and I—wanted everything that happened last night, so please don't worry about me—about anything, in fact.'

'What are you saying?' He sounded incredulous. 'That we should pretend all this never happened— that we never met, perhaps?' He walked over to her, cupping her unwilling face between his hands, staring down at her. 'Gemma *mou*, you know that is impossible. Too much has happened. We can never be free of each other, even if that is what we wanted—which I do not believe,' he added flatly. 'So, why will you not marry me?'

'For all kinds of reasons.' The gentleness of his hands against her soft skin made her want to weep, but she controlled the impulse rigidly. 'Because I have a life of my own—a career back in England, and—and I don't need you.'

'And what of my needs?' The smile curving his lips and gleaming in his eyes was a seduction in itself.

Gemma looked away hastily. 'I'm sure Fraulein Gretz will be only too happy to take care of them,' she said tonelessly.

He made a sound that was suspiciously like a choked back laugh. 'Perhaps she would, *agape mou*, if I gave her the opportunity, which I promise you I do not intend to do.'

'Not even at the cosy dinner you were suggesting next week?' As soon as the words were out, she regretted them, knowing that she had given him the chance to taunt her with being jealous.

'Not at any time. Gemma *mou*, I may not have lived like a saint, but I do not seduce women guests in my hotels. Besides, at this cosy dinner you speak of, I had planned to announce our marriage.'

'Is that why you suddenly want a wife?' she asked huskily. 'As protection against predatory blondes?'

He groaned. 'No, wildcat, it is not.' His eyes flicked restlessly past her to the bed, and his mouth curled wryly. 'Damn your brother. If he was not here, I would take you to bed and make love to you until you pleaded with me to marry you.'

'Then I can only be thankful he is here,' she said inimically. 'And you should be grateful, too, because marriage between us would be a disaster. We're strangers from two different worlds, who've just happened to—collide for a brief while, that's all.' She paused, struggling to control the faint quiver in her voice. 'Now, please leave me alone,' she added with desperation.

He gave her a hard, searching look, and she had to force herself to stand her ground and look back at him, as if she meant every word, as if she didn't care.

Then suddenly, starkly, he let her go, and she watched him cross the room, and go out, closing the door behind him.

She said under her breath, 'Oh God,' then her legs gave way, and she sank down, trembling, on to the floor, and stayed there, her arms wrapped round her body, rocking slightly like an unhappy child, while scalding tears emptied down her face.

*   *   *

A shower helped, later, and the tan-and-white dress, which was crisp and pretty, gave her courage too.

But when she got downstairs, only Mike was there, sitting on the terrace drinking coffee. 'He's gone down to the village to make sure the wedding truce is still holding up,' he said, passing her a cup of coffee. 'He's a dynamic bastard when he gets going, I'll say that for him,' he added with grudging admiration. 'I can't altogether blame you for having a little fling with him, Gem, no matter what the original reason. I shouldn't think he often has to ask twice, if ever.'

She said levelly, 'I suppose not.' She paused. 'Mike, can you drive the jeep?'

'Probably,' he said. 'Why?'

'I need to get to Heraklion to catch this plane.'

'Isn't Nikolaides driving you there?' He sounded surprised. 'He mentioned something about it.'

'Perhaps so,' she said. 'But I'd rather it was you, Mike. I don't really want to be alone with him again.'

'You can't get up to much in a jeep,' he said. 'But I'll mention it to him, certainly. I can't see why he should object. Under the circumstances he must be as keen to be rid of you, as you are to leave.' He frowned a little. 'I was hoping I'd be able to stay here again, but if he's in residence, I shall have to look elsewhere. Maybe someone in the village will put me up.'

'I'm sure they will,' she said drily. 'They'll probably be anxious to "make amends" too. But I don't think Andreas will be staying on here. He has an apartment in his hotel at Aghios Nikolaos. I expect he'll be returning there.'

He brightened. 'You think so? Well, here's

hoping. I like this place.' He yawned. 'I don't know about you, but I'm starving. I think I'll go down to the bakery and get some bread.'

'Maria usually brings it.'

'I expect Maria has other things on her mind today,' he said cheerfully, demonstrating, his sister thought wryly, yet again his unparalleled capacity for detachment. He went off whistling.

Gemma finished her coffee, then went upstairs to finish her packing. She put the lace tablecloth in on top of everything else and closed the case. She wanted to leave now, although it was far too early for her plane. She would rather drag round Heraklion, toting her case, than stay at the villa, listening to the moments pass, waiting for the time when she would never see Andreas again, she told herself wretchedly.

When she went downstairs, they had both returned, Mike with bread, and Andreas with a bundle wrapped in paper, which he handed to her.

'What is it?' She made a poor attempt at a smile. 'Another present from a wellwisher?'

He said coldly and briefly, 'Your bag. You could hardly leave without it.'

She bit her lip. 'Well, now I do have it, I'd like to leave right away please.'

He shrugged. 'If it is convenient for your brother, then I have no objections. Besides, I have other plans for the rest of the day,' he added softly.

In spite of what he had said earlier, she had an image of Helga displaying her golden body beside the pool, and winced inwardly.

Mike carried her case out and stowed it in the jeep, grumbling cheerfully at the weight of it.

Gemma faced Andreas. She felt helpless, totally

lost for words, and the dark cool face gave her no help whatsoever.

In the end, she managed a torn 'Goodbye,' then turned and hurried down the terrace steps and through the garden to where the jeep was waiting outside the gate. Mike was already in the driving seat, but as she took her place beside him, he uttered an impatient exclamation.

'I've left my wallet in the rucksack. Hang on, Gem. I won't be long.'

She hoped with all her heart that he wouldn't be. The pain was beginning already, cramping her throat, making breathing difficult. She put her folded arms on the dashboard, and rested her forehead on them, closing her eyes wearily.

Life went on, she told herself, and no one had ever died of a broken heart, or any similar self-inflicted wound.

But it would be easier once she was on her way.

She was aware of his return, aware of the jeep starting up, and she sat up slowly, pushing her tumbled hair back from her face as the vehicle began to lurch down the rough track towards the village.

She froze, her lips parting in a soundless gasp. She said, 'You! But Mike was driving me.'

'A last minute change of plan.'

'Like hell there is.' She wrenched at the door handle, almost breaking a nail. 'Let me out of here.' And as the jeep gathered speed. 'I said—let me out.'

'I heard you,' he hurled back at her. 'I should imagine the whole village heard you also. Now, be quiet.'

'I won't be quiet.' Her voice shook. 'Where is Mike? What have you done with him?'

'He is finishing his breakfast,' he said coolly.

'We talked on our way back from the village, he and I, and arrived at an understanding.'

'How nice for you,' she said wildly. 'Now, stop this bloody jeep. I am not going to Heraklion with you.'

'No, you are not,' he agreed. 'That is another change of plan. We are going to Rethymnon instead.'

She said dangerously, 'And why should we do any such thing?'

'Because my mother has a house there, and I am taking you to stay with her.'

The news struck her dumb, but not for long. 'You'll do no such thing,' she raged at him. 'I don't want to meet your mother, and I'm damned sure she won't have the slightest desire to meet me.'

'Don't be a fool.' He clashed the gears and swore. 'Every mother wishes to meet the girl her son intends to marry.'

'For the last time.' Gemma's voice rose. 'I am not going to marry you.'

She saw him grin. 'I am glad you say that for the last time, *agape mou*. I confess I would prefer you to take a more positive view of our relationship, because you, my wild dove, are going to be my wife just as soon as it can be arranged.'

Tears threatened perilously. She said in a low voice, 'You can't marry me, and you know it We—we're totally different.'

He shot her a smiling glance. 'Why, yes. You are a woman, and I am a man. That seems to be the usual arrangement.'

'Don't make jokes.' She shook her head helplessly. 'I'm trying to be serious.'

'Marriage is a serious business,' he agreed

solemnly. 'That is why I have avoided it until now.'

'But I'm not from your world,' she said desperately. 'Don't you see how impossible it is?'

He swung the jeep across the road, and brought it to a halt, just under the signpost where James and Hilary had deposited her an eternity before.

He turned to her, and he wasn't smiling any more. Under the smooth olive skin, his face looked taut and drawn.

He said, 'Without you, Gemma *mou*, I have no world. Don't you know that? I love you, and I am so afraid that if I let you go back to England, even for a few days, that I will lose you somehow. That when I follow, you will have escaped me at last, hidden somewhere, and I won't know how to find you.' He touched her cheek with his hand, and she realised he was trembling. 'Stay with me here, treasure of my life and let me teach you to love me. Let me make up to you for all the bitterness that has been between us.'

In a little shaken voice, she said, 'You say—you love me? But how can you? You don't know me.'

'What do I not know?' he asked. 'I know that you love your family, and that you have loyalty and integrity, and fierce courage. I know that you have a temper, and a sense of humour. I know that when we make love, you give yourself with your whole heart, even though you are still too shy to look at me afterwards. Whatever else there is, it will be my joy to learn as we live together.'

She made a little stifled sound. 'You're—very kind.' She didn't look at him. 'But you don't have to say these things. I know you only offered to marry me—to make amends—and because you think you may have made me pregnant.'

He said very gently, 'My sweet one, that is not

true. From the moment I saw you, looking at the Lily-Prince, I wanted you—before even I heard your friend speak your name, and knew for certain who you were.' He groaned. 'And when I realised that you were the girl I was seeking—I felt sick to my stomach. I hated Stavros and his claims on my friendship—hated myself—the whole mess which would stop me meeting you, and wooing you as I wished to do.' His voice deepened huskily. 'That first evening, when I asked you to pretend with me that we were simply lovers, with no complications except our need for each other, I meant every word, *agape mou*. Because, but for Maria and her stupid wicked lies, that is how it would have been for us. Can you deny it?'

'No,' she admitted helplessly. That day at Knossos, she'd already been tinglingly aware of him, although she'd made light of it to Hilary and tried to deny it even to herself, bewildered and disturbed by the strength of her reaction.

'And as for any baby——' His arm went round her shoulders, drawing her to him, and he kissed the corner of her mouth. 'Only God knows if you indeed carry our child under your heart, but I am selfish enough, *matia mou*, to hope that it has not happened yet, so that we will have some time to ourselves to enjoy each other, and to prepare a proper home for the children that will be given to us.' He brushed her mouth with his. 'The apartment at the hotel is unsuitable for a dozen reasons. I want a real home, and you in it. Am I still suffering from egotistical fantasies, my dove?'

She said, 'No,' her mouth trembling into a shy smile as she slid her arms round his neck. 'You make it sound like Paradise, Andreas *mou*.'

He drew her close, and she could feel the urgent,

steady beat of his heart against her breast. *'M'agapas?'* he asked her softly. 'Do you love me?'

'Yes,' she said on a little sigh. 'So much. And I've been so unhappy. I thought you were tired of me, and that was why you were sending me away.'

'Tired of you, wildcat?' His smile teased her. 'I could as soon be tired of life itself. No, I meant to behave so honourably. To send you home, so that I could follow. So that we could start again, with me asking your parents for you—convincing them somehow that I was a suitable husband. Convincing you too if necessary,' he added drily. 'I would have liked to have murdered Maria and Kemal with her, but also I was grateful to them, because the truth set me free to love you as I wanted. And, of course, it then followed that you had to be protected— especially from myself. As my bride to be, your body should have been sacred to me.' He uttered a soft groan. 'But when you came to my room last night, you were a temptation not even a saint could resist, and as I've told you, I've never pretended to be a saint.' His mouth twisted a little. 'So—that is why we go to Rethymnon, to my mother's house, where not even I would dare to be tempted.' He took her hands and raised them to his lips. 'And I think we will not distress either my mother or yours, by giving them any hint that we have already enjoyed our wedding night.'

It was her turn to tease. 'You have an unexpectedly conventional streak, *kyrie*.'

He grinned back at her. 'I intend to be a model husband, *kyria*—your husband.' He stroked her face with his hand. 'So, I ask again, Gemma *mou*, will you marry me. Will you be my life, as I will be yours?'

And she breathed her answer against his lips as she kissed him.

DARK PARADISE

DARK PARADISE

BY
SARA CRAVEN

MILLS & BOON LIMITED
Eton House, 18-24 Paradise Road
Richmond, Surrey TW9 1SR

*First published in Great Britain in 1984
by Mills & Boon Limited*

© Sara Craven 1984

*Australian copyright 1984
Philippine copyright 1984
Reprinted 1984
This edition 1992*

ISBN 0 263 77773 1

*Set in Monophoto Times 10 on 10 pt.
19-9204-61003*

Made and printed in Great Britain

CHAPTER ONE

THE wine in her glass glowed like a ruby. And had cost very nearly as much, Kate Marston reflected drily.

She'd been expecting a business lunch, but this was fast developing into an occasion, and she wasn't sure she could take it.

She wondered what would happen if she were to lean across the table and say to her companion, 'Clive, you're very sweet, and I like you. But it will never, ever be any more than that. So if all this expensive claret and sharing a chateaubriand is to promote a shift in our relationship, then they'd better go back to the kitchen'.

She wouldn't say it, of course. She was too fond of Clive to give him such a public affront, besides being fairly dependent on him financially, and extremely hungry as well.

She had been a young hopeful in her final year at art college when they had met. He was the youngest director of a well-known publishing firm specialising in children's books, and she'd been hawking a portfolio of her work around, looking for a job as an illustrator.

She was tired of hearing how talented she was, accompanied by regretful little speeches about economic recession and cutbacks, and she had expected little different from Barlow and Herries. Her confidence, her belief in herself had taken several hard knocks already, and she was surprised to get beyond the reception desk.

Her surprise deepened as the fair-haired, rather solemn young man into whose office she had been shown began to exhibit signs of positive enthusiasm as he examined the paintings and sketches she had brought.

'Do you know,' he had said at last, 'you could be exactly the person we need.'

He told her confidentially that they had just acquired

an established and popular author for their list who was proving troublesome to say the least. The lady in question had left their chief rivals after rows about publicity and the quality of illustrations for her books, and Barlow and Herries were naturally anxious to satisfy her on both these points.

Only it was proving more difficult than anyone had ever imagined.

'She's turned her nose up at all our regular artists,' Clive Joffrey had said rather bitterly. 'She claims she wants something original and unique to match her very personal style, and I quote. I think you might have what she wants.' He picked up one painting and studied it closely. 'This is a scene from one of her books, isn't it?'

'Yes,' said Kate, hope and excitement choking any deeper explanation.

He nodded. 'I like it. All that sweetness and light on the surface, and the sinister undertones.' He shuddered. 'God knows why kids go overboard for her, but they do. Her books would have given me nightmares when I was a child!'

Kate smiled. 'I love them.'

'Better and better. Make sure you tell her that when you meet. That's another thing she insists on—meeting everyone, checking on the vibrations. Awful woman.' He gave her a narrow glance. 'Think you could cope?'

Amazingly, she had, and was still doing so. Not that the dreaded Felicity, as she was known, was her only source of income. Clive had seen to that, recommending her to contacts in the magazine and advertising worlds, so that now, three years after that fateful interview, she had a flourishing freelance career as an artist.

The only fly in the ointment had proved to be Clive, whose personal interest in her had developed as rapidly as his professional interest had done. That was something she hadn't wanted at all, and she had done her best to dissuade him, but all to no avail. Clive might seem quiet, but he was also determined, she had discovered, and eventually she had succumbed in a moment of weakness to his gentle pressuring and agreed to go to the theatre with him.

That evening, and subsequent outings in his company, had proved pleasantly undemanding, and if Clive was content to be held at arm's length, then Kate supposed she had no real reason to complain.

Except that lately she had sensed a change in his attitude, a growing impatience perhaps with the course of their friendship, because it was nothing more.

This lunch today was a case in point. She was used to the publishing habit of conducting business discussions over well-cooked food in congenial surroundings, but these surroundings were more than congenial—they were luxurious, and the whole meal was developing all the hallmarks of a celebration of some kind.

Kate sighed inwardly. Clive's whole manner was portentous too, suggesting that it was all leading up to something. A proposal? she wondered wryly. And if so—what? Marriage, or something rather more casual. Because neither was acceptable.

And as if to confirm her worst fears, Clive lifted his glass and said, 'To us.'

She smiled wanly, and drank, without echoing his words. She wished she didn't feel so depressed. This was a fantastic restaurant, and the chateaubriand currently being dissected for them on a serving table looked delicious. Why couldn't she enter into the spirit of the occasion, and worry about overtures from Clive as and when they occurred?

There was a slight hubbub nearby and she glanced round to see a well-known film star making his way to a table, trying to pretend that he wasn't instantly recognisable.

Her mouth relaxed into a smile as she wondered how many other lunchers had shared her enjoyment of that air of total selfconsciousness. Not Clive. He was too busy fussing about the vegetables, she thought, as she glanced round the restaurant. But there were others exchanging amused smiles, and one girl in particular, her face alive with excitement and laughter as she leaned towards her companion.

Kate froze. Alison? she thought. But it can't be! For a moment she wondered if the wine could be giving her hallucinations, or if there'd been a maverick among the wild mushrooms she'd been served as a first course.

It couldn't be her sister-in-law sitting only a few tables away. For one thing, there was no way Jon, her stepbrother, could afford these prices . . .

Almost reluctantly, she looked again, aware of a sense of foreboding.

It was Alison all right. That blonde head was unmistakable, and so was the way she moved her hands when the conversation became animated.

Kate couldn't see her companion. There was a waiter in the way, and she watched tensely, willing the man to move.

'Mange-touts, madame?' The slightly reproachful tone of their own waiter indicated it was probably the second time of asking.

'Please,' she said, aware of Clive's puzzled look. She forced a smile. 'I'm sorry—I thought I saw someone I knew. But I was mistaken.'

The view to the table where Alison was sitting was unimpeded now, but she made herself pick up her knife and fork, taste the chateaubriand, pass an appreciative remark before she looked again.

There wasn't much to see. The back of a man's dark head, the breadth of his shoulders under an expensive jacket. And certainly not Jon. Which led to the question—what was her sister-in-law doing having lunch in one of London's top restaurants with another man after barely a year of marriage?

Not merely another man, either. That lightning glance had told her all the bad news. Alison was with Matt Lincoln.

Kate would have known that arrogant tilt of the head anywhere, she thought bitterly, even if Alison herself hadn't given the secret away. How many times had she

seen that same expression of pleasure and absorption
lighting up Alison's face, usually accompanying some
anecdote in which 'Matt said' or 'Matt did . . .'

Such a pretty girl, her family had agreed, and clever
too to hold down such a responsible job, because Matt
Lincoln, her boss, was a name to be reckoned with in
the world of television. He'd started out as a journalist,
switched to TV news reporting, and then moved into
the area of current affairs, producing and presenting a
hard-hitting series of documentaries which had already
collected a small clutch of prized awards.

Kate had watched and admired, even if she had
reservations about the man himself. He was clever,
ruthless and possessed of a sexual charisma that was
almost tangible, and she didn't like or trust men like
that—men who were invulnerable, who marched
through life like archetypal lords of creation.

His documentaries were brilliant, of course. He was
an ace investigative journalist, and his targets were left
with their villainies and weaknesses totally exposed.
People rarely emerged with credit once Matt Lincoln's
searchlight had been trained on them.

Kate had sometimes wondered what his victims did
with the ruin of their lives when it was all over. She'd
mentioned this once to Alison, who had stared at her in
amazement and asked what it mattered?

'They're crooks,' she had said with calm confidence.
'All of them, and the bigger they are, the harder they
fall. Save your sympathy for the people they've conned
and swindled.'

The spark in her blue eyes added silently, 'And don't
criticise Matt to me, because he can do no wrong.'

Alison was very different from the majority of the
girl-friends Jon had brought home, and this was what
had made Kate suspect that this time it might be
serious—at least with him. She wasn't so sure about
Alison's feelings. After all, she had a glamorous job.
She accompanied Matt Lincoln everywhere—even
abroad. She met everyone that he met, and clearly
enjoyed every exuberant moment of it, so would she be

prepared to jettison all that for marriage with an assistant solicitor in a suburban legal practice?

Kate loved Jon, and always had, but she had no illusions about him. He was attractive, without being an Adonis, and possessed of a quiet charm, but might not his personality seem pallid when compared with Matt Lincoln's arrogant forcefulness?

She knew without being told that Jon had misgivings too, although she hadn't the slightest doubt that he was in love with Alison, and one evening when they'd had the house to themselves, he'd confided in her.

'The trouble is I can't figure out the situation,' he'd said gloomily. 'She's worked with him closely for nearly two years, she's travelled the world with him, she mentions him in every other breath, and yet I don't know how heavily she's been involved with him—if at all.'

Kate felt her way carefully. 'Is it important that you do know?'

He was silent for a moment, then he said, 'Yes. I wish it wasn't.'

'Then can't you ask?'

'I've tried,' he said unhappily. 'Part of the problem is I feel a swine for probing. I keep telling myself that I love her, and therefore I should trust her. I really want to—and yet . . .'

Kate understood what he was trying to convey. Her mother had been a widow when she met Jon's father, but Michael Herbert had been divorced, and gradually it had emerged that his wife had left him for another man when Jon was quite small. Jon had been a reticent child, but gradually he had learned to relax under the influence of his stepmother's gentle serenity, and to accept and even return the affection which was offered.

Yet always at the back of his mind there had to be the memory of what his mother had done, she thought, which probably explained this strange streak of possessiveness he was displaying towards Alison.

She said gently, 'I don't think you have anything to

worry about. After all, it's the future you should be
concerned with, not what's past.'

He had smiled ruefully, running a caressing finger
down the curve of her cheek. 'Like you, Kate?' Then,
seeing her face change, he said swiftly, 'No, I'm sorry,
love. I didn't mean it.'

'No, I asked for it.' Kate forced a smile. 'It's really a
case of "Physician, heal thyself", isn't it? But the thing
is, Jon, you don't *know* that there's been anything
between Alison and Matt Lincoln. Not every secretary
has an affair with her boss, you know.' She giggled
suddenly. 'Has Alison ever speculated about you and
Miss Chalmers?'

Jon laughed too, his pleasant face relaxing. 'I doubt
it, but then if Miss Chalmers was in her thirties instead
of her fifties, and diabolically attractive to boot,
perhaps she might.'

Whatever his reservations, he had obviously managed
to overcome them, because he and Alison had been
married only a couple of months later, and Matt
Lincoln had been one of the guests at the wedding—as
Kate had good reason to remember, she thought with a
sudden stiffening of her spine.

Clive's voice cut plaintively across her reverie. 'I have
the oddest feeling I'm lunching alone. Come back to
me, Kate.'

'I'm sorry.' She ate another mouthful with feigned
enthusiasm, because she might as well have been
chewing cardboard.

'Still spotting familiar faces?' Clive signalled the wine
waiter to pour some more into her glass. 'This is the
place for them.'

'I think it is,' Kate said wryly, mourning her
wonderful meal. She would have to lie and say she
wasn't very hungry. She could hardly say, 'My sister-in-
law is over there having a whale of a time with the man
she used to work for, who may or may not have been
her lover, and knowing what this could do to Jon has
ruined my appetite.'

But that was the truth. Because Kate was ready to

swear it had been quite some time since Alison had worn that particular glow for her husband. 'Teething troubles,' Kate's mother had said, and she was probably quite right. For all Kate knew, Alison was lunching here with Matt with Jon's blessing and approbation, only she didn't believe it for one moment, because if there was going to be a bone of contention between the newlyweds, then it was likely to be called Matt Lincoln.

She supposed it would be the easiest thing in the world to walk across as they were leaving and say hello, and gauge what was going on from Alison's reaction, but she knew she wouldn't do it. She couldn't risk seeing a look of guilt on her sister-in-law's face, although Matt Lincoln would no doubt find the situation amusing in the extreme.

She could remember reading an article in a magazine quoting him as castigating what he termed 'Suburban morality' for concerning itself too much with trivial sins, and closing its eyes to the deeper crimes against humanity being perpetrated somewhere in the world each day.

Probably Matt Lincoln would regard the seduction of someone else's wife as a very trivial sin, she thought stormily.

'Is something wrong?' Clive's tone was worried. 'You look as if you're about to plunge that knife into someone!'

She forced a laugh. 'Well, I promise it isn't you, Clive. I'm afraid I'm just poor company today.'

'You're never that,' he said warmly. 'Is something bothering you? Can I help?'

She said, 'It's a family matter,' and determinedly changed the subject. The dreaded Felicity's latest book was a slight departure from her usual style, and Kate was wondering how far Clive expected the jacket and illustrations to reflect this. It was a good ploy and occupied them for the rest of lunch.

The next time Kate allowed her glance to slide towards the other table, it was to note with relief that it was unoccupied. Alison and her companion had departed—perhaps to go their separate ways, or perhaps not.

Clive said ruefully, 'All we've done is talk about work, and that's the last thing I intended.' He squeezed her hand. 'Perhaps I should wait for a time when I can count on all your attention.'

He wanted to call a taxi for her, but she refused, saying she felt like walking.

It was a beautiful day, crisply autumnal, reminding her of horse-chestnut trees and bonfires. Alison and Jon had been married on a day just like this, she recalled, and the sun had been so warm that the guests had spilled out on to the terrace and lawns of the riverside hotel where the reception was being held.

Kate had been chief bridesmaid, in a topaz crêpe dress with a high ruffled neck, her curling chestnut hair drawn into a casually pretty topknot. She didn't outshine the bride—Alison managed to look ethereal and radiant in her white silk organza—but she looked and felt good, and Jon's unattached friends buzzed round her like flies round a honeypot. After Jon and Alison had left for Paris, there was going to be a family dinner that evening, and Jon's best man, a friend since their schooldays, was escorting her in the traditional manner, and she declined all the other offers with smiling charm.

And all the time she was intensely aware that she was under surveillance.

If Kate was providing a centre of attention for the men, then Matt Lincoln was the same and more for the women. He was the celebrity guest, and it could only be a matter of time before someone actually asked him for an autograph, Kate thought cynically. Wherever he went there was an adoring group like satellite moons round a planet, but she supposed that wasn't altogether his fault. Even without the glamour imposed by television, Matt Lincoln was formidable, exuding a vibrantly masculine aura. No one with blood in her veins could have overlooked him even for a moment, and Kate was annoyed to find how often her own eyes were straying in his direction.

'For God's sake,' she adjured herself irritably, 'haven't you learned your lesson?'

And to make matters worse, each time she looked at him, it was to discover that he was watching her, a half smile playing about his lips as if he had discerned her inner struggle and was amused by it.

So she did her best to ignore him, and pretend that the buzz of talk and laughter around him did not exist, although she couldn't help but be aware of the almost electric excitement his presence engendered. But he was bound to leave soon, she told herself. A suburban wedding couldn't hold his interest or confine the air of restless energy which characterised him for very much longer.

Not for the first time, she wondered why he had accepted the invitation. The dinner service he had bought as a wedding present was displayed with the other gifts, so no other gesture was necessary. Alison's parents had issued the invitations, of course, and had been cock-a-hoop when he had accepted, but Kate knew that Jon had not been pleased, although he'd said nothing in the light of Alison's jubilation.

She had watched her stepbrother watching Matt kiss the bride, seen the rigidity of his features, and her heart had ached for him. Matt had been in Venezuela until the previous day, and had dashed back specially, she heard Alison's mother smugly proclaiming to a coterie of her friends.

'Why did he bother?' she asked herself savagely.

She had avoided him, and the inevitable introductions, since the reception began. She had no wish to become one of the admiring throng, she told herself, although even her mother who was not easily impressed had been won over, she noticed.

But at an intimate gathering like a wedding reception, she couldn't hope to keep out of his way for ever.

She was chatting to Simon, the best man, when she became suddenly aware that he was beside them. She was immediately irritated by Simon's deference, stopping in mid-sentence to turn to Matt Lincoln.

'Can I get you another drink, Mr Lincoln?'

'No, thanks.' Matt Lincoln shook his head, smiling. 'Jet-lag and alcohol don't mix too well.' He nodded towards the adjoining room where a small band had been playing softly during the reception. 'But some gentle exercise could be just what I need.' He looked down at Kate. 'We haven't actually met, but I'm sure this is our dance.'

The tenor of the music had changed, she realised as she took in what he had said. The energetic disco beat had changed to a slower dreamy rhythm, and people were moving closer, holding each other as they danced.

He would expect to put his arms round her, she realised, a kind of sick panic rising inside her at the prospect.

Her voice sounded thick as she said, 'I don't want to dance, Mr Lincoln. Why don't you ask one of your devoted fans? I'm sure any one of them would be only too delighted.'

The blue eyes narrowed slightly but he was still smiling. 'I can't really debate that without sounding like a slob. But the point doesn't arise, because the fact is I've asked *you*—Miss er . . .'

'Marston,' Simon supplied helpfully. 'Kate Marston.'

'Kate,' Matt Lincoln repeated musingly. 'A nice old-fashioned name.'

She said hotly, 'Please don't patronise me, Mr Lincoln. I'm not the subject of one of your programmes. And here's another fact, as you're so keen on them—I'm turning down your invitation.'

She'd never been so deliberately rude to anyone in her life, and she was aware of Simon gaping.

For a long moment, Matt Lincoln stood looking at her as she felt the betrayal of embarrassed colour rising in her cheeks, then he said coolly, 'I beg your pardon for having annoyed you.' And turned away.

'My God,' Simon said helplessly. 'That was a bit strong, wasn't it?'

Kate lifted her chin defiantly, crushing down an unexpected feeling of shame. 'I don't think any lasting damage has been done—not to an ego like his!'

Simon was looking at her as if she was a stranger who had suddenly developed horns and a tail. 'But he only wanted to dance with you, Kate. Hell's bells, you couldn't have cut him off more sharply if he'd made a heavy pass!'

'Well, I find his conviction that he's God's gift to women a bit strong too,' Kate retorted. 'Men like that are an abomination. One smile, an invitation to dance—and they expect you to—to roll over and beg!'

'Well—roll over anyway,' said Simon with a mock leer. 'I didn't know you were such a feminist, Kate.'

'I'm not,' she said shortly. 'But he—his whole approach—reminded me of—of someone I used to know.'

'Did you give him a hard time too?' Kate wondered if the alarm she heard in Simon's voice was altogether feigned.

She gave him a placatory smile. 'No.' She glanced round. 'I think Alison's ready to go up and change. I'd better help her.'

'Fine,' Simon agreed, and she realised ruefully as she left the room in Alison's wake that he was probably regretting that he had to spend the evening with her. And she wasn't altogether sure she could blame him.

By the time they came downstairs again, Matt Lincoln had left, to Alison's momentary pouting disappointment. Kate could only feel relief. She had almost been tempted to remain upstairs packing away the discarded wedding dress and tidying up generally rather than face him again.

She had imagined he had passed out of her life for ever. Now, it seemed, he was back with a vengeance.

Her steps began to slow. She had been walking aimlessly in no particular direction, or so she had thought. Now, as the glass and concrete block of the National Television building reared up in front of her, she wasn't so sure.

Was this what they called a Freudian slip? she asked herself wryly.

She stood staring up at the building, hating the way all those windows seemed to stare back like so many blank eyes, then gave herself a swift mental shake. She was doing no earthly good drifting round London, worrying about something for which there might be a perfectly innocent explanation.

The best thing she could do was go back to the studio and get on with her own work, her own life.

In other words, mind her own business.

The studio was one large attic room of a tall Edwardian house. It had windows on two sides and a skylight, and Kate loved it. There was another attic across the narrow passage, and this she used as a bed-sitter, sharing the bathroom on the floor below with the family who owned the house, Felix who was a newspaper photographer, his wife Maria and their two children. It was an arrangement that suited them all.

As Kate unlocked the front door and went in, Maria's voice called from the kitchen, 'How was the drunken lunch?'

Kate put her head round the kitchen door. 'Remarkably sober,' she said. 'Something smells wonderful.'

Maria grimaced. 'Not really.' She waved a spoon. 'Just an ordinary little meat sauce to go with spaghetti—it being the end of the month and all—but I think you'll be amused by its precocity. Want to join us, or are you too full of caviare and champagne?'

'I'd love to,' Kate said regretfully, and meant it, because Maria was generally an inspired cook even with the most average ingredients. 'But I thought I would go home this evening. It's been some time since I saw them all.'

'Fine,' Maria said amiably. She gave Kate a narrow look. 'There's nothing wrong, is there?'

'Of course not.' Kate achieved a laugh. 'I do go home occasionally, you know!'

'I didn't mean that. I just thought you looked a bit

fraught, that's all,' said Maria, stirring her sauce, and lowering the flame beneath the pan.

'Oh,' Kate pulled a face, cursing her landlady's perspicacity. 'It's just this new book—there could be problems. Nothing that I can't handle, of course.'

'Of course,' Maria agreed. 'Well, enjoy yourself this evening.'

Kate's mother was delighted to get her phone call. 'Darling, how marvellous! Jon and Alison are coming over too. It'll be a real family party.'

'Yes, won't it?' Kate agreed. She replaced her receiver slowly. She had intended to do some subtle probing, now it seemed she was going to be able to see them together and judge the state of their relationship for herself.

And probably Alison would be bubbling over with the story of her wonderful lunch, she told herself forcefully.

Her stepfather greeted her at the door with a warm hug.

'You've lost weight, my girl.' He held her at arms' length and stared at her critically.

Kate wrinkled her nose at him. 'That's what you always say. I only wish it was true.'

'Well, at least you'll get a decent meal inside you tonight,' he said triumphantly. 'Steak and kidney pie and all the trimmings. How's work going? Any interesting commissions?'

He poured sherry, and they took it into the kitchen and talked to Kate's mother as she bustled around, putting the last touches to the meal. She was a woman who had always found her fulfilment in caring for her family, and they'd often teased her about it, calling her 'an endangered species', which she accepted with unruffled calm.

Watching her, seeing her pleasure in the preparations she was making, Kate found herself thinking, 'Oh, let everything be all right! She and Dad love Jon. They're so proud of him. If anything went wrong in his marriage, they'd be so hurt, so bewildered.'

They heard his car pull on to the drive at the side of the house, and presently he came in. He was smiling and carrying a bunch of flowers for his stepmother, but Kate thought he looked tired.

He said ruefully, 'I'm on my own, I'm afraid. Ally sends love and apologies, but she's going to have an early night. She's got a splitting headache.'

'Oh.' Mrs Herbert looked downcast. 'I wonder what's caused that?'

Hangover? Kate supplied silently. Guilty conscience? Or had they had a blazing row, perhaps?

'Hi, love,' Jon bent and kissed her cheek. 'Anything exciting in your life?'

She shrugged. 'Depends on your view of excitement.' Keeping her voice casual, she added, 'I had lunch at Père Nicolas today.'

Jon whistled appreciatively. 'Very impressive! I hope you weren't paying.'

'Oh, Kate!' her mother wailed. 'Then you won't want another big meal. What am I going to do with all this pie?'

'I'm starving,' Kate assured her. 'No restaurant food could ever compare with yours, you know that.'

She would eat the dinner in front of her if it killed her, she promised herself. And it probably would, because she'd been counting on Jon saying something on the lines of 'Now there's a coincidence. Alison was lunching there too.' Whereas it was evident that he knew nothing at all about Alison's midday activities. Oh hell, she thought. Hell and damnation!

She finished everything on her plate with a struggle, and it was no consolation to note that Jon didn't have much of an appetite either. He talked cheerfully about the office, making them laugh with his story of a client who was always house-hunting, then finding some fatal flaw with the property of his dreams just before the contracts were due to be signed.

'And his own house is sold, so if he doesn't make up his mind soon, he could end up in a tent on the common,' he added with a gesture of mock despair.

'Talking of dream houses,' his father said. 'How's the decorating at your place coming along?'

Jon helped himself to cheese. 'It's rather ground to a halt at the moment,' he said, after a pause.

Mrs Herbert was piling used dishes on to a tray. 'But Alison was so keen, so full of plans when you bought it.' She laughed. 'I got the impression that she was into interior decoration in a big way.'

Jon said wryly, 'I think that was before she discovered how much there was to do, and what graft it was.' He paused. 'As a matter of fact, she's talking about going out to work again.'

'Getting her old job back?' his father asked.

'No.' Jon's denial was altogether too swift and too forceful, and he tempered it with a laugh. 'I mean, those sort of opportunities only come along once in a lifetime. I'm afraid she'll have to settle for something rather more humdrum.'

Kate pushed her chair back and rose. 'Leave the dishes,' she told her mother, 'I'll do them.'

'And I'll help.' Jon got up too.

Mrs Herbert smiled at them both affectionately. 'Just like old times,' she said.

Kate filled the sink with hot water, and whisked the washing up liquid into a lather.

Casually she said, 'Has Ally any idea what kind of job she wants?'

'We haven't really discussed it in any detail.' His voice sounded awkward. 'I don't think she'll find it very easy, with so many people out of work. And it isn't as if she needs the money—I don't keep her short of cash.' He stopped. 'I'm sorry, Kate, I shouldn't burden you with our problems. I suppose we're experiencing the "period of adjustment" that all couples go through.'

'You don't want her to work again,' said Kate.

He sighed. 'No, I don't. And I thought she didn't either, or so she always said before we were married. At first, she seemed absorbed in the house.' His mouth tightened. 'I suppose after working for a man like Lincoln, domestic life with me must seem very tame.'

Feeling her way carefully, Kate said, 'But I thought—Alison said something about starting a family as soon as possible.'

'That's right,' he said flatly. 'But it hasn't happened yet. Hell, we've only been married a year, there isn't that much damned hurry. But I suppose if she gets a job, it will have to be put off indefinitely. She seems to have decided that's what she'd prefer,' he added bitterly.

Kate swallowed. 'Well, she did have a pretty high-powered career. And I suppose with her contacts in television, it's not impossible . . .'

'Over my dead body,' said Jon, with stark emphasis. The weary look had deepened on his face. 'If she wants to work, I won't stop her, but she's not going back within a mile of Matt Lincoln. I was sick of the sound of his name before we were married. I'm not living with it now.' He took a dry tea towel out of a drawer. 'It's ironic, isn't it? We did *Othello* at school, and I had no sympathy for him at all. I kept thinking what a fool he was to get so stirred up by jealousy, and for so little reason. And now I'm exactly in the same boat!' He gave a shaky laugh. 'I can't even stay in the sitting room when he's on television!'

Kate mopped at an already clean plate as if she was trying to remove the pattern. 'Isn't that rather—irrational? After all, you don't know that there was ever anything between them.'

'As I've told myself a hundred times.' Jon sounded defeated. 'But it makes no damned difference at all. He's the sort of man women go for. He's got it all, looks, charm, charisma—and don't let anyone tell you that success isn't an aphrodisiac,' he added savagely. 'You met him at the wedding, didn't you? You saw the effect he had on everyone.'

Kate bent her head. 'Yes, I met him,' she agreed colourlessly.

'And didn't like him?' Jon gave her a curious look. 'My God, that must make you one in a million!'

'Perhaps.' Kate moved her shoulders. 'Actually, he reminded me of someone.'

'He did?'

She nodded. 'Drew Wakefield.'

'Him?' Jon frowned a little. 'Yes, I see what you mean. But I thought you'd forgotten all about him.'

'You don't forget about someone like Drew,' she said bitterly. 'Being involved with him is like being in a bad accident. You can be left with scars.'

'Kate,' Jon's eyes were gentle, 'that was over a long time ago. Let it go.'

She emptied the water out of the sink. 'Can you let Matt Lincoln go?'

He said wryly, *'Touché.'* Then he sighed. 'What fools we both are!'

She nodded. 'The coffee's ready. Why don't you take the tray through while I finish up here.'

When she was alone, she moved slowly, wiping down surfaces, and restoring the kitchen to its usual pristine condition.

It had been unfair of her, she thought, to aim that taunt at Jon, because although he didn't know it yet, Matt Lincoln was still very much part of his life. She only wished it were otherwise.

She rinsed out the cloth she'd been using and hung it to dry, staring out of the kitchen window at the dark garden beyond.

Well, she would make it otherwise. Jon loved Alison, and their marriage deserved a chance which it wouldn't have if the pernicious influence of someone like Matt Lincoln was allowed to take hold.

Drew Wakefield, she thought bitterly. Matt Lincoln. Birds of a feather, pursuing their destructive way through other people's lives, uncaring of the chaos they left behind.

Only this time—somehow—she wasn't going to allow it to happen. Scandal and bitterness weren't going to ruin her family's lives, she vowed silently, not if she could help it.

She thought savagely, 'To hell with you, Matt Lincoln!' then shivered suddenly as if a cold hand had brushed against her in warning.

CHAPTER TWO

'MATT LINCOLN's address?' Felix stared at her in amazement. 'What on earth do you want that for?'

Kate moved her shoulders evasively. 'Do you think you can get it for me?'

'I daresay I can. It'll be on file somewhere at the office, and if not, Lorna Bryce from Features was involved with him for a while. She'd know,' said Felix. 'But wouldn't it be easier just to call National Television?'

'Perhaps,' Kate's voice was noncommittal. 'I'm hoping it won't be necessary to call him at all.'

'I'm sure you are,' Felix said a mite caustically. 'Leave him to the Lornas of this world, darling. He's out of your league.'

'Don't be so rude, Felix,' Maria, who was crocheting by the fire, interrupted placidly. 'Kate's a lovely girl.'

'Have I ever denied it?' Felix gestured dramatically. 'So why throw her to the lions?' He grinned at Kate. 'Or do you like living dangerously, after all, and if so, what are you doing with boring old Clive?'

'You're a nosy swine,' his wife said in amiable condemnation. Her eyes shrewdly noted Kate's obvious embarrassment. 'I'm sure Kate knows what she's doing.'

Do I? Kate wondered dismally.

She had spent a miserable restless night trying and failing to decide on a particular course of action, and had wasted a working day too through her inability to concentrate properly.

All she knew was that some sort of confrontation was inevitable. Simply telling Jon what she had seen and letting him sort it out at whatever cost would be an unbearably sneaky thing to do, she thought. And seeking out Matt Lincoln at the television centre through layers of protective commissionaires and secretaries didn't appeal to her either. Her courage would have dwindled long before she reached him.

Her request to Felix to find out his home address— his telephone number was, naturally enough, ex-directory—had been made on the spur of the moment. And she wouldn't use it. It was purely something to be held in reserve, because first thing tomorrow she was going to talk to Alison.

It wasn't a prospect she welcomed. She had been Alison's chief bridesmaid, but that had been as a matter of form, she thought wryly, and hadn't prompted any real intimacy between them. Nor had they become any closer since. She had tried, but apart from the fact they seemed to have little in common, she had always sensed a slight reserve about her sister-in-law.

And after tomorrow, I suppose I'll be lucky if she ever speaks to me again, she told herself ruefully.

Every metre of the following day's bus and tube journey to the modern estate where Jon and Alison lived, she kept telling herself she didn't have to go through with it, that she could always turn back and allow whatever was going to happen to go right ahead without any interference from her.

The houses were attractively terraced, built on three sides of a square overlooking a lawned area with shrubs and a striking piece of modern sculpture. The individual gardens in front of the houses were more relaxed, several holding a scatter of children's toys, but the overall impression was one of quiet because most of the houses were occupied by working couples.

It occurred to Kate, not for the first time, that Alison might not find it merely quiet, but lonely during the daytime with the neighbouring wives out at jobs, or absorbed in their young families.

Perhaps she couldn't altogether be blamed for wanting to resume her career. Housework, shopping and decorating could hardly fill all her time, Kate thought with sudden compassion.

As she walked up the path, the front door opened,

and Alison appeared, smiling rather warily. 'Surprise, surprise!'

'We all missed you the other night,' said Kate. 'I thought I'd come and see how you were.' She saw Alison look puzzled, and elaborated, 'Your headache.'

'Oh, that.' Alison stood back to allow Kate past her into the house. 'It wasn't serious, just annoying.'

'I thought from what Jon said it was a migraine at the very least.'

'He exaggerates,' Alison shrugged. 'Sit down and I'll bring some coffee.'

'You must have known I was coming,' Kate joked, unfastening her jacket.

Alison's smile was wintry. 'I did. I watched you walk all the way round the central lawn. Do you know you're the only person who's come into the close this morning?'

Kate could believe it. While Alison was busy in the kitchen she glanced round the sitting room. It was immaculate as always, the furnishings and curtains looking brand-new, fresh flowers on the coffee table in front of the hearth, and a faint smell of lavender wax in the air.

She waited until her sister-in-law had set down the tray and poured the coffee, then she said, trying to sound casual, 'Jon says you're thinking of getting a job.'

The spoon Alison was using clattered into the saucer. She said, 'That's right.' There was a brief pause, then she said, 'As a matter of fact I might be getting my old job back.'

Kate stirred her coffee. 'With National Television?'

'With Matt Lincoln,' Alison said quickly and flatly.

'Oh,' said Kate, rather helplessly.

'It came right out of the blue,' Alison went on, a faint colour stealing into her face. 'Apparently none of the girls who've been working for him since I left have been the slightest bit of good. And he has an important assignment coming up in a couple of weeks—in the Caribbean. He wants me to go with him.'

Kate drew a deep breath. 'He does? And what did you say?'

'I told him I'd think about it.' There was a note almost of smugness in Alison's voice. 'What do you think about that?'

Kate shrugged. 'What's more to the point—what is Jon going to think about it?'

'Jon will just have to get used to the idea.' Alison's flush deepened. 'After all, marriage these days isn't a terminal condition. There is supposed to be life afterwards. And I'm going to go out of my skull if I have to spend many more days looking out of that window, watching people walk round the close!' She managed a little laugh.

Kate swallowed, 'Yes, I can understand that. But— but I thought it was your idea to give up your job when you got married.'

'It was, but I must have been insane,' Alison said with sudden sharpness. 'I suppose I thought . . .' She stopped. 'Well, that doesn't matter. One of the few benefits of being shut up alone here all day is that it gives you time to think, to realise what a fool you've been.' She took a breath. 'I should never have left Matt in the first place.'

Kate didn't like the sound of that. It implied that there had been more to their relationship than work.

'But we both realise it was a mistake,' Alison continued. 'And this Caribbean trip will be a good chance to make sure that we're—still on the same wavelength.'

Kate drank some coffee. 'Isn't the method rather a drastic one?' she enquired pleasantly.

It was Alison's turn to shrug. 'Perhaps. But Jon has his career. Why shouldn't I be allowed mine?' She paused. 'I thought you of all people would understand, Kate. After all, you have your flat, your work, your independence. Don't tell me you're dying to give it all up for a flowered pinny the moment your publisher man pops the question!'

There were undercurrents here beneath the mockery which Kate did not feel capable of fathoming.

She said, 'No, I can't say that. But on the other hand, I'm not sure I'd be contemplating a trip abroad with another man before my first anniversary either.'

Alison's giggle jarred. 'What a fuddy-duddy you are, after all, Kate! Haven't you ever heard of open marriage? It's far more interesting than the sort of prison most men want to shut you up in.'

'Do you feel as if you're in prison?' Kate set her empty cup back on the tray.

'Yes, if you must know,' Alison said shrilly, 'I do!'

Kate felt her way carefully. 'Have you told Jon how you feel? Perhaps . . .?'

'Of course I've told him, but it hasn't made an atom of difference,' Alison said angrily. 'He's always been spoiled, of course. He's had your mother, the classic happy drudge, waiting on him, and he thinks all women should be like her. Well, he's wrong!' Her voice rose sharply.

The biting reference to her mother caught Kate on the raw, but she controlled a hot rejoinder. She said, 'If Jon's views of marriage are old-fashioned, I think you need to go further back than that. His own mother walked out on him, if you remember.'

'I hadn't forgotten,' Alison said rather sullenly. 'And I can't say I altogether blame her, if Jon's father was as ridiculously possessive as he is.'

Kate was beginning to feel sick. Every word that Alison uttered seemed to be bad news. She tried to imagine Jon's reaction when Alison told him what she was contemplating, but failed completely. For his wife to resume work at National Television would have been sufficient blow, knowing how he felt about Matt Lincoln, but this proposed trip to the Caribbean opened up a whole new dimension, she thought, horrified.

She said calmly, 'I've never regarded my stepfather as being overly possessive, but then other people's marriages are generally a closed book.'

'How true,' Alison agreed. 'You're quite a philosopher, aren't you, Kate?'

Kate looked at her steadily for a moment, then she

said, 'You don't like me, do you, Alison? I wish I knew why.'

'Oh, but you're wrong,' Alison said, smiling. 'It's a great comfort to know that while I'm away with Matt, Sister Kate and the family will be around to give Jon consolation. Would you like some more coffee?'

'No thanks.' Kate got to her feet, buttoning her jacket. 'I really have to be going.'

'What a shame,' Alison said politely.

The breeze had risen she found when she got outside, and the initial brightness of the day had clouded over, and she shivered as she walked along, conscious that Alison would be watching every step she took. She kept her head down and lengthened her stride.

She found she was shaking inside as she stood at the bus stop for what seemed an interminable time. Alison's attitude bewildered her. Boredom might have made her sister-in-law resentful of the confines of marriage, but was that any real reason to rush on disaster as she seemed bent on doing? What had happened to the love she must have felt for Jon? Could that really have dissipated so quickly? And even if marriage hadn't lived up to Alison's illusions, surely after so short a time there was still something left to build on?

Or was Matt Lincoln's power over her really so absolute?

Kate couldn't be sure, but she told herself the fact that Alison hadn't instantly accepted his offer had to be a hopeful sign.

'Just as long as my interference doesn't push her into doing something stupid,' she thought gloomily, as the bus finally trundled into sight.

When she arrived back at the house, Maria was waiting for her.

'Felix phoned,' she said, holding out a slip of paper. 'With the information you wanted.'

'Oh,' Kate accepted it gingerly. 'That was quick work.'

'I think he had the impression that there was some sort of crisis going on,' Maria said drily. 'Is there?'

'Something of the kind,' Kate admitted. 'I wish I could tell you about it, Maria, but—but it's a family matter.'

'But not, thank God, the sort that Felix clearly imagines,' said Maria, an underlying note of laughter in her voice. She gave Kate's flat young stomach a long and meaningful look.

'No, of course not.' Kate was appalled. 'My God, I hardly know the man!'

'That could be best,' Maria nodded. 'That girl Felix mentioned—Lorna Bryce—apparently she was almost cut to ribbons when he finished with her, and Felix reckons that ordinarily she's quite a tough cookie.' She turned away, adding almost as an afterthought, 'Clive may not set the world on fire, but he doesn't leave charred remains behind him either.'

In the studio, Kate stood staring down at the piece of paper in her hand, sorely tempted to tear it into a hundred infinitesimal fragments.

But that wouldn't solve anything. She had no idea how deep the problems between Jon and Alison were, but she knew that this offer from Matt Lincoln could not have come at a worse time. If Alison were to accept, Kate was sure it would finish all hope of them ever working out their difficulties together. The marriage would end bitterly.

And she didn't believe for one moment that Alison was as indispensable as she had been led to believe. Matt Lincoln was an experienced and cynical man. He would know a discontented wife when he saw one, and know exactly what kind of lure to offer.

Drew had known too, she thought painfully. *'You have an exceptional talent,'* she remembered. And *'There's this amazing quality of innocence about you, Kate . . .'*

Tell a woman what she wants to hear, and she'll follow you anywhere, she thought.

And this was how Matt Lincoln was treating Alison. But why? Because he'd only discovered when it was too late and she was married to someone else that he really cared for her? Kate's mouth curled. Never in a million years, she dismissed. If he cared, then his first thought would be for her happiness—not a selfish desire to plunge her into the kind of ugly recriminations which were inevitable if she went away with him.

It was more probable that he wanted to boost his ego by proving to himself that he was irresistible. That he only had to beckon and even a bride of a year would run.

Distaste rose like bile in Kate's throat. But she knew what she had to do. For once in his life, Matt Lincoln was going to have to think again before causing havoc in people's lives. Slowly she opened her purse and slid the slip of paper inside.

The block of flats the taxi brought her to was a surprise. She had expected somewhere far more opulent and showy, but this place with its warm red brick, its balconies and windowboxes was positively old-fashioned, she thought as she paid off the driver.

She asked, 'Are you sure this is the place?' and he gave her a look, half indulgent and half irritable.

'Do me a favour, love! The name's on the wall over there if you don't believe me.' And he drove off.

Kate went in through the revolving doors. She stood for a moment assimilating her surroundings. Stairs on the left, she noticed, and lifts straight ahead.

'Can I help you, madam?' There was a long desk on the right, she saw, with a modern looking switchboard, and a uniformed man looking at her enquiringly.

She said lamely, 'I'm just visiting someone . . .'

He nodded politely. 'Of course, madam. If you could give me the resident's name, and tell me whether or not you're expected.'

The building wasn't as old-fashioned as she thought, she decided drily.

She said, 'I've come to see Mr Matthew Lincoln, and no, I'm not expected.'

'Then if I might have your name, miss, I'll just check whether it's convenient.' He sounded courteous but inexorable.

Kate swallowed a defeated sigh. 'It's Marston—Kate Marston.'

She stood, waiting and listening while he dialled and gave the message. He replaced the receiver and looked at her and she waited to be told that Mr Lincoln was not at home, or Mr Lincoln was busy.

He said, 'If you'd like to take the lift, miss. It's the second floor, and the door on the right-hand side of the corridor.'

She said dazedly, 'I—see. Thank you.'

She took a deep breath as she pressed the button for the second floor and heard the smooth whine of the doors as they closed. There was no going back now.

The palms of her hands felt damp, and she wiped them surreptitiously on her skirt, trying to marshal her thoughts, decide on the best tactic to use.

The lift stopped, and she got out and walked along the corridor. The lighting was subdued, and the carpet under her feet felt thick, muffling her footsteps.

She stopped outside Matt Lincoln's door and subduing an urge to run away very fast and very ignominiously, she lifted a hand to ring the bell.

But before she could do so, the door opened abruptly.

Matt Lincoln stood staring at her, the dark brows lifted questioningly. He was casually dressed this evening, with faded blue denims encasing his long legs, and a black woollen shirt unbuttoned to reveal the strong column of his throat.

Kate moistened her lips with the tip of her tongue. She said, 'Mr Lincoln, you won't remember me, but . . .'

'I remember you perfectly,' he said sardonically. 'You're the bridesmaid with an equal aversion to dancing and to me. What an unexpected pleasure. Won't you come in?'

He waved her into the flat, his mouth slanting mockingly at her obvious reluctance.

The room he showed her into seemed enormous, with pale walls and acres of olive brown carpet. Two big sofas upholstered in an abstract design of brown, orange and gold faced each other on either side of an imposing fireplace, and a huge antique desk, heavy with carving, stood beneath the window, but there seemed little occasional furniture and no clutter. A massive shelving unit occupied the length of one wall, part of it housing sophisticated hi-fi and television equipment, including a video tape recorder, and the rest crammed with books.

'At the flick of a switch, it transforms into a bed,' Matt Lincoln said smoothly. 'And mirrors come popping out of the ceiling.' He grinned maliciously at her startled expression. 'Relax, Miss Marston. This is my home, not Bluebeard's chamber. What the hell were you expecting?'

She said stiffly, 'I'm sorry if I gave the impression . . .'

He made a gesture of impatience. 'Forget it. Can I get you a drink?'

She shook her head. 'No, thank you. This—this isn't exactly a social call.' She swallowed. 'I expect you're wondering why I'm here.'

'I am indeed,' he said. 'But I'm sure you're going to tell me. Do you want to sit down, or is it the kind of thing that needs to be said standing?'

There was music playing softly in the background, nothing she recognised, a persuasive mixture of drums and guitars and some kind of wind instrument.

He said, 'Do you want the music turned off, Miss Marston? I guarantee that I won't ask you to dance again.'

She looked at him with fierce contempt. 'Very amusing! You find everything a great joke, don't you, Mr Lincoln?'

'No,' he said. 'And that particular incident even less hilarious than most. Anyway, we've established that you don't want a drink, and you don't want to sit down. I, on the other hand, intend to do both.'

She watched him pour a measure of Chivas Regal into a glass. He lifted the tumbler towards her with heavy irony. 'I drink to your good health, Miss

Marston,' he said. 'I imagine that's a safer proposition than our better acquaintance.'

He sauntered across the room and flung himself down on one of the sofas, casually insolent, leaving Kate on her feet and stranded in the middle of the room—as he'd no doubt intended, she thought furiously.

'Lost for words, Miss Marston?' He watched her over the top of the glass, the blue eyes examining her with frank arrogance—stripping her, she realised with mortification, slow colour creeping into her face. 'Now that must be a novelty.'

She lifted her chin, her hazel eyes flashing disdain at him. 'It doesn't take a lot of saying, Mr Lincoln. I'd like you to leave Alison alone.'

There was a long loaded silence, then he said, 'I think you'd better explain exactly what you mean.'

Kate swallowed. 'Please—don't let's be hypocritical. The fact is I saw you together at Père Nicolas.'

'A public restaurant,' he said. 'In broad daylight. No big deal.'

'No,' she said steadily. 'But I've seen Alison since—and she's told me everything.'

'Then perhaps in turn you could enlighten me.' He sounded almost indifferent, and she had to control a little spurt of temper.

She said flatly, 'She's told me that you've offered her her old job back, starting with a trip to the Caribbean in a week or two.'

'How indiscreet of her!' His voice slowed to a drawl. 'So?'

She stared at him. 'You do realise that if she goes with you, it will probably be the end of her marriage?'

'Ah,' he said. 'But has it been definitely established that she is coming with me?'

'The fact that it was ever suggested—that she's considering it, is bad enough,' Kate said fiercely, and he laughed.

'How very moral of you! Has it ever occurred to you that Alison is quite old enough to decide for herself what she wants from life—and whom, for that matter.'

'In normal circumstances, yes,' she said. 'But—but she doesn't seem very happy just now. Frankly, this—intervention of yours couldn't have come at a worse time.'

'I'd noticed she wasn't happy. Why should that be, do you suppose?'

Kate waved a dismissive hand. 'I don't know. But I'm sure that left to themselves, they can work it out. Only you're involved now and Alison has been under your sphere of influence so long that I don't believe she can think straight when you're around.'

'Not Bluebeard after all, but Svengali,' he said almost idly, staring at the amber glow of the whisky as if it fascinated him. 'Well, well. Does Alison know that you've come here, by any chance?'

'No, she doesn't.'

The blue eyes watched her coldly. 'Then she didn't fling herself on her knees begging you to save her from herself—and from me?'

'Of course not,' Kate said impatiently. 'I've told you, she doesn't realise . . .'

'What's she's doing,' he completed for her smoothly. 'Odd. When she worked for me before she seemed to be in reasonable control of her faculties. But fortunately, she has you to act as arbiter of her morals. May I ask why?'

Kate was slightly taken aback. 'Because Jon is my brother, and I don't want him hurt.'

His eyes narrowed. 'Don't you mean stepbrother?'

'Does it really make a difference?'

'A fundamental one, I'd have thought.' He gave her a long dispassionate look. 'Are you here at his request, perhaps?'

'No,' Kate said angrily. 'And you can thank your stars that he knows nothing about it. If he knew that you were planning to take Alison away with you, even on a legitimate business trip, he'd be ready to kill you!'

'Perhaps I should hire a bodyguard.' Matt Lincoln drank some more whisky.

'Perhaps you should just leave his wife alone.' She looked at him fiercely. 'It's not fair to tempt her like this when she's at a low ebb. And you don't really need her. There's probably a long queue of idiot women who'd give all they possessed to go to the Caribbean with you.'

'You flatter me.' The blue eyes glittered at her.

'No,' she said. 'I wouldn't imagine you get many refusals.'

'You, of course, being one of the exceptions.' The smile that twisted the firm, sensual mouth was not a pleasant one.

Kate shrugged. 'Let's just say I have a built-in immunity to men of your sort, Mr Lincoln, and leave it at that!' She paused. 'You have no real reason to ruin Alison's marriage, after all. You were never really serious about her, or you'd have asked her to marry you.'

'Perhaps I'm not the marrying kind.'

She shrugged, 'But Jon is, and Alison is his wife, and he loves her. It would be terrible for him if it all went wrong. Have you even considered what the consequences might be, if she goes with you?'

'Oh, I'm not that heedless, Miss Marston,' he said. 'I'd take adequate precautions against any—consequences.'

Kate almost ground her teeth. 'I didn't mean that, and you know it!'

'Yes,' he said, 'I know it.' He swallowed the remainder of his whisky and got to his feet in one fluid, angry movement. Alarmed, Kate took an involuntary step backwards, and he laughed.

'Scared, Miss Marston? So you should be. You have a bloody nerve coming here to preach to me about my morals, using your—disinterested affection for someone else's husband as an excuse. What a two-faced little bitch you are!'

'Attack, of course, being the best form of defence.' Kate spoke contemptuously, but her heart was thumping violently. 'What's the matter, Mr Lincoln?

Have I actually got to you? Could you be suffering a belated bout of conscience?'

'No,' he said grimly. 'Old-fashioned bad temper, coupled with another emotion you're probably too perfect to recognise, by your own reckoning anyway.'

He tossed the empty tumbler on to the sofa behind him without even sparing a glance to see if it had landed safely, and came towards her.

Kate gasped, and turned to run for the door, but he'd caught her before she even took two paces, taking her by the shoulders and swinging her round to face him. His face was a mask of anger, the blue eyes blazing.

He said with soft clarity, 'Not so fast, paragon. Let's see how secure that pedestal of yours actually is.'

She realised what he meant to do, and aimed a blow at him with her clenched fist. He avoided it easily, jerking his head to one side, swearing under his breath, and the next moment both her arms were pinioned behind her back, his hand clamped like a vice round her wrists. His other hand fastened in her hair, not gently, forcing her to be still as his mouth came down on hers.

She shuddered weakly, closing her eyes, bracing herself against the first bruising onslaught. Only it did not come. Instead his lips closed on hers with bewildering gentleness, exploring their softness with warm sensuousness.

She stood passively enduring the featherlight kisses pressed to the corners of her mouth, the delicate grazing of his teeth against the soft fullness of her lower lip.

She was desperately and shamingly aware that her breathing was changing, quickening as the long deliberate caress went on, and she tried to pull away. Immediately his grasp tightened in her hair, and with a little choked gasp of pain, she was forced to submit.

The pressure of his mouth against hers was subtly more insistent now, his tongue stroking teasingly along the contours of her lips, silently coaxing her to part them, and allow him a deeper, more passionate intimacy, and she felt her whole body shiver as she fought its traitorous urging to let him have his way.

She couldn't believe what was happening to her. She was being deliberately punished, and she knew it, yet deep within her, a soft, sweet trembling was beginning to take control, compelling her to move towards him so that their bodies touched as well as their mouths, prompting a first bewildered response to his kisses.

A little aching sigh escaped her, as her lips parted, yielding him the sensual dominance he sought.

But the mere fact of his victory seemed to be enough. Matt lifted his head and put her away from him, his smile slow and contemptuous as he looked down at her.

'No,' he said softly, 'you're not blessed with any special immunity, darling. Want to argue the point further—in bed, perhaps?'

'Let go of me!' Her voice cracked on the words.

He stepped back, raising his hands ostentatiously, his dark face sardonic. 'You're free, Miss Marston. Unless you have anything else you want to discuss with me.'

She shook her head, staring blindly down at the carpet. 'No—I was a fool to come here—I should have known—should have realised it wouldn't be any use.' Her voice shook. 'You really don't care, do you? You're so used to destroying people, ruining their lives in those programmes of yours, that it doesn't matter to you any more. I—I don't know how you can live with yourself.'

She went towards the door, and this time he made no attempt to prevent her from leaving. But Kate felt his anger following her like a shadow as she fled down the dim corridor towards the lift and some kind of safety.

She looked like death the following morning, but that was hardly any wonder considering how little she'd slept. And you didn't have to be actually asleep in order to have nightmares, she'd discovered too.

She decided she must have been suffering from temporary insanity. That was the only feasible explanation she could find for the way she'd acted. Just what had she hoped to achieve? she asked herself in a kind of despair. Some sort of appeal to Matt Lincoln's finer feelings? Some hopes, she thought with bitter irony. He was a tough ruthless man at the top of his profession. He had no need to bother with those kind of refinements, as his behaviour towards herself had clearly shown.

She groaned inwardly, feeling the hot colour surge in her face as she unwillingly recalled those few moments she had spent—not in his arms, certainly, because he'd never held her like a lover—but under his power.

She had been seduced, she was forced to acknowledge, and God only knew where it might all have ended if Matt Lincoln had not decided to call a halt.

It should have been me, she accused herself miserably. I might not have been able to use my hands or move my head, but I could have kicked him, bitten him, given him a swollen lip for the make-up girls to disguise.

Passive resistance had done no good at all. And at the end, she had been very far from passive, she remembered with shame.

And she had achieved nothing, except to reveal herself as the worst kind of naïve meddler, and to tell herself that she had meant well wasn't the slightest comfort. Didn't they say the road to hell was paved with good intentions?

The cheerful babble of the coffee percolater did nothing to raise her spirits, and she switched it off irritably, giving the inoffensive machine a subdued glare.

From now on, she resolved, she was going to mind her own business, no matter what happened. And her business was her work, and the illustrations that Barlow and Herries were waiting for.

Her chin set determinedly, she marched across the landing into the studio. It wouldn't be the first time she'd soothed away some inner pain with the anodyne of work, and from what life had taught her already, it wouldn't be the last.

Normally, she worked fast, with ideas crowding on

her as she sketched and discarded, using sheet after sheet of paper as she tried to capture the spirit behind the typed words of the script. But she couldn't pretend she possessed anything like her normal concentration, she thought wearily, as she crumpled yet another sheet and hurled it towards the brimming wastebasket.

The tap on the studio door was almost a welcome interruption. It would be Maria, Kate thought, flexing her shoulders as she straightened up from her drawing board. She had heard her go out earlier, and guessed she was on her way to the shops, and in particular the small home bakery just round the corner to collect some bread for them both.

Bread and honey, she decided as she called 'Come in,' and some of the previously rejected coffee. Probably Maria would join her.

All the breath seemed to escape from her body in one jolting gasp as Matt Lincoln walked into the room.

She slid off the stool, uncomfortably aware of the increased rate of her heartbeat.

'What the hell are you doing here?'

'I met your landlady on the steps. She told me to come straight up.' He smiled thinly. 'Were you hoping to have me arrested for trespass?'

'Well, she had no right,' Kate said stormily. 'Will you please get out of here right now!'

'Well, you're consistent, I'll give you that,' he said grimly. 'Morning, afternoon or evening, it's always the hard word.'

'What else to do you expect?' Kate glared at him. 'How did you find out where I live?'

'I could ask you the same question,' he drawled. 'But I won't. Let's just say I'm as good a detective as you any day of the week, and call it quits, shall we?'

She stared at him bitterly, resenting the intrusion, although she knew she had brought it on herself by her own actions. He looked incredibly tall, the sloping attic ceiling emphasising his height, and he seemed to fill the available space completely. Her space, Kate thought angrily. Her privacy.

'Quits, then,' she said with an effort. 'Now will you please leave—I have work to do.'

He took in the litter of crumpled paper around her feet and trailing to the wastebasket. 'Going well?' he asked pleasantly.

'A new project,' Kate said shortly. 'And early days yet.' She paused. 'Please will you go.'

'Presently,' he said. 'When I've said what I came here to say.'

'There's no need for any further conversation,' she began.

'I don't agree.' His tone was smooth but definite, and it seemed to convey a warning. Kate felt herself tense. He glanced round the studio. 'Is there any coffee going? I've had no breakfast.'

'Too busy looking for me, no doubt,' she said tautly.

'Too busy, certainly,' he said laconically.

She hadn't the slightest desire to give him coffee, but she knew that any kind of protest would only make her appear mean-minded and foolish, so with a little shrug she led the way across the landing to her bed-sitting room, silently thanking her stars as she did so that in spite of everything, she had still found the time that morning to make her bed and leave the room tidy. She walked over to the worktop and flicked the switch with operated the percolater. Out of the corner of her eye, she could see Matt Lincoln looking round appraisingly, lowering the zip on his casual jacket, and her heart sank.

'Perhaps you'd like to help yourself when it's ready,' she said hurriedly. 'I really do have to get on and . . .'

'Not yet.' His tone was cool but utterly implacable, and he was between her and the door. 'As I said, we have some talking to do.' He pulled a chair across and sat down, straddling it, his folded arms resting on its back, grinning sardonically at her expression of dismay.

'Very well,' she said, pretending a calmness she certainly didn't feel. She didn't like the way he was watching her as she moved about putting milk in a jug,

taking two pottery mugs out of her china cupboard.
The faded yellow sweatshirt wasn't particularly revealing, but her jeans clung to her hips and thighs like a
second skin, a fact which he was frankly and openly
appreciating. Kate gritted her teeth.

The coffee was percolating, sending a beguiling
aroma through the room. She wanted to relax—after
all, this was her home—but she couldn't, not with him
there. His presence was like an irritant. He seemed to
charge up the atmosphere, destroying the workmanlike
but peaceful ambience she had been at pains to create
for herself.

She poured the coffee into the mugs and handed him
one, her face stony. He took it with a brief word of
thanks, declining milk and sugar. Kate leaned against
the worktop, sipping her own drink, feeling its warmth
comfort her and give her heart, while she waited for
him to speak.

He said softly at last, 'I was deeply moved by your
eloquence last night.'

'Oh?' Her expression was suspicious, her tone
antagonistic, and he laughed.

'You don't believe me? But you underestimate your
own powers of persuasion, darling. If you think it
would be such a disaster for Alison to go to the
Caribbean with me, then I shall not take her. It's as
simple as that.'

Kate put her mug slowly down on the worktop. 'I
don't think I understand.'

'I'm a reformed character. Your impassioned plea
has made me see the light. My home-wrecking days are
behind me.'

Kate's lips tightened. 'This is clearly some kind of
weird joke, and I don't find it very amusing.'

'I've never been more serious.' The blue eyes glittered
oddly as they surveyed her. 'I am not taking Alison to
the Caribbean. That's what you wanted, isn't it?'

'Why—yes.' She was taken aback, and growing more
and more uneasy.

'Then you have your wish.' He paused, then said

smoothly, 'There is, of course, one minor condition.'

'Oh?' Kate swallowed. 'What is it?'

He smiled, his eyes appraising her body again with unconcealed sensuousness. He said gently, 'On condition that you come with me instead.'

CHAPTER THREE

FOR a long moment, Kate couldn't think of a single thing to say.

Then, at last, she managed, 'You—really—are joking.'

'Not in the least.' He was no longer smiling. The dark face was set and almost cruel. 'That's the way it is, darling, I am off to the Caribbean on the fifth of next month, and I haven't the slightest intention of travelling alone. If you want Alison to stay at home and go on practising the role of the virtuous wife, then you'll go with me. If you don't then she will. See how easy it all is?'

'Easy?' Her mouth was so dry, she could hardly force the word out. 'My God!' Then something snapped inside her, and she picked up her mug of coffee and threw it at him.

He had the reflexes of a cat. As her hand came up he was already moving. The coffee went everywhere, the mug smashed against the opposite wall, and he was unscathed.

Not only unscathed, but grinning in unholy amusement as he looked at the mess she'd made. 'You've got a violent streak, darling. Your parents must have been clairvoyant when they named you after a shrew. What a way to behave when you've just been offered the holiday of a lifetime!'

Kate regained her self-control with a superhuman effort, digging her nails painfully into the palms of her hands.

'I wouldn't have described your offer in quite those terms. I thought it more of an insult.' She lifted her chin, speaking coolly.

His brows rose. 'Obviously you've never been insulted. But there's no need to smash things. All you

43

have to say is "no", and the offer to Alison will stand. Why complicate matters by breaking the crockery?'

She said huskily, 'You couldn't imagine for one moment that I'd agree.'

'Now there you're wrong.' He threw back his head and looked at her, his eyes narrowed. 'I got the distinct impression last night that you'd do anything in your power to prevent me from ruining your—stepbrother's marriage. I merely decided to test the depth of your commitment.' He shook his head. 'I'm not impressed.'

'I'd do anything within reason, naturally.' Kate bit her lip. 'But this suggestion of yours is—sick. It's twisted!'

Matt burst out laughing. 'Now how do you make that out?' he wanted to know.

'Because you only said it to embarrass me—to punish me,' she answered in a low voice.

He shrugged. 'Partly true, perhaps. But certainly not the whole truth.' He paused. 'I fancied you at that wedding, as you know perfectly well. And last night's —admittedly brief—encounter has whetted my appetite as far as you're concerned.'

'But not,' said Kate, 'mine for you.'

Matt shrugged again. 'Then the answer's "No" and Alison goes with me.' He looked at her meditatively. 'She won't be quite so—lively a companion, but at least she's never tried to deny her own responses.'

'Are you implying that I do?' Kate demanded furiously.

'Yes,' he said. 'When I saw you at that wedding, it was a mutual thing, and you know it.'

'No,' Kate said.

'Oh, but it was.' His voice was gentle, but there was a steely note underlying it which chilled her. 'I wasn't the only one looking, darling, and every sidelong glance I had from you was drawing me across the room like a bloody magnet. I wanted to find out all kinds of things about you, and not merely what you looked like without that silky thing you were swathed in—although that was part of it,' he added, a self-derisive smile tugging at the corners of his mouth.

'And I, of course, was supposed to be flattered by your attentions,' Kate said stonily. 'The famous Matthew Lincoln honouring us all with his presence at a suburban wedding. God, what an ego you must have! Believe me, Mr Lincoln, setting you up was a pleasure.'

'I believe it.' Matt's mouth twisted. 'But now it seems to be my turn, darling, and I intend to make the most of it.' He put the mug down on the table. 'Thank you for the coffee,' he went on with a mocking glance at the stained wall behind him. 'And the proposition I've made you still stands. You have the next twenty-four hours to decide if this marriage you have such faith in is really worth saving or not. The decision is yours.' He walked across to the wall-mounted memo pad she kept beside her food cupboard, and wrote a number on it. 'Call me,' he said, and left.

Kate sagged back against the worktop, hearing his footsteps receding down the stairs with a feeling which mingled relief and other emotions not so easily definable. She could hardly believe what had happened.

Matt Lincoln didn't—couldn't expect that she would agree, she thought desperately. He was merely tormenting her. He had to be.

She filled a bowl with water, took a cloth and some liquid cleanser and began to clear up the mess she'd made. The brilliantly coloured handwoven blankets she'd bought on a trip to Greece the previous year and which she used to disguise her bed as a couch during the day were soaked with coffee, and would need to go to the cleaners, and she bit her lip as she stripped them and folded them.

All she had to do was dial the number he had left, and tell Matt Lincoln to go to hell. Except that wouldn't be the end of it because of Alison's involvement.

She groaned. That, of course, was the joker in the pack. The fact that she knew about Alison. That it was in her power to stop her sister-in-law from messing up her life completely, because Kate had no doubt that that was what was at stake.

Matt Lincoln wasn't a lover from the past, desperate to rekindle an old passion no matter what it cost. She could have understood that, if not condoned it. But it wasn't any romantic elopement he was planning. Alison had said an assignment, but that, she suspected, was merely to provide an element of respectability.

No, he was off to the Caribbean and he wanted a woman to go with him. It was as simple as that, to use his own phrase. He lived a high-powered life, but now he was in the mood for some relaxation. Sun, sand and sex, Kate thought wryly. Wasn't that what the travel brochures offered, even if it wasn't quite as overt as that?

And Alison's marriage made no difference to his plans, because the fact was that Alison herself didn't matter. She'd been chosen because she was an available female body, and that was all.

But anyone else would do as well. His insulting offer to herself had made that more than clear. She still could hardly believe it. Did he really imagine for one moment that she would agree, that she'd take a step that would transform their relationship from that of antagonistic strangers to the kind of total intimacy which made her mind reel?

It was impossible. No one would do such a thing, and that was why he'd suggested it, of course.

She rinsed her cloth and wrung it out as if it were Matt Lincoln's neck.

No doubt the foolish weakness of her capitulation the previous night had prompted him. Probably he thought that her dislike of him, and everything he represented as a man, was only a façade, and that one kiss would transform the Sleeping Beauty into the ideal travelling companion, she thought savagely.

God, he was a bastard, and she wished she'd kicked his shins to splinters!

Yes, she'd been shaken out of her usual cool control, but only by surprise. The last thing she had expected had been for him to kiss her. He had caught her off guard, that was all, she assured herself, and that was why she had behaved so stupidly.

And he had all the experience in the world, a small voice reminded her. That long, sensuous kiss had taught her that Matt Lincoln would be the kind of lover against whom a woman would measure all other men for the rest of her life . . .

She stopped short, frowning. Those were avenues of thought she definitely did not want to explore, she told herself decisively. She wasn't interested in him as a human being, let alone a lover.

All she wanted was that he should forget about Alison, and it was too late now to wish that she'd never got involved, to regret with all her being that she had ever sought him out.

What satisfaction his arrogant ego must have derived from her intervention, she thought angrily. He was well revenged for the snub she had administered at the wedding. By revealing her concern for Alison, she'd given him a stick to beat her with, and he hadn't hesitated to use it.

She'd done no good at all, she thought dolefully. In fact, if she was honest, she'd probably made matters worse.

She sighed and poured the bowl of water away down the sink. She hadn't made a perfect job of clearing up, but then she hadn't been entirely concentrating on what she was doing.

She looked at the phone number scrawled on the memo board, and her brows drew together angrily. He knew damned well she would never use it. She must have been mad to allow him to amuse himself at her expense, to pretend that he could really be persuaded to think again about his selfish pleasures.

It would serve him right, she thought, if she was to call his bluff.

She picked up the damp cloth she had been using and went to wipe the board clean, then stopped abruptly, her brain working furiously.

Well, why not? Why shouldn't she do just that? God

only knew he'd asked for it, she assured herself almost feverishly.

She poured herself another mug of coffee, and sat down to think. There was nothing to prevent her from going. Her passport was in order, and she'd been vaguely considering taking some sort of break, although nothing as opulent as a Caribbean island.

Not that she'd be spending very long there, she thought grimly. It would probably only be a matter of hours before Matt Lincoln discovered that she was not the pushover he thought, and that he'd been set up all over again. He wouldn't be pleased, but there wouldn't be a great deal he could do about it.

Unless he chose to play rough, a warning voice reminded her, but she dismissed it. She might not like him, but she gave him credit for not having the instincts of a rapist. Oh no, he wouldn't use force, she thought. He would rely on his own physical attraction, and his undoubted powers of persuasion to get her into his bed, and when he failed, he would be only too glad to see the back of her. And she could then decide whether to continue the holiday on her own, or return home.

A small triumphant smile curved her mouth. Oh, but she'd make him sorry! After the big build-up she was planning, the final let-down would be all the greater. And now that she was warned about his tactics, her resistance would be impregnable. After all, she knew all about freezing off unwanted advances, she was an expert on the subject and Matt Lincoln would never find her defenceless again.

She stared at the numbers on the memo board, memorising them, rehearsing the moment when she would ring him and tell him that she was prepared to go with him. Sacrificing herself for Alison, naturally, she thought ironically, but underneath her words there'd be just the tiniest hint that she hadn't been able to help herself.

But would he believe her? Would he really be arrogant enough to think that one kiss had turned her on so much that she wanted to share more than just a touching of lips with him?

Well, she would just have to see, but she didn't anticipate any real difficulty. She could make him think she'd been intrigued by his audacious suggestion, and he would think that her conquest was as good as achieved. He wasn't used to rejection, and if she played her cards right, it was the last thing he would be anticipating.

I'll be shy, she decided with relish, and just a little tremulous, so that he won't push too hard at first. And when he finds my door locked I can always tell him that strange hotels make me nervous. With luck, I could keep him dangling for days—and nights.

She finished her coffee. She wouldn't ring right away, of course. She'd leave it until the last minute so that he'd know the kind of heart-searching she'd had to go through, she thought, stretching luxuriously. As she did so, she caught a glimpse of herself in the mirror opposite, saw the smooth length of thigh and leg in the tight jeans, the thrust of her breasts against the sweatshirt that her movement had produced, and remembered the way Matt Lincoln had looked at her.

She straightened abruptly, colour tingeing her face. She knew exactly what that long, calculated assessment had meant—that he was undressing her mentally, imagining her naked, and the thought made her stir restlessly, aware of an odd heat spreading through her body.

He would not be very pleased, she thought, to discover that imagination was all he would be left with, and it occurred to her forcibly that she could be playing with fire.

She stood up, resolutely shrugging the moment of doubt away.

So is he, she promised silently. So is he.

In the end it was simplicity itself. Matt was clearly surprised at her flattering words, but he covered well, she had to admit grudgingly.

She had expected some kind of interrogation about her motives, but none was forthcoming. Instead he had sounded almost brisk as he asked about her passport and told her the time and other details of the flight they would be taking.

'We're going to St Antoine,' he added. 'It's not a very sophisticated place, so you won't need a great deal of gear.'

'Oh.' Kate digested that. She'd expected they would be going to Barbados or Antigua—one of the islands geared to the tourist industry.

'Disappointed?'

'Certainly not,' she said brightly. 'I—I'm sure it will be fascinating.'

'I'll do my best to make it so.' She heard the amusement simmering under his tone, and scowled at the receiver in her hand. 'If you've got a map, look in the region of St Lucia, preferably with a magnifying glass.' He paused. 'I'm going to be pretty tied up between now and then, so I think it's safer if I say we'll meet at the airport, somewhere round the flight desk. They like you to check in about an hour beforehand.'

Kate was taken aback. She'd expected he would want to see her and had marshalled her excuses accordingly.

She said coolly, 'Fine. I'll be there.' She hesitated. 'What are you going to tell Alison?'

'I'll think of something. It won't be a problem.' His voice was almost casual, she thought furiously. Not for him, no. Off with the old love, and on with the new, or so he thought. The fact that he'd raised all kinds of hopes in Alison and was now going to disappoint her was a matter of indifference to him.

Uncaring swine! she raged silently.

Suddenly suspicious, she said, 'You don't intend to tell her the truth, I hope?'

'That you're going in her place? It would hardly be tactful, but perhaps you're into total honesty.'

I'm into the exact opposite, she assured him under her breath.

She said, 'I'd really rather she knew nothing about it. In fact I'd rather no one knew.' She hesitated. 'I don't make a habit of this sort of thing . . .'

'Then I'll have to make sure it's special.' Matt's voice

deepened huskily, and she swallowed, aware of a returning unease as she contemplated just what she was letting herself in for. 'Oh, and Kate,' he continued after a pause, 'I meant what I said about travelling light. Don't bother with unnecessary refinements—like night-dresses, for instance. I'm sure you'll find the nights on St Antoine quite warm enough.'

She was thankful he couldn't see her, because she was blushing.

She managed to keep her voice light. 'I'll bear that in mind.'

'Do that,' he said. 'See you at the airport.' And rang off.

Kate would have liked to have wrenched the telephone off the wall and jumped on it.

She began to break the news gradually to family and friends that she was going away for a while, talking with deliberate vagueness about off-season rates to Spain and Greece, emphasising that her plans were fluid and she had no idea exactly how long she would be away.

Deception was absurdly easy, she discovered miserably. Everyone took it for granted that she was entitled to a holiday after a busy year, and no one probed or asked awkward questions, although Clive had verged on the reproachful, dropping hints that if she'd waited a while he might have been able to go with her.

At least she'd been spared the hassle of dissuading him about that, she thought unhappily.

The worst experience had been facing Alison. She felt so guilty when she encountered her sister-in-law that she was sure it would show in her face. Her guilt increased when she saw how miserable Alison looked.

Matt's rejection must have hit her hard, she thought, but surely it was better for it to happen now before any real harm was done.

She waited to see if anything was said about Alison's return to work, but the subject wasn't mentioned, and at last when they were alone in her mother's kitchen for a few minutes she raised it rather diffidently herself.

Alison shrugged, 'I haven't made any definite plans yet.' She bent her head, and Kate saw that her pretty face was painfully flushed. 'But I've decided against that trip I mentioned. It—it wouldn't be fair on Jon.'

It was a gallant attempt at face-saving, Kate thought wryly.

She said, 'I'm sure you're doing the right thing, Ally.'

And wished she could think the same about herself.

Because to say she was having second thoughts was putting it mildly. Every time she passed a travel agent, or saw a picture of a sun-kissed beach fringed by palms in a magazine, or even an advertisement for swimwear, she was assailed by all kinds of qualms about what she was doing.

It had occurred to her more than once that she didn't have to go through with it. Now that Alison knew she wasn't going, the problem was solved. She could pretend to be ill, she thought, or simply not turn up. He wouldn't miss the flight to come looking for her, and if there were recriminations on his return, she could say she'd mistaken the time of their departure.

She was amazed at the extent of her own deviousness. And I used to be such a truthful person, she thought ruefully. Another black mark against Matt Lincoln.

But as the days slid away with frightening rapidity, she found she was retrieving the lightweight case she used on trips abroad from the big storage cupboard on the landing, and beginning to assemble, at least in her mind, the things she would take with her.

She didn't need to do any shopping. The bikinis and leisure clothes she'd bought for the Greek holiday were still as good as new, and this was just as well, because she didn't want any large items of expenditure cutting into her savings. She wanted to have enough money to allow her to hand Matt the cost of her ticket at least when they came to the parting of the ways on St Antoine.

He might be out of luck, and out of temper, but there was no reason for him to be out of pocket too, she told herself.

But she didn't understand fully why she was going, except that everyone was expecting her to be away, and she would undoubtedly have to explain why she was still around. Either that, or she would have to take one of the trips to Spain or Greece that she was supposed to be contemplating.

It appeared that she was bound to go somewhere—so it might as well be the Caribbean, she told herself, and if a warning voice in her head suggested that she should enquire more closely into her reasoning, she crushed it down.

But as she approached the flight desk at the airport and saw Matt's tall figure, her nerve almost faltered. Panic settled like a leaden ball in her throat, and she was sorely tempted to turn and run before he saw her.

Yet even as the thought crossed her mind, he had turned and was lifting his hand in greeting.

Kate gripped the handle of her case more tightly and walked slowly forward, trying to appear composed. She had a score or two to settle, she reminded herself. Wasn't that worth a little aggro?

She was aware she was looking her best in a cream, figure-skimming dress buttoning from neck to hem down the front, her chestnut hair drawn chastely back from her face by tortoiseshell combs, and Matt Lincoln's smile was frankly appreciative as he came forward to take her case from her.

'Beautiful and punctual,' he said softly. 'I can hardly believe my good fortune.'

Patronising pig! Kate thought, lowering her lashes demurely. Make the most of it while you can.

She waited passively while the formalities of their trip were completed. Eventually Matt came across to her.

'We have some time before our flight is called,' he said, glancing at his watch. 'Shall we have a drink?'

'Coffee would be fine.' While she was anywhere near Matt Lincoln, she intended to keep her consumption of alcohol to an absolute minimum.

His brows rose, and he was laughing. 'Are you going to drink it or throw it, this time?'

'Drink it.' She permitted herself a small smile in response. 'That was a pretty silly thing to do, wasn't it? My only excuse is that—well, I suppose I was knocked sideways a little by your sudden appearance.'

'I know what you mean.' His glance was dry. 'I felt exactly the same the previous night. However, everything turns out for the best in this best of all possible worlds.'

'Yes,' Kate hesitated. 'You must have been surprised to get my call . . .'

'Amazed,' he said. 'And naturally delighted. Some time you can tell me what caused the change of heart.'

'That's quite simple,' she said swiftly. 'You wanted to know how deeply committed I was to helping Jon and Alison—well, this is the answer.'

'The only one?' He smiled suddenly, the blue eyes caressing her, and she felt the breath catch in her throat at the sheer force of his attraction.

She said, 'That's a leading question,' and looked away hurriedly.

'I specialise in them,' said Matt. 'Here's the coffee-shop, but I can't guarantee what the liquid they serve here will taste like.'

The place was crowded and heads were turning as they walked to the counter. Kate didn't kid herself that the people were looking at her, either. Matt was instantly recognisable, she realised.

She sat at a table and watched him fetch the coffee. While he was paying, two young girls came up and asked for his autograph, and he coped with the request with courteous patience.

'Sorry about that,' he said as he put the cups down on the table. 'It doesn't really go with maintaining a low profile. And that is what you wanted.'

'Yes.' Kate stared down at the surface of the table, tracing a meaningless pattern on it with her forefinger. 'This—this hasn't been easy for me. I mean—we're strangers.'

'That's something this trip is designed to cure.' He sounded faintly amused.

'Isn't it rather a drastic way of getting acquainted?' she murmured, still not meeting his eyes.

'I didn't have a great deal of luck with the more conventional methods,' he reminded her silkily.

And your luck hasn't changed by one iota, Kate thought with satisfaction as she drank her coffee.

She had never known time pass so slowly. Usually when she was waiting for her flight to be called, she wandered about exploring the airport, browsing round the bookstall, letting the excitement, the anticipation of the trip build up. She liked watching her fellow passengers too, and sketching them sometimes in the little book she invariably carried in her shoulder bag for the purpose. It was with her now, but she doubted whether she was capable of drawing even a line.

This time she was the one being watched, she realised, and envied too. The lucky lady with Matt Lincoln. She just prayed she wouldn't be seen by anyone who would recognise her.

It was almost a relief to find herself on board the aircraft. Almost but not quite. She fumbled with the seatbelt, thinking, 'That's it—no turning back now.'

As the plane began to taxi, she closed her eyes, sinking back into her seat.

'Nervous?' asked Matt.

'Yes,' she said. But not of flying, she added silently. She was acutely, frighteningly aware of every inch of the strong lean body relaxed in the adjoining seat, so close that it was difficult to move without brushing against him.

'Don't be afraid,' he said. He picked up her hand, clutching tensely at the armrest, and touched it with his lips. Kate had to bite her tongue to stop herself from crying out, from flinching away from him. He was frowning a little, his face concerned. 'They'll be serving drinks soon.' He gave her a faint smile. 'I recommend a stiff belt, or even two.'

She nodded wanly. Nine hours to St Lucia, she thought, and then the change-over to the smaller plane which ferried people between the islands, and every

minute spent with her senses screaming at this
unwanted proximity. How was she going to bear it?

But bear it she did, helped by the fact that he made
no further attempt to touch her after that brief caress.
The stewardess brought magazines, and she read them
as well as one of the paperbacks she'd brought with her.
Meals were served, and although she wasn't hungry, she
made herself eat, telling herself that she needed to keep
her strength up. Matt read too, mostly files he took
from his bag, bulging with typewritten sheets and press
cuttings. He smiled at her occasionally, and asked if she
was all right, and they chatted over the food, but apart
from that she could have been travelling alone, she
discovered with relief.

At last, inevitably, she fell asleep, wandering through
a confusion of small troubled dreams until she heard
Matt's voice telling her it was time to fasten her seatbelt
again.

She opened her eyes slowly and reluctantly, and
found to her horror that she had slipped sideways as
she slept, and that her head was on his shoulder and she
was being supported by his arm round her. She almost
shot upright, stammering something, feeling colour
blaze in her cheeks. She couldn't cope with the seatbelt
and he leaned across and fastened it for her, giving her
a sardonic look as he did so.

No doubt he was wondering why she was making so
much fuss about a doze on an aircraft when tonight she
would be sharing his bed, Kate thought with a touch of
hysteria.

She stumbled down the steps of the plane into warm
darkness.

'Take it easy.' His hand was on her arm steadying
her, and she wanted to scream, 'Don't touch me!'

She felt weird, disorientated and close to cracking as
she waited for their luggage to be retrieved.

'Come on.' Matt joined her carrying the cases.
'There's a taxi waiting.'

She gave him a startled look. 'A taxi—is that what
you call the plane?'

'No,' he said. 'I mean a taxi—a thing with four wheels and a driver. We're spending the night here and taking the morning plane to St Antoine.'

Kate stared at him. She'd been counting on the extra journey, however long it took, to eat into the night, postponing the first inevitable confrontation between them.

She drew a breath. 'You didn't tell me.'

He shrugged. 'You didn't ask. Does it matter?' He studied her, frowning. 'And even if we'd been booked to fly on tonight, I think I'd have postponed. You look like hell.'

'Thank you,' she said between her teeth, and he laughed.

'That's more like it! Can you make it to the taxi or shall I carry you and come back for the bags?'

'No.' She gave him a muted glare, hardly bothering to pretend any more.

She sat gazing out of the taxi window into the darkness, eaten up by tension. She'd hoped for a long journey, but it was only a short one. They were stopping in front of a long, low building festooned with lights. A man with grizzled hair, wearing white jeans and a striped tee-shirt, was opening the car door and helping her out, welcoming her to some hotel whose name she didn't catch.

As she stepped into the air-conditioned foyer, she was aware of a wide expanse of tiled floor and greenery everywhere.

The receptionist was smiling widely. 'Welcome back, Mr Lincoln. Too bad you're not staying longer this time.' His grin encompassed Kate too. 'Good evening, madame.'

A pen was put into her hand and she signed a registration card. The receptionist handed Matt a key and a bellhop appeared from nowhere, hoisting up their cases. He was smiling too. Everyone was smiling except her, and she felt totally and utterly frozen, because she'd just grasped the significance of that single key.

She'd taken it for granted that they would be

occupying separate rooms, at least for appearances' sake. She'd counted on it.

'No lift,' said Matt. 'But there's only one flight of stairs. Think you can manage it?'

She said faintly, 'No—I don't—I can't . . .'

His voice was soft, 'Yes, you can, darling,' but there was a note in it that made her shiver. Dazed, Kate looked at him, her eyes widening as they met his.

He wasn't smiling either. His blue eyes were like chips of steel, his mouth hard and set.

He said, 'Let's go up to our room, my sweet. I can't wait to be alone with you.'

And his hand closed like a vice on her arm, urging her up the stairs in front of him.

CHAPTER FOUR

IT was a large room, and the biggest thing in it was the bed. It dominated everything else, and Kate had the feeling that wherever she stood, even if she turned her back, she would still catch sight of it from the corner of her eye.

There were other things to notice too. Flowers everywhere, for instance, and a basket of fruit, and champagne on ice.

She thought, 'It's like a bridal suite,' and had to quell the nervous laugh rising up in her throat, because there was nothing to laugh at. She'd got herself into this impossible situation, and now, somehow, she had to get out of it again.

She walked over to the windows which opened on to a balcony. The night air was warm and still. In the distance she could hear the faint sound of music—a drumbeat—and farther off what might have been the sound of the sea.

Behind her, she heard Matt tip the bellboy, and tell him they didn't want to be disturbed. She heard his cheerful 'Goodnight' and the closing of the door, and she waited, a strange aching trembling spreading through the pit of her stomach.

Matt said softly, 'Alone at last.'

Kate turned slowly and faced him, her arms folded defensively across her diaphragm. There were marks on her wrist where his fingers had gripped her, she noticed with a kind of astonishment.

He took off the beautifully cut lightweight jacket he had been wearing and tossed it on to the bed, then began to loosen his tie. The blue eyes held hers enigmatically.

He said, 'You're very quiet, darling. Tired after the flight? Then an early night's just what you need.'

59

Her lips parted helplessly, but she couldn't think of anything to say, although speech was essential and growing more so by the second.

Matt said, unbuttoning his shirt, 'I need a shower. Do you want to use the bathroom first?'

'No—yes—I mean . . .' Kate floundered to a halt.

The dark brows lifted interrogatively. 'Yes, what exactly do you mean?'

She swallowed, 'I didn't expect—this.' She gestured around her.

'Don't you like the room?'

'I—I expected one of my own.'

'You did?' He shook his head slowly. 'That wasn't in the deal.'

Her lips felt dry, and she moistened them with the tip of her tongue. 'About that . . .'

'Yes?' His shirt joined his jacket and tie on the bed. Hands on hips, he watched her. His mouth was smiling, but his eyes held the same steely coldness which had startled her down in the foyer. 'What about it?'

Kate lifted her chin. 'I think you know already,' she said.

'That you intend to renege on our bargain?' His voice was cool and contemptuous. 'Yes, of course I know. You could hardly have made your intentions more obvious.'

'Oh?' She looked at him warily. 'I don't know how . . .'

'Your performance so far hasn't been particularly impressive,' he said evenly. 'Or did you think I was so eaten up with my own sexual conceit that I would simply accept it at its face value? No, darling, you didn't fool me for a moment. I knew quite well I was being set up, and why.'

It annoyed her to think he had found her so transparent, but she didn't see how else she could have behaved.

'Then we know where we stand,' she said. She held out her hand. 'If you'll give me my case, I'll go down to the desk and see about another room.'

'Save yourself a trip,' he said. 'There are no other rooms.'

'Oh,' Kate said uncertainly. She paused. 'But there'll be other hotels.'

'Plenty of them,' he agreed. 'But you're going nowhere—at least not tonight. Tomorrow you're flying to St Antoine with me, just as we arranged.'

She said hotly, 'I'll do nothing of the sort! You must be mad if you think . . .'

'You haven't the least idea what I think,' Matt Lincoln said with icy emphasis. 'All you did was make some wild assumptions, and I decided to let you.' He walked towards her, and Kate shrank. He noticed the swift, instinctive movement and his face hardened, but he made no attempt to touch her as she had been dreading. There was a chair near the window, made from bamboo and deeply cushioned, and he dragged it forward. 'Sit,' he told her briefly. 'And listen.'

'I'd rather stand,' Kate said defiantly.

'I'm not interested in your preferences,' he said flatly. 'Sit!'

There was something in his face which prompted obedience. Kate sat, glaring at him.

He gave her a faint smile. 'You've learned your first lesson, darling. And now I'll tell you why you're here, and why you're staying, and it has nothing to do with my unbridled lust for your undoubtedly delectable body.'

The note in his voice made her cringe inwardly. She wanted to tell him she wasn't going to remain there and be insulted, but it sounded absurd, a comedy line, and this wasn't funny at all. She'd never felt less like laughing in her life, and this whole humiliating situation was entirely of her own creation, which made it even worse.

He said, 'I'm going to St Antoine to work, but it's not a thing I want generally known. So—you're my cover story. For anyone who wants to know, I'm in St Antoine to enjoy the sun, and a romantic interlude with my new lady.' He paused. 'That's your role, and I expect you to be rather more convincing in it than you've been so far.'

She stared at him, her eyes widening. 'You expect me to pretend that—that I'm in love with you?' she demanded huskily.

His mouth twisted mockingly. 'I think that's straining credibility, don't you? A state of mutual physical enrapturement might be easier to aim for, perhaps.'

Kate swallowed. 'I'm glad you think so.'

He said gently, 'I hope you'll think so too. Play the part as I've written it, and you'll have nothing whatever to fear from me. Is that clear?'

'And if I won't?'

He shrugged, his face hardening again. 'Then we'll play it for real.' His gaze stripped her. 'It would be no hardship, believe me.'

She said hoarsely, 'If you're prepared to use force, how do I know I can trust you?'

'You don't,' he told her laconically. 'Will it reassure you if I say I've never used force with a woman in my life?'

She produced a travesty of a smile. 'Not particularly.' She was remembering that kiss, and knew that he was, too, and the realisation galled her. Her hands were clenched together in her lap. Staring down at her tightly woven fingers, she said, 'Do I really have no choice? What's to stop me walking out of here right now?'

'I am.' He smiled down at her silkily. 'I'm sure you're not penniless, but you wouldn't get far without your passport.'

'My God,' Kate said unevenly. 'You really are a bastard!'

'It's been said before,' he dismissed briefly. He gave her a long steady look. 'And if it comes to it, you're no lady yourself. We made a bargain, even if you had the terms slightly wrong, and you were going to run out on it.' He shook his head reprovingly. 'Welshers aren't nice people.'

Kate said with a snap, 'What would you know about nice people?' She drew a deep breath. 'May I know what this hush-hush job is on St Antoine? As I'm going to be so closely involved with it, I feel I have a right to know.'

'On this trip, you have only the rights I choose to accord you,' said Matt. 'And to quote your own words—how do I know I can trust you?' He watched her flush angrily and laughed. 'No, darling, I think I'll keep my own counsel, at least for the time being.'

'Will you please stop calling me that!' Kate muttered between gritted teeth.

'What would you like me to call you?' he asked pleasantly. 'It can hardly be Miss Marston in the circumstances. How about "My sweet" or "my dear love"? '

'Oh, make it what the hell you want,' she sighed wearily. 'And when we get to St Antoine, I want my own room.'

'Tough,' he said succinctly. 'The booking has already been made, and it stands. You'll have to cross your fingers that there are twin beds.'

She bit her lip. 'And tonight?'

'You really think you're irresistible, don't you?' Matt looked down at her smiling, and she looked away, hating the disadvantage she was at, loathing the sheer masculine challenge of him. All the time they'd been talking, she had been deeply conscious of the fact that he was shirtless, unwillingly aware of the breadth of his shoulders and the taut muscularity of his chest and abdomen. If they'd been talking on a beach, she wouldn't have given his state of semi-undress a second thought, probably, but here in this room, at this time of night, it seemed a threat, which was exactly what he intended, she suspected. 'But you really have no need to worry. It's been a long journey, and I'm too tired to contemplate even a mild pass.'

'I'm grateful for the reassurance,' she said sarcastically. 'But it doesn't alter a thing. I've no intention of sharing a bed with you.'

His grin widened. 'Why? Isn't it big enough for you?'

It was almost as big as the island itself, not merely

king-sized, but emperor-sized, and she was probably
being ridiculous. He obviously thought she was, but she
didn't care.

He added cheerfully, 'But please yourself, of course. I
hope that chair remains comfortable.'

Kate was taken aback. She said, 'I thought you might
have offered me the bed.'

'Did you now?' He sauntered across the room. 'Well,
half of it is as far as my generosity runs.' He picked up
a couple of pillows and arranged them with ostentatious
care down the centre of the bed. 'Not the Berlin Wall,
but an adequate barricade, I'd have said. And if you
don't want to use the bathroom, then I do.'

He opened his case, pulling out a silky robe and
shaking the creases out of it. No pyjamas, she registered
with a sinking heart, but then after his comment in
London about 'unnecessary refinements' she supposed
that would have been too much to ask for.

When she was alone, she sat staring at the floor and
wishing that she was dead at worst, or that she'd never
got involved at the very least. She groaned. The next
two weeks, dancing to whatever tune he chose to play,
promised to be unbearable, a humiliating, embarrassing
experience.

Her only comfort was the thought that Alison was
still safely with Jon, because this would have been a
very bad scene for Alison. Matt Lincoln certainly
wouldn't have made any guarantees to her about his
conduct, even if she'd wanted him to, she thought
miserably, remembering the way Alison had been
looking at him in the restaurant. She acquitted Alison
of actually contemplating infidelity in cold blood, but at
the same time her sister-in-law was bored and peeved
with marriage, and she would be vulnerable to the kinds
of pressure that these circumstances would produce.
Someone as blatantly attractive as Matt Lincoln with
all that undoubted sexual charisma wouldn't even have
to try very hard, she thought.

But she wasn't like Alison, or like any of the other
girls he fancied for a while. She wasn't vulnerable. She

was impervious to any amount of his kind of charm, and for that she had Drew Wakefield to thank, although it had never occurred to her that she would ever be grateful for the lesson he'd taught her. Drew had always been her secret shame, but now he was her secret weapon, and one that she could well need before she was finished.

She shivered, wondering why she was sitting there, thinking all these disturbing things when she could have been searching in his case, his jacket for her passport. Not that it would have been there, she realised wearily. It would be downstairs in the hotel safe, and retrieving it without a damned good reason wouldn't be easy.

She heard the bathroom door open and Matt returning. One swift sidelong look under her lashes told her all that she needed to know, that he was wearing the silk robe and nothing underneath it.

She heard the tinkle of ice cubes and the subdued pop of a cork, and realised he was opening the champagne.

He said, 'I'm drinking to the success of this assignment. Do you want to join me?' He smiled. 'Champagne makes a fantastic nightcap—beats warm milk into a cocked hat!'

Kate said stonily, 'I'm not in a celebratory mood. I don't want any champagne.'

'As you please.' He paused. 'When you think of something you do want perhaps you'd let me know.'

He was laughing at her, and she glared at him, remembering the first time she'd looked across a room and seen him with a glass of champagne in his hand, and felt the unwilling tug of attraction.

As she felt it now, she realised incredulously. She swallowed, gulping air, fighting down bewilderment and dismay. The implication in his words had been that some day she might want him, and it was fortunate he'd never know how close to the truth he was.

Her heart was beating extra-fast suddenly, and in her ears it seemed as audible as that distant insistent drumbeat. She leaned back in her chair, breathing deeply, struggling for composure. And she'd just been congratulating herself on her own invulnerability where he was concerned, she thought bitterly.

She was in danger, real danger, and she couldn't deny it, but at least she realised it, and forewarned was forearmed—wasn't it?

Matt lifted his glass in a mocking toast. 'To us,' he said, and drank, almost as though he'd been reading her thoughts.

Kate's colour rose, and she got to her feet in one swift movement and went over to her case, busying herself with unlocking it and searching for her toilet bag, finding her nightdress and robe, although if she was going to be spending the night in that chair, then she would do better to remain fully dressed.

The bathroom door had a bolt, and she pushed it into place, uncaring whether he heard or not, feeling a sense of security for the first time.

She unbuttoned her dress slowly and wearily. It had been a long and tiring flight, she thought, and probably accounted for that extraordinary moment of weakness just now. She would feel entirely different in the morning.

She sighed as she stepped under the shower, letting the warm water stream soothingly down her body, lifting her hair away from the nape of her neck with both hands. With no fear of interruption, she had not bothered to draw the shower curtain, and as she turned under the pouring water, she caught a glimpse of herself in the long mirror opposite. She wasn't narcissistic. She took her slim good-looking body with its high round breasts, gently curving hips and long slender flanks very much for granted, but tonight she looked steadily, examining herself, wondering how a man would see her. 'Delectable,' Matt Lincoln had said, but he'd been sneering. And if Alison was a reflection of his taste, then she was too thin. Alison's curves had a hint of the voluptuous, and she was a spasmodic dieter, constantly complaining about her weight.

Kate turned off the water and stepped out, reaching

for a towel. It felt damp against her skin, and with a shock she realised it was the one Matt had used. His male scent seemed to cling to it, enveloping her, and with a gasp she flung it away.

She cleaned her teeth with her usual meticulous thoroughness, then brushed her hair until it swung in a shining curtain. There was a scent spray in her bag, one of her favourite fragrances, and almost before she knew what she was doing, she was using it, letting a perfumed cloud mist her throat, her shoulders, her breasts cupped in the fragile bodice of her nightdress.

With a little groan of self-contempt she capped the spray, thrusting it back into the bag with shaking fingers. She snatched up her robe and put it on, knotting the sash round her small waist with unnecessary vigour.

When she went back into the bedroom, Matt was already in bed, the thin sheet clearly outlining the lean relaxed lines of his body. He was propped on one arm reading, and drinking occasionally from the glass in his other hand. He didn't even glance up as she came in, and she saw that in spite of her refusal, a glass of champagne had been placed temptingly on the low table at the other side of the bed.

The chair by the window was beginning to look singularly uninviting, she thought with a tiny grimace.

She wanted to burst out laughing. The whole thing was so incredible, more way-out than anything she could have imagined.

She thought, 'My first night in the Caribbean, and I'm spending it in bed with a man who, if not exactly a stranger, is certainly an enigma to me, and sipping champagne. What could be more decadent?'

Matt's back was turned towards her, but she still felt absurdly selfconscious as she took off her robe and slid gingerly under the sheet. She was waiting for some sardonic comment, but he gave no sign he was even aware she had joined him, and she felt an odd sense of anti-climax. She glanced over her shoulder at the strong, tanned curve of his shoulder and spine, experiencing once again that betraying leap of the senses.

Physically, she felt bone-weary, but her nerves were taut, her mind jumping.

How could he lie there, she raged inwardly, reading so casually, as if this was an everyday occurrence? But then, a sly inner voice reminded her, it probably was. According to the gossip columns most of his loves had lived-in, including the Lorna Bryce that Felix had mentioned. What was it Maria had said? That she'd ended up 'cut to ribbons'? Kate could believe it. Perhaps that was how Matt signalled indifference, the beginning of the end, with the book, the glass of wine and the deliberately turned shoulder.

Only in her case, he was signalling that it was never going to start, and she should have been overjoyed at that because he'd got her into an impossible situation, and she disliked him anyway.

He knew that, of course, and he was probably deriving some kind of sadistic pleasure from her embarrassment. It was mortifying to know that he'd been ahead of her, every step of the way, duping her, making her believe exactly what he wanted, react in the way that he wanted.

He was moving, and her whole body tensed as she wondered what she would do if he touched her. But he was only turning off the bedside lamp, and his 'Goodnight' was as brief and courteous as if he'd simply been thanking her for a pleasant evening.

Kate turned off her own light, and the darkness closed in on her, hour after hour of it as she lay listening to the soft regular sound of his sleeping breath, and trying to make sense of the welter of confused thoughts and emotions in her tired mind.

The air-strip on St Antoine was tiny, and Kate braced herself as they came in to land, fearing the worst. But they were down with scarcely a bump almost before she knew it, and she opened her eyes weakly and stopped clutching the armrests.

Matt was watching her, brows raised. 'You really are a nervous traveller!'

She gave him a muted glare. She was nothing of the sort, but the events of the past twenty-four hours would have made anyone into a nervous wreck.

She'd no idea what time she had finally fallen asleep, but she had an uneasy feeling that daylight hadn't been far away. It had been the hardest thing in the world to wake up, and face the breakfast of hot rolls, fresh fruit and coffee which had been served in their room. By some cosmic injustice, Matt looked a million dollars, refreshed and alert, she noted sourly.

The terminal buildings were amazing—a collection of prefabricated huts which looked as if one good wind would see them off for ever. And immigration procedures were casual in the extreme, Kate discovered, fuming.

'So much for your elaborate cover story,' she said sarcastically, as they stood outside in the sunshine waiting for a taxi. 'They couldn't have given a damn who you are or why you're here. They barely glanced at your passport.'

Matt grinned. 'Think so? I can guarantee at this moment, the word is being passed along the line.'

Tight-lipped, she said, 'Egotist,' and turned her attention to her surroundings.

She'd discovered long ago that it was unfair to judge any place by the area immediately around the airport or the railway station, but St Antoine seemed to have jumped that particular hazard. The dusty road which led, Matt told her, into town, was fringed with trees and flowering shrubs, and in the distance tall hills which just missed being mountains hung like blue shadows in the haze of heat.

She tried to recall some of the information she had acquired about St Antoine from the library. Centuries ago, cane and coffee had been grown, and buccaneers had used the oddly named Paradis Anchorage, but those stirring times were long over, and fruit growing, fishing and boat chartering were the main industries now.

They were staying at the Paradis Hotel, Matt had told her over breakfast, which stood on the beach in the next bay to the harbour. It sounded wonderful, and in any other circumstances it would have been, but she had felt she was having the prison described where she was about to serve a sentence. Not a long one, she was forced to admit. Two weeks were not an eternity, but she suspected they could seem like it, and if every night was going to be like the one she had just passed, she would surely crack from the strain.

The taxi was another eye-opener. It was painted a vivid yellow which made the sun look pale, and Kate blinked faintly and queried, 'What on earth——?'

Matt grinned. 'It's one of a fleet,' he explained. 'They call themselves the Banana Bunch. They do car rental as well, and I thought we might hire a jeep and do a tour of the island.'

'All in the line of work?' she queried, poisonously sweet.

'Naturally,' he said, leaving her unsure whether the offer of sightseeing had been an olive branch or not. Probably not, she decided.

The driver was lanky and cheerful, with a permanent grin. He had one of those miniature cassette players tucked into his shirt pocket and earphones on, and he sang along to a variety of tunes, making up in rhythm what he lacked in pitch.

Kate would have enjoyed the performance thoroughly if it hadn't been for the fact that Matt had put his arm round her as soon as they'd got into the car. It was draped across her shoulders quite casually, but his thumb was stroking along her collar bone and the hollow at the base of her throat, and his fingers weren't an inch from the swell of her breast, and she was finding it difficult to breathe suddenly, even though he'd murmured, 'Just local colour,' as his mouth grazed her ear. The instinct to strike out, to push him away had been almost overwhelming. She sat dry-mouthed and rigid in the curve of his arm, enduring this whisper of a caress, oblivious of the scenery or anything else except the sensuous probing of his fingers under the neckline of her shirt.

Last night they had slept together in an enormous bed, but he had been nowhere near as close to her as he was now, and his nearness, the scent of his skin, was acting on her like a drug, making her feel lightheaded, strange, totally unlike herself. It would be easy, so fatally easy to turn her head and put her mouth against the long column of his throat, discover whether his pulses were thudding as erratically as her own.

She was shaken at the strength of the impulse, and a little frightened too. She had never felt like this before. Certainly with Clive there had never been this terrifying urge to touch him, to learn the shape of his body with her hands, to let her mouth, her tongue discover the taste of him.

Her hands closed round each other in her lap, gripping until the knuckles turned white, and she sensed Matt's swift downward glance, and heard the dryness in his tone as he said, 'Relax. We've arrived.'

The Paradis Hotel wasn't over-large. There was a reception block, long and low and gleaming white which also contained the dining room, a hairdressing salon and some boutiques, and two small wings of bedrooms. The rest of the accommodation was in bungalows scattered through the grounds which led through a fringing of shrubs and palm trees directly on to the beach of silver sand.

The bungalows were white too, with green shutters opening on to terraces with padded chairs and loungers. The interior gave an impression of space and coolness in spite of the heat. There was a living area, furnished with a settee and chairs in the ubiquitous bamboo, and from this doors led into a compact bathroom tiled in a colour like the delicate inside of a shell, and the bedroom.

'Twin beds,' Matt pointed out sardonically, when they were alone. 'Another blow struck for chastity!'

Kate unlocked her case and began taking out her things and hanging them away in the fitted wardrobe.

After the way her thoughts had been running in the taxi, that was almost funny, she reflected wryly, but fortunately there was no way he could know that.

He was lounging on one of the beds, watching her. He said with a slanting smile, 'You don't think you'll be bored?'

She shook out a dress and slid it on to a hanger. 'I'll try and keep myself amused,' she countered lightly. 'Without, of course, interfering in your work.'

'I don't imagine you'll do that.' Matt lifted a shoulder in a negligent shrug. 'But I am a little concerned about your co-operation—or lack of it.'

'If you mean that little interlude in the taxi,' Kate said tautly, 'what did you expect—a full-blown necking session?'

'Hardly,' he said. 'But I'd prefer it if you didn't jump a mile every time I touch you. That's always given you away, as a matter of fact. Even if I'd been the kind of arrogant, randy idiot you had me marked as, I'd still have been able to recognise that you were trembling from panic rather than passion.'

'You're more used to the latter, of course.' Kate began to put the bikinis she'd brought into one of the drawers.

'If you say so.' He sounded amused. 'But you need to loosen up, otherwise there isn't a soul in the world who'll believe we're lovers once they see us together.'

She looked down at the scraps of brightly coloured fabric in her hands. 'And is it really so important that they should do so?' She let her scepticism show.

'I've told you it is.'

'Yes, you've told me,' Kate said. 'But you still haven't told me why it's so necessary—what you're doing here.'

'No,' he said. And that was all.

She turned and looked at him. 'You're not prepared to take me into your confidence?'

'Not yet.'

'But you'd have told Alison all about it, no doubt.' She wished she hadn't said that as soon as the words were uttered, because it sounded more like a jealous whinge than a statement of fact.

'Alison again,' he said softly. 'You really are obsessed with her, aren't you, darling? Almost as obsessed as she is with you.'

'What do you mean?'

Matt shrugged again. 'Think about it,' he advised. 'It will give you something to do in the long night watches—far healthier and more constructive than wondering if and when I'm going to leap on you.'

Colour burned in her face. She said, 'While we're on the subject, there is a settee in the other room.'

His brows rose mockingly. 'I'd noticed. Which of us are you suggesting should use it?'

She hesitated. 'I suppose—to be fair—we should take turns. A week each, perhaps.'

Matt gave her a grim look. 'Sometimes,' he said softly, 'I get the impression you don't hear a word I say.'

'That's not true.' She held herself very straight. 'You accuse me of being uptight, but is it any wonder?' She swallowed. 'I—I guarantee I'll do my best to play my part during the day, but at night I want some privacy.'

'That's too bad,' he said flatly.

'You won't even discuss it?'

'There's nothing to discuss,' he said wearily. 'As far as outsiders are concerned, I've come here with you to have a holiday and an enjoyable love affair. I want to give the impression that I'm absorbed with you to the exclusion of everything else, that work couldn't be further from my mind. They're not likely to believe it, if it's realised that we sleep in separate rooms.'

'You talk as if we'll be watched,' she protested. 'As if anyone will know.'

'It's a small island,' said Matt. 'There'll be waiters bringing our breakfast, and maids coming in to clean. You think they don't gossip?'

'Probably,' said Kate. 'But what does it matter? As it happens, I think you're less concerned with your cover story than you are with a possible slur on your virility. You can't bear anyone to think you haven't scored.'

The blue eyes glittered, and she saw a muscle move beside the firm mouth. She'd made him angry, she judged, and suddenly she wished very much that she hadn't.

He said softly, 'You really have a rock-bottom opinion of me, don't you, darling? I may as well justify it.'

He swung himself off the bed and came towards her. Kate shrank, but there was no retreat possible. She was trapped between his advancing figure and the bulk of the wardrobe unit behind her.

She said pleadingly, 'Matt—I'm sorry . . .'

'No, you're not.' He shook his head. 'But you will be.' One arm went round her, the other under her knees, scooping her up as effortlessly as if she had been a child.

He walked with her to one of the beds and dropped her, sprawling, on to the coverlet. For a second she lay there, robbed of breath and her dignity, then she twisted violently, attempting to roll across the bed and gain the floor on the other side, away from him.

But he was too quick for her. His hands caught her by the shoulders, dragging her back, pinning her easily against the yielding softness of the mattress. Then with one supple movement he was kneeling astride her, imprisoning her struggling body between his knees.

Kate was breathing hard, her breasts rising and falling quickly, as she glared up at him.

She said huskily, 'Well, we seem to have established that you're stronger than me, if there was ever any doubt. Do you intend to go on with this macho display, or are you satisfied?'

He said between his teeth, 'No darling, I'm far from satisfied. And this dress you're wearing is an invitation in itself.' The long fingers reached down and unfastened the button at the top of the bodice, then moved down, releasing the one at the hem of the skirt, rucked up to mid-thigh by her struggles.

Her little startled gasp broke off in her throat. She said, 'No—please—no . . .'

'But my pleasure is otherwise,' he told her softly, mockingly. Unhurriedly, he undid two more buttons, brushing the loosened edges of the dress away from her body. Her face burned, and she sank her teeth into her lower lip as another two buttons gave way. The fire was spreading to her body, because he was touching her now, his fingertips moving softly, sensuously over her skin, her shoulders, the curves of her breasts·where they rose above the demure broderie anglaise trimming of her bra, along the smooth, exposed length of her thighs. Her pulses were behaving oddly, her heart fluttering against her rib cage like a trapped bird, and there was a queer trembling ache deep inside her.

She turned her head away, feeling the softness of her tumbled hair under her cheek, closing her eyes as she did so, because she didn't want to look at him, didn't want him to see her eyes.

He was seducing her with his touch, she thought, dry-mouthed, tantalising her with this slow, calculated removal of her clothes, teasing her into wanting more. And she wanted so much more, she realised as his hand moved to the last remaining fastening at her waist, and her dress fell away.

He said, 'No protests, Kate? No last-minute pleas for mercy?'

She said nothing. Even if she could have trusted her voice, she wouldn't have known what to say.

She felt him move. She wasn't a prisoner any more, because now he was lying beside her, his hands sliding the brief sleeves of the dress down from her shoulders, freeing her arms. He touched her face, cupping her chin, turning her gently but inexorably towards him, and then his mouth covered hers. A long quiver ran through her body as her lips parted under his, shyly at first, then completely as his intimate invasion of her mouth kindled her response.

Her fingers curled into the woven fabric of the coverlet and her body tensed as his fingers traced the cleft between her breasts down to the clip which fastened her bra. He was teasing again, playing with the clip, allowing his fingers to explore so far and no further inside the fragile cups. His other hand skimmed the flatness of her stomach, and curved about the rounding of her hip.

She felt a little moan rising in her throat. The blood was singing in her ears, her senses were clamouring for a fulfilment they had never known.

He said her name against her lips, then the clip on her bra was twisted free and she gasped as she felt his hands on her naked breasts. His touch was a sensuous agony. He moulded and caressed, brushing his palms softly across her nipples, and for the first time she put her arms round him, her hands moving over his shoulders and clasping finally at the back of his head, her body lifting towards his in an arc of sheer abandonment.

She wasn't sure when she first became aware of the voices and the laughter. At first, they seemed to be in another world, then Matt lifted his head sharply, saying, 'What the . . .?'

The bedroom door bounced open and two women appeared in the doorway, carrying towels and linen. Looking over Matt's shoulder, Kate saw their embarrassed faces, their mouths forming 'o's of sheer consternation, then they were backing away hurriedly, and the door was closing.

Matt said something succinct and obscene under his breath, then he was off the bed and across the room in pursuit.

Kate watched him go, feeling dazed and breathless and curiously bereft. She half sat up, propping herself on one elbow, and as she did so, she caught a glimpse of herself in the dressing table mirror, and gulped, realising for the first time what they must have seen— the tumbled hair, the flushed, aroused face, her body naked except for a pair of flimsy briefs.

She crimsoned, fumbling in the folds of the coverlet for her bra, and huddling into it, struggling clumsily with the suddenly recalcitrant clip. Her dress was on the floor, and she kicked it out of the way as she slid off the bed and ran to her case, dragging out her robe.

A stranger's face looked back at her from the mirror as she tried to drag a brush through her tangled hair, then the image blurred under a mist of humiliated tears. She swallowed, fighting them back, as she heard Matt returning.

He kicked the door shut behind him. He said grimly, 'It was a wrong number. They actually wanted the bungalow next door.'

'Really?' Kate gave her hair a vicious tug with the brush. 'How very convenient!'

He came to stand behind her, putting his hands on her shoulders, and she twisted away from him. 'Would you mind not touching me?' There was a note of hysteria in her voice, and he frowned, the blue eyes searching her face.

He said quite gently, 'Don't you think you're overreacting?'

'No,' she said, 'I don't. You wanted gossip, didn't you? You wanted your unknown victim to be assured that you were here to have an affair and not to pursue him—or her. Well, you've achieved that beyond your wildest dreams.'

He looked at her incredulously. 'You think that I—arranged that? Kate, for God's sake, it was one of those things—an unfortunate coincidence.' He hesitated. 'For a variety of reasons, I'm more sorry than I can say that it happened.'

She picked up a pot of cream and began to remove what was left of her make-up. 'I expect you are,' she said expressionlessly.

'While you, of course, are totally unaffected.' His voice was cynical suddenly. 'We're back to the buttoned-up Miss Marston, the wedding guest's scourge, are we?' He shook his head. 'No way, Kate. That undesirable female has gone for ever, and bloody good riddance!'

'Transformed by you, I suppose?' Kate screwed the

lid back on the jar as if it was someone's neck. 'So what do you do for an encore, Mr Matt Personality of the Year Lincoln—kiss frogs and turn them into—princesses?' She drew a deep breath. 'My God, I despise men like you!'

'I think we've established that already—more than once.' His voice was icy. 'So what happened a few moments ago? Did you allow it to slip your mind?'

There was no answer to that. But for the interruption, she would have given herself to him, and she knew it. As, unfortunately, he did too.

She said bitterly, 'Oh, you're very persuasive. Your technique is probably faultless. But then it should be, with all the practice it's had.'

'Thanks for the unsolicited testimonial.' He was very white under his tan, and his eyes were blazing. 'I've never slapped a woman in my life, but I could really make an exception with you, Kate.'

Her glance slid away, her voice was ragged. 'Just leave me alone!'

'That,' he said flatly, 'I can guarantee. I wouldn't have you, darling, even if you came gift-wrapped. But that doesn't mean you're being let off acting the part I brought you here to play. In public, we're lovers. In private——' he shrugged, 'you can crawl back into your shell.' He glanced at his watch. 'I'm going up to the hotel bar for a drink. Join me when you're ready, and we'll have a long lunch, gazing into each other's eyes.'

'And if I refuse?' Kate's chin lifted defiantly.

He said softly, 'Don't even consider it. And don't think to get your own back on me by broadcasting the real reason we're here, because that would really make me angry, and you wouldn't like that.'

For a long moment his eyes held hers, then he turned away and she heard the door slam and his quick stride going away.

A long, sick shiver shook her from head to foot, and she sank her teeth into her bottom lip, fighting for self-control, fighting, too, against an overwhelming urge to cry out, to call him back.

She put her elbows on the dressing table and hid her face in her hands.

She thought, 'My God, what am I doing? What have I done?'

CHAPTER FIVE

SHE looked reasonably composed, Kate thought, as she walked through the grounds up to the hotel. She had changed into a bikini, covering it with a simple shift, striped in blues and greens, because she imagined that if she managed to get through the lovers' lunch he had described, they would probably spend what remained of the afternoon on the beach.

She couldn't find him right away, and she felt somewhat at a loss as she wandered through the reception area and the public rooms. One of them contained a bar, but it was deserted except for a lanky young man, hardly more than a boy, coiled moodily round a bar stool, staring into a drink.

He cheered perceptibly when he saw Kate, smiling hopefully at her. He looked lonely and at a loose end, and under different circumstances, she might have stayed for a chat and a drink, even though he was younger than her by at least a couple of years.

At last one of the smiling reception staff directed her to the terrace bar at the side of the hotel, overlooking the sea. Nearly everyone seemed to be there, sitting at the tables under the roof thatched with palm fronds, and Matt stood up as she appeared, and came across to her, taking her hand and bending to kiss her. She forced herself to remain passive under the swift, cold brush of his lips, although to any onlooker his greeting would have appeared tender in the extreme, she thought bitterly.

He gave her a steely look as he straightened. 'Come and meet everyone,' he suggested.

She was the cynosure of all eyes as she arrived at the table. Most of the smiles were friendly, she thought, as she returned greetings and listened to introductions, but a few of the women were giving her narrow-eyed looks as if they couldn't understand what a spectacular-looking man like Matt Lincoln was doing with an ordinary girl like her.

Don't worry, she wanted to assure them. I don't understand it either—especially what almost happened not an hour ago.

The least welcoming smile belonged to someone called Imogen who was dark, and as glossy and groomed as a magazine cover. She was with Robert who tended to be on the plump side, and Kate knew from a single exchange of glances that Imogen considered Matt a far more attractive proposition and was pardonably annoyed that he had company.

A girl who had been introduced as Fran, fair and pretty, leaned forward. 'Is this your first time on the island? You'll love it. It's still quite unspoiled, the tourist boom hasn't quite got here yet, but there are some marvellous places to eat.'

'You sound like a holiday brochure,' Imogen said sourly, her dark eyes pricing Kate's chainstore shift with probably total accuracy.

Fran shrugged, unruffled. 'Who cares? I love the place, and I want everyone else to do the same.' She beamed at Kate. 'What made you come here?'

Kate said feebly, 'It was Matt's choice. I—I didn't . . .'

'Well, we're glad you did,' Fran interrupted gaily. She shot Matt an impish look. 'An actual celebrity—unless, of course, you count Mr Big,' she added carelessly.

Kate swallowed. 'Mr Big?' She chanced a look at Matt, but his face was impassive. 'Who is that?'

Fran shrugged again. 'No one seems to know—or they aren't telling. But he seems to be behind most of the development round here. We went to see one of the old sugar plantations yesterday—they have it working as it used to be, but it isn't always open to visitors, and when we asked why not, they just muttered something about the boss's orders. Apparently it's on part of his land and he values his privacy. But it's certainly worth a trip.'

'Then I'm sure it will be one place that we'll be visiting,' said Kate, the irony in her tone for Matt alone. She was half expecting someone in the group to say, 'Hey, you're in the media. Do you know who this man is?' but no one did. Matt was chatting easily to some of the other men about hiring a boat at the Anchorage, about scuba diving and fishing, as if relaxing and enjoying himself were the only things on his mind.

'And tonight there's going to be a jump-up,' Fran went on, her eyes sparkling. 'That's local for party. There was one the other night, and it was super. A lot of local dancers came in and entertained, and a steel band. There were even a couple of fire-eaters, and we all did the limbo.' She sighed. 'Not like the islanders, though. They don't seem to have any bones at all.'

Imogen wasn't interested in the islanders' anatomical structure. She was watching Kate. 'Do you work in television?' she asked abruptly.

There was enough bite in her tone to still the conversation round them, and Kate found herself flushing slightly.

Before she could reply, Matt said, 'Not on your life. I have a strict house rule never to get involved with my staff. Kate's an artist.'

'An artist?' Imogen's eyes studied her disdainfully as if searching for splashes of paint.

Kate forced herself to smile pleasantly, disguising her anger at Matt's blatant hypocrisy.

'Actually I illustrate children's books. Perhaps you've heard of Felicity Fawcett?'

'No,' said Imogen, although of course she must have done. Felicity was hardly publicity shy, and her books were immensely successful.

'I have,' Fran interrupted eagerly. 'My little cousin adores them. And you actually do the drawings? She'll be thrilled when I tell her I met you.'

'So she should be,' said Matt. 'Kate has an amazing talent.'

He looked at her and smiled, his gaze suggesting that

they shared all kinds of intimate secrets, and there were some appreciative grins, mostly from the men around the table. She stared down at the drink which had been placed in front of her, hiding the angry embarrassment in her eyes.

The conversation became general again. Matt had said St Antoine was unsophisticated, but there seemed to be more going on than he'd thought, and there were a lot of invitations coming their way—fishing trips, swimming parties, dinners in town, jeep trips to the hills and to the rain forest at the other end of the island. If they accepted them all, then Matt wouldn't have time to get anywhere near this Mr Big, if he was the unknown target, Kate thought. But, of course, Matt wasn't doing anything of the sort. He was charming, he was interested in every suggestion, but committing himself to nothing. He was making it clear that he'd come there to be alone with Kate, not become part of a crowd, and no one was going to blame him or argue with that.

Kate sighed soundlessly, and sipped her drink. It tasted of fruit—mainly pineapple—but there was a potent kick underlying it all, which she felt she might be glad of before she was finished.

If she'd been on St Antoine with Matt for all the right reasons, the next half hour could have been one of the most magical ones of her life, because he was making love to her with every look, every smile. But that was his talent, she thought furiously. That was what he did on television—manipulating people, making them believe what he wanted.

And he was clever at it, she thought—God, he was! Only a short time before, he had sent her almost mindless with wanting him—not because he had expected them to be interrupted. On reflection, she acquitted him of that. But it would be far more convenient for him if she was his mistress in fact instead of just in pretence. He wouldn't be accustomed to sharing a room but not a bed, and in spite of everything he had said, he probably thought that any protests she might make would be merely token.

That had been Drew's attitude, and he'd been angry, violently and obscenely angry when he had discovered he was wrong. Even now, the fleeting memory of it had the power to make her freeze, every sense, every nerve flinching.

Matt said, 'Lunch,' and his hand closed over hers, pulling her gently to her feet.

'Oh, are you going already?' someone asked in a disappointed tone, and Matt said, 'I think I'd better feed her before she passes out on me.'

Fran was demanding, 'Are you going to come to the jump-up tonight?'

He smiled at her lightly. 'Doubtful. I think we'll probably have an early night.'

Kate half expected some ribald response to that, but no one said a word as they moved away.

He said, 'So what's the nightmare?'

'I don't know what you mean.'

'Of course you do,' he said impatiently. 'Just for a moment back there, you looked as if you were going to keel right over.'

She shrugged, making her voice expressionless. 'Perhaps I don't like a lot of strangers looking me over, speculating about what I'm like in bed.'

He looked faintly amused. 'Not even when they think you're a million dollars?'

'Especially not then.' She paused. 'And do you mind if I forgo lunch? I'm really not hungry.'

'I'd mind very much.' He sounded amiable, but his fingers tightened inexorably round hers. 'However justified your grudge against me, starving yourself won't help.'

When she saw the buffet spread temptingly under the trees, she had to be glad that he'd overruled her. She adored shellfish and there seemed to be an infinite variety to choose from, together with exotic salads and great bowls containing various sauces. Kate filled a plate, knowing that Matt was watching her, and expecting some mocking remark about her lack of appetite, but he said nothing.

As they sat down at a table, she said shortly, 'So, it's this Mr Big that you're after?'

'It is.'

'What makes him so fascinating? The fact that he's putting this island on the map?' Kate stared at him. 'Hardly the thing that interests you, surely?'

'On the face of it, no,' Matt agreed. 'And if this Mr Big was just any entrepreneur with an eye to the tourist industry, I wouldn't give him a second thought. But he isn't.'

Kate dissected a lobster claw. 'And you still aren't going to tell me who he is?'

'That's right.' He smiled coolly at her. 'You tend to overreact, and it's something I don't need.'

She said tartly, 'You mean there could be danger?'

'There often is.'

She drew a deep breath. 'Well, thanks a lot!'

'On the other hand,' he said, 'it could all be a damp squib, a figment of someone's overwrought imagination. But if I start getting close, I'll warn you. I might even put you on the next flight out. So you can keep those nightmares strictly under control.' He paused. 'And who's Drew?'

She dropped her fork, stammering, 'What do you mean?'

'You said his name in your sleep last night.' The blue eyes watched her shrewdly, and she wanted to lift her hands and cover her face.

She said at last, 'He was just—a man I used to know.'

'I'd gathered that,' Matt drawled. 'Not, surely, the man in the restaurant?'

Her lips parted. 'You saw us? You recognised me?'

He gave her an ironic look. 'Did you think you'd be easy to forget? And I noticed you noticing us, too, so I wasn't altogether surprised when you made contact.'

'Did Alison see me?' she demanded huskily.

'No,' he shook his head. 'Alison had—er—other things on her mind.'

'Naturally.' Her voice sounded thick. 'And while we're on the subject, what did you mean by that crack of yours about house rules? I didn't find it funny.'

'I didn't mean you to.' He shrugged. 'Nevertheless it happens to be the truth.'

'All right,' she said, 'so you didn't have an affair with Alison while she was working with you. Very honourable, I'm sure. But that didn't stop you moving in later.'

Matt put down his fork. 'You brought the matter up,' he said. 'So let's get the whole thing straight once and for all. I have never had, or ever contemplated having, any kind of affair with Alison. I can't of course speak for any plans she might have made. In fact I got a strong hint more than once that she was available, but I never at any time followed it through.'

'But you were bringing her here . . .'

'No,' he said, 'I was not.'

Kate looked at him in utter bewilderment. 'I don't understand . . .'

'Of course you don't,' he said with a kind of weary exasperation. 'That's what I've been trying to tell you. This is how it was—Alison showed up at the Television Centre one day. She was clearly unhappy and angling for an invitation to lunch, and against my better judgment, I decided to take her out. It was obvious that marriage hadn't lived up to her expectations, and she was hinting broadly that she'd like her old job back. I'm well satisfied with Carole, my present secretary, and I let her know plainly that there was no chance. She seemed to accept it. But I did not mention this trip to her, or ask her to go with me. I've no idea where she learned about it, except that she was in Carole's office for a while, chatting to her, and she probably used her eyes and ears to good effect.' He paused. 'She was never slow on the uptake. There was literature about St Antoine lying around, and tickets. If she'd asked a direct question, Carole would probably have seen no harm in answering it. After all, Alison taught her the job before she left.'

'I don't believe you,' said Kate.

He shrugged a shoulder. 'Then ask her yourself. And

don't expect me to explain why she should have told you a string of lies. As I've said, she didn't seem happy, and no doubt she felt she had her reasons.'

There was still food on her plate, but she pushed it away. She felt sick.

She said, 'It can't be true.' But she knew that it was, knew that if she was confronting Alison at that moment, what she would hear. Her voice began to shake. 'Why didn't you tell me . . . Why did you let me think . . .?'

'Because you made me bloody angry,' Matt told her. 'Arriving at the flat and accusing me like that. I decided you needed a lesson.'

Dull colour rose in her face. 'You don't go in for half measures!'

He looked at her grimly. 'You asked for it, darling. You had me tried and condemned from the first moment we met. I wasn't even allowed to speak in my own defence.'

Kate bit her lip. 'I'm sorry.'

'No, you're not,' he said derisively. 'A little mortified, maybe, a little less armoured in self-righteousness, but there aren't any real regrets, so don't pretend.' He pushed back his chair and stood up. 'I'm going to make a couple of phone calls and see about hiring some kind of vehicle. I'll meet you on the beach in an hour.' He paused. 'Don't look so shattered!'

'What do you expect?' She glared at him, and he began to laugh.

'That's more like it! You'll fight back, darling. I have the greatest faith in your recuperative powers.' His eyes met hers, held them, and the smile hardened on his mouth. He said softly, 'On the subject of regrets, I have a major one—that I'll probably never have ten minutes alone with the bastard who gave you that chip on your shoulder about men.'

He walked away, and Kate watched him go, suddenly and stingingly aware in spite of what he had said of a number of very real regrets, none of which seemed to make any sense at all.

The beach was wonderful, Kate decided as she sat in the shadow of a palm tree, allowing the coarse silvery sand to drift through her fingers. The sun was wonderful, the sea looked wonderful, and in other circumstances this could have been the holiday of a lifetime. It would still be a trip to remember, she thought ruefully, but for all the wrong reasons.

There weren't many people on the beach, and a kind of warm somnolence hung over the afternoon. Only brief snatches of conversation and muted laughter reached her ears above the soothing whisper of the sea, and a solitary windsurfer moved across the sunlit dazzle of the water.

Kate shaded her eyes and watched him, admiring his expertise. She'd never tried windsurfing, or water skiing either, which was another activity the hotel provided, but this could be the time to start, because she intended to fill her days as full as possible to stop herself thinking, brooding.

Not that it would be easy. Her head was still whirling in confusion over Matt's unwelcome revelation. In her mind, she had gone back over everything Alison had said, trying to find some clue, some explanation, but there was none. For whatever reason, her sister-in-law had deliberately misled her.

She led me up the garden path, Kate thought wryly, and I—I not only walked through the gate, I slammed it behind me and locked it too.

She pushed a hand through her hair with a little sigh. Oh God, what a fool she'd been, naïve and totally credulous, only too ready to believe the worst.

She'd wanted to think badly of Matt, to have all her inbuilt prejudices about him confirmed because he reminded her of Drew who had hurt without compunction, who had not cared for anyone or anything except his own interests.

Those prejudices had been her barrier to retreat behind, the weapon she had used on that instinctive immediate attraction. Matt Lincoln had spelled danger to her from that first moment, so the attraction between them had to be destroyed, because this time she was going to walk away unscathed.

She groaned silently. And what had happened to all those hard-headed sensible resolutions? They had led to a closer involvement than she could ever have dreamed of. She was here in a trap of her own making, and she would have to endure it until he chose to set her free.

If she was ever free again.

A shadow fell across her, and she tensed. A bottle of sun oil dropped into the sand beside her.

'You'll need to use that,' said Matt. He spread the large coloured towel he was carrying and lowered himself on to it. Clad in minimal black trunks, his broad-shouldered, narrow-hipped body looked magnificent.

Kate asked inanely, 'How did your phone calls go?'

'Reasonably,' he said.

'In other words, mind your own business.'

'Something like that,' he agreed.

'Except that you've made it my business—bringing me here, and forcing me to act in this charade!'

'Oh, really?' he said mockingly. 'So far, darling, there's been no force, and precious little acting either. I'm hoping for a marked improvement—now that we know each other better. And now, you'd better put some oil on. This sun is fierce.'

She shrugged. 'I don't burn that easily,' she said, and could have bitten her tongue out when she saw his slow smile. She uncapped the bottle and poured some of the fragrant oil into the palm of her hand. It felt good on her skin. She never tanned deeply, but usually her body acquired a warm honey-golden colour after a few days in the sun.

Now, she felt selfconsciously pale in the brief turquoise triangles which constituted her bikini, aware that Matt, propped on an elbow, was watching her, and wondering, if he was remembering, as she was, how he had undressed her only a few hours before, touching her, cupping her breasts in his strong fingers as if they were the petals of flowers. Her hand shook suddenly as she smeared the oil across her bare midriff.

He said, 'Shall I oil your back?' and she jumped, fumbling a little as she put the cap back on the bottle.

'Thanks, but no. I'm not planning on any serious sunbathing today.' Her voice sounded husky, and the words seemed to tumble over each other. She was expecting some sardonic remark, but all he said was, 'In that case, you can oil mine instead.'

He rolled on to his stomach, pillowing his head on his arms. Kate stared at him, the smooth bronze skin, the play of muscle engendered by his slightest movement, and knew she couldn't do anything of the kind.

She said, 'I don't think . . .'

'I'm not asking you to think,' he cut across her with sharp impatience. 'It's a thing any woman would do for her man, so you can do the same, instead of telling the world that you can't stand touching me at any price,' he added harshly, and Kate winced.

She began to apply the oil, her hands moving tentatively and reluctantly across his body, its warmth and strength tantalising her fingertips. Her face was impassive, tightly controlled, but she wished she was wearing her sunglasses, because she was terribly afraid he might turn his head and look into her eyes and see for himself the effect this sensuous contact was having on her, know that she was longing to bend her head and run her lips across the width of his shoulders and down the long, firm column of his spine. She wanted to let her soft palms caress him, learning every bone and sinew, and having to pretend an indifference bordering on aversion was almost killing her suddenly.

She smoothed the oil down to the narrow line of his trunks, then recapped the bottle, asking coolly, 'Satisfied?'

'Far from it.' Matt turned swiftly, catching her off guard, his hands reaching up and taking her shoulders, pulling her down on top of him, crushing her breasts against his hard chest, while his mouth touched hers in a passionless travesty of a kiss. The whole embrace could hardly have lasted more than a few seconds, but it seemed an eternity before he let her go.

He said laconically, 'Don't look so stricken, darling. The ordeal is over—at least for the time being.'

Kate caught her breath. 'Perhaps you could warn me if there are to be any—similar demonstrations,' she said huskily.

'Sure. Consider yourself warned.' Matt relaxed back on to his towel.

'That isn't what I meant . . .'

'Do you think I don't know that?' he asked contemptuously. 'But if you expect me to signal every advance, you can forget it. As you're the new lady in my life, I shouldn't be able to keep my hands off you, and no one would expect anything different. Just be thankful you'll have your nights to yourself.'

'Yes,' she said thickly, 'I will.' She rolled on to her back and lay looking up at the sky, feeling humiliated tears pricking at the back of her lids. At last she said, 'I've been thinking about Alison.'

'Not altogether surprisingly,' he said. 'What conclusions did you come to?'

'Not very many at all,' she acknowledged with a little sigh. 'I can't understand why she should have told me all those things when they weren't true.'

'It's not that difficult,' he said. 'Jealousy often motivates the most extraordinary behaviour.'

'Jealousy?' She turned her head. 'You mean she was jealous of your new secretary?'

'No, darling, I mean that she's jealous of you.'

Kate said flatly, 'That's ridiculous. She has no cause . . .'

He shook his head. 'I don't think Alison would agree with you. Before she got married, before she was even engaged, she used to talk about you a lot—your looks, your style, your career—and the fact that you were only Jon's stepsister, and no blood relation. She talked about that more than anything.'

Kate was very still. 'She thought that Jon and I . . .?'

'Of course she did. After all, you'd lived in the same house for a number of years; there had to be some kind of bond between you. I don't think Alison ever figured out what it was, not even after she was married.'

'That's because there was nothing to figure,' Kate said wearily. 'Jon's my brother, no more and no less, and Alison has no reason to believe otherwise.'

Matt gave her a straight look. 'And the fact that if your stepbrother had a problem he was more likely to turn to you and the rest of the family for help than to his wife—did she imagine that too?'

Kate bit her lip. 'Is that what she says?'

'She says she began to feel that your family was a kind of charmed circle in which she would always be an outsider.'

Kate was silent for a moment. 'That's not fair.'

'People who are in love and jealous and miserable are often unfair.'

'And Jon has a point of view, too.' She stared at him defiantly. 'He was convinced that you'd had an affair with Alison, that she couldn't get you out of her mind.'

Matt shrugged. 'She was probably trying to fight fire with fire. She was jealous and uncertain, and she wanted her husband to feel the same. It may not be very rational, but it's understandable.'

'And you have every sympathy with her,' Kate said bitterly.

'No,' he said. 'When she worked for me, she did what she was told with reasonable efficiency, but with very little effort she could have developed into a pain in the neck. I made sure that didn't happen while she was still employed by the television company, but I couldn't control what she did once she'd left, and she seems to have been having an emotional field-day. I have little sympathy for that, and none at all for the way she's involved me.'

Kate was feeling bitter herself, but just the same she was glad Alison wasn't around to hear that. However foolishly she had behaved, that tough intolerance would have bruised her.

She said slowly, 'You don't forgive easily?' and she was no longer thinking of Alison.

'You feel that I should?' He looked at her, his lip

curling mockingly, as if he read a plea for clemency into her words, and she flushed.

'I suppose it would depend on the extent of the injury.' And how much, she wondered, would it cost for the blow to his masculine pride that she had dealt? She wrenched her thoughts back hurriedly to the original topic. 'Are you going to say anything to Ally?'

For a moment, he looked surprised, and she knew that Alison couldn't have been further from his thoughts either. Then he shrugged again. 'Probably not. She would seem to have enough troubles already.'

Fortunate Alison, Kate thought, her heart pounding, because the glitter in the blue eyes was warning her that she couldn't hope to escape so lightly, as she was already more than aware.

In spite of the heat of the sun, she shivered suddenly and sat up.

'I—I think I'll go for a swim.'

'Fine,' he said. 'Don't get out of your depth.'

She gave him a brittle smile. 'Please don't worry about me,' she said, just as if he had actually been expressing real concern about the strength of her swimming. 'I'm a survivor.'

She walked down the beach towards the water, feeling his eyes on her with every step she took, her hands clenching in tension at her sides.

His warning was too late, she thought. She was already well out of her depth, and floundering.

CHAPTER SIX

FROM her seat in the stern, Kate watched the snowy wake of the boat foaming behind them as they sped across the water.

She wasn't particularly accustomed to speed on land, let alone the ocean, and the first few times she had been a little nervous. But seeing how calmly and expertly Matt and Winston, the coloured skipper from whom they had chartered the boat, handled the powerful craft, she had grown rapidly to enjoy these outings.

The level of Matt's expertise had surprised her. She hadn't expected him to be so much at home on the water, and had said so, and he had laughed.

'I was brought up beside the sea. The family business was a boatyard, and my brother runs it now.'

It was shattering to reflect how little she really knew about him. She had only been aware of the public image, and it had angered her, enabling her to ignore the possibility of the private man behind that image. Not that Matt seemed keen to make that aspect of himself known to her. Any details about his background, his likes and dislikes, were divulged almost reluctantly.

Even after a week of the closest proximity, it was evident that he still didn't trust her particularly, Kate thought bitterly.

For instance, she still had no clearer idea of what they were doing on the island, apart from having a wonderful time, or pretending to do so, she amended.

She didn't know how he usually went about investigating his victims, but she had a shrewd idea that it was not by water-skiing or scuba-diving, or exploring the island in the jeep hired to them by Winston's brother-in-law. He took photographs, but so did every other tourist, and Kate herself featured in most of them.

She had fully expected to be left to her own devices

94

while he pursued his own private enquiries, but it had never happened. If his aim was to convince some unseen watcher that they were inseparable, then he had certainly succeeded, she thought irritably.

She didn't know which was the harder to bear—the long daylight hours when other people were around, and she had to act the part of Matt's holiday lover, or the nights when she lay in bed, staring sightlessly at the passage of the moonlight across the floor of their room, and listening to Matt's deep regular breathing.

But all the agonising was on her side, she knew. Matt was totally casual about the proximity he'd forced on them both, even though sharing a room and not a bed must have been a new experience for him, too.

In the circumstances, he had been considerate, she thought. If he had wanted to go on punishing her, he could have created all kinds of difficulties, embarrassed her a dozen times a day, but he hadn't. In fact he had gone out of his way to ease any small awkwardnesses that threatened, and she knew she should have been grateful.

But it was a fact that the pleasant yet aloof courtesy he showed her when they were alone could signal only one thing—his indifference.

It was easy for him to be polite because he didn't care—because he didn't want her. He wasn't even sufficiently interested in her to persuade her into a casual affair, and although Kate might assure herself vehemently that it was the last thing she wanted, it was nevertheless humiliating to realise she didn't even possess that much attraction for him.

But it was hardly surprising, she told herself. She'd behaved badly towards him since day one, and Matt Lincoln had no need to bother about ladies who consistently gave him a hard time. There were plenty who would be only too eager to please, and Kate could name several staying at the hotel right there and then. Imogen had departed a couple of days before, still trailing her discontent like a shadow, but there were still covetous glances being directed from any number of directions, and the ambiguity of her position made them oddly hard to bear.

If she and Matt had been lovers, then their relationship would have provided her with some kind of security. She could have been able to signal tacitly, 'This is my man—so hands off!' But she had neither the confidence nor, she felt, the right to do any such thing.

And if she had been able to go on hating him, resenting him as she had done originally, then predatory glances from other women could have been shrugged off as typical, justifying all her prejudices against him.

But she couldn't accuse him of encouraging them, she acknowledged reluctantly. He took his part in the flirtatious banter that went on, but he never initiated it, and he shielded Kate from the goodhumoured ribaldry of some of the other men.

Not that they spent much of their time with the other guests at the hotel. They were out most of each day, contenting themselves with a simple lunch of fruit, or, if they were on the boat, fish which Matt and Winston had caught, cooked deliciously over a driftwood fire in some secluded cove. And they didn't always dine at the hotel either, which Kate found a relief, because invariably after dinner there was dancing, and she found that a candlelit table for two overlooking the water in one of the Anchorage restaurants was infinitely less threatening to her peace of mind than moving slowly to music, held close in Matt's arms.

Matt knew about body language—it had been the subject of a lighthearted discussion during one lunchtime that they had spent at the hotel, and he had talked about how he could read whether he had managed to put his television interviewees at their ease or on their guard from their physical attitudes as he talked to them. There had been a lot of laughter, and taking up exaggerated stances of relaxation and aggression by the others, but for Kate it had been a warning.

Because soon, if she wasn't careful, Matt was going

to read the growing desperation in her, the uncontrollable yearning as she melted into his arms, and then she would be in trouble.

Because he would either take what she was aching to give him, or he would reject her, letting her down gently, no doubt, but firmly just the same, and she didn't know which would be the most damaging.

With each day and night that passed, the desire to belong to him was increasing, and she was ashamed of the urgency of her response each time Matt came near her. For so long she had held her emotions under such strict control that she was shocked to discover how fragile her defences were. She had remained unscathed in the past, because there had never been any real threat.

Not even, she was beginning to realise, from Drew.

She could even look back with detachment now, remembering every painful detail—but, for the first time, without wincing.

Drew had arrived at the art college during her second year. He was a visiting lecturer, on an exchange visit from America, and he had a confident, sexy Californian gloss which had knocked them all off their feet.

Fancying him had been more than fashionable—in fact, a positive epidemic, Kate recalled, and she had joined in like all the others, although she never made one of the admiring crowd which usually gathered round him in the college canteen, or at social functions. She had her own circle of friends, her own passion for work to absorb her.

She still couldn't fully understand why Drew had singled her out, unless, initially, it had been a genuine recognition of her talent. He had made it seem so, but she could never be sure. She had been flattered by his praise, and by the increasing attention he'd paid her.

With the distance of time, she could acknowledge that flattery had played a bigger part in her infatuation than she had realised at the time. But then she had only known that she blossomed each time Drew looked at her with that smile in his eyes, or spoke to her with that special warmth. None of her previous experiences with the male sex had taken her further than a few kisses. She was almost pitifully naïve, aware for the first time of the urgings of her body, but unsure how to cope.

She had begun to meet Drew outside college hours. He took her to exhibitions and concerts, and introduced her to the kind of small Italian and Chinese restaurants that she would never have found on her own. They seemed to talk about everything in the world—or perhaps she talked, and he listened—but in spite of her shy probing, he said little about California and his own work there. He wasn't evasive so much as dismissive— as if the here and now were all that mattered. It was heady stuff.

And it deafened her to the warnings that were beginning to come her way. Someone hinted that Drew had a wife back in California, and there were rumours that Kate wasn't the only girl in his life here either. 'One of Drew's harem,' she heard herself described as, and it stung, even though she didn't believe it. She had had to put up with a lot of jealousy and spiteful remarks ever since it had become known that she was seeing Drew. So it was easy to dismiss the latest warnings as mere envy, instead of asking herself if there couldn't be a grain of truth in her friends' guarded remarks, because by now she was too bemused by love to care.

She wanted desperately for Drew to tell her he loved her too. She had a favourite fantasy where they married and went back to California together. She saw them living in a house overlooking the ocean. There would be a terrace, she thought dreamily, where she could paint . . .

But the declaration she longed for did not come, although the pressure on her to make love with Drew was increasing all the time.

She did not know what held her back from the ultimate commitment. She was unable to explain her inner confusion. She loved Drew, so why this reluctance to express her love in physical terms? Drew teased her about being an old-fashioned girl, but she could sense he was growing impatient, and she wished she could explain, and be reassured by him in some magical way.

But Drew had not been in the reassurance business. He was looking for easy sexual conquest, and Kate's reluctance was a thorn in his flesh, a slur on his virility. What little patience he possessed was soon used up, although Kate only realised this when she found herself actually fighting him off.

It was the most frightening experience of her life. He was a stranger suddenly, all the easy charm submerged by more primitive forces, uncaring that he was bruising her, hurting her. He swore at her, telling her to relax, but it was impossible. Shock had locked her muscles, and tautened her body into rigidity. His hoarse, excited breathing seemed to fill her ear. Her voice, pleading with him to stop, to leave her alone, sounded weak and fragile in contrast. His body crushed her, making her feel sick with disgust. She moaned helplessly, feeling scalding tears pouring down her face, her hands clenched into fists pushing unavailingly at his shoulders.

Then, suddenly, it was over. Drew rolled away from her, cursing under his breath, telling her harshly to get out. For a moment, she was too stunned to move, then she dragged herself to her feet, straightening her clothes, noticing almost mechanically that there were a couple of buttons missing from her shirt.

Outside it had begun to rain, and she wasn't prepared for it. Shaken and shivering, she waited at the stop for a bus that was inevitably way behind schedule, and a kindly woman asked if she was ill. She knew she would have to pull herself together before she reached home if she was to avoid arousing her parents' concern. And Jon's. She shuddered to herself, thinking of Jon's reaction if he knew what had happened.

She could hardly believe it herself. But at least it had made one thing clear: Drew did not love her and he never had. The things he had said, the things he had tried to do to her had proved that. She bit her lip, tasting blood, as she remembered with anguish the last thing he had said to her as she stumbled to the door of his flat, 'Why the hell did I ever waste my time on you, you stupid, frigid little bitch!'

It was that which had made her understand that she was just another sexual adventure—a challenge for him because she was a virgin. But he had never cared for her, and that was the hurt which would linger corrosively, long after the shock and bruises of his attempted violation had faded.

Going on with her college course wasn't easy, because Drew took his revenge in any number of ways, ignoring her in private, and ridiculing her work in class.

Whenever she saw him, he was the centre of an adoring female circle, obviously intent on showing her what she had missed by her recalcitrance, she thought bitterly. He would soon be going back to the States, so he wasn't even bothering to be discreet any more. If she'd dreamed she'd been the only one in his life, she knew better now. Drew had been right about that at least—she had been stupid—stupid and blind not to see him for what he was.

Worst of all, it was assumed by most people at the college that she had had a full sexual affair with Drew, and had been discarded by him when she had failed to live up to his exacting standards. At first, when the rumour got back to her, she denied it vehemently, but she soon realised that few people were inclined to believe her, aware that even her friends were regarding her with a certain scepticism. She supposed she couldn't blame them. She had been so besotted by Drew that it hardly seemed credible even to herself that she could have denied him anything.

Nor could she expect much sympathy for her daily humiliations at his hands. The girls who had envied her were glad to see her unhappiness, and even her friends felt that she had probably asked for it by getting involved with Drew in the first place.

It had been a hard and bitter time for Kate, and her work had proved her only salvation. And even when Drew had gone, and she knew that she would never have to set eyes on him again, or suffer his sly taunts, she wasn't altogether free of him. One of the girls in her year who had been most recently involved with him had a nervous breakdown, and threw up her course, and it was said that another girl had had to have an abortion.

Every new whisper filled Kate with anguish. She despised Drew for the way he used women, but she despised herself far more for her own weakness.

She had allowed his cloud to hang over her ever since, making her wary of every relationship, reluctant to commit herself even lightly.

And when she had seen Matt at the wedding, she had instantly judged him as coming from the same mould, and condemned him.

Well, she knew better now. Because if Drew had brought her to St Antoine, she wouldn't have been permitted to spend her nights unmolested.

She started violently as Matt's hand descended on her shoulder.

'I've spoken to you twice already.' His voice held a trace of impatience. 'In case you hadn't noticed, we've dropped anchor.'

Kate said, 'Oh,' feeling foolish.

Winston, who was putting things in the dinghy, looked round with a flash of white teeth. 'She's in a dream, man,' he said, giving Kate a knowing look.

Matt leaned down and took off her sunglasses, looking at her naked eyes with deliberate assessment. She knew he saw the shadows, the strained look, and she saw his mouth tighten.

'No,' he said abruptly. 'She's awake.' He handed the big frames back, and she replaced them hastily, thankful for their concealment.

Matt helped her into the dinghy, but Winston made no attempt to land with them when they reached the shore. Kate watched in surprise as he began to row back to the boat with a cheerful wave.

'I thought you were going to dive to those underwater caves you were discussing.'

'Later,' Matt said. 'Winston has a cousin living not

far from here, and he's gone to pay him a visit, and pick up some fresh local crab for lunch.'

'It sounds wonderful,' said Kate, with a bright smile. He gave her a weary look. 'Does it?'

He began to walk up the gently shelving beach, and Kate followed, her feet sliding a little in the soft sand.

'What do you mean?'

He sounded grim. 'I mean this has hardly been the trip of the decade so far.'

She bit her lip. 'Because you haven't got near your Mr Big yet? But—but there's still time, isn't there?'

'I'm beginning to doubt it,' he said flatly. 'Unless I get a breakthrough soon, the whole thing's been a waste of time.'

'Is it really so important?' Kate asked doubtfully.

Matt shrugged. 'It would have been to me—and to the company if I'd managed to pull it off. A genuine old-fashioned scoop. A dead man brought back to life again, courtesy of National Television.'

'A dead man?' Kate stared at him, her brows wrinkling questioningly.

'Except that like Mark Twain, reports of his death were greatly exaggerated,' Matt said. 'The man I'm here to see is Jethro Alvarez.'

Kate gulped. 'The South American dictator? But he's dead—he must be! They found the burned-out wreckage of his plane in the jungle after the coup and . . .'

'I'm not denying what they found,' Matt agreed. 'What I'm saying is that Alvarez was never in that plane. The things they found were no real identification, but the new régime couldn't wait to write him off, so they never looked further than the fact that it was his own private aircraft. I say he's here, in hiding, biding his time. Because a man like that isn't going to be satisfied with this little corner of Paradise for long.'

Kate could only agree. Jethro Alvarez had been a big man in every sense of the word. The small, backward nation he ruled with total authority was rarely out of the news because of him. He had put Santo Cristo on the map. He had risen to power from the kind of obscurity which encourages the wildest rumours. He was part Spanish, and part Irish, it was believed, a bearded giant of a man with fists like hams which he didn't hesitate to use when he was displeased. He had enjoyed his years as El Presidente to the full, and Santo Cristo had flourished to a certain extent. Alvarez had a persuasive tongue and he had talked foreign investment into his country, drilling for oil and mining for minerals, although fruit crops would always be its largest export.

His fall had been as spectacular as his rise in the end. There had been an army revolt and a coup, with fighting in the streets. For a while, no one knew what had happened to Alvarez, and it was supposed that the rebels had captured him with his family, then the news came that his plane had crashed in a mountainous jungle region while he was trying to escape.

And since that time, Santo Cristo had been torn by a sporadic civil war, with left-wing insurgents fighting the ruling army junta.

She said, 'But what gave you the hint that he might be alive, after all?'

Matt shrugged. 'Instinct at first. The crash seemed— too convenient, somehow. I'd met Alvarez during my time as a foreign correspondent, and he struck me as a man who'd have his retreat well planned and foolproof. He knew exactly how shaky his position really was. He ruled through his personality, claiming he was the people's friend, but he was under no illusions about them. He knew that as a nation, they hadn't even got to first base. The vast majority might be sorry to see him go in a desultory way, but they wouldn't fight to support him. And he was right. No one lifted a finger to oppose the coup, and all the fighting since has been done by small fringe minorities.'

'And was it instinct which brought you here to look for him?'

Matt shook his head. 'It was part coincidence, part detective work. I came here first a couple of years ago purely on holiday, but even then things were changing. It was clear someone was investing in the place, lifting it out of the doldrums, but I couldn't find out who, and that seemed odd, because usually these entrepreneurs are only too pleased to take public credit for their efforts. Then I remembered that Alvarez had married a white Creole girl, after his first wife died, and I decided to dig a little deeper. What little I managed to learn convinced me that I wasn't mad, that the mystery man round here could well be Alvarez. The tricky part was always going to be getting close enough to persuade him to answer some questions.'

'Do you think he knows that's why you're here?'

'He can't be sure, any more than he was a couple of years ago, otherwise he'd have been out of here on the next plane looking for another bolthole. That's been my private nightmare while trying to persuade London to back me in this—that someone else would get to him first—or frighten him off. But, touch wood, it hasn't happened yet.' He sent her a sardonic grin. 'So this masquerade of ours has been a partial success at least. Aren't you glad that your sacrifice hasn't been utterly in vain?'

Kate didn't look at him. She unrolled her towel and spread it on the sand, mumbling, 'Oh, it hasn't been that bad.'

'Hasn't it?' His tone was ironic. 'No one taking a long, hard look at you would ever believe it! Just now, on the boat, you were out on your feet. Why don't you spend your nights sleeping? Or is it really so impossible for you to relax when I'm around?'

Kate shook her head, saying something inane about strange beds, and he gave an exasperated sigh.

'Oh, for God's sake! We'll give it a couple more days, and if I'm still no closer to this interview, then we'll go home. And in the meantime, I'll use the couch in the other room. Will that make things better?'

'No,' Kate thought with a sudden pang. 'Infinitely, desperately worse.' But all she said quietly was 'Thank you.'

She unbuttoned the matching shirt she wore with her coral bikini, and slipped it off. Matt was stripping too, down to the usual brief trunks, and she studiously avoided looking at him, because, if he looked back, he might see something in her eyes besides the strain engendered by lack of sleep.

When he said abruptly, 'I'm going for a swim,' and started off down the beach, she wasn't really surprised. He tanned swiftly and deeply and his skin was like mahogany already, but he didn't work at it. He was too active to enjoy simply lying around in the sun.

His seaside childhood had paid off, she thought, because he was a good swimmer, strong but safe, with a healthy respect for the sea. She had spent a lot of time in the water over the past week and her own swimming had improved out of all recognition, although Matt and Winston kept a watchful eye on her, she realised.

Probably if she asked them to teach her to dive, they would have done so, but she didn't want to be a drag, and she wasn't entirely smitten with the idea anyway.

She turned on to her tummy, reaching behind her and undoing the strings of her bikini top. She was selfconscious about doing this when Matt was around, although he had never made any edged remarks about her coyness. Many of the girls at the hotel sunbathed topless, but there was no way that she would do so. Considering she had been through art college, and attended innumerable life classes, she was absurdly inhibited, she knew, but there was little she could do about it.

She had brought a book with her, a paperback family saga set against the Industrial Revolution with all the characters having a uniformly grim time, and she read a few pages, getting more and more depressed as she did so. It was the first of a series, so presumably at least some of them survived their vicissitudes, she thought, closing the book with a little sigh.

She pillowed her head on her folded arms, staring gloomily in front of her, considering what Matt had said. Was he really prepared to abandon his quest and go home? It seemed incredible, but that was what he had said. She should have been overjoyed. She would be getting out of an impossible situation, and her work was waiting for her in London, and yet she wasn't aware of any lifting of the heart. Quite the reverse, in fact.

After the shock of learning about Alison's devious behaviour, and the shaming realisation that she had been unfair to Matt all along, she had had time to think—to hope that she was being given another chance. Because Matt had been quite right when he had accused her of fancying him at the wedding. She had been attracted—shatteringly so. Which was why she had overreacted when he came across to her. Because she was terribly afraid that the defence mechanism which had served her so well since Drew was going to let her down.

Because she had wanted with every fibre of her being to be held in his arms, even for the duration of a dance. And the reason she had come here with him had been a twisted desire for revenge on him, because he had made her feel vulnerable again. She remembered the vindictive pleasure she had felt in planning his ultimate downfall. Only it hadn't worked out that way, because that bewildering, devastating attraction had still been there, seething just below the surface of her mind.

Sometimes, when she was alone like this, she let her mind drift, fantasising about what it could have been like between them, pretending that the bitterness, the misunderstandings had never existed, and that the only reason they were here was because they wanted to be together.

And that, she thought wryly, was the sheerest fantasy, because Matt's attitude since that first day had adhered strictly to the limits of their agreement.

She sighed abruptly and reached for her bag, dragging out her sketchbook. It was almost empty, and it should have been half full, especially if they were going to be leaving soon. She had intended to collect a whole range of memories and impressions, using drawings as other people might use cameras. Her own personal record of an unforgettable few days out of her life.

Not that she needed one. If she never drew another line, she knew that everything that had happened since they arrived on St Antoine was imprinted indelibly on her memory for ever more.

The prospect of returning to London with only memories, and the occasional glimpse of Matt on television to sustain her, seemed unutterably bleak. The life she had made for herself, which had always seemed so sufficient, so satisfactory, now seemed empty and sterile. It wasn't, of course, she assured herself robustly, and once she was back in the swing of things, this sundrenched madness which had possessed her would begin to fade.

Everything faded in time. She had thought she would never forget Drew, and the hurt and humiliation he had dealt her, and yet she had been able to remember every detail of their abortive relationship almost without a pang.

But then it hadn't been love she'd felt for Drew, she realised, but only infatuation, and she wondered with bewilderment why she hadn't been able to see that before.

She started out to sketch the scene in front of her—an odd-shaped rock backed by a clump of palm trees—but when she glanced down at the sheet in front of her she saw, with a kind of shock, Matt's face. It wasn't a portrait by any means, but unbeknownst to herself it had been taking shape under her hand, conveying all his restlessness, his vitality and thinly veiled impatience. She had made him frown slightly, she saw, and his mouth was a downward slash of pure arrogance.

If she had had to draw him, she wished it had been smiling, giving her the look of warm intimacy which told the world they were lovers. But that was all part of the fantasy. This was the real Matt Lincoln, dynamic and ruthless—and in total occupation of her heart and mind.

She thought, 'I love him,' and it was as if all the random thoughts, all the fantasies, all the doubts and uncertainties which had assailed her were a kaleidoscope which now, suddenly, fell into place and into focus, enabling her to see them properly for the first time.

The seeds had always been there, she thought numbly, but it was this hothouse proximity they had been in which had forced them to such rapid and startling growth.

Because in every way that mattered, Matt was still a stranger to her. She stared down at the harsh familiar lines of his face and knew a kind of despair.

She was so absorbed that she was totally unaware of his return until his shadow fell across her, and his voice, drawling slightly, said, 'Hardly a flattering likeness!'

Kate started, dropping the sketchpad, aware that her heart was thumping, her forehead beaded with sudden perspiration. She turned swiftly, facing him, and it was only when the questioning mockery on his dark face changed to a very different expression that she remembered too late that her bikini top was still lying on the towel beside her. She only had to reach for it and she would be safely covered again, but she was still held by her dream of delight, and the girl who lived in that dream gloried that Matt should look at her body and find it beautiful.

Her hands went up, not to cover herself, but to lift her tumbled hair back from her shoulders in a gesture of sheer invitation.

She saw Matt's blue eyes darken, and a tiny muscle tauten beside his hard mouth, and she met his gaze fully, no longer caring that the dream had become reality, and that she was incapable of disguising her feelings any longer.

He dropped to his knees beside her, and his hand reached out, touching her face, running cool fingertips down the curve of her cheek, and she turned her head, kissing the stroking hand, moving her tongue against his salt-damp palm.

For a long, tense moment he was still, hardly breathing, it seemed. Then he moved, and she was in his arms, and he was kissing her pliant mouth with fierce, demanding passion. Kate yielded almost deliriously, her arms going up to circle his strong shoulders, the blood singing crazily in her ears.

Matt lifted her, half turning her in his arms as he put her gently down on the towel, following her down almost before she could reach for him, his mouth searching hers completely, demanding its every secret, just as he would soon explore her willing body.

She had craved to feel his hands on her naked flesh for an eternity, and as his fingers worshipped her small, pointed breasts, a little moan of pleasure escaped her.

His lips traversed the offered arch of her throat and moved down to her sunwarmed shoulders, learning every curve, every angle and hollow. The dark head moved lower, and his tongue was a sweet torment in the cleft between her breasts before pursuing a slow sensuous path across her flat abdomen to her navel.

He lifted his head and looked at her, his face fevered and intent, then he bent to her again, his mouth adoring the aroused thrust of her nipples, the movements of his lips and tongue creating a delicious agony against her heated skin. Her hands locked round his neck, holding him to her, stroking the damp dark hair growing down to his nape.

No fantasy had prepared her for this, the depth of her own emotions, the strength of her own sensuality. She had not dreamed she could feel so strongly, that she could ache for this man with every fibre of her being. Because of Drew, because of his cruelty and insensitivity, all the passion in her had remained dormant, but she was awake now, alive for the first time, her senses demanding and responding, her flesh eager.

Matt's mouth burned on hers again, caressing its parted contours with sensuous delight, and his hands gentled her body, moulding every line and curve, sliding down to where the fragile strings fastened the lower half of her bikini on her slender hips. He loosened them slowly, brushing the flimsy triangles of material away, as if they were thistledown.

The sun was glowing against her closed eyelids, and the whisper of the sea seemed very far away. Her body convulsed in a shiver of pure sensual yearning as he began to touch her delicately, erotically, and very gently, as if he knew that these intimate caresses were a whole new dimension for her.

Her hands clung to his shoulders, because she was drowning and he was her rock. Her mouth tasted the salt on his skin in a small frenzy of desire. She could deny him nothing, and her slim body arched towards his in silent offering.

He drew a long, deep breath, and she felt the sudden tautness in his shoulder muscles as, unbelievably, he lifted himself away from her. Her eyes flew open, searching his face, seeing the guarded expression there, and trying to fathom it.

She said, 'Matt?' on a little breathless question.

His breathing was ragged, and the blue eyes were heavy with desire as he looked at her, but she had lost him, she realised with a pain that was almost too much to bear. He was back in control again.

He said, 'Kate—I'm sorry. I never intended this—you know that. God help me, I . . .' He paused, brushing a hand across his face, as he searched for words—words to cushion the blow, she thought with agony.

Her voice shaking, she said, 'You don't have to say any more. I—I understand.'

The humiliation of it made her feel cold and sick. She had thought Drew had made her suffer, but it was nothing to the way she felt now. She couldn't look at Matt as she retrieved the discarded scraps of her bikini and put them on, her fingers clumsy as she fumbled with the strings. Not that he was watching her. He had turned away abruptly and was staring out to sea, his back turned to her.

When she had been in his arms, she had felt no sense of shame about her nakedness, but now she couldn't be sufficiently covered, and she snatched up her shirt, sliding her arms into the sleeves with guilty haste. She stood up, grabbing at her novel, her sketchpad, and stuffing them into her shoulder bag. Matt rose to his feet, too. His face was bleak, his mouth taut and compressed as he looked at her.

He said quietly, 'Don't run away from me, Kate. I want to talk to you—I have to explain . . .'

'No explanation needed.' Her voice was a tone higher, and sounded brittle. 'It—it just stopped being a good idea—for both of us. This is your trip, and you made the rules.' She swung the bag on to her shoulder. 'I'm going for a walk.'

He took her gently by the shoulders. 'Don't go—not like this.'

'Please don't touch me!' She wrenched away from him, despising herself for that traitorous clench of the flesh that the merest brush of his hands induced.

For a moment they stood glaring at each other, then Matt turned away, muttering something violent under his breath. He bent and picked up an inoffensive stone, and sent it flying towards the sea with one powerful twist of his body.

Kate began to walk along the beach, shoulders hunched, stumbling a little, not looking back. She was terrified he might come after her, because she might cling to him, beg him to take her, beg him for his lovemaking even though there was no love to sweeten it.

She began to walk faster and faster until she was almost running—away from him, out of the dream, and back into the nightmare.

CHAPTER SEVEN

SHE was panting and breathless by the time she reached the rocky outcrop which blocked the way into the next cove, but she had no intention of turning tamely back.

Matt wasn't following, or he would have caught her by now, but she wanted to put distance between them, to find somewhere private and far away where she could lick her wounds in peace.

The rocks were high and not an easy scramble, and the water which foamed around their base was deep, because the beach shelved sharply, making wading difficult. Kate anchored her bag slantwise across her body and decided to climb.

She thought she heard Matt shout something in the distance, but she pretended not to hear, concentrating on finding hand and toe holds. She scraped her shin and the knuckles on one hand, and she welcomed the physical pain because it distracted her momentarily from the ache inside her.

She hauled herself on to the top of the rock and found another problem awaiting her. The sea had forced a channel through the promontory, and there was a gap of several feet to be traversed before she could reach the other cove. She looked down into the water and grimaced, remembering Winston's warnings about sea-urchins and their poisonous spines. Surely there must be some other way across.

There was some kind of stunted tree projecting almost horizontally from whatever soil it could find behind her, and after a moment's hesitation she grasped the unprepossessing trunk, bending it experimentally, trying to test whether it would take her weight. It looked precarious in the extreme, but rather to Kate's surprise, the roots showed no signs of budging. The tree's hold on life must be hardier than its appearance gave credit for, she decided, but it was still risky, and any sane person would climb down again, in more ways than one. Only she would rather dare a ducking at best and the sea-urchins at worst than do any such thing, she told herself fiercely.

She grasped the trunk with a silent prayer, reminding herself it really wasn't very far, then swung out towards the opposite rocks, hand over hand. Even in that brief distance, her arms felt as if they were being torn out of their sockets, and she had to grit her teeth in order to struggle on. She collapsed on her knees on the rock, breathing hard, and promising herself that there was no way she would take the same route back.

The climb down to the sand after that was a doddle. It was a much smaller cove, this, its beach almost bisected by a grove of palm trees growing down to the water's edge.

Kate walked slowly towards the trees, sucking her grazed knuckles, trying to calm herself, and get back on emotional balance. But every time she thought of her eager, wanton response to Matt's lovemaking, she wanted to die of shame.

Why, oh, why had he come back just at that moment to find her off guard and vulnerable? He probably thought the fact that she had been half naked was quite deliberate, an attempt to provoke him into making some kind of advance to her, and her total lack of inhibition in his arms could only have confirmed this for him, she thought unhappily.

But whatever the provocation, he hadn't allowed himself to be carried away for long, she reminded herself with some bitterness. He hadn't been sufficiently interested to indulge himself with a brief passionate interlude on a deserted beach, but what else could she have expected? Since the day they had arrived, he had shown her quite clearly that he found her only too easy to resist. And the fact that she had fallen deeply, disastrously in love with him made not the slightest difference.

She had sensed a need in him, as raw and urgent as

her own, but that was because he wasn't used to being celibate. Any girl, discovered in those circumstances, would have done as well. He had wanted a warm female body, but nothing more, and certainly no emotional commitment, and perhaps her eager untutored passion in his arms had betrayed her, warning him that to take what she was offering might bring unwanted complications.

The thought lashed at her, and she started to run again, up the beach and into the shelter of the palms which closed around her like a sanctuary.

The clustering trunks were denser than she had imagined, and it was suddenly dim and much cooler. She paused, getting her bearings, hearing the excited chatter of a bird nearby. She moved forward carefully, keeping a watchful eye on the tangle of roots and undergrowth at her feet, awake to the possibility of unseen hazards. Poisonous insects, she thought, or even—snakes. She remembered the guide at the old sugar plantation they had visited a couple of days ago explaining how mongooses had been imported into many of the islands to kill the *fer-de-lances* in the canefields, but that wasn't to say they'd all been wiped out, she thought gingerly.

She stood still for a moment, shivering a little, wishing she was back on the beach in the heat and light of the sun, tempted to turn back. Then she shook herself, and plunged forward again.

St Antoine wasn't a big island. There couldn't be a square foot of it unexplored, yet she still had the feeling that she was the first person ever to walk through this palm grove. Virgin territory, she thought wryly, until one saw the footprint in the sand.

And as if to underline the point, somewhere quite near at hand she heard a dog bark happily, excitedly.

It was the last thing she had expected. There were dogs on the island, of course, usually asleep in patches of shade, or hanging hopefully round the stalls on the street markets, waiting for scraps, but few of them seemed to have the energy to do more than snarl at each other occasionally.

Whereas this barking seemed to betoken a certain *joie de vivre*.

Kate made her way towards the sunlight, pausing for a moment in the shade of the palms, an incredulous smile curving her lips.

Beyond the trees the beach seemed to stretch endlessly, a perfect playground for a boy and his dog. It was a beautiful animal—a German Shepherd, obviously in the peak of condition, leaping and frisking round his master, who was throwing a piece of driftwood for him to retrieve.

Kate sat down on a fallen trunk and watched them, her artist's eye entranced by the sheer exuberance of it all. She found that she was automatically reaching into her bag for her sketchpad. She wanted to capture all that life and happiness if she could. Her work at home was usually detailed and exacting, but this would be an exercise in movement and flow, an impression created in a few brief lines.

Her pencil began to move hesitantly at first, and then with more confidence as she saw the sketch taking shape, and realised that it was working. She hadn't made a sound. She didn't want to intrude or interrupt, and she thought they were probably enjoying themselves so much that they wouldn't even notice that she was there. She could make her drawing, and then her escape.

But before she could finish, she heard the tone of the barking change and knew that inevitably she had been seen. The dog was loping towards her to investigate, and his master was just behind him.

As he got closer, Kate registered that he seemed vaguely familiar, yet she couldn't imagine where she could have come across him. He also looked frankly astonished, she noticed, as if she'd just dropped down from Mars.

He said sharply, 'Quiet, Caesar!' to the dog, who instantly subsided, then he looked at Kate. 'How did you get here? This is a private beach.'

'I'm sorry.' She got up. 'Some friends of mine are

diving nearby, and I felt like a walk. I didn't realise there was any restriction.'

He spread his hands rather helplessly. 'You didn't see anyone? You weren't told to turn back?'

'No one at all.' She tried a smile. 'Is that a guard dog?'

'A pet,' he said flatly. 'You're staying at the Paradis, aren't you?'

'So that's where I've seen you before. I was trying to think—but I couldn't remember Caesar. Are you staying there too?'

'No.' He shook his head. 'I live near here. But I sometimes go there for a drink.' He paused, then added stiffly, 'My family owns it, you see.'

Now she did remember him. 'I saw you in the bar the first day I was there,' she said. He'd been on his own. He'd given her that hopeful smile. 'You seemed rather more friendly then.'

He flushed. 'I'm sorry, but there are difficulties. People are not intended to come here. I cannot understand how it could have happened. My father will not be pleased; he—values his privacy.'

'Then don't tell him,' Kate said lightly. 'I'm sorry I butted in. I'll go now.' She stood up, making to slip her sketchbook back into her bag.

He was looking at it. 'You are an artist? You've been making a drawing?'

She pulled a rueful face. 'I'm afraid so. I suppose it must seem a cheek, but it was such a nice scene—free and happy.'

'Yes,' he said in an odd tone. 'I come here often with Caesar—to be free. May I see your drawing?'

Kate handed over the book with a feeling of resignation, half expecting him to tear the sketch out. He studied it for a few moments, then the shy smile she remembered began to spread.

'This is good,' he said. 'This is really wonderful! It is Caesar—and myself also, although you cannot see my face. Are you a professional artist?'

She nodded. 'I illustrate books, among other things.'

'Then they must be very good. I should like to see some of them,' he said promptly.

Kate laughed. 'I'm afraid they're for children, not adults.'

He shrugged. 'Sometimes the things of childhood remain the best.' He glanced again at the sketch, hesitating. 'I would like to show this to my father. He would be most impressed, I know.'

Kate smiled. 'Keep it.' She held out her hand. 'If I could just have the book back.'

The hesitation was even more noticeable. 'I was thinking that perhaps you yourself might show it to him. It is nearly lunchtime. You could join us. We have so few visitors.'

Kate was taken aback. 'I—I don't think so . . .' she began.

'There is some difficulty?' He looked crestfallen.

'I did mention that I wasn't alone,' she said gently.

He cheered up at once. 'No problem. We will invite your friend also—especially if she is as beautiful as you.' His smile had lost most of its shyness and was frankly admiring. Kate found herself wondering how old he was.

She said, biting her lip. 'My—friend is a man.' He looked wary, and she said, 'That obviously makes a difference. In the circumstances, I think perhaps I'd better re-join him for lunch instead. But do take the drawing.'

He made to hand the book over, but between them they bungled it and it fell to the sand. The boy bent to retrieve it with a muffled exclamation. When he straightened, his face wore an odd, startled expression.

He said, 'You made this drawing also?'

Kate saw that the book had fallen open at the portrait of Matt.

She gave a taut smile. 'Of course.'

'You—know this man? He is perhaps the friend you spoke of?' The words were quick and staccato, and Kate raised her brows.

'Yes, as a matter of fact. What of it?'

The boy shut the book and thrust it into the

waistband of the denim shorts he was wearing. He said, 'Then I must insist that you have lunch with us.'

Kate took an indignant step forward, then halted as a low warning rumble issued from Caesar's throat. 'What the hell do you think you're doing? Please may I have my property back?'

'Later, perhaps,' he said dismissively. 'Now you will come with me.'

Kate gasped. 'I'll do nothing of the sort!'

'I think you will.' He looked past her towards the palm grove and gave an almost imperceptible nod. She turned, and saw that a tall man had emerged from the trees and was watching them.

For a crazy moment she thought it was Winston, because he was of similar build, dressed in white pants and a striped cotton shirt. But as he walked towards them, Kate realised her mistake. He was burlier than Winston, and he certainly wasn't smiling as Winston would have been.

And, she realised with heart-stopping shock, he was carrying a gun.

They left her alone in the room. It was long, low and beautifully furnished, with sofas and chairs in silky pastels, but it was a prison just the same. One wall seemed to be composed entirely of glass, and Kate looked round for something to smash it with, but the elegant room contained nothing more lethal than a cushion.

The house itself had been quite a shock. From the beach there had been no sign of it, and as she had been taken through the clustering palms and along a narrow path, Kate had known real terror. But with the dog Caesar padding in front of her, and the man with the gun following behind, any attempt at flight seemed madness.

The high wall seemed to grow out of the ground in front of them like a special effect in the theatre. The old grey stones were like the rampart of some forbidden castle, Kate thought, as a heavy wooden door creaked open to admit them.

She tried to tell herself that she had fallen asleep on the beach, and that everything which had happened in the last two hours was just a bad dream, which would soon dissolve back to normality. Tried to tell herself, but failed.

The house was real enough, an enormous white villa, built on two storeys, the upper one of which was graciously balconied, and rioting with flowering vines. It wasn't the sort of grim fortress, Kate thought, that one would associate with a former dictator who had gone into hiding. There were several men tending the immaculately laid out gardens, but their interests weren't wholly horticultural, she realised, as they straightened, giving her and her companions keen-eyed looks as they passed by. She couldn't see any guns, but she had no doubt they were there just the same.

Inside the house, she was briefly aware of cool marble floors, and pale walls forming a background for displays of what appeared to be pre-Columbian pottery. Kate wondered cynically as she was hustled past whether Jethro Alvarez had visited the Santo Cristo museum as well as the treasury before his hasty retreat.

On her own, she wandered restlessly up and down the room, stopping every now and then to peer through the big glass doors which led on to a paved patio, well supplied with cushioned chairs and loungers. Beyond the patio, the ground seemed to fall away sharply, and she guessed that a steep path or steps led down to another part of the garden.

She stared unseeingly at the patio, thinking about the irony which had brought her here instead of Matt. She shivered, wondering how soon he and Winston would miss her and come looking for her. She had no idea what the time was—her watch was in her bag, which had been taken from her—but she guessed it was past the time when they usually ate.

And if they did come looking, would they know where to search?

She knew suddenly that the answer to that was 'yes'. That while the other choices of picnic coves might have been random, today's had not. Matt knew the island well, and Winston had been born here, so they both knew exactly what they were doing when they had set out from the Anchorage that morning. The underwater caves had merely been an excuse, she thought, recalling Matt's offer to abandon the story, his mention of needing a breakthrough soon. Clearly he had decided to force the pace a little.

She heard the door behind her unlock, and turned quickly, trying to look composed. The boy came in. He had changed into dark trousers and a shirt which made him look older.

He said, 'We're having lunch by the pool. My father and his wife are both anxious to meet you.'

He walked over to the patio doors and pressed an unseen switch in the frame which caused them to slide back, then stood waiting for Kate to precede him into the sunshine.

She noticed that he hadn't said 'stepmother' and that there had been a note of constraint in his voice, and wondered about it as they crossed the patio.

There were steps, a lot of them, wide and shallow and bordered by banked shrubs, and at the bottom she could see the azure gleam of water. It was a wide oval pool, the surrounding area flagged by coloured stones in various muted shades. At one end, a kind of pergola had been constructed, protected from the full heat of the sun by an elegant awning, and two figures were sitting there.

Aware that she was under close scrutiny, Kate lifted her chin and stared back.

Jethro Alvarez was a bull elephant of a man. She had only ever seen blurred newspaper photographs and occasional glimpses of him on television, but he had clearly put on weight in exile. One of the island shirts, gaily patterned, strained over his heavy body, and the bright, shrewd eyes seemed almost hidden amid rolls of flesh. Hands like hams, their backs lightly sprinkled with black hairs, clasped the arms of the chair he was sitting in.

Beside him, the woman appeared almost ethereal, but a closer look revealed a figure that bordered on the voluptuous in her jade green raw silk dress. Kate saw a beautiful, rather sulky face, the full mouth tightening in angry petulance.

On the table between them stood Kate's bag, looking prosaic and a little sorry for itself in such exotic surroundings. She felt her temper rising. She thrust her hands into the pockets of her shirt, and looked mutinously at Jethro Alvarez, who was making an effort to rise to greet her.

'Miss Marston?' The faint Irish burr in his voice seemed deliberately emphasised, she thought. 'Welcome to my house. May I introduce my wife, Leanne. My son, Carlos, you have already met, I think.'

Kate said stonily, 'How do you do.'

He smiled, showing strong, rather crooked teeth. 'We were about to have an aperitif before lunch. I hope you'll join us for both.'

'I'm not dressed for a lunch party,' Kate said. 'Nor am I hungry.'

'Then we shall have to tempt your appetite,' Jethro Alvarez said genially, subsiding into his chair which groaned under his weight.

He turned to a respectfully hovering servant. 'Bring Miss Marston a dry Martini, Jakey, and I'll have the same. And a Campari soda for my wife.' He picked up Kate's bag and held it out to her. 'This is yours, I believe?'

'You know it is.' She made no attempt to take it. 'I hope it told you whatever you needed to know.'

He laughed, the shrewd eyes appraising her. 'It told me remarkably little. Except that you seem to be a tidy person. For an artist, that is surely unusual.'

Kate shrugged. 'Boring, you mean? Conventional?'

'Hardly that. If you were those things you would not be staying on the island with my old friend and adversary Matthew Lincoln. When I was acquainted with him he was not, of course, the celebrity in your country that I understand he has become.'

'He's certainly very successful,' Kate agreed woodenly.

'And very ambitious, I think. It was a quality in him that I always admired. He stood out among the other foreign correspondents with whom I came in contact. But this time he has overreached himself.'

Kate raised her eyebrows. 'Really? In what way?'

He sighed. 'Must we prevaricate, my dear Miss Marston? His visit to St Antoine was made with the object of seeking me out, as we both know quite well.'

Kate stood her ground. 'I don't know anything of the sort.'

He gave her a weary look. 'Your loyalty does you credit, Miss Marston, but I would have found your profession of ignorance more believable if you hadn't accepted my identity and my continued existence quite so unquestioningly.' He smiled again. 'You follow me?'

She felt a dull flush stain her cheeks, but she returned his mocking stare inimically.

'Of course you do,' he went on blandly. 'And now that we have established where we stand, I hope we can relax a little. Your drink, Miss Marston—and, Jakey, bring the lady a chair.'

Kate accepted the glass she was offered and the seat, because it would have seemed foolishly churlish not to, but she couldn't relax.

'Would you prefer to join us under the awning?' Alvarez asked courteously. 'I prefer the shade, and my wife, like many Creoles, likes to guard her complexion.'

Kate wasn't altogether surprised. Leanne Alvarez might look sullen, but she had a skin like a magnolia.

Carlos, she realised, had disappeared, presumably back to the house. It was silly to regret his absence, because he was no ally, yet she did. But for the sketch of Matt in her book, he would have let her walk away from the beach earlier, she was sure. She sighed inwardly. That sketch had trapped her in more ways than one.

'You are a talented artist, Miss Marston.'

It was as though the big man in front of her could read her thoughts, and she jumped a little.

'Do you go in for portraiture as a general rule?'

'Er—no, I was telling your son. I illustrate books and do other commercial work.'

'Perhaps you have missed your vocation.' Alvarez produced the sketchpad suddenly, rather in the manner of a conjuror taking a rabbit from a hat. 'The likeness here is unmistakable.'

'I think successful portraits require rather more than that.' Kate sipped her Martini, made in the American way, and heady stuff.

'You don't regard this as a success?' He held up the pad.

No, she thought, it came from pain and longing and unrequited love.

Aloud, she said calmly, 'I find it hard to be objective about that particular drawing, for obvious reasons.'

As she spoke, her eyes met Leanne Alvarez's gaze and encountered a look of such smouldering resentment that she almost gasped out loud.

'Look at this, *querida*.' Alvarez gave the drawing to his wife. 'You remember Matthew Lincoln, of course. Isn't this the image of him?'

Leanne hardly glanced at it. She shrugged. 'Perhaps. It was a long time ago.'

Alvarez watched her, still smiling. 'Not so very long, *querida*. But soon you will be able to make an up-to-date judgment—when he also joins us.'

'You think that he will?' Kate took another sip of her drink.

'I know it,' said Alvarez. 'If only to satisfy himself that his lady is safe. And then you will both be my guests for a little while.' He sighed. 'I shall be sorry to leave this place. I did not believe any place other than Santo Cristo could ever seem like home to me, but I was wrong.'

'So you mean to keep us here while you move on somewhere else?' Kate said slowly. 'But isn't that just delaying the inevitable? If Matt found out you were alive and where you were living, then others will too. You can't stay in hiding for ever.'

'I have no intention of doing so,' Alvarez said sharply. 'I have other plans, but they are still at a delicate stage. Your lover's intrusion has come at an inopportune moment.' He shrugged wryly. 'But I have been fortunate so far.'

'Perhaps he won't come here.' Kate was playing with the stem of her glass. 'Perhaps he's gone back to the Anchorage in the boat and is phoning the world press at this very moment, telling them all where you are.'

He shook his head, smiling. 'You underestimate your charm for him, I am sure. What do you say, Leanne?'

Leanne remained silent, but hunched an irritable shoulder. She didn't say much, Kate reflected, but she could look volumes.

'We will delay lunch for a little while and wait for him.' Alvarez was saying.

Kate shrugged. 'Fine—but you might get very hungry.'

Alvarez shifted in his chair, his smile widening as his gaze went past Kate. 'I think not,' he said softly.

She put down her empty glass and turned. Matt was walking towards them, Carlos by his side. She jumped up and ran to him. 'Matt!'

He said sharply, 'Are you all right?' He held her away from him, his eyes searching her face.

She nodded, fighting tears. 'I'm sorry—I've made such a mess of everything, haven't I?'

'That,' he said, 'remains to be seen.'

Holding her hand, he walked towards Alvarez. 'Good afternoon, Señor Presidente. How nice to meet with you again. I'd expected it to be in the next world rather than this one, however.'

Alvarez chuckled, his bulky body shaking with mirth. 'For a little while, my friend, perhaps. But you were not deceived for long, may the devil fly away with you. Now I must go on my travels yet again.'

Matt's eyebrows lifted. 'I fail to see why. Why not a spectacular resurrection, courtesy of National Television?'

Alvarez's shoulders shook. 'Because, *amigo*, it would be the shortest resurrection in the history of the known world. My enemies would see to that, if only because they had been made to look foolish by so readily accepting my death. How long do you think I would last once they learned where I was?'

'As long as you wanted,' Matt said blandly. 'How many attempts did you survive in Santo Cristo? Three, was it, or four?'

Alvarez laughed. 'In those days, my friend, we lived in interesting times, but no longer.' He gave a deep sigh. 'I am an old man in exile, broken in health, broken in spirit. The will to fight has gone out of me.'

'Señor Presidente, you're breaking my heart,' said Matt in frank appreciation. He shrugged. 'But if that's your last word, then I'll just have to accept it.'

Alvarez nodded. 'You were always a realist, my friend. And now let us relax and enjoy this beautiful day that the good Lord has sent us, and the lunch which my chef has prepared,' he said prosaically.

Leanne Alvarez stood up, smoothing her jade dress over her rounded hips.

'I will order it to be served,' she said, her voice low and husky. She looked full at Matt, her full lips parting in the first smile Kate had seen from her. 'Welcome, Matthew. It is good to see you again.'

Matt took her extended hand politely in his. 'Señora Alvarez.'

'Oh, come,' she pouted. 'It was always Leanne in the old days.'

His mouth twisted slightly. 'You were not married in the old days.'

'Jethro,' Leanne swung towards her husband, 'tell him there is no need for this formality.'

Alvarez's face was enigmatic. 'As she says, *amigo*, there is no need for such—old friends to be on such formal terms.'

As she glanced from one to the other of them, Kate's uneasiness increased rapidly.

The speed with which lunch was served almost took

her breath away. A table appeared and was laid with
the efficiency of long practice, and chairs were
assembled around it. Kate had imagined she wouldn't
be able to eat a thing, but to her surprise she found she
was doing full justice to the consommé, and to the
poached red snapper in its creamy sauce with saffron
and clams, so much so that she was forced to say a
regretful no to the flan made with coconut purée which
followed. Matt and Jethro Alvarez talked easily
together, discussing the changes that had come to the
island over the past few years, although Alvarez's role
in these changes was touched on only lightly. Seated
between Leanne and Carlos, Kate found herself rather
isolated. Leanne toyed with her food, her extravagantly
lashed eyes flickering between Matt and her husband,
while Carlos applied himself to his meal in sullen
silence.

Kate ventured a few remarks to him, but received
only monosyllabic replies. The contrast between the
carefree boy on the beach and his present attitude
was quite incredible, and she wondered how easy she
found it to live in his father's shadow. Or was it
Leanne who brought about the change in him? she
asked herself, remembering his odd reference to his
father's wife.

The meal over, coffee was served, and a box of long,
dark cheroots was brought. Alvarez took one. 'A
reminder of home,' he remarked, gesturing to Matt to
help himself. He gave a sentimental sigh. 'They were
good days, *amigo*. It is a long time since I had a chance
to talk about them with someone who remembers too.
You will stay for a day or two—indulge an old man's
whim for nostalgia?' He bowed gallantly towards Kate.
'And your lovely companion, of course,' he added.

Kate tensed, and she glanced at Matt, wondering
how she could warn him about Alvarez's real
intentions, willing him to look at her. Their eyes met,
and he raised an eyebrow coolly, questioningly, before
transferring his attention back to Alvarez.

'Our privilege, Señor Presidente.' He lifted his cognac

in a toast. 'I shall need to telephone the hotel, of course, to explain our absence.'

'That will be done,' said Alvarez, smiling.

Matt continued unruffled, 'And I've arranged to call a friend of mine at the Anchorage this evening. He's a nervous guy, and unless he hears from me in person, he might start alerting all sorts of outside agencies!'

There was a long, heavy silence, as the two men looked at each other. Kate felt a trickle of perspiration slide into the cleft between her breasts.

At last Alvarez shrugged. 'Then, naturally, you must make your call,' he said with a touch of resignation. 'I am a realist also. I hope you will confine the call to essentials.'

Matt said with a faint smile, 'You have my guarantee.'

Alvarez drank his coffee and heaved himself out of his chair. 'And now you must excuse me. I always rest these days after lunch. But my house, my gardens are at your disposal. Swim in the pool, use my library, the projection room if you wish. And we will meet at dinner. Come, *querida*.' He held out an imperative hand to Leanne, who rose to her feet without any great enthusiasm.

'Just a minute.' Kate found her voice. 'You—you can't keep us here like this. It's ridiculous!'

Jethro Alvarez gave her a reproachful look. 'Señorita—as my honoured guest.'

Matt intervened, 'I think Kate is a little overwhelmed by everything that has happened, Señor Presidente. And a little concerned over the fact that we have only the clothes we stand up in,' he added.

Alvarez made a negligent gesture with the cheroot. 'There is no problem—no problem at all. Carlos and my wife will be happy to loan you anything you need for your stay, isn't that so, *querida*?' he queried, drawing Leanne's hand through his arm.

Leanne's dark eyes travelled down Kate's slender figure with open mockery. 'It will be my pleasure,' she said. 'My maid will bring a suitable selection of clothes to your room during the afternoon.'

'Thank you,' Kate managed. She was shaking inside, not so much with fright as with temper.

'Well?' said Matt when they were alone. 'Shall we do as the man says and look round, or do you want to rest, too?'

She faced him stormily, breasts heaving. 'I just want to get out of here!'

'I imagine Jethro's private army might have something to say about that,' he said, shrugging. 'He'll let us go when he's good and ready and not before. His motives for keeping us here interest me,' he added thoughtfully.

'Well, allow me to explain them to you,' Kate said tautly. 'We're to remain here while he takes off for an unknown destination, and next time he does not mean to be found.'

Matt smiled slightly. 'Perhaps.'

'He told me so himself,' she said, stung.

'I'm sure he did, but that doesn't mean he intends to do it. It's just one of several possibilities, as he and I are both aware.'

'Well, I wish you'd left me out of your little games,' Kate muttered crossly.

'So do I,' he snapped. 'Why the hell did you have to go dashing off like that, anyway? And what were you doing clambering all over those rocks? Didn't you realise you could have fallen and damaged yourself, you little fool?'

'Compared with what's happened, that's the option I'd have gone for,' she said moodily. 'You never had the slightest intention of abandoning this story, did you?'

His hands descended on her shoulders. 'I meant everything I said. As you must have guessed by now, Winston didn't bring us to the cove by chance this morning, but I swear I never intended for you to be involved. I'd arranged that while I was trying to get in here, he would take you back to the Anchorage and on to the hotel. And I'd left instructions at the desk. You could stay, or you could fly out, whether or not I was free to join you. That's what I'd planned.'

'Then it's a pity it didn't work out like that.' She wriggled free, glaring at him. 'I could have been safely on my way home now, instead of cooped up here in this—prison!'

'Kate, calm down!' He sounded almost pleading. 'It won't be as bad as you think—and I promise it will only be for a couple of days.'

'A couple of days?' she threw back at him recklessly. '*Only* a couple of days? A couple of hours would be too much! Can't you see that it's you that I want to be free of? You!'

'Is that a fact?' The blue eyes were chips of ice. 'Well, that's just tough, my little shrew, because we're stuck with each other as never before. And believe me, you can be no sorrier about it than I am!'

He turned and walked away. Kate watched him go, tears blurring her eyes, her mouth silently framing his name, and all the secret, yearning words of love that she dared not utter.

CHAPTER EIGHT

THE afternoon dragged wretchedly past. Kate made another abortive attempt to read her book, but she found it impossible to concentrate. The image of Matt's face, harsh and bleak, kept intruding between herself and the printed page, and those last dismissive words echoed tormentingly in her ears.

At last she put it aside and went for a walk, but she found the awareness that she was always under scrutiny, the figures moving unobtrusively never too far away, distinctly unnerving, and she gave up and went back to the poolside.

Presently Jakey appeared, bringing a tray of iced tea, and towels in case she wanted to bathe. The water looked inviting, it was true, but Kate found it easy to resist. Her present state of unhappiness would probably make her sink like a stone, she thought.

There was no sign of Matt, but then what else could she have expected after what had passed between them? And she could never explain that her almost hysterical outburst had been triggered off because she had sensed something approaching tenderness in him which was more than she could bear.

To protect herself, she had to convince him that her unguarded response to him that morning on the beach had been prompted by the senses only, and not the emotions.

Things were foul enough without Matt realising that she had fallen in love with him, and perhaps pitying her, she told herself. And if her bitter words resulted in him holding her at arm's length for the remainder of their stay on St Antoine, then she might be able to keep her secret, and return to London relatively unscathed. 'Might' being the operative word, she thought ruefully.

She had nearly betrayed herself earlier when she had

run to him, but hopefully he would interpret that as sheer relief.

With a sigh, she took out her sketchpad and made a quick drawing of the area round the pool, but the sketch seemed flat and lifeless. She was about to rip it up in disgust when she heard the sound of a masculine tread approaching, and instantly directed all her attention to her drawing, forcing her fingers to move steadily, even though she could not control the wild beating of her heart.

She was startled, and a little relieved, when the dog Caesar ambled up and put his nose in her hand. Carlos was not far behind him.

'Heel, Caesar,' he ordered sharply. 'I am sorry—we are interrupting you.'

'No.' Kate put down her pad, but he was turning away. She raised her voice slightly. 'Please come back.' And when he showed no sign of doing so, she added, 'After all, you forced me to come here. The least you can do is talk to me!'

He swung round, almost gaping at her for a moment, then his face dissolved into amusement, and he was the cheerful boy she had seen romping with Caesar on the beach again.

He came back and pulled up a chair, the dog flopping easily into the nearest patch of shade.

He said, 'And for that I am really sorry, but you must understand I did not know what to do.' He flushed slightly. 'When I saw you at the Paradis, I did not know that you were the companion of Señor Lincoln.'

'Well, how could you? We'd only just arrived,' she said. 'Come to that, I didn't know who you were either.' She hesitated. 'You just looked as if you needed company. I thought perhaps you'd come on holiday on your own and found out it was a mistake.'

'No,' Carlos said quietly. 'I am not supposed to visit the hotel, in case I am recognised, but sometimes when this house becomes more than I can bear, I escape for a while.'

Kate gave him a sympathetic look. 'Are you supposed to be dead too?'

Carlos shook his head. 'I was at school in the United States when the news came of the revolution, and the crash. My father had taught me a code whereby I could recognise valid messages from him. I was just beginning to realise what had happened, to grieve for him and all I had lost, when such a message came.' He spread his hand expressively. 'You cannot imagine how I felt. One moment I was in despair—then, suddenly, there was hope.' He gave a twisted smile. 'That was before I knew what our life would be.'

There was a pause, then Kate said awkwardly, 'On the surface, it seems very comfortable here.'

'For the tourists no doubt it is a paradise,' Carlos said abruptly. 'But it is not Santo Cristo where I was born. I no longer have the life I was used to there—and,' his face became bitter—'other things have changed also.'

Kate knew intuitively that he was talking about Leanne, and she said nothing. After a pause he went on, 'I suppose I should have expected—but I did not. After my mother died, there were always women, but I could understand that. I never thought that he would marry again—or marry such a woman.'

There was another pause, then Kate said awkwardly, 'Because your stepmother is so much younger than your father, perhaps?'

He shook his head. 'That would not have concerned me.' He took a breath. 'But to put a woman like that— a woman who had been a singer in a cheap bar—in my mother's place, that is what matters.'

Kate said half to herself, 'If she was an entertainer, that's probably how Matt came to know her.'

Carlos said bitterly, 'Without doubt. The club where she worked was much frequented by the foreign press. She was probably his mistress before she became my father's.' He looked up at Kate's sharp intake of breath. 'But you must have realised that?'

She said, 'Yes—I suppose so.' She rallied herself. 'But it was over a long time ago, Carlos, and whatever she did before she became married to your father shouldn't really matter. He's a shrewd man—he must have known about her past, and if it's made no difference to him, then perhaps you should try to accept it too.'

He said, 'If it was only the past, perhaps I could, but she has never been faithful to him.' He flung up his head and looked at her. 'That is why I am sorry that I made you come here, because if she wants Matthew Lincoln, then she will take him and you will be hurt.'

Kate stared at him. She said quietly, 'Don't you think you're letting your dislike for her—twist your viewpoint? Even if she and Matt were once intimate, they wouldn't—they couldn't . . .' Her voice trailed away helplessly.

Carlos said, 'You do not know her. I tell you, you do not know her—what she is capable of.' His voice sounded intensely weary. There was silence for a moment, then he said, 'But I am being dismal. When you said you wished to talk, it was not of such matters as these, I think. Would you like to swim? It will soon be time to change for dinner.'

Kate didn't want to swim, but she realised Carlos was making a real effort to overcome his mood of bitter introspection, so she agreed, and discovered that the exercise and relaxation provided by the water were just what she needed.

Carlos found a large coloured ball, and they played noisy and idiotic games, while Caesar padded gravely up and down the side of the pool as if he was considering joining them.

Kate felt almost regretful when Carlos announced that it was time they were going in. He swung himself athletically on to the side of the pool and reached down to help her out, pulling her up beside him.

She said, laughing, 'You know, you're stronger than you look.'

He said softly, 'And you, Kate, are very beautiful.' He bent his head and kissed her, his mouth tentative. She didn't want the embrace, but avoiding it would have meant stepping backwards into the pool, which was ridiculous. She didn't return the kiss, and after a moment he let her go, and handed her a towel.

They had been in the pool longer than she'd thought. Deep shadows were beginning to spill across the flags as the sun went down.

Carlos said, 'You love him very much, this Matthew Lincoln. And I wish you did not, because I am afraid—very much afraid—that you will be unhappy.'

Kate looked at the encroaching shadows, and shivered, pulling the enveloping towel closer round her body. She picked up her bag and discarded shirt.

She said, 'I think I'd better go and find my room.' She sent Carlos a quick meaningless smile, then walked ahead of him up to the house.

The room Jakey showed her to was dim, the shutters drawn to close out the sunlight. Kate heard the splash of water, and guessed that Matt was using the shower in the adjoining bathroom. She went slowly across the room and opened the shutters wide, letting the remaining sunlight illumine the room.

It was a glamorous room, rather too much so for Kate's taste. All the elaborate fitted furniture was white trimmed with gilt, and the huge bed was draped in gold silk with an enormous matching swathed canopy.

A number of dresses had been hung on the front of one of the wardrobes, and Kate examined them. They were expensive and well made, but they had been chosen for Leanne's size, and Leanne's colouring, and the styles were over-elaborate.

Kate sighed soundlessly as she went through them. She supposed it shouldn't matter, but she loathed the idea of having to appear at dinner dressed in Leanne's hand-me-downs. Dejectedly, she picked out the simplest, a floating affair in pale green crêpe-de-chine with a silver belt which could, she hoped, be cinched in tightly to give the illusion of a fit.

But there was worse to come. On the bed Kate found undies, brand-new and still in their original wrappings. She looked at them with dismay. She had never thought her own underwear dowdy, but these bordered on the exotic. There was even a nightdress, black and sheer, slashed provocatively from waist to hem at each side.

She heard a sound behind her and turned. Matt was standing in the bathroom doorway, watching her. He wore a towel draped round his hips and nothing else, apparently.

Kate swallowed, dropping the scraps of silk and lace she was holding as if they had burst into flames.

'Oh—hello.' She tried to sound casual, but embarrassment won.

'Welcome to our mutual cell,' he said coldly. 'Before you start pushing the panic button, allow me to point out that other door. It leads to a small dressing room, which also contains a small bed. I shall be using that.'

Kate bit her lip. 'I see.'

'That,' said Matt, 'is a debatable point.'

He moved towards the door he had indicated, and she said, 'Matt——' quickly before her courage deserted her.

The face he turned to her was not encouraging. 'Well?'

She said huskily, 'I just want you to know that—that I'm sorry for what I said earlier.'

'Are you?' His shrug professed pure indifference. 'It really doesn't matter. And I probably should apologise to you. This trip has been an unmitigated bloody disaster from beginning to end, and I should never have brought you.' He gave a short laugh. 'That should teach me to give way to dangerous and stupid impulses!'

Kate winced inwardly. She said, 'But has it really been so disastrous? You've achieved what you wanted. You're here in this house.'

He gave her a cold, ironic look. 'And you think that's all there is to it?'

She frowned. 'You mean that you still won't get your interview? That perhaps we'll go down to dinner and find we're the only ones here?'

'I don't think the Señor Presidente will go to those extremes, just yet,' said Matt. 'I think he's too intrigued with the situation to run out on us. But of course I could be wrong.' He lifted one shoulder in a shrug. 'I seem to be making a habit of it lately.' He moved to one of the wardrobes and collected a handful of the clothing it contained. 'I'll move these things into the dressing room. It has its own door to the gallery, so I shouldn't need to disturb you again.' He sent her a brief, wintry glance, and went into the room he had indicated, shutting the door behind him with un-necessary firmness.

Kate sank down on the bed, a trembling sigh escaping her lips. There was no need to have closed the door. The barrier was there already, and more impenetrable than any conventional wooden panels.

But wasn't that what she wanted? she asked herself dejectedly. She needed to keep Matt at a distance if she was to retain some semblance of pride or self-respect. Only a matter of hours ago, she had been willing to give him everything—her body, her soul and her heart—and he had walked away.

A casual encounter with someone as sophisticated and experienced as himself he might have welcomed. But he didn't want any semblance of involvement. And he certainly didn't need love.

She showered, applied the modicum of moisturiser and lip-colour she had in her bag, then reluctantly got into the green dress. Belted as tightly as it would go, it wasn't too bad, she supposed, surveying herself dejectedly, even though the wide scooped neckline slid off first one shoulder and then the other, making it impossible for her to wear a bra.

She smoothed the soft fluid lines of the material over her slim hips, twisting slightly to see how low the neckline dipped at the back.

The knock on the door was a surprise. She had heard Matt leave his room some time before, but perhaps he had relented and come back for her, she thought hopefully.

She opened the door and came face to face with Leanne.

Resplendent in a tight-fitting dress in a deep shade of cerise, the other woman was smiling.

She said, 'I came to see that you have everything you need. May I come in?'

'Of course.' Kate stood aside rather awkwardly. 'You—you've been very kind.'

Leanne shrugged gracefully. 'It is only for one evening, after all. My husband is arranging for your luggage to be brought here from the Paradis.'

'He is?' Kate bit her lip. 'Then it seems that he really does expect us to stay?'

'Did you doubt it?' Leanne rummaged in her bag, producing cigarettes and a lighter. 'You smoke? No?' She lit her own, inhaling deeply. 'You do not seem very happy at the prospect of staying in this house? Yet you accompanied Matthew of your own will. You knew what the risk might be.' The dark eyes glittered slightly. 'Or did you imagine he would not succeed in his aim?'

Kate shrugged lightly. 'It doesn't really matter what I thought,' she parried. 'We're here now, and I must just make the best of it.'

Leanne blew a smoke ring. 'Does not Matthew's company compensate for any—inconvenience?' There was a sudden sharpness in her voice which did not escape Kate.

She felt sudden colour rise in her face. 'Of course.' Leanne's smile widened, and her gaze went past her to the closed dressing room door, and lingered there quite deliberately.

Kate felt herself stiffen.

Leanne spoke again, her tone conveying amused puzzlement. 'You are not at all his usual type.' Her eyes looked Kate over from the crown of her head to her bare feet.

Kate moistened her lips. 'Perhaps his—tastes have altered.'

'I think they must have done.' Leanne moved slightly, stretching her body voluptuously, conveying a wealth of pleasurable reminiscence in one brief movement. 'He has lost none of his attraction. He is still all the man any woman could ever want. Or don't you agree?'

'Naturally, I agree,' Kate said woodenly. She took a scent spray from her bag and applied a cloud of fragrance to her wrists and throat, as if she didn't have a care in the world.

She could feel Leanne's eyes on her, devouring her, as she tossed the spray back into her bag, found the flat sandals she'd been wearing all day, and slid her feet into them.

Leanne said gently, 'And what about you, little English Kate? Are you all the woman he needs? Somehow I doubt it.'

Kate's voice sounded strange in her own ears. 'Why don't you ask him?'

Leanne's smile was catlike. She leaned forward, stubbing out her cigarette on a crystal ashtray on the dressing table. 'Perhaps I don't need to ask. I knew him well, remember.'

'But I have him now,' was what Kate wanted to say, but the words choked in her throat, because they were lies, and somehow Leanne would know, just as she knew now the total sterility of their relationship and was amused by it.

Leanne came to stand beside her. Kate looked at their mirrored reflections side by side, her own slenderness enhanced by the ill-fitting green dress contrasting with Leanne's confident beauty in the cerise silk which clung to her full breasts and rounded hips.

Leanne said with husky mockery, 'And I will tell you something else—I do not think his tastes have changed at all. And I want him back.'

Kate found her voice at last. 'Don't you think your husband might object?'

Leanne shrugged. 'Why should he? He loves me and he wants me to be happy—and as he is no longer capable of satisfying me himself . . .' She shrugged again, indicating all kinds of possibilities.

Kate said huskily, 'You're revolting!'

'And you are a child,' Leanne retorted. 'But why should we quarrel, when I can help you?'

'Help me?' Kate stared at her. 'Why should you want to do that?'

'Because your presence here is an impediment,' said Leanne, the look in her eyes frankly calculating. 'It would suit me very well if you were elsewhere, and as that is clearly your wish also, there is no reason why arrangements agreeable to us both cannot be made.'

'I see.' Kate was gripping the edge of the dressing table. 'I leave, so that you can play your games with Matt. You're taking rather a lot for granted, aren't you? It doesn't occur to you that Matt could have other ideas?'

Leanne laughed. 'You credit him with too great a sense of honour! He remembers as well as I do how it once was between us, and he wants me. We shall be discreet—Jethro will not be hurt, if that is what you are thinking—and then I will persuade my husband to do as Matt wishes and allow himself to be interviewed.'

Kate said slowly, 'You actually want him to do the interview—even though it could be dangerous for him when his enemies find out he is still alive?'

Leanne looked at her scornfully. 'You call this being alive—buried here in this house, seeing no one, going nowhere? How little you know! Jethro has taken his chances in the past, so why not again?' The lovely face was hard, suddenly, the calculating look even more pronounced. 'He is an old man—and sick. He has had his life, and a good one. Why should I not have mine?'

'With Matt as part of it?'

Leanne's full lips curved smilingly. 'Why not, if we find after this time that it is what we want?'

'Why not indeed?' Kate said wearily.

'I think we begin to understand each other,' said Leanne with satisfaction. She put up a hand, smoothing an errant strand of hair into place. 'I knew that you would be sensible and realistic. You have had your time with Matthew, but now it is over, and men become very bored with women who cling when they should let go.' She moved towards the door. 'Are you ready to come downstairs?'

Kate's lips moved. 'Presently.'

The door closed, and Leanne had gone. Kate released the edge of the dressing table, and flexed her aching fingers. Her head was throbbing, and she felt a little sick.

Carlos had been right, she thought. She had been a little shocked by the way he spoke of his stepmother, and yet he had said little more than the truth. *'If she wants Matthew Lincoln, then she will take him, and you will be hurt,'* he had said, and the pain was already beginning.

Was this why Matt had turned away from her on the beach that morning—because he knew that soon Leanne would be back in his life? It began to seem like it. Momentarily he had been tempted to take her, but a closer involvement might have interfered with his plans, so he had rejected her.

She bit down hard on her lip. It couldn't be true. That was Leanne's kind of thinking. She infected everything. And it was years since she and Matt had been lovers. How could she be so sure that he would want the relationship revived?

Perhaps because he's told her, a sly little voice within her suggested. Perhaps that's why you didn't see him all afternoon—because he was with her. And anyway, she isn't the woman any man could forget in a hurry.

She didn't want to go down to dinner, but she knew if she stayed in her room that it would be a victory for Leanne, and she wasn't defeated—not yet, at any rate. She gave herself a long, last unhappy look, and left the room.

Jakey was hovering in the hall as she came downstairs, waiting to usher her to the right door. She took a long, deep breath as he stood aside to allow her to precede him into the room. It was like being in one of those nightmares where the curtain was about to go up on the first night of a play, and she was waiting in the wings, stunned by the realisation that she didn't know any of the lines she was supposed to say.

And dressed in the wrong costume too, she thought with self-derision, as they all turned to look at her.

Jethro Alvarez occupied centre stage, his massive bulk accentuated by a burgundy velvet dinner jacket.

'Miss Marston, at last,' he said. 'We were wondering if we should send out a search party.' He was smiling as he spoke, but the dark eyes were enigmatic as they surveyed her. 'Carlos, my son, get the young lady a drink. She looks as if she could use one.'

'Come and tell me what you would like. A Martini, perhaps?' Carlos led her over to a well-loaded drinks trolley. 'I thought you would never come down,' he said in an undertone.

Kate flushed slightly. 'I—I was trying to make this dress wearable,' she said, trying for lightness. 'I'm afraid I haven't succeeded too well.'

'You look charming.' Carlos' eyes rested on her appreciatively, as she nervously adjusted the slipping neckline. 'Like a little girl dressed up in grown-up's clothes.'

She winced. 'That's what I was afraid of.' She took the Martini he handed her, and gave him a nervous smile. 'Well—cheers, I suppose.'

Although she had deliberately avoided looking at him, she had known from the moment she entered the big room exactly where Matt was—standing near the window talking, inevitably, to Leanne. Now, every fibre of awareness in her warned her that he was approaching.

He too was wearing evening clothes—a white dinner jacket over close-fitting dark pants, and a frilled shirt. Apart from the long-ago wedding, it was the first time she had seen him so formally clad, and the effect was devastating.

She turned defensively to face him, the tip of her tongue moistening her dry lips.

His dark brows drew together as he looked down at her. He asked, 'Are you all right?'

'Never better,' she returned with false brightness.

His mouth turned down derisively. 'Now that's open to question.' The blue eyes flicked over her. 'I clearly got the better bargain under the clothes loan scheme.'

Kate flushed. 'Naturally.' She made to turn away, but his hand closed round her arm.

He demanded, 'What else is wrong? Still brooding over the evil fate which has trapped you here?'

Kate turned away. She didn't want to look into his eyes. 'Perhaps.'

She heard him sigh with something like exasperation. 'Then it's something you're going to have to come to terms with. You've managed so far. Why is it suddenly so difficult?' He was standing so close to her that she could feel the warmth from his body, breathe the faint scent from the soap he had used.

She wanted to scream at him, 'Because I was hoping and praying that this was going to be the beginning of the beginning for us, and instead it's the beginning of the end, and I don't think I can bear it!'

A sigh wrenched itself up from the soles of her feet, and she turned slowly to face him. And past him, over his shoulder she saw Leanne watching them, the beautiful face predatory and triumphant, and anything she might have said, any link she could have forged between them seemed to freeze in her throat.

Her voice shook. 'Because I'm sick and tired of this stupid game we've been playing. I want to get back to real life—my life—again.'

The blue eyes glinted suddenly. 'And to this man—this Drew, whoever he is?'

He meant Clive, she thought, but it didn't matter. Each was as unimportant as the other. At least her time with Matt had taught her that. Drew had done her a mischief, but because she had been young and vulnerable she had built it up in her mind into a major tragedy. Drew's treatment of her had been like a wasp-sting—painful but transitory. But with Matt, any wound would be mortal.

'Why not?' she said, and shrugged, aware that the damned dress was slipping again. 'He wants me—and it's good to be wanted,' she added recklessly.

Matt's mouth curled. 'Tell me about it some time,' he invited thickly, and walked away from her.

Kate sipped her drink, more shaken by the little encounter than she cared to admit. She watched Matt walk across the room to Leanne, and saw her lips part in a welcoming smile. She was smitten with a spasm of jealousy, almost physical in its impact. Her teeth sank into the softness of her inner lip, and her fingers tightened round her glass. She turned abruptly, and ran head-on into Jethro Alvarez's frankly appraising stare. He lifted a massive hand and beckoned to her. Reluctantly Kate crossed the room to his side, and took the chair he indicated.

'Relax,' the deep voice told her with a trace of amusement. 'Use all the chair, not just the edge. Believe me, Miss Marston, I mean you no harm. But there are—circumstances which force me to protect myself. I wish I could explain more fully, but at present it is not possible.'

'You don't need to explain anything to me.' Kate shook her head. 'It's my own fault that I'm here.'

'Not wholly.' Alvarez stroked his upper lip. 'My friend Lincoln can be—most persuasive, I know.' His tone was dry. He didn't appear to be watching Matt with Leanne, but Kate knew that he would be aware of every look, every gesture, even if he could not hear what they were saying. The shrewd eyes returned to Kate's face. 'You have—known him long?'

Without considering her words, she said, 'All my life, I think,' then paused, a hectic flush running up under her skin. 'I mean . . .'

'I know what you mean, and it is nothing to be ashamed of.' His voice was quiet, almost reflective. 'Does that surprise you? Had you written me off as a sick old man, a failure, living on past dreams?'

'In no way,' Kate denied with a vehemence that surprised her.

'Good,' said Jethro Alvarez, and grinned at her. 'Now what do you propose to do with yourself while Matthew attempts to talk me into being interviewed by him? You wish to paint? I can get you canvas—colours. Tell me what you want.' He gave her a sly look.

'Perhaps I should commission you—a portrait of my beautiful wife maybe. What do you say?'

Kate said diplomatically, 'I'm not really into portraiture!' She smiled. 'But if you ever decide to write your autobiography, then I'll be glad to design the jacket.'

'Autobiography!' Alvarez made it sound like a dirty word. 'That is an occupation for those whose lives are over. Mine is not—yet. I may still amaze the world. Do you find that hard to believe?'

'While you're hiding here, pretending that you're dead—yes,' Kate said daringly.

For a moment, the heavy brows drew together in a frown, and she waited for some kind of explosion. Then he said softly, half to himself, 'Yes, it was a mistake. But then I was so very tired of it all. I no longer wanted to fight to stay the top man. I wanted some peace in my life, some privacy. I imagined how it could be—but, naturally, I was deluding myself. We cannot escape reality. It must be faced—survived.' His voice lowered almost to a growl, and for a moment he sat staring in front of him. Then he moved, levering his heavy body out of the chair. 'Come, we will go in to dinner. You must eat, my child. You are too thin—even in your own clothes!'

He kept her beside him at dinner, talking to her, drawing her out, asking her opinion on books, current films, and the political situation in Europe. She didn't fool herself that he really wanted to know what she thought, but their conversation engaged her attention and stopped her from looking too often at the other end of the table where Leanne was talking to Matt, her voice intimately lowered, her eyes gleaming into his, her fingers stroking caressingly at the sleeve of his jacket.

Alvarez's face was impassive, but Kate knew that he must be just as aware of what was going on. Perhaps Leanne was right, and her ways of diverting herself no longer mattered to him, but Kate wasn't sure she believed that. In spite of Alvarez' frequent references to himself as an old man, as being tired and sick, she sensed a raw energy in him that in no way matched his self-denigration.

She thought in a kind of agony, 'Matt—be careful!'

They began the meal with stuffed crab, and went on to slices of smoky duck breast cooked with pears in a rich sauce. Kate murmured appreciatively about the food, and swallowed it without really knowing what she was eating, thankful for the wine which enabled her to wash it down past the solid knot of misery which had formed in her throat. When the fruit sorbet which had completed the meal had been cleared away, Alvarez announced that coffee would be served on the patio. He took Kate's hand benevolently. 'And then? You can watch the latest Spielberg movie in my projection room, or there could be music.'

What she really wanted was to go to her room. She needed a sanctuary in which to lick her wounds—those already inflicted, and those to come. But it was clear she wasn't going to be allowed to run away just yet, so she smiled and opted for the music.

It drifted into the night air from concealed speakers, not loud but with a slow insidious beat. Leanne was on her feet almost at once.

Kate steeled herself, waiting for Matt to rise and take Leanne in his arms. She was moving to the music, her body sinuous in the cerise dress, her smile a challenge and an invitation.

Alvarez said drily, 'My wife finds it impossible to forget her days as a cabaret artist.' He smiled slowly. 'She must find the restricted life here—dull.' He lifted a hand, signalling imperiously to Matt to come and sit beside him. As Matt obeyed, Alvarez looked at him, sighing deeply. 'Ah, my friend. What am I to do with you?'

'I'd say the choice was give me my interview, or send me on my way.' Matt leaned back in his chair with indolent grace, his blue eyes fixed on the older man's swarthy face.

'If only it were that simple!' Alvarez shook his head, as if genuinely regretful. 'But I have others to consider.

How can I expose my wife to danger? My only son? Once my enemies know where I am, I am a dead man.'

'Your security has always seemed pretty impregnable in the past,' Matt observed, putting his coffee cup down on a side table.

'I thought so, yet you have managed to penetrate it.'

'Yes,' Matt agreed, 'I did. I'm still wondering how it happened.'

Alvarez shrugged, 'One should never take anything for granted. The lapse will be investigated, you may be sure.'

'I'm no longer sure of anything.' Matt lifted his brandy glass, watching the swirl of the liquid in the bowl as if it fascinated him.

Alvarez laughed. 'Now that is an admission,' he said with open satisfaction. 'And I confess that I am intrigued too. That is why you are still here, and why I remain also. Of what interest can I be to anyone any more? I am finished. My life is over. What questions could you possibly ask me?'

'I can think of several,' said Matt. 'Top of the list—what happened to the Santo Cristo treasury?'

Alvarez' shoulders shook. 'Treasury, my friend? It never existed. My poor bankrupt country survived on hand-outs from wealthy nations trying to assuage their guilt about the third world—your own included.' He paused. 'Naturally, I had already made provision for my own future. But then even the lowest grade civil servant in Britain receives a pension. Why should I be different?'

'Why indeed?' said Matt with irony. He glanced round. 'This makes a pretty palatial almshouse.'

Kate was getting increasingly nervous, but Alvarez seemed amused.

'Do you grudge me my final resting place, my friend?' he asked plaintively.

'No,' Matt said. 'I simply don't believe that this is it.'

There was a long silence. Alvarez's hand came up and stroked his chin. He said softly, 'Matthew Lincoln, how I wish I knew if I could trust you!' He turned his head slowly and looked down at Kate. 'Would you trust him?'

There were so many answers she could give, she thought, suddenly frozen. 'I hardly know him,' was one; 'He fooled me into coming here with him,' another. Or there was, most damning of all, 'Your wife is planning to betray you with him.' The pain of that made her wince, but she knew what she had to do, what she wanted to do, because, right or wrong, she loved him.

She looked at Matt, seeing the guarded look in his eyes, the half-derisive curve of his mouth as he waited to hear what she would say.

She said, 'I'd trust him with my life.' And knew achingly that it was only the truth.

CHAPTER NINE

THERE was a long silence. Kate saw Matt's eyes narrow, his dark brows snap together in a frown.

Jethro said, 'You are a fortunate man, my friend, to have inspired such faith.'

Leanne's laugh was almost strident. 'How solemn you are, *querido*! And how easily beguiled. We are wasting the evening and the music with all this talk.' She was smiling, but the look she shot Kate was minatory and hostile. She held out a hand to Matt. 'Come and dance with me,' she coaxed.

'Yes,' Alvarez leaned back in his chair, smiling a little, the heavy lids closing over his eyes, 'go and dance.' He raised his voice slightly. 'Carlos!'

It wasn't until Carlos appeared from whatever corner he had been hiding in that Kate realised Alvarez intended him to dance with her. She flushed as he sulkily offered her his hand.

'I was just going up to my room.'

'Nonsense,' Alvarez dismissed bracingly. 'Dance, child. Enjoy the music. It will give me pleasure to watch you.'

She got reluctantly to her feet, conscious of the ill-fitting dress, and they began to move awkwardly together.

After a few silent moments Carlos said in a low voice, 'She is disgusting, that woman, she has no shame. How can my father bear it?'

Kate chose her words carefully, 'Perhaps—when you love someone very much—you are prepared to forgive them, whatever they do.'

'You think he cares for her in that way?' he demanded incredulously. 'It is impossible! He is not a weak man, and tonight her behaviour has been blatant.' He paused. 'I did warn you how it would be.'

148

'Yes,' Kate acknowledged miserably, 'you warned me.'

'And yet you say you trust him,' Carlos went on, half to himself. 'It is incredible! But perhaps you don't yet realise what she is capable of.'

Kate sighed. 'I think I do.' She could see the way Leanne was dancing with Matt, her body against his, her arms linked round his neck.

Carlos muttered, 'She is shameless—evil.'

'Perhaps so,' Kate said wearily. 'But I don't see that saying these things over and over again helps at all.'

He gave her an offended look, and relapsed into silence.

When the music ended, Kate excused herself as diplomatically as possible, and said goodnight to Alvarez.

'So soon, child?' He sounded disappointed, and she gave him a faint smile.

'It's been a pretty shattering day.'

He nodded. 'Then sleep well, and tomorrow we will talk again.'

And say what? she wondered as she walked across the patio towards the house. To her surprise, she found Carlos at her shoulder.

'I think I can manage to find my way back to my room unaided,' she said more sharply than she had intended. She wanted to be alone, and she certainly didn't want to hear another diatribe against Leanne.

'My father expects me to escort you,' Carlos announced.

'I see,' Kate said bitterly. 'I don't intend to pinch the silver, you know. Do you treat all your guests this way?'

Carlos halted, his gaze going sharply to her face. 'Guests? What guests? I don't understand what you mean.'

'Joke,' she said with a sigh. 'I'm not surprised you didn't recognise it. They're pretty thin on the ground round here, I'd imagine.'

'A joke—I see.' His brow cleared. 'I am sorry I didn't understand. Naturally there are no guests. It would be impossible.' He paused, then added with odd insistence, 'You do believe me, don't you?'

'Of course I do,' said Kate with a little shrug. 'Why shouldn't I?'

It was a relief to reach her room, and she gave him a brief smile and a determined, 'Goodnight, Carlos.'

He took her hand and stood looking down at it. 'It is still early. Couldn't we talk for a while?'

'No, we couldn't,' she said gently. 'I'm really tired. I'll see you tomorrow.'

'I thought you liked me,' he protested sulkily.

Kate groaned inwardly. 'I think you're very nice,' she began temperately.

Carlos said almost fiercely, 'And I think you are beautiful,' and his hands came down on her shoulders, pulling her towards him. Caught off balance, she half fell against him, and his mouth descended eagerly on hers.

Matt said arctically, 'I'm sorry, I didn't realise I was interrupting something.'

He was only a couple of yards away, standing with his hands on his hips, watching them. Carlos let Kate go as if he had been stung. If she hadn't been so furious, she could almost have felt sorry for him. Desperately trying to recover his poise, he said, 'I did not realise you were there.'

'So I gather.' Matt's face was glacial, his mouth in a taut line of anger. 'Have you finished saying goodnight to Miss Marston?'

'Oh—yes.' Carlos' gaze slid embarrassedly away from Kate's. 'Er—sleep well.' He turned and scuttled away, head bent.

Kate moistened her lips with the tip of her tongue. 'Thank you. I—I don't know what came over him.'

The dark brows lifted arrogantly. 'No? I suggest it was exactly the same thing that prompted him beside the pool this afternoon.

'I'd be grateful if you didn't encourage the little idiot,' he added, after a pause while Kate digested what he had said. 'It could cause complications.'

Kate gasped. 'I haven't encouraged him!' she began heatedly.

He shrugged. 'You didn't slap his face either. You let him kiss you earlier, you've been dancing with him, and you allowed him to walk you to your room. He must have thought it was his birthday.'

She stared at him. 'How did you know he'd kissed me?'

'Our room overlooks the pool,' he said. 'Or hadn't you noticed? I happened to be on the balcony. I had a circle seat. Leave him alone, Kate. He's immature and confused—totally bad news as far as you're concerned.'

'Oh, thanks for the good advice!' Her voice shook. 'And who made you the arbiter of everyone's morals around here—after the way you've been behaving with—with that woman!'

'You have some complaint?' asked Matt, too pleasantly.

She hesitated, sensing danger. 'It's none of my business.'

'You seem to have made it your business,' he said flatly. 'Not long ago, you were telling Jethro that you trusted me. You were amazingly convincing. Now you seem to be accusing me of playing around with his wife.'

She muttered, 'She's been throwing herself at you ever since you got here.'

He shrugged. 'That's no great problem, although it's something I should have foreseen, perhaps. But if you're thinking Jethro still harbours any illusions about her then forget it. He recovered from those a long time ago—probably even before they were married.'

'Is that supposed to be some kind of excuse?'

'No,' he said. 'Because I don't need one. Leanne is what she is, and no one can change that. Jethro may have thought differently once—I suspect he had some crazy idea about turning her into another Evita—but he knows better now.'

'But he loved her once,' Kate said stubbornly.

'I'd hardly describe it quite so romantically.' His voice was cynical.

'And your relationship with her?' Kate lifted her chin defiantly. 'How would you describe that?'

He gave her a long, level look. 'What do you want me to say, Kate?' His voice roughened. 'That it was entirely platonic? It wouldn't be the truth, so why should I lie about it? God knows it was over a long time ago.'

'Was it?'

He was very still for a moment. 'What the hell are you saying?'

She bit her lip. 'It's obvious that Leanne doesn't think it's over.'

'And that makes it so?' He gave a short laugh. 'Thanks. What was that you were saying a little while ago about trust?'

'Wasn't it what you wanted me to say?' Kate stared down at the floor.

His hand took her chin, forcing it upwards, making her meet his gaze. 'No,' he said harshly, 'I'd have preferred you to mean it. For one crazy moment, I thought you did. But it was all part of the performance, wasn't it?' He paused. 'Wasn't it?'

For one long moment Kate was tempted to tell him the truth, to let the depth of feeling he had aroused in her spill over into words, to throw herself on his mercy. But the burning memory of his rejection of her only a few hours ago still lingered. She couldn't face another, even greater humiliation.

She said again, 'I thought it was what you wanted.'

Matt was silent for a moment or two, then his hand fell away.

He said, 'Then you'll be glad to know that you don't have to perjure yourself any more. The agreement ends here. It's—outlived any usefulness it might conceivably have had, and frankly it's becoming an embarrassment! He gave her a bleak look. 'Goodnight.'

She watched him walk across the room, and vanish into the dressing room. The door closed behind him with a click.

She was alone, and she began to shiver uncontrollably.

She felt mentally and physically exhausted, but she couldn't sleep. She dozed, began to dream uneasily and awoke with a start as if someone had put a hand on her shoulder.

She sat up, the single sheet covering her sliding away from her naked body. Leanne's black nightdress was draped across the dressing stool. She couldn't have borne to have it anywhere near her.

The night was quiet. The air was warm and still. She swallowed, breathing deeply, trying to relax herself, but she felt as taut as a drum. She glanced restlessly round the room, wondering what had woken her, running her tongue over her dry lips.

Then somewhere close at hand she heard a woman's laugh—soft, amused, seductive.

Kate tensed, then she slid out of bed, taking the sheet with her, winding it round her body, and tiptoed over to the door of the dressing room. For a long moment she stood listening, hardly breathing, but she heard only silence and the deep heavy beat of her own pulses.

She put out a hand and gently tried the door. It gave instantly, swinging noiselessly open. Kate swallowed, feeling like Bluebeard's wife. If Matt woke up, if he saw her standing there, wrapped in a sheet, what would he think? And what could she say? 'I thought I heard Leanne, and came to see if you were together.' Never! She would just have to pretend that she was sleepwalking, or had heard a strange noise and was frightened. She hitched up the sheet and stepped forward uncertainly, words of apology for having woken him already forming on her lips. And then she stopped, because they weren't necessary. The sheet was turned back and the pillow dented, but the bed was empty. Matt wasn't there.

Kate turned with a gasp, half expecting to find him standing behind her, grimly asking what she thought she was doing, but she was alone.

She backed out of the room, closing the door behind her, her legs curiously weak. And heard the laugh again, and recognised this time the direction it was coming from.

The sheet trailing on the floor around her, she crossed to the window and opened the long shutters a fraction, easing herself through the opening on to the balcony.

Below the pool rippled and shimmered in the moonlight, and she paused, staring down, telling herself that she was mistaken, obsessed.

But she wasn't imagining the faint splashing sounds, or the way the pattern of the ripples was breaking up on the water. As she watched, Leanne grasped the rail at the side of the pool and pulled herself out with easy grace. She stood on the edge in the moonlight, twisting her dark hair into a rope to wring the water out of it, completely naked and aware of it, confident in her own beauty.

And not alone. Transfixed on her balcony—what had Matt called it—'a circle seat'?—she saw a movement under the pergola, saw a tall figure, heard a man's voice speak, although the tone and the words eluded her

Leanne Alvarez shook her hair over her shoulders and walked to the pergola. Kate's clenched fist went up to her mouth to prevent her crying out. She saw the shadows move again, and Leanne's triumphant smile. She heard her voice. 'Darling, you must not be so impatient. After all, it is your own fault that we have been apart for so long.' Numbly Kate watched her walk up the shallow steps of the pergola to be snatched passionately into the darkness of an embrace, then she forced her nerveless limbs to move, stepping back silently into the security and dimness of the bedroom, away from the betrayal of the moonlight.

It hurt to breathe. It hurt even to exist. Like an automaton she walked to the bed, and sank down on it, still wrapped in the sheet, curling involuntarily into the comfort position of childhood. For a moment she lay still, then one tearing dry sob after another shook her body.

Matt with Leanne down there, uncaring who might see them. A little moan escaped her throat. It had taken no time at all for Leanne to re-establish her power over Matt, she thought desperately. He had said their affair was over, but Leanne had known that it was not.

Kate buried her face in the pillow. So much for love and trust and hope, stifled almost at birth. What a fool she'd been to think that Matt was different! How naïvely she had accepted his control where she was concerned as proof that he was not just another womaniser like Drew. Well, she knew better now.

If Matt had wanted her, he would have taken her. God knows, she had given him sufficient opportunity. But instead he had taken Leanne who was beautiful and amoral, and who had promised to give him what he wanted.

A long deep shiver went through her. She wanted to get away from this house, and its strange twisted relationships. She wanted to go home, to work and sanity, and a measure of calm. The last twenty-four hours had been like living in some wild, lurid dream, but she was awake now, and she needed to escape.

And escape above all from the sheer confusion of emotion inside her—the jealousy, the frustration, the passionate crying need for this man of all men, who would never love her or belong to her as she so desperately wanted.

She thought, 'I must get away. I must—or I shall go mad!'

It must have been almost dawn before she fell at last into an uneasy sleep, listening vainly all the time for the sound of Matt's return to his room.

She was woken by Jakey, bringing a tray of fruit juice and coffee to her, with the information that breakfast was being served on the patio.

She knew she wouldn't be able to manage a mouthful of solid food, but she was glad of the coffee. Its warmth and fragrance seemed to put fresh heart into her, and she poured a second cup and took it into the bathroom with her while she showered and cleaned her teeth.

All she had to wear again was the coral bikini and its covering shirt, and she put them on with reluctance, only to find when she re-emerged into the bedroom that Jethro Alvarez had been as good as his word and her luggage was waiting for her.

Another obstacle to her departure had been removed, Kate thought, dropping to her knees beside her case. She stripped off the bikini, rolling it into a ball and thrusting it down the side of the case, putting on instead a sleeveless shift dress in a stinging lemon yellow. She tied her hair back at the nape of her neck with a matching scarf, and concealed the ravages of the previous night behind her sunglasses before going downstairs.

She had no wish to meet the other members of the household, but common sense dictated that she couldn't spend all day in her room. The last thing she wanted was for Matt and Leanne to guess that she knew about their relationship. She needed to leave St Antoine with some remnants of pride intact.

As she walked down the stairs, Carlos seemed to appear from nowhere, and she guessed with irritation that he'd been waiting for her.

'Kate.' His expression was sheepish. 'I want to apologise about last night. I'm sorry—I didn't mean to make trouble.'

He looked so downcast that she took pity on him. 'You didn't. It was all right.'

'He wasn't angry?' Carlos whistled. 'He must be very sure of you if he can find his woman in another man's arms and—shrug it off. I—I would not be able to control my temper.'

Kate could well imagine it, but she didn't say so. There couldn't be that much difference between her age and Carlos's, but she felt a million years older.

On the patio, the first person she saw was Matt. Casual in denim jeans and a matching shirt, its sleeves rolled back to the elbows, he was deep in conversation with Jethro Alvarez.

Kate felt her face freeze. How could he? she thought helplessly. He spent last night making love to his wife, using her in order to get to him.

'Ah, the little Kate.' Alvarez beckoned her to him. 'You slept well?'

'Like a log,' she said. A log caught in a strong river current, and heading for the rapids, she thought.

'You would like breakfast?' He gestured to a well-laden table in the shade. 'There are fresh rolls—fruit, but if you want Jakey will bring you eggs, or perhaps fish.'

Kate refused politely, saying mendaciously that she rarely ate at breakfast-time, but accepting another cup of coffee. She could feel Matt watching her, but she avoided his gaze.

'You look very beautiful this morning,' Alvarez went on. 'But a little overdressed, perhaps. Are you not going to swim?'

The thought of using the pool, of even being in its immediate environs after what she had witnessed there the previous night, made her feel sick, but she forced a smile to her lips.

'Not today. In fact I might keep out of the sun altogether. I think I've been overdoing it.'

Jakey arrived at that moment with fresh coffee, and as he was pouring it, Alvarez turned to speak to him, and Matt leaned forward, his hand covering hers where it lay on the arm of the chair.

He said in an undertone, 'Are you all right? You're not feeling ill?'

'I feel fine.' Her voice sounded higher-pitched than usual. 'I just had rather a disturbed night, that's all.' And make what you want of that, she thought savagely.

'I'm sorry to hear it,' he said quietly. 'Kate—I think we need to talk.'

'What a coincidence,' she said too brightly. 'I was thinking exactly the same. And when do you suggest we have this little tête-à-tête?'

Matt gave her a wary look, the blue eyes guarded. 'What the hell's got into you today?' he muttered.

Jealousy, she thought, unrequited love, a sense of despair—and a number of purely female emotions that you wouldn't understand in a thousand years, because to you women are bodies and nothing more.

'Good morning, everyone.' Leanne stepped smilingly out on to the patio. She glanced round and gave Kate a condescending nod. As she passed Matt's chair, she ruffled his hair. 'Did you sleep well, *querido*?' Her tone held open mockery. How could she be so blatant? Kate wondered numbly, staring down into the dark swirl of coffee in her cup. She risked a glance at Alvarez and saw his face was bland, giving nothing away. 'Doesn't he guess?' she wondered. 'Or doesn't he care?'

Leanne bent to give her husband a careless kiss on the cheek, before sinking into a chair and demanding food to be brought to her.

'What a wonderful morning!' She stretched luxuriously, the full breasts lifting under her thin dress as she did so. 'I am so hungry, I could eat a horse!'

Kate drank her coffee in a swift gulp, and stood up. 'I—I think I'll go for a walk.'

'I'll come with you.' Matt rose purposefully to his feet.

Leanne pouted. 'But you're all running away. Is it something I said?' Her eyes surveyed Kate mockingly.

Alvarez patted her hand. 'They wish to be alone, my dearest. I am sure that you can understand that. You can keep me company for a while.'

Leanne looked frankly sulky, but she subsided, and began to make inroads into the plates of food which Jakey had brought her.

Kate plunged blindly down the steps leading to the garden, pausing only for a moment to choose a path at the bottom which would lead away from the pool area. Matt caught up with her, his hand descending on her shoulder.

'If the heat's getting to you, then you shouldn't be dashing about,' he told her.

'It isn't the heat,' she said. 'It's this house, this whole situation. I've had enough. I want out—preferably today.'

He stopped abruptly, staring down into her face. 'Just like that? There could be problems.'

'What's new about that?' she demanded passionately. 'But you got me into this, so now you can get me out of it.'

'Calm down!' he snapped. 'Admittedly you can't wander about at will, but conditions here aren't that intolerable. And I can't pull out now. Alvarez is just on the point of changing his mind about giving this interview. I know he is.'

'I'm quite sure of it,' she said bitterly. 'It's all working out beautifully, isn't it? You'll have to forgive me if I find that your methods leave a lot to be desired. Or is all fair in love and journalism?'

Matt said wearily, 'I wish I knew what the hell you were talking about. I also wish you'd stay. Alvarez likes you. You could be of immense help.'

'Playing the phoney girl-friend?' she flung at him scornfully. 'It never had much appeal as a role, but now the very idea is disgusting!'

Matt's face was grim. 'I'm sorry you think so, but the fact remains we had a bargain.'

'Had is right,' she said bitterly. 'I think under the circumstances the terms are forfeit.'

'What circumstances?' he demanded impatiently. 'What the hell are you getting at?'

She said unevenly, 'I'm talking about you—and Leanne Alvarez, you hypocrite! That's why you want me to stay, isn't it? Because with a live-in girl-friend on the premises, Alvarez won't be looking too closely at your relationship with his wife. No matter how indulgent he is with her, I doubt if he'd take kindly to a resumption of your affair under his own roof.'

'I doubt it too,' Matt said drily. 'And what makes you think that I'd be happy about it either?'

Kate said wretchedly, 'Because I saw you. I woke up last night and you—weren't in your room. And when I went out on the balcony, you were with her, beside the pool.' She moistened her lips with the tip of her tongue. 'You—you should have remembered that the room overlooked it.' She looked at him, noting unhappily his stillness, the pallor beneath his tan. 'Aren't you going to say something?'

'You appear to have said it all.' His mouth twisted. 'Kate, I wish I could explain to you, but at the moment it's impossible. You said you trusted me. Can't you go on doing so for a little while longer?'

'No!' The word came almost explosively. 'You sicken me—both of you, and I won't act as cover any more. You can't expect me to.' She paused. 'And if you don't arrange for me to get out of here, then I shall go to Alvarez and tell him the whole story—and then see if Leanne can persuade him to give you your interview,' she added bitterly. She glared at him fiercely. 'Do you understand me?'

His voice was sardonic. 'I'd say you'd made the position more than clear. Perhaps I should thank you for warning me. If you'd simply gone straight to Alvarez, things could have become—difficult.'

'I'm sure they could,' she said. She wanted to burst into tears, but she hung on to her self-control. 'So you'll do as I ask?'

Matt shrugged. 'I'll try, but the final decision is up to Alvarez. You must realise that.' His tone hardened. 'After all, you're the bright lady. You're the one with all the answers.'

Kate said in a stifled voice, 'I seem to be. And I'd rather go on with this walk on my own.'

His face was hard. 'I won't argue, Kate.' He swung on his heel and walked away from her.

Her lips parted. She knew an aching desire to call him back, but she was aware that for her own peace of mind, she had to resist. Everything that needed to be said had already been uttered. All that remained was 'Goodbye'.

She was in her room, endlessly packing and re-packing

her case, when Jakey tapped on the door and told her that the Señor wished to speak to her.

'Oh.' She got up nervously. 'I'll come at once.'

She was expecting him to conduct her downstairs, and was surprised when he led her past the stairs and along the wide gallery to a door at the far end. He knocked, and stood aside for her to go past him into the room.

Her first impression was that the room was all glass, because there were windows on three sides looking straight towards the ocean. Her second, that there were flowers everywhere.

'Orchids,' Alvarez greeted her. He was lying on a sofa in the middle of the room wearing a flamboyantly patterned silk dressing gown. Matt was lounging in a chair nearby. 'My little hobby.' He gestured round.

'They're fantastic!' Kate stared round in amazement. Fantastic was the right word, she thought, because many of the blooms were almost too exotic for real beauty, looking rather as if they had been constructed from silk and velvet than from a living entity.

'You will forgive my informality,' Alvarez went on. 'I have been enjoying a massage, and I like to rest for a while afterwards.' He paused, and the shrewd eyes surveyed her, lingering, she thought selfconsciously, on the shadows beneath her eyes. 'Matthew tells me you wish to leave us, *querida*. I hope it isn't true?'

'It's quite true.' Kate sat down on the chair he had indicated. 'I'm a working girl, *señor*, and I need to get back to work.'

'And you cannot spare even a few days out of this busy life?' Alvarez spread his hands in a reproachful gesture.

'I've already spared all the time that's available.' She managed to make her faint smile regretful. 'Coming on this trip in the first place—was an indulgence.'

'But you found our friend here irresistible.' Alvarez chuckled richly. 'Ah, Matthew, if I were a younger man, I could be jealous of you. Can't you use your charm on her, man—persuade her to stay?'

Matt shrugged cynically. 'Kate is very much her own lady,' he said. 'If she feels she must leave, then I won't stand in her way.'

'Then I must agree.' Alvarez sighed deeply. 'Perhaps it is for the best—safer in every way if she leaves us now.' His eyes met Matt's and they exchanged a long look. He turned back to Kate, shedding his almost reflective air like a skin. There was a suddenly harsh note in his voice. 'So—tomorrow you will leave us. Carlos will escort you to St Lucia and see you on your way. And you will say nothing—nothing, you understand, about what you have seen or heard here.' He looked at her sharply. 'If you—forget, I shall be angry, and it is best that does not happen, especially for Matthew here, who remains with me for a while. Remember that if you are ever tempted to be indiscreet.'

Kate swallowed. 'I'll remember,' she said faintly. 'But—but can't I leave today? I'm quite ready.'

Alvarez' lips thinned with displeasure. 'I said tomorrow, and that is what I mean. You have rejected my hospitality, Miss Marston. Take care you do not compound your fault.' He waved a regal hand. 'Now, you may go. You also, Matthew, but we will talk again later.'

When they were outside, Kate said shakily, 'My God, he can be formidable!'

'Santa Claus he's not,' Matt agreed flatly. 'I hope you don't intend to flog your amazing story to half Fleet Street, otherwise the consequences for me could be unpleasant. He really wasn't fooling.'

She stared up into his face. 'Then why stay and risk his anger?' she asked shakily.

He shrugged. 'Because it's what I have to do. While there's a chance of that interview, I'm not leaving.' He glanced at her, his face hardening. 'So make what you want of that, my little scandalmonger.'

'At least I'm not a hypocrite like you!' she flung back at him.

'Can I have that in writing?' he came back at her

savagely. They were back at her room, and before she could say anything, he had opened the door and pushed her inside. She stumbled slightly, glaring at him.

'Take your hands off me, Matt Lincoln!'

'You have a nice line in clichés, Kate,' he said insolently. 'And you're going to need them all!'

He pulled her into his arms, crushing her mouth with his. She gasped, trying to release herself, pummelling his chest with clenched fists, but the only effect of her resistance was the tightening of his arms round her and the deepening of his kiss.

The slow intimate movement of his lips against her was a bewilderment against which she could not remain proof for long. She could feel the anger draining out of her to be replaced by a deep, bitter-sweet yearning. Her hands locked at the back of his neck, and her lips parted in surrender as she returned his kiss.

Her body trembled as she clung to him. He lifted a hand and stroked her face, her throat, his fingers moving to the nape of her neck to loosen the confining ribbon and allow her hair to tumble over her shoulders. He lifted his mouth from hers, and drew her gently forward so that her body rested totally against his. She turned her head blindly, her lips seeking the warm skin inside the open shirt with a kind of fever.

All her life, it seemed, she had been running scared, hiding behind manufactured defences, choosing the safety of the emotional shallows. The tide of yearning sweeping her away now might mean disaster, but she no longer cared. She was in his arms, and that was all that mattered. If these few brief moments were all that she could have of him, then she would keep them in her heart for ever.

She heard him murmur her name on a long shaken sigh, then his mouth closed on hers again with a deep sensual urgency, and she responded with a fierceness that matched his own, her body moving against his in restless abandon.

She felt the zip slide at the back of her dress, felt the brush of the material against her skin as he slipped it from her shoulders. Her head fell back helplessly as his lips explored the long, sweet line of her throat. His hands cradled her bared breasts, caressing them as if they were flowers, brought to bloom for his private delight. Her body shivered with pleasure at his touch. Her hands slid inside his shirt, stroking the long hard line of his shoulders, the muscular wall of his chest, exploring him with equal frankness, and hearing him groan softly in response.

His arms circled her with savage tenderness, swinging her off her feet. He carried her the few paces to the bed and put her down with infinite gentleness, his face flushed, the blue eyes passionately intent as he came down beside her.

Kate yielded to him totally, all inhibitions flown as he caressed her body, his mouth possessing hers in heated demand. She was weightless, floating on the sea of sensation he had aroused in her, waiting without fear for the inevitable culmination.

When she felt him lift himself away from her, her hands clung.

'Where are you going?'

Matt said softly, 'Nowhere.' His hand slid down her body from her shoulder to her rounded thigh in a gesture of total possession.

Through half-closed eyes she watched him move round the room, drawing the shutters against the sunlight, locking the door, and, finally, shedding his clothes. Then he came back to her.

Kate said huskily, 'You're beautiful.'

'Really?' The long arms wrapped round her, drawing her against him. 'Is that the artist speaking, or the lady?' His mouth teased hers, his tongue flicking along her lower lip.

She whispered, 'Both.' And her body arched against his in mute invitation, total giving.

In Matt's arms, she lost all sense of time and place, learning through the hungry expertise of his hands and mouth how many levels of arousal there were, how many avenues of pleasure to be explored. But even as she dissolved in pleasure, her body aching sweetly for the final consummation, she was aware of the restraint he had placed on himself, the almost savage self-control he was exerting because of her inexperience.

And then, as if he sensed the need for patience was past, and that her desire was as complete as his own, his body covered hers. Wordlessly, she touched him, guided him, welcomed him, moving in accord with him even as his initial gentleness splintered rawly into driving passionate urgency.

Her voice broke on a little cry. 'Oh yes, darling, yes!'—and was engulfed in a pleasure so intense that it seemed her body might shatter like fragile glass.

She returned to normal breathing consciousness slowly. Matt's sweat-dampened body still rested languorously against hers. His eyes were closed, the dark arrogant lines of his face transmuted into a kind of vulnerability. She touched his mouth with her finger, tracing its strong curve, and felt him smile at the shy caress.

She smiled too. She felt triumphant, victorious. 'He's mine,' she thought. 'He belongs to me.' And then, with a sudden chill, she remembered Leanne.

She thought, 'I won't run away. I'm going to stay and fight her. I won't let her have him.'

Matt said softly, 'You've gone very tense.' He propped himself up on an elbow, his other hand cupping her chin. 'Not hating yourself?' he probed. 'Or hating me?'

Warm colour invaded her face. 'No.'

'Good.' He bent and kissed her lingeringly. 'Are you hungry?'

'Yes,' she admitted, amazed to discover that she actually was.

'I mention it because it's lunchtime, and Jethro will be sending out search parties for us.' He kissed her again. 'Perhaps we should put on some clothes and start behaving like house guests.'

'Perhaps we should,' Kate agreed in a subdued voice. She didn't want to leave this room, she thought. She wanted to remain here in Matt's arms, safe from the mysteries and undercurrents in the rest of the house.

His hands smoothed gently along the skin of her shoulder. 'What are you thinking?'

'Not a great deal,' she said evasively, unwilling to confess her own reluctance to allow the outside world to impinge upon them again.

He grinned, his eyes caressing her. 'Then you do it beautifully. I could watch you all day.'

'Then why don't you?' she challenged lightly.

He groaned. 'Witch! I wish it were as simple as that. But I'm here to work, in case you'd forgotten. And you——' he bent and touched his lips to the rosy peak of one breast—'are a distraction.' His voice deepened huskily. 'It's probably as well you're catching that plane tomorrow.'

Kate stiffened. She said, 'What do you mean? I thought—don't you want me to stay?' She despised herself for the words as soon as they were uttered. They sounded like a plea for mercy.

She saw, with a sinking heart, the way his dark brows had drawn together in a frown. He said, 'What I want really doesn't matter. It would be better if you went to St Lucia and caught the plane as arranged.'

'Better for whom?' she demanded. 'And in what way?'

His mouth tightened. He swung himself lithely off the bed, reaching for his clothes. He said, 'It would be safer. And it would avoid further complications.' He looked at her, the blue eyes travelling broodingly down her body. 'Complications which I'd intended to avoid,' he added.

The room was warm, but she felt cold. The victory she had gloried in no longer existed. All their passionate coming-together represented to him was—a complication.

Because during his stay in this house, he was Leanne's lover, for whatever motive, and the most that Kate could hope to be was a diversion from his purpose.

A sob rose in her throat and was ruthlessly suppressed. She'd made a fool of herself, that was all. She'd allowed her senses and emotions to overpower her reason, and now she had to pay the price.

Matt had taken her, but it was over now, and he wanted her no longer. He didn't want possible recrimination, or emotional hassle when she discovered she had to share him. It was better—safer—for her to be out of the way.

She snatched up her dress, holding it against her defensively.

'I understand,' she said tautly. 'I'm sorry if I've upset your plans in any way.'

Matt said harshly, 'You've been doing that since the moment we met.'

He jerked her into his arms, crumpled dress and all, and his mouth took hers angrily, bruisingly. Then he released her so abruptly that she nearly stumbled, and went away from her across the room, unlocking the door, then closing it behind him, without even a backward glance at her.

Kate sank down on the edge of the bed, still clutching her dress against her body. She stared ahead of her into the mirror of the dressing table at the stranger who confronted her there, with her bruised bewildered eyes and trembling mouth.

She said, 'It's over. All over,' in a voice she didn't recognise.

And knew with absolute finality that she couldn't spend another night in this house.

CHAPTER TEN

'BUT are you really sure that this is what you want?' Carlos gave Kate a worried frown.

'Yes,' Kate said firmly. 'Quite sure. Now will you help me, or not?'

He sighed. 'Yes—if you are so determined. But I don't understand. Why is it so important that you leave today and not tomorrow as arranged?'

Kate turned away. 'I can't explain,' she said tonelessly. 'You'll just have to take my word for it that it's more than important to me—it's necessary.'

'I see.' There was a pause, then he said awkwardly, 'I hope it is not because of anything I have said. Sometimes—sometimes I don't always think straight. I say stupid things. I imagine stupid things.' He laughed uncomfortably. 'Like linking Matthew Lincoln with—with Leanne. Where that woman is concerned I lose all sense of proportion.'

Kate shook her head. 'Not always.' She tried to smile, to control the sudden tremble of her lips. 'Sometimes you hit the nail right on the head.'

Carlos went very still. 'What do you mean?'

She said wearily, 'I mean I saw them—last night, from the window of my room. They were down at—at the pool together.'

Carlos said hoarsely. 'They were? You—you saw them, you say?'

'I saw enough,' Kate said. She moistened her dry lips with the tip of her tongue. 'And when I—taxed Matt about it, he didn't deny it.'

She looked at Carlos, and saw him almost gaping at her, his jaw dropping. She went on, 'But then why should he? I don't own him, after all, and as you said, Leanne can probably help him to that interview.'

There was a silence. Then he said slowly, 'I wish I had never spoken to you about it.'

'No,' Kate said, 'I'm glad you did. At least I wasn't under any illusions. So you'll drive me to the airstrip?'

'I'll do better than that,' he said with sudden briskness. 'I'll telephone to the airport at St Lucia and see if there are any seats on the early evening flight. We could still make it, if you can get ready in time.'

'My case is already packed. I only have a few last things to put in it,' Kate told him. This sudden enthusiasm after his early reluctance to help her had her a little bewildered.

When she had first sought Carlos out after lunch was over, and told him she wanted to leave that afternoon, he had protested. Arrangements had been made, he insisted, and his father would be offended and angry if there was any alteration. He would think his hospitality was being spurned. But now . . .

'Fine,' said Carlos. 'After I've called the airport, I'll have them bring a car round.' He shrugged. 'As you've decided, then no more time need be wasted. We may as well get on our way.'

She watched him leave the room. The dog Caesar pattered after him, then changed his mind, and came back to Kate, dropping his muzzle on to her knee. She stroked him, looking into the intelligent eyes.

She thought, 'No time to waste, so why am I sitting here like this?'

And the answer came, 'Because you're a fool. Your experience with Drew taught you nothing. You still want your illusions. Because you let Matt make love to you, take you to paradise and back—you want that expanded into loving—caring and sharing, everything there is. You want him.'

Caesar whined sharply as if he sensed her inner misery, and she touched the long muzzle, soothing him.

She went slowly up to her room. It felt as impersonal as any hotel stopping place. It was hardly believable that she could ever have been so ecstatically, passionately happy here, or suffered so much either. Not a trace of either seemed to hang in the warm air. Her open case in the middle of the floor was an intrusion. She fetched her sponge bag from the bathroom, searching the empty drawers in the dressing table, anxious not to leave so much as a tissue.

She caught a glimpse of herself in the mirror and leaned closer, examining her face. They said making love changed you, she thought. But she didn't think they meant the kind of bleak vulnerability she saw in her eyes. She didn't look like a girl with a lovely secret.

She bit her lip and got up from the revealing mirror. She fastened her case and took a last look round, realising with a brief grimace of distaste that she had forgotten the dress and other things which Leanne had loaned her. She had put them in the wardrobe out of sight, but she ought to take them back. Unless she asked Jakey to do it as she was leaving, she suggested to herself. But that was the cowardly way. After all, she knew the worst now.

'What more can she do to me?' Kate asked herself with a kind of desperate levity.

She hung the dress and nightgown over her arm and started off down the gallery. She wasn't sure which Leanne's room was, but it had to be near Jethro's, and she could retrace her steps there. Had it only been that morning that she had stood among all those orchids and been given her release? It seemed a lifetime ago.

She turned a corner, and stopped dead, the startled breath gasping out of her as if someone had driven a fist into her solar plexus. Matt was there. He and Leanne were walking slowly down the gallery together, talking quietly, their attention centred so deeply on each other that they certainly weren't aware of her standing, rooted to the spot, behind them.

Hardly daring to breathe, she stood, watching helplessly as they reached a door which Leanne opened. Smiling, she took Matt's hand and drew him after her into the room beyond, closing the door behind her, closing out the world, and Kate with it.

Kate turned and ran. She didn't care how much noise she made or who heard her. She ran back to her room, where Carlos was waiting for her, a trace impatiently.

'There's a seat on tonight's plane,' he greeted her without preamble. 'At least you won't have to look for a hotel room in St Lucia.'

'No.' Kate dropped the clothes she was carrying across the bed as if they scorched her. 'Can—can you see that these are returned to your stepmother, please?'

He moved restively. 'Don't call her that—I hate the word. It makes me sick to my stomach!'

She said, 'Then why do you stay? Why don't you persuade your father to let you go away—make a different life for yourself?'

He said, 'I wish it were that simple. But my father needs me, and that's why I stay here. And there may come a time when he'll need me more than ever. I—I wish I could explain, but it's impossible.' He paused, then said bitterly as if he sensed she had reservations, 'Do you think I haven't wanted to escape? I have—so often. I tell myself that no one knows who I am, that my papers give me a new identity. But at the same time, something hints to me that the world outside these islands contains a lot of my father's enemies, and that they might trace him through me.' He hesitated. 'Or perhaps that's just what I tell myself, and the truth is that I'm a coward, and worse than a coward.'

He stopped abruptly, and picked up her case. 'Is this everything? Are you ready to go?'

Kate nodded, and he gave her a searching look. 'You don't wish to say goodbye to anyone—Matt Lincoln, perhaps?'

Her voice barely audible, she said, 'I'd rather just—leave.' She hesitated. 'Your father . . .'

'Will be resting,' he interrupted swiftly. 'It would be better not to disturb him. I will make your excuses when I return, then only one of us will have to bear the brunt of his anger.'

Kate tried to smile. 'I'm sorry if it's going to mean trouble for you. I didn't intend that.'

Carlos shrugged dismissively. 'It does not matter.'

He led the way downstairs and she followed, aware of Jakey's surprised stare as they passed him on their way to the front door. Kate got into the passenger seat of the car. She was in a ridiculous agony of apprehension as Carlos stowed her case in the boot, terrified that Jethro might find out somehow, and prevent her departure. She was almost sick with relief when he took his place behind the wheel and the car moved off.

She sat staring down at her hands tightly clenched in her lap, without speaking or looking up until the house and its environs were safely out of sight.

'Well,' Maria said critically, 'I can't say that your holiday appears to have done you much good.'

Kate made herself smile. 'You know what they say,' she returned lightly. 'That you always need another holiday to recover.'

'Hm.' Maria looked her up and down. 'So what went wrong? Did they give you a room over the disco?'

Kate bit her lip. 'N-no, nothing like that. I'm all right,' she said hastily. 'I'll be fine after I've had some sleep. The flight back was a bit tiring.'

'From Spain?' Maria's brows soared.

'From anywhere, I hate flying,' Kate told her, and escaped to her flat.

Maria's concern wasn't altogether surprising, she conceded, eyeing herself ruefully in the full-length mirror. She looked like a ghost with a tan.

She had finally relaxed as the plane from St Lucia taxied for take-off, realising that now there was no possible chance of Matt appearing to demand an explanation as she had feared—or hoped, she thought with self-derision.

She would carry that image of him disappearing into a room with Leanne like a scar for the rest of her life, yet it had made no basic difference to the way she felt about him. She had dozed uneasily on the plane, and each time she had dreamed that she was in Matt's arms and that he was making love to her.

She thought drearily, 'At least I have the memory of it to remember.'

She did the minimum of unpacking, had a warm bath

and went to bed, and this time exhaustion had its way with her, and she slept deeply and dreamlessly in familiar surroundings.

She realised when she woke that she had slept the clock round. Maria was knocking on the door with an invitation to supper that night.

'No, of course it's no trouble,' she broke reassuringly across Kate's protests. 'Felix has invited some people from the paper, so an extra one will make no difference. And I'd have arranged something anyway if I'd known you were coming back.'

Kate spent a leisurely day. She did some chores and shopped for food. She supposed she should phone Clive and tell him she was back, and ready to start the new illustrations, but she was oddly reluctant to take up the old threads again quite so quickly. For a couple of days, she thought, she would live in the past, examining everything that had happened, and generally getting her head together. She owed herself that. She didn't want to see people, especially her family, until she had come to terms with it all and learned to dissemble. It would have been a relief to have gone home and cried, put all her hurt and bitterness and disillusion in her mother's lap as she'd done when a child, but she couldn't do that any more, because it wasn't fair to worry her mother with her problems. She had never said a word about Drew for fear of upsetting her, and she would pursue the same policy over Matt.

And if her mother's natural shrewdness led her to ask questions, she would simply say that there had been a man, but it hadn't worked out.

As simple as that, she thought, and knew that it wouldn't be simple at all.

She was taken aback that evening to discover that one of the other guests was Lorna Bryce. She wondered awkwardly if Maria remembered the conversation they had had concerning her, but Maria's introductions were so casually performed that Kate assumed she had probably forgotten all about it.

Lorna was a vividly attractive girl, blonde and chic,

and Kate found herself wondering why Matt had ever let her go.

Lorna's smile was friendly too. 'Maria says you've just come back from Spain. I was in Marbella for a while last year, and loved it. Whereabouts were you?'

Kate hesitated, hideously embarrassed, aware that her mind had gone a complete blank. She supposed she could mention one of the well-known resorts like Benidorm or Torremolinos, and hope that Lorna hadn't been there too, and expect her to quote hotels and restaurants.

Lorna gave her a puzzled look. 'What's wrong? Is it a secret?'

'Not—not exactly.' Kate decided to come clean. 'As a matter of fact, I didn't go to Spain at all. I went somewhere else.'

'Oh, I see.' Lorna's smile was shrewd and understanding. 'And unless I miss my guess, there's a man involved.'

Kate sighed ruefully. 'Am I that transparent?'

'I recognise the signs,' said Lorna. 'I took a hell of a toss some time ago myself.'

Kate winced. She had a crazy desire to say, 'Snap.'

Lorna went on, 'Everyone told me what a fool I was being, but I wouldn't listen. I really thought it was the real thing, and that I'd be his one and only for ever.' She laughed drily. 'I soon learned differently!'

Kate stared down into her glass of wine, wondering what would happen if she ran out of the room screaming. Of all the women in the world, Lorna's confidences were the last ones she wanted to hear about.

Lorna added almost casually, 'I hope yours wasn't married too?'

'Married?' The sound came out almost as a squeak. Kate paused, recovering herself. 'No—no, of course not.'

Lorna shrugged wryly. 'It happens. It happened to me. I believed every word he said, especially the ones about leaving his wife. Needless to say he had no intention of doing so. I was one in a long line.' She paused. 'When the crash came, I was fortunate in having some good friends to pick me up again. I'll always be grateful to them.' She smiled. 'Felix and Maria were among them—and Matt, of course,' she added casually.

Kate went very still. 'Matt?' She was afraid Lorna would hear the shake in her voice.

'Matt Lincoln, she said, name-dropping.' Lorna wrinkled her nose. 'He was fantastic, though. He made me want to go on living, and there were times when I hadn't wanted that at all.' She was silent for a moment while Kate tried to collect her reeling thoughts. 'I suppose if you've only ever seen him on television, he comes across as a bit of a ruthless bastard, but privately he's not like that at all.' She smiled reflectively. 'It was good of him to stand by me, particularly as a lot of people thought that he was the man I'd fallen for, and blamed him accordingly. And, even though he was one of the few who knew Jeff's real identity, he still didn't give me away, although it can't have been pleasant for him.'

Kate swallowed. 'N-no.' Her mind was reeling, trying to make sense of what Lorna was saying, and failing. She wanted to ask more, but she had to be careful. Lorna had recovered from her hurt, and could speak frankly about it, but it would be a long time—perhaps never—before Kate could take anyone similarly into her confidence about Matt.

And at that moment, Maria came to call them into the dining room for supper, and she and Lorna were sited at different ends of the table, so any further exchanges were impossible.

Her neighbour at dinner was another colleague of Felix's, a young photographer called Mark. He was unostentatiously good-looking, and amusing, and Kate soon realised she was being chatted up, and in an odd way it was balm to her spirit. Maria's *coq au vin* was wonderful and so was the lemon syllabub which followed it, and Kate found she was beginning to relax.

She was almost sorry when the party broke up around midnight. Mark had never left her side, so there was no chance of another private talk with Lorna, which, on balance, was just as well.

There wasn't a lot she could have said without either betraying herself, or giving away the fact that Felix and Maria were among those who had been taken in by the whole affair, she thought.

She parted from Mark pleasantly, without making any definite response to his suggestions that they should see one another again. He was clearly disappointed, but promised that he would telephone her. Well, he might, or he might not, she decided as she went up to her flat, and when he did was time enough to worry about whether to accept his invitation or not.

The next day she went to see Alison. She felt the sun warm on her back as she walked across the big square of grass, and wished she knew exactly what to say. She rang the bell and waited, edgily.

The front door opened and Alison stared at her, her eyes widening, her face breaking into a smile.

'Kate—you're back. How smashing! Come in. Would you like some coffee?'

Kate could hardly believe her eyes and ears. Alison looked a different girl. The sulky air which had hung around her at their previous encounter had vanished. Her hair had been re-styled, and she looked glowingly alive and happy.

'Was Spain wonderful?' she went on, leading the way into the house. 'Jon and I were wondering about a few days in Majorca perhaps in September, if all goes well.'

Kate followed her into the kitchen and watched while Alison flitted about, getting out beakers and plugging in the percolater, and chatting inconsequentially about this and that.

'You haven't done anything more about finding a job?' she asked at last, as Alison poured the coffee.

There wasn't even a momentary embarrassment in Alison's face. 'No, I've given up the whole idea now— for a very good reason.' That smile lit up her features again. 'Oh, Kate, you're the first one to know—apart from Jon, of course. I'm going to have a baby! I've just had the test confirmed, and it's definite. I'm so happy I could die!'

Kate took the beaker she was handed almost mechanically. She said, 'Ally, that's wonderful! I thought . . .'

'You're remembering how I was a few weeks ago,' Alison diagnosed correctly. 'I'm sorry if I gave you a hard time. I was certainly giving myself a worse one. You see, Jon and I had been trying for this baby— and—well, it hadn't happened, and I was beginning to panic, think there might be something wrong. And you know how it is. Every magazine article—every television programme seemed to be about the problems of infertility. I began to think I was getting a complex. And then Jon started saying he thought it was too soon to have a family, and that he wanted me to himself. I was just totally confused, and miserable. But when I realised there might be a baby on the way, he confessed that he'd been worried, and he'd just been trying to make me feel better. Wasn't it ridiculous?' She laughed, her face tender.

She chattered on, and Kate drank her coffee, knowing that she could not spoil that precious new-found contentment with recriminations about Matt Lincoln. Alison had probably put the whole incident out of her mind, she realised, and it would be unkind and unfair to resurrect it, and remind her of behaviour which she would be ashamed of now.

'Do the rest of the family know you're back?' Alison asked at last. 'We're going over to see them tonight for a meal—and to tell them the good news. Why don't you come as well?'

'I have something planned for this evening,' Kate said mendaciously. 'But you could tell Mother that I'll be over towards the end of the week.'

Tonight was Alison's time, she thought. Tonight, she would be the centre of attention, basking in everyone's happiness and approval, and Kate couldn't cope with it, although she was thankful her sister-in-law seemed to have regained her equilibrium.

She drank a second cup of coffee, and said she had to be on her way, firmly refusing all Alison's pressing offers of lunch, and an afternoon visit to the local shops to look at cots and prams. As she turned to wave goodbye to her sister-in-law, she reflected wryly that the next nine months were probably going to be the longest on record, then chided herself for being malicious. She shouldn't blame Alison for what had happened between herself and Matt. It was her own fault for jumping with both feet into a situation she didn't understand. And now she had to live with the consequences.

The days passed slowly. Kate got back to work with utter determination. Clive was delighted that she was back, and bombarded her with invitations, none of which she accepted. Eventually, she supposed, he would take the hint, and realise that their relationship would never be more than a business one. Mark was equally persistent, in spite of her excuses, and Maria was clearly disappointed that Kate didn't take him up on any of his offers of dinner, or the theatre.

'I thought you were getting on well,' she mourned.

'He's very nice,' Kate offered placatingly. 'But I'm just not ready to be involved—with anyone,' she added, feeling a faint tinge of colour steal into her face.

Maria gave her a look filled with foreboding. 'I hope you haven't done anything silly,' she remarked with sudden abruptness, and to Kate's relief, left it at that. Going to the Caribbean with Matt, falling crazily in love with him, giving herself to him even though she knew he had no serious interest in her, would definitely come under the heading of 'anything silly,' she thought wretchedly.

Going home was the hardest, convincing her mother that she was fine and life was coming up roses, joining in her pleasure over Jon and Alison and the coming baby. Time and time again, she longed to tell her everything, but it was impossible. She could never tell her mother the whole story without hurting and worrying her, and that was the last thing she wanted to do.

The only bright spot in a bleak landscape was the fact that her preliminary sketches for the new book were better than ever, and even Felicity was pleased.

But there wasn't an hour went by that she didn't think of Matt, and wonder where he was and what he was doing. He had to be back in London by now, with his interview on tape, or without it. As the days lengthened into weeks, she was tempted to telephone him at National Television, ask for his extension just to hear his voice again, but of course she did no such thing. She still had a little pride left, and besides, she reminded herself practically, it was unlikely that Matt would answer his own phone. His secretary—Carole, he'd called her—would do it for him.

Meanwhile, she watched television almost obsessively, waiting to see him or even hear some brief mention of his name, or a trailer of a programme he was involved with. But she was invariably disappointed.

It was as if he'd vanished off the face of the earth, Kate thought, and shivered as she wondered what kind of revenge Jethro Alvarez might take against a man who had become his wife's lover. These were uncomfortable thoughts, and it was a relief to know that she was going to have supper with her parents, instead of sitting in the flat brooding. Even listening to Ally listing the latest treatments for morning sickness was better than that.

All evening Matt was on her mind, this inexplicable sick anxiety about him destroying her appetite. Her mother looked reproachfully at her barely touched plate as they cleared the table.

'Darling, I'm sure you're not well,' she began as they washed up together in the kitchen. 'You haven't been yourself since you came back from your holiday. Do you think you picked up some kind of virus while you were away?'

Kate shook her head. 'I don't think so.'

'Well, I think you should see a doctor,' her mother

said decisively. 'You're certainly not eating properly, and you don't look as if you're sleeping either.' She was clearly warming to her theme when her husband came into the room.

'Great excitement in the sitting room,' he said wryly. 'I put the television news on, and it appears that Alison's former boss has got himself involved in some South American revolution.'

It seemed impossible that the glass Kate was holding wasn't lying in shattered fragments on the floor, but she found she was still holding it. She set it down quietly and carefully on the draining board, and put the tea-towel beside it. She wanted to run, but she made herself walk.

Jon looked round as she came into the room, grimacing slightly. Alison was on the edge of her chair, her eyes fixed tensely on the television screen.

'Can you believe it?' Jon said. 'That dictator fellow who was supposed to be dead has been in hiding all this time, and he's staging a comeback. And guess who just happens to be on the spot—the great Matthew Lincoln, of course.'

'Oh, hush!' Alison hissed.

The screen was filled with a picture of a city, which Kate guessed was the capital of Santo Cristo. As she watched it dissolved away, and Jethro Alvarez took its place, wearing some kind of military uniform. And all the time in the background, Matt's voice, distorted and sometimes indistinct. Dimly Kate heard phrases— 'control of the radio station,' 'government forces falling back,' 'fighting in the streets,' 'some loss of life already.' She heard other things too—the muffled rattle of gunfire, louder explosions which had to be falling shells.

She watched the picture fade and the screen grow dark, and suddenly she was part of that darkness, falling into an endless void.

'I still think you should let me call the doctor,' Mrs Herbert said anxiously.

Propped up by pillows, Kate gave her a wan smile.
'Really, I'm all right.'

'All right indeed!' Her mother pursed her lips.
'Fainting away like that! I told you that you must have
picked up some kind of virus. Well, you're not going
back to that flat of yours, and I've telephoned your
landlady and told her so. You're staying here so that I
can look after you.'

Kate sighed, 'Mother, I have to go back. I have work
to do.'

'Nothing that can't wait.' Mrs Herbert's face wore an
expression of steely determination. 'Your career won't
be furthered by you making yourself thoroughly ill.'

'No, Mother,' Kate agreed with unwonted meekness.

'And now I'm going to heat up some milk,' was Mrs
Herbert's final stern decree as she departed.

Warm milk and her old room. It was like plunging
back into childhood, Kate thought when she was alone.
Except that no childish crisis in her life had ever hurt
like this one. She kept seeing Matt, lying on his back in
some dusty street with blood on his face.

She could hardly believe what she had seen and
heard, and yet she knew it must be true, and that
Alvarez must have been planning it all along. In fact,
when she looked back, she could remember things he
had said about his plans which she had not
understood.

But then, she thought ruefully, she had understood
very little of what was going on at the house on St
Antoine.

But she had never dreamed that Alvarez intended to
re-invade Santo Cristo, or, most incredible of all, that
Matt would accompany him. Perhaps Alvarez had
forced him, she thought, then castigated herself for
being a fool.

It was a chance no newsman would be able to resist,
and Matt knew Santo Cristo well because he had been
stationed there as a foreign correspondent.

Even if the revolution failed, he would know where to
go—how to survive, she told herself with a kind of

desperation. He had to know, because if anything happened to him . . . Her eyes closed and scalding tears began to trickle down her face, as she prayed silently, 'Keep him safe. Oh, please, keep him safe!'

The next day's papers were full of the coup in Santo Cristo, and Jethro Alvarez's apparent return from the dead. Matt's interview with him had been shown the previous night on television, and the papers quoted extensively from it.

There had been secret meetings going on for months, with rebels from the present government, and high-ranking officers in the armed services going to St Antoine to discuss the details of Alvarez's return.

Kate thought, 'No wonder Carlos got so edgy when I talked about visitors! He must have thought we knew something.'

At her mother's insistence, she spent the day resting, trying to resist the temptation to put on the television when the newscasts were on and find out what was happening.

During the afternoon, Alison arrived. Kate's heart sank when she heard her voice in the hall, and saw the speculative glance her sister-in-law cast her as she came in.

'Hello,' Alison said awkwardly. 'Are you feeling better? You gave us quite a fright.'

'I frightened myself,' Kate admitted. She made herself smile 'I think my mother's right, and I have some kind of virus.'

'Oh, really?' Alison didn't bother to disguise her scepticism. She shrugged. 'Well, I suppose you know your own business best, but don't forget I know Matt well—I worked for him—and work always comes first with him, as a number of his girl-friends have found to their cost. He won't be pinned down to any safe, domestic number.' She paused. 'I suppose you were with him, not in Spain at all. And I always thought butter wouldn't melt in your mouth! Well, you live and learn.'

She gave Kate a cool, brief smile and went into the kitchen to talk to Mrs Herbert.

Kate had to force herself to sit quietly through the news that night. The latest bulletin from Santo Cristo included the first pictures of the fighting, and they made her feel sick, but the news was that Alvarez was back in control, and the former government leaders were under arrest. The reporter making the broadcast was a stranger, young and blond. Matt Lincoln's name wasn't even mentioned, she realised, her heart thudding with unease. Where was he? What had happened to him?

In spite of the warm milk, she slept badly that night, disturbed by violent dreams of death in the streets. And next morning, she told her mother that she was going back to the flat.

'But I thought you'd stay till the end of the week,' Mrs Herbert wailed.

Kate shook her head. 'If I stay any longer, Clive will begin to panic. And I can't afford any more time off. I have my living to earn.'

'Oh, Kate!' Her mother bit her lip. 'You still don't look well. You're so drawn!' She hesitated. 'Alison was hinting that there was a man involved. Oh, darling . . .'

Kate almost ground her teeth. 'Damn you, Alison!' she thought savagely.

Aloud, she said, 'Well, Alison has a vivid imagination, that's all. Please don't worry about me any more.'

Even so, it was late afternoon before she finally got away, after steadfastly refusing to stay for supper. There'd be something in her store cupboard in the flat, she thought, or if not, she'd call at one of the local takeaways.

The journey back to the flat seemed interminable. It began to rain, and she felt damp and despondent as she made her way up the path to the house. The outer door was locked, so Felix and Maria must be out, which was a relief in a way. They would have been watching the news too, and she couldn't endure any kind of inquisition about it.

There was a note on the hall table, written in Maria's flaring script. 'You have a visitor,' followed by a number of exclamation marks.

Kate looked at it stupidly. What did it mean—that someone had called or telephoned? Then why hadn't Maria put the name? She sighed. It was probably Clive, panicking about the illustrations. She would phone him tomorrow, she decided. She was too tired and too wretched to do it that evening.

She walked slowly up the stairs, and pushed open the living room door. It was dim in the room, the curtains half-drawn across the windows, and she saw a movement and screamed, her hand flying to the switch, flooding the room with light.

Matt said wearily, 'I'm sorry if I frightened you. It's the last thing I wanted.'

He'd been lying on her bed, she realised. The movement she had glimpsed had been him sitting up, swinging his legs to the floor. He looked terrible. He was pale and unshaven, and his eyes were red-rimmed with weariness.

She whispered, 'What are you doing here?'

'Waiting for you,' he said. 'I thought you'd never come. Your landlady phoned your home, and they said you were on your way, but that was ages ago.' He threw his head back and looked at her. 'I began to think you'd run away again. It was all part of the nightmare, to get here at last and find that you were gone.'

She said, 'I don't understand. I thought you were in Santo Cristo.'

'I was,' he said briefly. 'But I never intended to stay. The media have rediscovered the place in force by now, and I took the first flight out.'

Kate said, 'You realised what was going on, didn't you? You knew what Alvarez intended?'

'I took an educated guess,' he said. 'It was clear we'd stumbled into the middle of something, and that it would only be a matter of time before Alvarez told me what it was.'

'After Leanne had persuaded him,' she said, staring down at the floor as if it fascinated her.

Matt said cynically, 'I think you vastly overestimate

her powers of persuasion. And she hadn't a clue what was going on anyway.'

'But that was why you got the interview.' She still couldn't look at him. 'Because she helped you.'

'I fail to see how,' he said after a moment's pause. 'But I don't really want to talk about that hysterical bitch. I want to know why you ran away like that without a word to anyone.'

'Carlos knew,' she muttered.

'What the hell's that got to do with it?' demanded Matt with a snap. 'You were supposed to be leaving the following day, and you know it!' He gave her a long look. 'In fact from what I remember, you weren't keen on leaving at all.'

The colour rose miserably in her face. 'I changed my mind.'

'And I want to know why.' He moved towards her, and she took an involuntary step backwards. He stopped, his face hardening. 'After what happened between us, I'd have thought I rated an explanation at the least, if not a goodbye.'

'Well, that's simple enough.' Kate lifted her chin. 'The explanation—you wanted me gone, and I wanted to go. And goodbye,' she added defiantly. 'Now perhaps you'd go. I'm tired.'

'I haven't come halfway across the world to be dismissed like that,' Matt said roughly. 'What the hell's the matter with you? Didn't it occur to you that I had good reason for wanting you safely out of the way?'

'Oh, yes,' she said bitterly. 'And I know what it was.' She glared at him, fighting her tears. 'I saw you—remember?'

He said slowly, 'I gather we're back to Leanne again. Well, I don't know what you saw, or what you dreamed perhaps, but it wasn't me. I was not with Leanne, at the pool, or anywhere else for that matter, although I admit I wasn't in my room.' He paused. 'As it happens, I was with Jethro. He sent for me, and we talked until dawn, establishing terms, although he still didn't tell me everything. Naturally, he was still wary in case I jumped

the gun and took the surprise element out of the
invasion, but it was clear he was prepared to give me an
exclusive, if I promised him the guarantees he wanted in
return.' He shrugged. 'Of course, I agreed. I'd have
probably stood on my head if he'd asked me to, but I
would not have seduced his bloody wife, or allowed her
to seduce me.'

There was another pounding silence, and Kate felt
screaming tension rising inside her.

Matt went on evenly, 'I don't know who you saw
with Leanne that night, although I can guess. When
you accused me, I thought you were suffering from
delusions—sunstroke perhaps, and then I realised what
the truth was. But the fact that you could even think it
was me proves up to the hilt that you still have this
lousy image of me, that you're still convinced that
anything female will do.'

He paused again, then added with biting coldness, 'In
view of what happened between us, presumably you
include yourself in that category.'

Her   flush   deepened.   'That—shouldn't   have
happened . . .'

'You don't have to tell me that,' he said with weary
exasperation. 'It was a situation I'd been trying to
avoid for all kinds of reasons—but principally,
I suppose, because I wanted you to know that I
regarded you as more than a desirable body.
I wanted, like a fool, to prove that I cared about you.'
He added ironically, 'But that was before you decided
to pair me with Leanne.'

She said unhappily, 'But I did see you, Matt. Oh—
not that night, perhaps. It was dark, and I never saw
him clearly, and I—I took it for granted that it was you.
But the next afternoon, you were with her then. I saw
you go into her room.'

He said with chilling emphasis, 'You saw me go into
Jethro's room. Yes, Leanne was there too for a few
minutes. She is Jethro's wife, after all, even if she loses
sight of the fact most of the time. But if you'd hung
around for a little while longer, you'd have seen her

leaving—alone.' He paused. 'And as Carlos then drove you to the plane, presumably she remained alone.'

Her lips parted in a soundless gasp. 'Carlos? You mean . . .? Oh, but that's impossible! He hates her.'

'I'd say he was obsessed with her,' Matt said drily. 'And burdened with guilt. As for hate—well, it shares a pretty thin dividing line with certain forms of love. And knowing Leanne and her—propensities, I'd say that once Jethro lost interest in her, she'd have found it quite amusing to beguile that poor young idiot.'

Kate said shakily, 'That's sick.'

'That's Leanne.'

She looked at him desperately. 'But she told me she wanted you. She told me that was her price for making sure that you got your exclusive.'

'But my bargain was with you.' Matt walked over to her, and this time she made no attempt to retreat, but stood her ground, looking up at him mutely, her mouth trembling. He snapped 'You little fool, couldn't you see what she was? How the hell did you lend credence to anything she said to you—let her get to you like that?'

Kate shook her head miserably. 'I don't know—but she was so sure—so convincing . . .'

'Then perhaps she should go back on the stage,' Matt said. 'She'll need something to do, now that she knows she won't be joining Jethro in Santo Cristo.'

'She won't? And Carlos?'

'Is with his father, who is probably quite aware of what's been going on. I told you he had no illusions about her. Certainly he won't blame the boy for what happened.'

'What will happen to her?'

'Frankly, I neither know nor care, though I don't doubt she'll get by. What does interest me,' Matt went on slowly, 'is why, believing that I was involved in a sordid mess with Leanne, you let me make love to you?' There was a silence, and he said implacably, 'I'm waiting for an answer.'

She swallowed convulsively, 'I—I thought I'd never see you again. I wanted something—something to remember . . .'

'You could have tied a knot in your handkerchief,' he said. 'You didn't have to fall into my arms giving me everything I'd longed for, and more. So why did you, Kate?'

She said wretchedly, 'Because, damn you, it didn't matter what you did—I loved you anyway. And that's why I ran away—because I couldn't bear to stay and watch her—take you from me.'

'My darling,' Matt said. 'My sweet, crazy little fool! Don't you know that no one can do that? My God, when you vanished, I imagined all kinds of things—that you'd found you hated me after all. I've been through torture these past weeks. And now you tell me you ran because you were jealous!'

'I know I've been a fool,' she whispered. 'But it did hurt . . .'

'It hurt me too,' he said. 'When I saw you with Carlos, when you told me you were coming back to this guy in London—what's his name—Drew?'

She shook her head. 'That was over a long time ago—and there's no one—no one at all.'

'Now that's a pity,' he said. 'Because I've been hoping and praying that there was me.' He cupped her face in his hands, looking deeply into her eyes. 'You shouldn't have run, Kate. You should have let me tell you how much I loved you—how much I wanted you to wait for me.' He groaned. 'The invasion was sheer hell. I'd never bothered about danger before, and I'd been in stickier situations many times, but this time it was different, because I'd had you, and I was terrified that something would happen, and I would never see you again.' The blue eyes darkened. 'I also had to come to terms with the fact that I'd taken you utterly selfishly, and that I might have made you pregnant.'

Kate was trembling, a wild exultant happiness flooding through her body.

She said, 'It never even occurred to me.'

'Nor to me at the time,' he admitted, grimacing. 'I've no excuses to offer, Kate, except that I wanted you so much I simply ignored all other considerations.'

'Then why—that morning on the beach . . .?'

He groaned, 'Because Winston could have returned at any time—and for all I knew we might have been under surveillance. I wanted time for us, darling, and a modicum of privacy.' His voice roughened. 'The hardest thing I ever did was send you away, but knowing how far advanced Jethro's plans were, I couldn't risk you staying in case something went wrong. I didn't want to leave you behind on the island, but on the other hand it was impossible to take you to Santo Cristo with me. But at the same time, I needed you desperately, I needed to know that you belonged to me completely.' He sighed. 'I was going to tell you all these things that night—our last night together, as I thought. I intended to give you my family's address as well. I thought perhaps you might have gone to see them—to stay with them for a while.'

'I'd have liked that.' Her voice broke suddenly, and he gathered her warmly, closely into his arms, cradling her head against his chest.

'Hush,' he said gently. 'Hush, my darling. I'm here now, and we can go to see them together—tomorrow perhaps, when I've had some sleep.'

'Yes,' she said wonderingly. Tomorrow was a golden word, she realised, ablaze with all kinds of promise. She said softly, 'Matt—stay with me tonight.'

'Sweetheart, I can't.' His lips touched her hair. 'I need a bath, a change of clothes and a shave—besides, I'm dead on my feet.'

She reached up and kissed his rough cheek lingeringly. 'I'm tired too, but I need to sleep with you. I want to know I'm not dreaming this, and that when I open my eyes tomorrow you'll be there.'

His smile, his voice were both infinitely tender. 'I'll be there, darling, always. And I'll never let you get away from me again.' There was a sudden note of laughter in his voice. 'You realise that if I stay the night, you'll have to marry me?'

She pantomimed amazement, laughing up at him. 'I will?'

Matt said, 'You will.' And the warmth of his mouth on hers sealed the vow fcr the rest of their lives.

A NEW LOOK TO OUR AUTHOR COLLECTION SERIES

Watch out for our new look author collections from June 1992.

Best selling authors Catherine George and Sally Wentworth launch our new look books and to complement the new design we are also giving it a new name; suggested by you, our valued readers, the collections will now be called "DUETS".

SO LOOK OUT FOR...

The Catherine George Duet featuring:
DEVIL WITHIN
GILDED CAGE

The Sally Wentworth Duet featuring:
DARK AWAKENING
THE HAWK OF VENICE

FROM JUNE 1992

Price: £3.50

Next month's Romances

Each month, you can choose from a world of variety in romance with Mills & Boon. These are the new titles to look out for next month.

THE GOLDEN MASK ROBYN DONALD
THE PERFECT SOLUTION CATHERINE GEORGE
A DATE WITH DESTINY MIRANDA LEE
THE JILTED BRIDEGROOM CAROLE MORTIMER
SPIRIT OF LOVE EMMA GOLDRICK
LEFT IN TRUST KAY THORPE
UNCHAIN MY HEART STEPHANIE HOWARD
RELUCTANT HOSTAGE MARGARET MAYO
TWO-TIMING LOVE KATE PROCTOR
NATURALLY LOVING CATHERINE SPENCER
THE DEVIL YOU KNOW HELEN BROOKS
WHISPERING VINES ELIZABETH DUKE
DENIAL OF LOVE SHIRLEY KEMP
PASSING STRANGERS MARGARET CALLAGHAN
TAME A PROUD HEART JENETH MURREY

STARSIGN
GEMINI GIRL LIZA GOODMAN

Forthcoming Titles

COLLECTION
Available in April

The Sara Craven Collection

ALIEN VENGEANCE
DARK PARADISE

The Sandra Field Collection

AN ATTRACTION OF
OPPOSITES
ONE IN A MILLION

BEST SELLER ROMANCE
Available in May

TEMPERED BY FIRE Emma Goldrick
THE LONELY SEASON Susan Napier

MEDICAL ROMANCE
Available in May

THE SINGAPORE AFFAIR Kathleen Farrell
CAROLINE'S CONQUEST Hazel Fisher
A PLACE OF REFUGE Margaret Holt
THAT SPECIAL JOY Betty Beaty